Praise for *The Blacktongue Thief*

"Dazzling. I heartily recommen̲̲
—Robin ̲ ̲ ̲ ̲ ̲ ̲
̲ ̲

"Wow! Truly outstanding. I can't say enough good things about
The Blacktongue Thief. Damned good stuff."
—Glen Cook, author of *The Black Company*

"A delight from start to finish. Buehlman takes the well-worn tropes
of fantasy and weaves them into a new and vibrant tapestry."
—Anthony Ryan, *New York Times* bestselling
author of *Blood Song*

"Fast and fun and filled with crazy magic. I can't wait to see what
Christopher Buehlman does next."
—Brent Weeks, *New York Times* bestselling
author of the Lightbringer series

"Chock-full of wry wit, foul language, and characters who arrive
on the page with savage, sordid pasts hot on their heels. Often hu-
morous, occasionally horrifying, and sometimes incredibly poi-
gnant, I love *every single page* of this book. Every sentence, even.
It's *that* good."   —Nicholas Eames, author of *Kings of the Wyld*

"Equal parts fairy tale, D&D adventure, and acid trip. Buehlman
has successfully blended the essences of these elements into
something at once familiar and fresh. I look forward to returning to this evocative and f*cked-up world!".
—Jonathan French, author of *The Grey Bastards*

"*The Blacktongue Thief* is a master class in voice and thoughtful
world design, with a wonderful cast and a protagonist who grabs
you instantly. Fans of Lynch's *The Lies of Locke Lamora* will love
this one."   —Django Wexler, author of *The Thousand Names*

Other Books by Christopher Buehlman

THE
Blacktongue
Thief

Christopher Buehlman

TOR

A TOM DOHERTY ASSOCIATES BOOK
NEW YORK

THE BLACKTONGUE THIEF

Copyright © 2021 by Christopher Buehlman

Map and calendar art by Tim Paul

Calendar illustrations by Christopher Buehlman

A Tor Book
Published by Tom Doherty Associates
120 Broadway
New York, NY 10271

www.tor-forge.com

Tor® is a registered trademark of Macmillan Publishing Group, LLC.

The Library of Congress has cataloged the hardcover edition as follows:

Names: Buehlman, Christopher, author.
Title: The blacktongue thief / Christopher Buehlman.
Description: First edition. | New York : TOR, a Tom Doherty Associates Book, 2021.
Identifiers: LCCN 2021008835 (print) | LCCN 2021008836 (ebook) |
    ISBN 9781250621191 (hardcover) | ISBN 9781250621184 (ebook)
Classification: LCC PS3602.U3395 B53 2021 (print) | LCC PS3602.U3395 (ebook) |
    DDC 813/.6—dc23
LC record available at https://lccn.loc.gov/2021008835
LC ebook record available at https://lccn.loc.gov/2021008836

ISBN 978-1-250-79997-5 (trade paperback)

Our books may be purchased in bulk for promotional, educational, or busi-
ness use. Please contact your local bookseller or the Macmillan Corporate and
Premium Sales Department at 1-800-221-7945, extension 5442, or by email at
MacmillanSpecialMarkets@macmillan.com.

First Tor Paperback Edition: 2022

Printed in the United States of America

For Jennifer,

at last,
under this and any moon.

———•———

LUNDAY	HARTHDAY	KNOTSDAY	RINGDAY	OATHDAY	WIDDERSDAY	LAMBSDAY	FRULDAY	SATHSDAY
1	2	3	4	5	6	7	8	9
10	11	12	13	14	15	16	17	18
19	20	21	22	23	24	25	26	27
28	29	30	31	32	33	34	35	36

1

The Forest of Orphans

———•———

I was about to die.

Worse, I was about to die with bastards.

Not that I was afraid to die, but maybe who you die with is important. It's important who's with you when you're born, after all. If everybody's wearing clean linen and silk and looking down at you squirming in your bassinet, you'll have a very different life than if the first thing you see when you open your eyes is a billy goat. I looked over at Pagran and decided he looked uncomfortably like a billy goat, what with his long head, long beard, and unlovely habit of chewing even when he had no food. Pagran used to be a farmer. Frella, just next to him in rusty ring mail, used to be his wife.

Now they were thieves, but not subtle thieves like me. I was trained in lock-picking, wall-scaling, fall-breaking, lie-weaving, voice-throwing, trap-making, trap-finding, and not a half-bad archer, fiddler, and knife-fighter besides. I also knew several dozen cantrips—small but useful magic. Alas, I owed the Takers Guild so much money for my training that I found myself squatting in the Forest of Orphans with these thick bastards, hoping to rob somebody the old-fashioned way. You know, threaten them with death.

It pays surprisingly well, being a highwayman. I was only a month in with this group, and we had robbed wagons with too few guards, kidnapped stragglers off groups with too many, and even sold a merchant's boy to a group of crooked soldiers who were supposed to be chasing us. Killing never came easily to me, but I was willing to throw a few arrows to keep myself out of the shyte. It's the way the world was made. I had more than half what I needed for my Lammas payment to the Guild to keep them from making my tattoo worse. The tattoo was bad enough already, thank you very much.

So there I was, crouched in ambush, watching a figure walking alone down the White Road toward us. I had a bad feeling about our potential victim, and not just because she walked like nobody was going to hurt her, and not just because ravens were shouting in the trees. I had studied magic, you see, just a little, and this traveler had some. I wasn't sure what kind, but I felt it like a chill or that charge in the air before a storm that raises gooseflesh. Besides, what could one woman have on her that would be worth much split seven ways? And let's not forget our leader's double share, which would end up looking more like half.

I looked at Pagran and gave him a little shake of my head. He looked back at me, the whites of his eyes standing out because he'd mudded himself, all but his hands, which he left white to make handcanting easier. Pagran used a soldier's handcant he'd learned in the Goblin Wars, only half like the thieves' cant I learned at the Low School. His two missing fingers didn't help matters. When I shook my head at him, he canted at me. I thought he said to repair my purse, so I checked to see if money was falling out, but then I realized he was saying I should check to see if my balls were still attached. Right, he was impugning my courage.

I pointed at the stranger and made the sign for magicker, not confident they would know that one, and I'm not sure if Pagran did; he told me there was a magicker behind me, or at least that's what I thought at first, but he was actually telling me to put a magicker in my arse. I looked away from the chief bastard I was about to die with and back at the woman about to kill us.

Just a feeling I had.

To walk alone down the White Road through the Forest of Orphans, even on a pleasantly warm late-summer day in the month of Ashers, you would have to be a magicker. If you weren't, you'd have to be a drunk, a foreigner, a suicide, or some sloppy marriage of the three. This one had the look of a foreigner. She had the olive tones and shaggy black hair-mop of a Spanth. With good cheekbones, like they have there, a gift from the old empire, and there was no telling her age. Youngish. Thirty? Built small but hard. Those sleepy eyes could well be a killer's, and she was dressed for fighting. She had a round shield on her back, a gorget to save her throat a cutting, and if I didn't miss my guess, she wore light chain mail under her shirt.

The blade on her belt was a bit shorter than most. Probably a *spadín*, or bullnutter, which would definitely make her Ispanthian. Their knights used to be the best horsemen in the world, back when the world had horses. Now they relied on the sword-and-shield art of Old Kesh, known as Calar Bajat, taught from the age of eight. Spanths don't take threats well—I was all but sure if we moved, it would be to kill, not intimidate. Would Pagran think it was worth bothering? Money pouches hung on the stranger's belt, but would Pagran order the attack just for that?

No.

He would be looking at the shield.

Now that the maybe-Spanth was closer, I could see the rosy blush on the wood rim peeking over the stranger's shoulder marking the shield as one of springwood. A tree we cut so fast during the Goblin Wars it was damned-near extinct—the last groves grew in Ispanthia, under the king's watchful eye, where trespassing would get you a noose, and trespassing with a saw would get you boiled. Thing about springwood is, if it's properly cured and cared for, it's known to stay living after it's been cut and heal itself. And as long as it's alive, it's hard to burn.

Pagran wanted that shield. As much as I hoped he'd move his cupped palm down like he was snuffing a candle, I knew he would jab his thumb forward and the attack would start. Three scarred brawlers stood beside Pagran, and I heard the other two archers shifting near me—one superstitious young squirt of piss named Naerfas, though we called him Nervous, kissing the grubby fox pendant carved from deer bone he wore on a cord around his neck; his pale, wall-eyed sister shifted in the leaves behind him. I never liked it that we worshipped the same god, they and I, but they were Galts like me, born with the black tongues that mark us all, and Galtish thieves fall in with the lord of foxes. We can't help ourselves.

I pulled an arrow with a bodkin point, good for slipping between links of chain mail, and nocked it on the string.

We watched our captain.

He watched the woman.

The ravens screamed.

Pagran jabbed the thumb.

What happened next happened fast.

I pulled and loosed first, feeling the good release of pressure in my fingers and the bite of the bowstring on my inner arm. I also had that warm-heart feeling when you know you've shot true—if you haven't handled a bow, I can't explain it. I heard the hiss of my fellows' arrows chasing mine. But the target was already moving—she crouched and turned so fast she seemed to disappear behind the shield. Never mind that it wasn't a large shield—she made herself small behind it.

Two arrows hit the springwood and bounced, and where my

own arrow went I couldn't see. Then there went Pagran and his three brawlers, Pagran's big glaive up in the air like an oversized kitchen knife on a stick, Frella's broadsword behind her neck ready to chop, two others we'll just call Spear and Axe running behind. The Spanth would have to stand to meet their charge, and when she did, I would stick her through the knee.

Now things got confusing.

I saw motion in the trees across the road.

I thought three things at once:

A raven is breaking from the tree line.

The ravens have stopped shouting.

That raven is too big.

A raven the size of a stag rushed onto the road.

I made a little sound in my throat without meaning to.

It's an unforgettable thing, seeing your first war corvid.

Especially if it's not on your side.

It plucked Spear's foot out from under her, spilling her on her face, then began shredding her back with its hardened beak. I woke myself out of just watching it and thought I should probably nock another arrow, but the corvid was already moving at Axe, whose name was actually Jarril. I tell you this not because you'll know him long but because what happened to him was so awful I feel bad just calling him Axe.

Jarril sensed the bird coming up on his flank and stopped his run, wheeling to face it. He didn't have time to do more than raise his axe before the thing speared him with its beak where no man wants beak nor spear. His heavy chain mail hauberk measured to his knees, but those birds punch holes in skulls, so what was left of Jarril's parts under the chain mail didn't bear thinking about. He dropped, too badly hurt even to yell. Frella yelled, though. I glanced left and saw Pagran bent over, covered in blood, but I think it was Frella's—she was bleeding enough for both of them, spattering the ground from a vicious underarm cut that looked to run elbow to tit.

As the Spanth switched directions, I caught a glimpse of her naked sword, which was definitely a *spadín*. Sharp enough to stab, heavy enough to chop. A good sword, maybe the best short sword ever made. And she could use it. She moved like a blur now, stepping past Frella and booting her broadsword out of reach.

Spear, her back in tatters, was just getting up on all fours like a baby about to try walking. Beside me, Nervous cried out, "*Awain Baith*," Galtish for "death-bird," and dropped his bow and ran, his older sister turning tail with him, leaving me the only archer in the trees. I had no shot at the Spanth, who kept her shield raised toward me even as she lopped Spear's hand off below the wrist. Funny what the mind keeps close—I glimpsed the shield closer now and saw its central steel boss was wrought in the shape of a blowing storm cloud's face, like the kind on the edge of a map.

Pagran had taken up his dropped glaive and was trying to ward the corvid circling him. It bit at the glaive's head twice, easily avoiding Pagran's jab and not seeming to notice my missed arrow—these things don't move predictably, and at twenty paces, an arrow doesn't hit the instant it flies. Now the war bird grabbed the glaive-head and wrenched sideways so Pagran had to turn with it or lose the weapon. Pagran turned at just the instant the Spanth leapt fast and graceful as a panther and cut him deep just above the heel. Our leader dropped and curled up into a moaning ball. The fight on the road was over.

Shyte.

I nocked another arrow as Spanth and bird looked at me.

The bow wasn't going to be enough. I had a fine fighting knife on the front of my belt; in a tavern fight, it would turn a geezer inside out, but it was useless against chain. At my back, I had a nasty spike of a rondel dagger, good to punch through mail, but against *that* sword in *that* woman's hand, not to mention the fucking bird, it might as well have been a twig.

They moved closer.

I could outrun the Spanth, but not the bird.

THE BLACKTONGUE THIEF 19

I pissed myself a little, I'm not ashamed to tell you.

"Archer," she said in that *r*-tapping Ispanthian accent. "Come out and help your friends."

That they weren't really my friends wasn't a good enough reason to leave them maimed and wrecked on the White Road, nor was the fact that they deserved it. The Spanth had fished an arrow from the bloody tangle of shirt under her arm, matched its fletching to the arrows still in my side-quiver, and said, "Good shot."

She gave me the arrow back. She also gave me a mouthful of wine from her wineskin, good thick, black wine, probably from Ispanthia like she was. Pagran, grimacing and dragging himself to lean against a tree, got nothing. Frella, who seemed within two drops of bleeding herself unconscious, got nothing, even though she looked hopefully at the Spanth while I tied her arm off with one stocking and a stick. The wine was just for me, and only because I had shot true. That's a Spanth for you. The surest way to make one love you is to hurt them.

To speak of the injured, Jarril was still unconscious, which was good—let him sleep; no stander wants to wake up a squatter, especially one barely old enough to know the use of what he'd lost. Spear had picked up her lost hand and run into the forest like she knew a sewer-on of hands whose shop closed soon. I don't know where the bird went, or didn't at the time. It was like it disappeared. As for the Spanth, she was off down the road like nothing happened past a scratch and a bloody shirt, but something *had* happened.

Meeting that Ispanthian birder had just changed my fate.

2

The Bee and Coin

———·———

Getting Frella and Pagran back to our camp was no easy matter. I gave Pagran back his glaive to crutch himself along on and had to let Frella lean her weight on me over a mile of uneven ground. Luckily, she was skinny—fit for palisades, as soldiers say, so she was less of a burden than she might have been. My masters at the Low School would have chided me for helping those two. They would have seen that getting trounced on the White Road was the end of our none-too-jolly band and that the archers who ran away, being brother and sister, were loyal only to each other and likely to help themselves to whatever we'd left behind before scampering off to the next adventure.

What I'd left behind was my fiddle, a fine helmet I'd hoped to sell, and a jug of Galtish whiskey. I didn't really care about the helmet, and there was barely enough burnwater left to wet my lips, but that fiddle meant something to me. I'd like to tell you it had belonged to my da or something, but my da was a sad bastard miner and couldn't play the arse-horn after a quart of beans and cabbage. I stole that fiddle. Walked off with it while a mate argued with a music student about whether his singing at a tavern had been in key. For the record, it wasn't, but it was a damned fine fiddle. So much so that, after our con, I paid my mate his half of its worth rather than sell it. And now it was likely off to be sold for next to nothing and the two shytes who will have taken it so far ahead of me I had little chance to catch them.

* * *

Cadoth was the first town west of the Forest of Orphans and the last town in Holt proper before you get to the yet gloomier forests and broad highlands of Norholt. You can tell how big a town is by how many gods have temples there and how big those temples are. For example, a village with one mud road, one tavern that's really just the back of a fat man's house, and a dying ox everyone shares at plowing time will have an Allgod church. No roof, logs to sit on, an altar with tallow candles and a niche where different gods' statues will go depending on the holiday. Those statues will be carved from ash or hickory, with generous breasts on the goddesses and unthreatening pillicocks on the gods, except Haros, who will be hung like the stag he is, because everyone knows he screws the moon so hard she has to sink beneath the hills and rest from it.

A slightly bigger town, one with a full-time whore who doesn't also brew beer or mend shirts, will have an Allgod church with a thatched roof and a bronze disc in a square of lead or iron, plus a proper temple to whichever local deity they feel will defecate least upon their hopeful, upturned faces.

Cadoth was as big as a town gets before someone decides it's a city. A proper trade town at a proper crossroads, it had an Allgod church crowned with a bronze sun, a huge tower to Haros topped with wooden stag horns, plus temples to a dozen other divinities scattered here and there. Notably absent were Mithrenor, god of the sea—nobody much bothers inland—and the Forbidden God, for obvious reasons.

One thing a town this size *will* have is a proper Hanger's House, as the Takers Guild Hall is called, and I would need to head there to discuss my debt to them. My adventures with Pagran and his cutty, stabby, punchy crew had gone well enough that summer, until we got our arses pulped and handed to us by the Spanth and her murder-bird. Now Nervous and Snowcheeks, the sibling archers who'd scampered when the bird joined the fray, had all but cleaned me out. I needed money—fast—and playing a few hands of Towers would be a good way to start.

I knew I'd find a game at the Bee and Coin because a Bee and
a Coin were two of the cards in the Towers deck, besides the
Towers, the Kings and Queens, Soldiers, Shovels, Archers, Death,
the Traitor, and, of course, Thieves, signified in common decks
by an illustration of a grasping hand.

Not everyone in the tavern would be a cards player. A few sheep-
herders and root farmers faithful to the gods of sour frowns held
down edgeward tables, talking low about rain and weevils, their
never-washed woolens insulated with decades of hand-wiped meat
grease. Two younger bravos near the bar had short copper cups at
their belts, used in Towers to collect coin. Despite their swords,
these fellows seemed leery of a trio of hard-looking older women
*clink-clink*ing away at Towers around a worm-bitten table.

I was leery, too, but I wanted a game.

"Do you care for a fourth?" I said, mostly to the bald killer
shuffling the deck. She looked at my tattoo. She had every right
to slap me for it but didn't seem keen on it. Neither of the other
two playing cards wanted a beer more than they wanted a cordial
start to the game, so neither of them claimed the prize either.

Baldy nodded at the empty chair, so I put my arse in it.

"Lamnur deck or Mouray?" I said.

"What'chye fuckin' think?"

"Right. Lamnur."

Nobles and such used the Mouray deck. Better art on that one.
But folks with permanent dirt on their collars played the Lamnur
deck, simpler images, two queens instead of three, no Doctor
card to save you if you draw Death. For my part, I prefer the
Mouray deck, but I'm partial to second chances.

"Now pay the price," she said.

I dug sufficient coins out of my purse to ante.

Clink-clink!

She dealt me in.

I won two of the three Tourney rounds and folded the third so not to seem to be cheating, but the War round's chest was too fat to pass up. The pale blondy woman with the scar like a fishhook bet heavy, thinking herself invincible with the last King in the deck, but I dropped the Traitor on her, archered off the Queen that would have caught the Traitor, took that King, and won. Again. A lot.

"The fuck'r ye doin' that, ye slipper?" the bald one said, leaving out the *how* like a good Holtish street thug. *Slipper* wasn't such a nice thing to be called, either, but then I had just bankrouted her.

"Just lucky," I said, not lying.

More about luck later.

She hovered between stabbing me and slapping me, settling finally on exile.

"The fuck out th'table" she said, as in *I should get,* so I pouched my winnings up in my shirt, slid them into my belt-purse, and walked away smiling, followed after by several comments about my father, none of which I hoped were true. They all wanted to slap me, but were too enthralled by the game; they would stay nailed to the table until two of them were destitute, and then they'd likely fight. Little wonder preachers of so many gods rail against the game—it had killed more folk than the Murder Alphabet. I almost said it killed more than goblins had, but that would be too gross an exaggeration even for me.

I made my way toward the bar, and what should I see leaning on its rough wood, past a large fellow built for eclipse, but the Spanth from the road. We shared an awkward nod. The space at the bar next to her, the one I had been just moving to occupy, was suddenly taken by some rentboy with too much black makeup around the eyes. Those eyes inventoried the birder and found much to approve. She was a very handsome woman in her way, what with her black hair and seawater-blue eyes, but I hadn't worked out if she would look better if she didn't seem sleepy or if the heavy-lidded look gave her a certain charm. Men love a woman who doesn't seem to give a damn, so long as she's hand-some. We also love a happy woman, so long as she's fair, or a sad pretty one, or an angry girleen with a good face. You see how this works. So, yes, the Spanth was fair. But if she had to summon a smile to put out a fire, half the town would burn. She didn't seem to notice the keen young pennycock next to her, rather occupy-ing herself with her wine and staring into the middle distance. Troubled girl with good bones. The lads love that.

I found another place to stand.

A Galtish harper of some talent was singing "The Tattered Sea," a song that had become popular after enough men had died to make calling humanity *mankind* sound a bit off. The word in vogue these last twenty years was *kynd*.

Her voice wasn't half-bad, so nobody threw a bottle at her.

One day upon the Tattered Sea
I waded out upon the waves
A comely young man for to see
Who looked to me more knight than knave

Now swam he toward a maiden brave
Who treaded water in the brine
I should have left, my shame to save
But I swam after, close behind

For I was young and poorly bred
With much to learn of lechery
Beneath the waves I dunked my head
And what there should I hap to see?

I found a tail fin fairly twinned
Where I had sought four legs entwined
Said I, "O, brother, are you kynd?"
Said he, "No kynd, but surely kind

I'm kind enough to send you home
Though kynd above I seem to be
You'll find no pleasure 'neath the foam
Nor husband in the Tattered Sea"

Then kindly did the mermaid speak
To teach a daughter of the kynd
"Go back to land and loam and seek
A legsome lad more fond than finned"

So turned I from the ocean cool
Much wiser than a maid might wish
For I swam out and found a school
Where lustily I sought a fish

She got a few coins in her hat and too few claps, even counting mine, so she gathered her harp and went on to the next tavern and hopefully a more grateful audience.

I saw that, in one corner, a spellseller of the Magickers Guild—her face powdered white, her thumb and first two fingers of her left hand pinched together to cant her Guild allegiance—had lit a beeswax candle with a braid of hair tied around it to advertise she was open for custom. It wasn't a moment before a young woman in rough-spun wools slipped her a coin and started whispering her wants in the witch's ear.

Just after I ordered and got my first taste of the decent red ale they served at the Bee and Coin, a nasty-looking little fellow in waxy, stained leathers came up to my other side at the bar, staring right at my tattoo. It was a tattoo of an open hand with certain runes on it, and it sat on my right cheek. You could only see it by firelight, and then it showed up as a light reddish-brown, not too prominent, a bit like old henna. You could miss it altogether. Unfortunately, this fellow didn't.

"That's the Debtor's Hand, yae?"

Yae, he said, a northern Holtish affectation. It seemed they were all Norholters here, which figured—we weren't so far from the provincial border.

I was required to acknowledge the tattoo, but I didn't have to be sweet about it.

"Yae," I said, stretching it out just a little so he couldn't tell if I was mocking him or if I was a fellow rube.

"Ye see that, barkeep?"

"I do," she said without looking back. She was up on a stool now, fetching the Spanth's wine from a high shelf.

"Anybody claim the Guild-gift yet?" the rube said.

"Nae," said the barkeep, yet another Norholter. "Not tonight." Now Leathers took my measure. I leaned back to give him a look at the blade on my belt, a fine stabber and slasher. A serious knife. A knife-fighter's knife. I called her Palthra, Galtish for "petal"— the rondel at the back of my belt was Angna, or "nail"—and I had two wee leather roses inlaid on Palthra's sheath. Not that Leathers would likely see more than the sheath and handle. I'd be unthumbed if I pulled a blade on any who slapped me in the Takers' name, and should I bleed them, I'd be poked by the Guild wherever I poked them for the slap.

But did this kark know that?

"Then I claim the Guild-gift. Debtor, in the name of the Takers, ye'll have this."

Yah, he knew it.

He looked back at the prettier of the two girleens he had been nose-rubbing with, then, never taking his eyes off her, he flashed out his hand and popped my cheek. It stung, of course, especially the ring that cut my lip against my tooth a little, but the slaps never hurt as much as the knowledge that a moron got to paddle my cheeks and I could make no answer. I wasn't even allowed to speak to him again unless he spoke first.

The barkeep poured the fellow his half pint of beer, on the Guild, putting enough head on it to let him know what she

thought of him making Norholters look like cowards for striking those not allowed to return the favor. The rube drank from
it, painting his near hairless upper lip with foam, which he then
wiped with his sleeve.

"Man ought to pay what he owes," he said with the conviction
of the freshly twenty, as much to himself as to the room generally, but that was all I needed. He wasn't supposed to speak to me
after. Now I could talk.

"Man also ought to have a bit of callus on his hands," I said.
"Yours look borrowed from a high-nut boy."

He seemed surprised I answered, but covered as well as he
could, raising his half pint at me like he got what he wanted and
didn't care what I said, but he cared, all right. Someone had snig-
gered at what I said, and the laugh cut him, especially in front of
his henlets. Oh, I knew his sort. Family had a bit of coin, but he
was such an arsehole he'd up and left the inn or the chandlery or
whatever business his bunioned mother ran because he couldn't
stand to be told what to do. Might have found his way to a Guild
straw farm to get filled up with useless tricks and style himself
a thief, but he couldn't hack even that and got bounced before
his debt could sink him. Gone long enough now that his clothes
reeked, but he still hadn't pawned his last good ring. Was one hard
week away from turning cunnyboy or sell-sword, but wasn't sweet
or clever enough for the first or strong enough for the second.

I was a half heartbeat away from pitying him, but my face still
stung from his bastard hand, so I said, "You can have another
slap at me, as far as the Guild's concerned. Seems a shame you
wasted your first one doing so little harm, you fatherless kark."

A kark is a wet fart, by the way, if you've never been to Galtia
or Norholt. The kind you think will be one thing but turns out
to be the other, to your shame and sorrow. It's why a Galt says,
"Close the whiskey jug," not cork it. We say cork and kark almost
the same, and most of us don't hate whiskey so much we'd go
putting a kark in it.

Several at the tavern hooed at that, shepherds and farm women mostly, not the sort to forgive weakness. He couldn't let that be the last word, or he'd likely have one or two of them to reckon with as the taps kept flowing. A smart lad would've hustled the girls off to whatever hayrick awaited their exchange of crotch-fleas. But he wasn't smart.

"I wasn't trying to hurt ye, I just wanted the beer. But I'll hurt ye if y'like, y'shyte-tongue Galtie knap."

The Spanth opened the wine with her teeth and poured her-self a gurgle, one eyebrow raised in amused curiosity. She likely won't have known that a knap was a tit, nor will she have known that the word I was about to use meant a particularly cute tuft of pubic hair.

"I doubt that, sprumlet," I said. "I've had a hard piss hurt me worse than you look like to. But if you'd care to try, I'm all face for your knuckles. So why don't you come and have another throw before your little sisters get the idea they're at the wrong table."

I touched my black tongue to the tip of my nose and winked at him.

That did the trick.

He rushed across the tavern and punched at my jaw. I shrugged up and leaned so my shoulder caught most of it. I won't bore you with a blow by blow, except to tell you that he flailed his little cat paws at me, and soon, we ended up tussling on the floor, me grabbing his head close, now an arm, grabbing his head again. He smelled like week-old sweat and like his leathers had had the mold at some time or another, and they never really come back from that, do they? The barkeep was all "Here, here!" and "Now, now!" until she flubbed us apart with the end of the flail she'd had mounted over the brassheet mirror, probably the very one she'd parted goblin hair with in the Daughters' War.

I got up holding a hand to my bloodied lip, evidently worse off than Stinkleathers, and he flipped his longish hair back in a move that a cockerel would have been proud of. Since he'd been the first to throw a punch and he was obviously a twat, the bartender gave him a shove toward the door. He collected the girleens on his way out, saying, "Regards to the Guild," in such a nasty way I was now sure he'd been chewed by the Takers and spat out.

"Sorry you didn't get to finish your beer," I said to his retreating back.

I looked up where the Spanth had been standing, but she had slipped out during the fray. A woman who's got someplace to be. A woman who doesn't want to be recognized. Intriguing. I saw the fancy man with the made-up eyes looking at me with the same casual disinterest he might have shown a dog who wandered in. I winked at him. He sneered and looked away, which was what I wanted him to do, because I had to palm something from my mouth to my pouch.

It was Stinkleathers's ring.

Goblin silver.

Probably the most valuable thing he still owned.

Worth letting him hit me a few glancing blows at bad angles I entirely controlled. I had given his finger a good pinch as I stripped the ring so he would still feel it there, he wouldn't notice its absence until he hit the bedstraw if I were lucky.

And I was.

Very, very lucky.

In many ways, I'm perfectly ordinary. A bit shorter than most, but Galts run small. Thin as a stray dog. No arse to speak of, so I need a belt to keep my breeches north of Crackmere. I'm a decent fiddler, as I've said, and you wouldn't punch me in the throat for singing near you, but you wouldn't be like to hire me for your wedding either. Some things I'm shyte at. Not laughing when I find something funny, for example. Adding figures in my head. Farmwork. Lifting heavy weights. But thieving? That I've a talent for. And part of that talent is a pure gift for and awareness of luck. Luck is the first of my two great birth-gifts—more about the second later.

Luck is very real, and anyone who tells you differently wants all the credit for their own success. Luck is a river. I can actually feel when I'm in it and when I'm out of it, too. Think about that for a moment. Most people try something difficult or unlikely with very little notion of whether it'll work or not. Not me. When I feel the inner sunshine of good luck under my breastbone, I know that, yes, I can snatch that woman's pouch and that it's got a diamond or three gold lions in it. I know I can make the far jump to the next roof and that my foot will miss the loose tiles. And I know when I sit down to shuffle a Towers deck, the other fellow's going to drown in Bees and Shovels and probably get a visit or two from our old friend Death.

Playing games of chance wakes luck up in me, and soon, it's running out of control. You can only win so many hands or dice-throws before the others are ready to cut your throat. Worse, running through my luck at the gaming table means I'll be well out of it when I need it. When I feel the empty chill of luck running thin, I know a walk on an icy path is like to split my tailbone. I keep my head down, because I've good odds to meet a man I ran a confidence game on the year before or some girleen I left things sour with.

It was luck that got me moved from a straw farm to a True School when I joined the Takers Guild. Normally, see, they recruit all the lads and lasses they can get to sign for the Low School, but only three of the nine schools are true. The straw farms teach basic lock-picking, basic climbing, some knife-fighting, but nothing advanced. No spells. No trap-finding or animal-talking, no cozening, no misdirection. Just loads of conditioning. You graduate from a straw farm strong, fast, tough, lightly skilled, and heavily in debt. If you can pay your debt somehow, good on you. When you can't, you're indentured. This means the Guild has at its beckon many thousands of leg-breakers, prostitutes, and hard laborers. They can summon a mob to terrorize a town, then disperse and hide them before the baron's spearmen show up.

Myself, I went to a True School.

Or at least I think I did.

But I am nonetheless very much in debt, as they want us all to be.

Here, read for yourself.

> Our Most Esteemed Kinch Na Shannack,
> Third Year Physical,
> First Year Magus,
> Debtor
>
> It is with great reluctance and no small disappointment that we, the bursars of the Pigdenay Academy of Rare Arts, in fealty to the Takers Guild, inform you that the meat of your debt has outgrown the shell of your willingness to work and is at risk to crack your body.
>
> As your last five seasonal payments to us averaged less than two trounces each, at this laggardly march, you will not clear your debt of eighty-five trounces gold, one gold queening, one silver knight, and three silver knaves (plus interest), for a period of some sixteen years. Our actuaries need not be bothered to tell us this is beyond your likely life span and at the outer limit of your plausibly useful years in the profession. It is only at the argument of one of your former masters that we have measured your remunerative value alive and unmaimed beyond your cautionary value harmed for all to see or dead for all to know.
>
> You are therefore commanded, on pain of unthumbing, to deliver yourself to the closest chartered Guildhouse for a lookover and a tongue-wag, the most likely outcome being a deed indenture of the greater sort. Our intelligence places you on the White Road and suggests that Cadoth may be the advertised Guildhouse most near your person. Of course, prompt payment, upon your arrival, in the amount of

Two lions gold and five owlets silver

or

One trounce gold, two queenings gold, one shilling silver

will render the conversation far more cordial and do much to reassure us as to your good intentions toward your promise. We need not remind you that the skills gifted to you within our walls render most students capable of discovering monies enough to clear their names within seven years leisurely or three years hard and lucky, and that our lenience in only burdening you with the mark of the open hand will not long persist without some laudable action on your part.

Tenderly (for now),

The Humble Bursars

of

Your Masters in Arts Rare and Coveted

By our hand

This First Lūnday of Ashers, 1233 Years Marked

It was now the eighteenth, exactly halfway through Ashers. Lammas month was coming fast, and with it, a new payment due the Guild.

Stinkleathers's ring had been a good start, but I was going to have to do some stealing in Cadoth.

And I was going to need a buyer.

3

Tick-Turd

---·---

"Goblin silver, eh?" said the oldish woman scowling through a lens at Stinkleathers's ring, not that she needed a lens to know it had been worked under a goblin's hammer; goblin silver gave light back green, and some thought its weird beauty put gold to shame. And by some, I mean me. The light of her candle-lamps showed off my open-hand tattoo to great effect as well. "And yer on the bad side of the Takers. Ye want work?"

She didn't really want to hire me for anything. She wanted to know how hungry I was. She didn't get her shop full of high-end stolen goods by hiring people she didn't know.

"I'm already working, but thank you."

"Think nothin' of it."

Turns out that's exactly what I thought.

"Who's working ye, then? Ye with Cobb?"

"Ten shillings," I said, "and I'll be grateful for any owlets."

She laughed, showing the brown nubs that passed for teeth.

"Owlets I got, but yer nae getting ten. More like six for this."

"We both know it's worth fifteen to you, and you'll sell it for a queening and a gold whore. My game is I ask for one shilling more every time you offer less than I say. Now I want eleven. If you prefer to give me twelve, offer me seven."

"Why, ye little tick-turd," she said.

"I don't charge for you calling me things, I like being called things. But if you want this beautiful bit of silver greening, I need eleven, preferably—"

"Owlets, yae, I know, ye little—"

"If you call me a tick-turd again, it's twelve. I only love laziness in myself."

She shut her nub-box, then squinted at me.

A snoring came down at us through the roof-boards.

Her eyes unsquinted.

"Yes, I know, he was going to follow me out and give me rough hugs in the alley if you said so. I did a little sleep spell while you goggled my ring. A cantrip. Small magic. Thief magic. Wouldn't have worked on a strong-minded fellow, but that one's overfond of his beer and stretching his shirts a bit, judging by his snore. Fat men have a singular snore."

As if to illustrate, the snore hitched, paused, then sawed down louder.

"I'll give ye nine just to get ye and yer eastie talk out of here the faster, ye Galtish tick-turd."

"You'll give me thirteen because you threw low and then repeated yourself."

She moved like she meant to toss me out herself, but then settled back in place.

"Ten, and that's robbery enough."

"Fourteen. And if you hesitate again, I might start thinking how the shop on Featherbow Street there under the bell tower might like to have a look at this. Spider sign over that one—Cobb's, yeah? Rival of yours? Used to be a lover when you could both see what you peed with? Just that little bit of sour warmth in your voice when you mentioned him earlier. The fact you haven't kicked me out yet tells me you'll pay fifteen like I said, but if you're quick and smart, I'll take fourteen because I'm sentimental and you remind me of the smelly old woman who took my virginity."

She pressed her mouth shut by sheer tonnage of will, counted out fourteen shillings, none of them owlets, and shoved them at me, pocketing the ring. I pursed up my money, wondering if she was really going to let me go without a last rejoinder.

She wasn't.

She hissed the next bit like an Urrimad basket-snake.

"I can see ye think yer clever, and praps y'are, but by my lights, yer nothin' but a dirty, blacktongue thief and will ne'er be more."

I smiled an oily smile, half bowed, and stepped out backward, just dodging a strand of drool probing its way down from a murder-hole in the ceiling.

I heard something break against the door after I shut it.

I truly love the thrill of commerce.

Now I was off to the Takers Guild to see how much of their carefully rationed goodwill I might buy back.

4

The Hanger's House

"How's your face?"

I was sitting at a table in the Hanger's House. The building was quite near the front gate, sitting in plain sight. This was the official, lower-level way to reach the Takers Guild. Of course, the Guild is where you think they aren't, but they're also where they say they are, which means they have little to fear from barons and dukes, and they have even been known to flout a king. No crown sits so sure that a knife in the dark may not topple it.

I had noted the square wooden sign with our hanged man holding his own noose. Good sign, that, different colors of wood inlaid and a border of gold leaf. Also, a gold livre-coin nailed to the hanged man's free hand because nobody would dare to take it. A Gallardian lion, I noticed. Did I mention I love those? The woman sitting across from me reading my lamb-parchment ledger sheet was distractingly pretty. She appeared to be about nineteen, but the hairs on the back of my neck told me she was magicked, so she might have been older than the cronish owlet-miser I had just left.

"Nobody's managed to slap it off me yet, so no complaints."

The girl might have broadened her waifish smile a hairs-breadth; she might not have. Behind her, an Assassin-Adept, who had so little fat on her you could count her muscles through her tight but giving woolens and silks, lounged against the bar, just lounged lazy as the long day, as if she weren't threat made flesh. It was hard not to stare at the adept; you could tell from her blackened neck, cheeks, and forearms she was inked almost from crown to soles in dark glyphs that would let her disappear, drink poison, spit poison. I had seen an adept at the Low School fly. Actually fly. There were maybe a hundred of them in the world. Or maybe only twenty. Whoever knew wasn't saying. I stopped reading the glyphs on the adept's skin before anyone caught me doing it. I wondered what the clock tattoo on her chest did.

The false waif checked the seal on my document against the one in the huge book slouched open before her, then wrote *1T 1Q 14s* on each. She passed a witness coin bound to her wrist over the trounce, queening, and fourteen shillings on the table, then fed them to a leather sack, which she tossed to the Assassin-Adept, who ferried them behind the bar and appeared to descend stairs, though she had just as likely disappeared upstairs.

"Staying tonight, Prank?" the maybe-young woman said, definitely broadening her smile. A Prank is the lowest thieving rank, but a true thief, not a Scarecrow, and that's something. I was made a Prank at the Low School in Pigdenay. Assuming I clear my debt, complete another year of study, and/or pull off a notorious caper or three, I promote to Fetch. Then, should I further distinguish myself in all the wrong company, I may earn the title of Faun. A Faun in myth has deer's legs—you'll not easily catch a Faun. Has a nice ring, doesn't it? One of the Guild's strengths is its poetry—it makes you feel you belong to something not only unopposably strong but also wickedly sly and clever.

Most of the best of us are content to remain Fauns because the last level is for ascetics and the half-mad.

The last rank of thieves, called Famines, takes an oath of hunger, and they further swear to pay for nothing. What they cannot steal, the rest of us provide for them, but even the older and slowed-down among them earn their keep by running schemes, planning for the able-bodied, and teaching. I'd learned under the baton of a Famine or two.

My interviewer hadn't closed the book yet. "It says you favor tall girls. Is that true?" Even as she spoke, her legs lengthened, and she was looking down at me where we had once been level. I felt a pleasant but embarrassing sensation that caused me to cross my legs. "It's a new moon tonight, you know. Most propitious for first couplings. One gold queening and I'm yours 'til midnight."

"If you knew what I've done to get that money."

"If you knew what I could do to make you forget."

"Who's going to watch the shop? While I wreck your womb and enslave your heart, I mean?"

"I had them both removed. And she will," she said, nodding at an older but still-lovely woman who had appeared behind the bar. A second look confirmed it was the same girl who sat across from me now, only twenty years older. This "girl" was no mere secretary or whore; she was quite probably a Worry (a high enforcer), taking direct orders from the Problem (think mayor). My skin flushed warm with an ugly, seething jealousy. However she had doubled herself, whether grafting, echoing, or somehow bending time, I would never do magic that strong. Never.

"Never," I said.

"Never what?" she said, pressing her tongue to the corner of her mouth and letting it retreat.

"I'll never get this tattoo off me if I don't . . ." I trailed off, watching the place her tongue had been, enjoying the hum of the erotic cantrip she was working on me.

"Pay the family?" her mouth said.

"Yes."

"What if I told you that I had work for you?"

"I'd say keep talking for as long as I get to watch your mouth move."

"I have work for you," she said. Before I could respond, she pressed a witness coin to my head and magicked pictures into my mind.

I saw.

I saw.

I was running in the cold at sunset.

I was a woman, a youngish girl pressing a witness coin into my head and turning to look behind me.

Somebody yelled at me in Oustrim's language, Gunnish, which I don't normally speak, telling me not to look.

I saw a tower of two colors in ruins, its stones collapsed. I saw a massive statue toppled on its face. The king's bodyguard formed up, presenting wing-tip spears to a shadow coming out of the dust; they were marching backward with great discipline, despite their terror. Huge drums beat, strange horns lowed, and everyone was yelling. Stones flew through the air, and arrows. A ram horn sounded a lamenting retreat.

More shadowy figures could be seen beyond the wreckage of the keep, each of them the height of two men and built like barrels. They held axes with bronze heads the size of children's coffins and slings that could hurl stones a man would want two hands to lift. Some held the trunks of trees to their belts as cabers. One chucked just such a tree, and it spun and hit the halberd-men, killing or crippling as it went. The rest of the king's guard ran.

A hand clutched at me and spun me, and a woman with a big emerald on a gold choker shouted into my face with wine-breath to run, just run, and somewhere, a child screamed. Everything went black, and then I was standing on a sort of rocky hill watching small figures stream out of the broken city in the last light, watching large ones stream in. Fires chuffed black pillars into the sky, reflected on the face of a large, calm lake or bay. Crows and gulls wheeled over a battlefield just beyond the breached west walls. I was cold.

Next, I was a blond girl in wobbly candlelight, looking into a mirror with this coin stuck to my head, blood from a scratch on my hairline slimed on my skin. I wore the emerald choker. I was aware of a dagger at my left side, a dagger I knew how to use very, very well. I said my name, which wasn't mine, and my hair turned brown. I said, in Gunnish, that I had paid my debt. I stared at the tattoo of a rose on my cheek, barely visible in the candlelight. I said, "Get it off me." I said it again, dead-eyed, and I shuddered. And everything went dark.

A witness coin was powerful magic, and so far as I knew, its images were always true. I had just seen something not known in Manreach for seven hundred years and more. This was a giants' *army*. One giant was formidable enough, but they were said to live in small clans beyond the Thrall Mountains, content to milk their giant hilloxen and enslave small folk stupid enough to go too far west. Five or ten at once was the most you were like to see. That they had banded together and crossed those treacherous mountains in sufficient numbers to lay low a city's walls, crush its guard, and send its people running to the foothills, that was something awful and new to living generations.

Had we survived thirty years of tussle with the biters just to be tread over by bigguns? Not that Holt and the eastern kingdoms were soon to fall under their shadow—Hrava, the capital city of Oustrim, was eight weeks' hard travel west of Holt by ass or ox-cart, a season's walk, or a rotten month at sea away. Six kingdoms lay between here and there. But how numerous was this army? What did it want? Could the kingdoms stop it if it meant to tram-ple east and east all the way to the Mithrene Sea?

She interrupted my reverie, taking the witness coin back and giving me a not unfriendly pinch.

"We believe a certain Spanth you met on the road is going to Oustrim, probably to the city of Hrava. You will go with her. Win her confidence if you can—if not, follow her unseen and await further instruction," the not-waif said. "The assault of that kingdom by giants has set large wheels in motion, and the Guild has an interest in how those wheels turn. The particulars of your mission are better not known to you at this time—if it becomes necessary to tell others why you are going, tell them you are to recover certain magical items held in the reliquary of the king of Oustrim, among them the Keshite arrow wand, a ring of Catfall, and the Hard-Stone Torque."

"That last, what's it do?" I said. "Make old husbands stand like young ones?"

"No. But I like the way you think."

The way her tongue kissed her upper teeth when she said *think* made it so I couldn't stop looking at her mouth again.

"Time is not your friend, Kinch," she said. "The Spanth will not dawdle, but see that you push her when you may to make haste, and do not delay her by your own folly, or it will cost you more than coin. Today is the nineteenth of Ashers, and the moon shows the inky face we nightlings love so well. Try to make Hrava by the first of Vintners, two bright moons hence, though the gods only know what will happen there by then with the city now fallen."

"All your talk of moons has lit my blood," I said to her. "Half a queening? For just half the night?"

She smiled at me now with a mouthful of rotten teeth, worse even than those of the pawnbroker.

"You get what you pay for," she said.

I practically ran out of there.

5

A Fox to Run With

---•---

"Are you going to Oustrim?" I asked the Spanth.

This was at the inn I had tracked her to, the Roan Horse, a handsome old wooden firetrap much loved by travelers keen to spare their purses. I was sitting in a chair by the Spanth's bed when I spoke, and it really wasn't a fair question, considering she was sleeping.

Quick as summer lightning, she caught me up by the heel and dangled me upside down out of the window I had opened. What she didn't know was that I hadn't spoken until I was ready to wake her—I'd already had a peek around her room and looked through her meager worldly goods. No bath in this place, but a bowl of murky water where she'd washed, bloody wrap-linens soaking in it, fresh ones on her arm where my arrow pricked her. Her shield leaning against the wall. That pretty *spadín* of hers naked on the bed beside her—very like a Gunnish seax, but more elegant. An angular sword, the blade just shy of two feet long, broader near the foible, with a stout spine, a fuller, and a wicked point that called to mind a shard of broken glass. How fast she would have driven that into my heart had I breathed wrong as I leaned over her!

But there's the thrill of the profession.

Her pouches hadn't been hard to peek into. She had less money than you'd want if you were going far, at least on her belt. I didn't take any. It wasn't so much money that she wouldn't miss whatever I took, and I wanted her on my side. It's hard for me to leave money in its bag, though. I've got some sort of disease about money, a love for coin that has little to do with commerce.

I just love the way it looks, and feels, and smells. I hoped one day to hoard enough of it to run through my hands with no need to spend it.

She had Ispanthian silver—three lotuses and two king's heads complete with long-haired mustachioed King Kalith at his mustachiest—but also Holtish shillings, a few copper shaves, and even one Gallardian lion worth all the rest combined. I smelled that one, ran my thumbnail on its ridges, even put it in my mouth and savored its taste. That one was gold. Don't worry, I dried it on my shirt before I put it back, though I stared at it again. I love the way the lion looks like he's smiling. I love the three swords vertical and one cross dagger on the back.

Gallardians know their money, best engravers and sculptors in the east, as good as the ones in Old Kesh, before the Knock. My favorite coin is the Gallardian owlet, which isn't even gold. Just silver. But whoever carved the stamp for that one must have loved owls, it looked just like one, you expected the bastard to hoo at you. And on the tails side, a tree with a crescent moon behind. I hate spending owlets when I get them, but eventually I have to, I always run out of money. Whatever was in the messenger bag would have to stay her secret; she had been sleeping on it.

It didn't sit heavy where she wore it, so not many coins if it were coins. Probably had bearer notes from a bank or jewels or some other light currency, but you never know what's in a person's most guarded pouches. Where I thought to find money, I've nipped sacks containing locks of horse mane, a bag of sand, a pouch of baby teeth. The strangest thing was a dried heart, almost certainly human. I'm glad *that* fucker didn't catch me.

But then, none of them catch me.

Where was I? Right, upside down. And don't picture the Spanth holding me by the ankle one-handed like some Thrall Mountains quarter-giant. No, she had me two-handed, elbows braced on the sill. I didn't struggle. Just crossed my arms. Felt rather good, actually, all the blood going to my head.

"Are you bound for Oustrim?" I said again. "And where'd the bird go?"

"Shut up about the bird."

"Fine. What's your name, then?"

"You don't need to know it."

"All right. But are you going to Oustrim?"

"You're a Guild thief. You have training and magic. If I drop you, it won't hurt you, will it?"

"If I say no, will you think of a different way to hurt me?"

"Maybe."

"Then yes, it will hurt me very much. Please, brave knight, do not drop me on my melon."

She dropped me, but I don't hold that against her.

We were only on the third floor.

Using the wall to brake myself, I landed on my feet and rolled. Then I climbed back up to the window, pretty fast. She had her sword ready, but not in my face or anything. She knew I could have killed her while she slept. Not that she was careless, she'd locked the window tight, I'm just hard to keep out. And even harder to kill. If you speak Galtish and know my name, you probably figured that out already.

In our blackish, brackish tongue, a *kinch* is a loop in a rope, or a noose. It can also mean a tangle or an unexpected problem, which I certainly was for my mother, being only three months younger than my parents' wedding day. I suppose *unexpected trouble* describes Galts generally, at least as we've been found by our conquerors from Holt. It took the Holtish fifty years to subjugate our lands, and they've spent the three centuries since regretting it. No good at taking orders, blacktongues, we'll never be invading anybody—but we're hell on our own soil. Galts are natural archers and good at throwing anything from a stone to a spear to a rotten squash. Fine musicians and riders, too, back when horses ran on the plains.

That, of course, was before the goblins came.

They say Galts are what's left of elves, with our gently pointy ears and small bones. My hair's browny copper, more red in the light, and my beard comes in ginger, what little I can grow. Not that the question of elves had been decided—most university twats said no, some said mayhap, but every village near a peat bog had the legend of some old tuber-farmer hauling up a wee manlike thing with bog-blackened skin, sharp ears, and the finest jewelry you've ever seen. Not that anyone you knew personally had seen one, and the jewelry had always been stolen or sold. But what did I know?

Nothing but my name.

"My name is Kinch, or Kinch Na Shannack, or fucking Kinch if you prefer. It won't be the first time I've heard it," I said.

She grunted.

I sat cross-legged on the sill, looking at the Spanth with my big, lady-killing green eyes. Eyes light like western jade, I'd been told.

"Shall we journey west together?"

She considered me. "What will you do for me?"

"It's what we'll do for each other."

"So tell me."

"I'll watch while you sleep. Sleep while you watch. I'll lie to you when it doesn't matter, but I'll also lie for you when it does. If you let me do the talking, I'll make sure you miss the penny-cock with the pizzle-itch and get the best wine in the merchant's barrel. You'll never again meet a door you can't get through nor a wall you can't get eyes over. I need your arms, yes, but you need my nose. If you do the worst of the fighting, I'll make sure you know where your foes are coming from and cull the weak ones. I won't be your dog, but if you're half the wolf I think you are, you've found a fox to run with."

She said, "Ask me again tomorrow," and went to sleep with her back to me.

6

The Wasted Plum

---·---

The next day, adolescent, yellow-shirted runners from the Runners Guild came to Cadoth, and after the baron broke the seals on the messages they carried, the baron's town mouths stood atop step-boxes to read the hastily prepared bans. The mouth I heard first was a plumpish girl with deep lungs. Her inbreath reminded me of a dragon getting ready to breathe fire.

"Listen all! Listen all! Word has reached the fair and serene Baron Anselm of Cadoth and His Most August Majesty, King Conmarr of Holt, that the lands known as Oustrim! Have been most treacherously invaded! By armies from beyond the Thrall Mountains!"

This girl was loud, her voice ringing off glass panes and stone walls, her mouth opening so wide as she spoke, I could see her back teeth.

"The capital city, Hrava, has fallen! And the king is feared dead! A merchant from Molrova, a man well known to the person of the baron, has had a runner last night! And assures us that the walls of his kingdom, the Oxbone Walls, just east of Oustrim, have not been darkened! And that they cannot be breached!"

"Was it goblins?" a woman shouted. She had a thick Unthern accent and wore their traditional dress-like long-coat over her traditional Unthern gut. Her status as a foreigner didn't excuse her from the baron's justice, however, and the mouth pointed her baton at her so that two guards most folks hadn't noticed before scurried over and shook her until she thumbed half a silver out of her pouch. You don't interrupt the bans, not in Cadoth.

Everyone knew the lands of kynd stopped at the Thrall Mountains, so whatever came east wasn't human. Goblins weren't west, though, and not much north. Oustrim was cold, and those mountains were colder. Goblins don't like snow, or so I had heard. Goblins came from the Hordelands in the south, the huge island also known as Old Kesh, beyond the Hot Sea.

Right where we kicked them back to.

For now.

These people had not seen the hard truths of the witness coin as I had. They did not yet know that giants had spilled east. But some were figuring it out, and the rest would know soon.

"The baron stands with King Conmarr and knows you stand with him, each man, woman, and child. None are so faithful as Cadothmen! Nor so brave! For the falcon of Cadoth! Harralah!"

The crowd harralahed. The mouth stepped down and hurried off to the next square, step-box in hand, the guards trotting behind her. The roughed-up Untherdam supported herself on the ring of a long-unused horse-head hitching stone while she tested a burp to see if it would turn more material.

And the crowd talked.

I caught bits of it.

"Far too much like the start of the other business for my tastes."

"Rally? Y'think they'll call a rally?"

"—been training at the bow since I was a pup. What's it for if not for such?"

"Yer still a pup, girl, and wise tongues don't wag so. Wouldn't *be* training at the bow if they hadn't spent all the lads on goblins in the Threshers' War twenty years back. They went from the fields and shops in their hundreds of thousands and tried to smother the biters in numbers. And they fell in the corn and on the grass and in sand. They fell in mud and on stone, and sickened in their camps, and brought back whip-cough and worse."

"But then they let the women fight in the Daughters', and women are better."

"No better nor worse. In the Daughters', ye had the birds. And training. And men fought beside you, too."

"I have training. I can put a bodkin through a thrown plum."

"That just shows how soft y'are, ready to waste a plum."

The oldster had the right of it. Not enough hands to bring the crops in during the Threshers' War, and most of Manreach went hungry. We'd had it better in Galtia, with game in the woods and fish in the river.

"I'll kill a goblin," boasted the girleen.

"That's as they said, to a man, and all gone to the worming vaults now."

"S'not goblins," another old man said.

"Nae, s'worse."

"Nothin' worse."

"There's worse."

"How so?" said the girl.

"Goblins you look down at—what's past the Thralls looks down at you."

The gaffer who said that last was a one-legger, his empty pants leg pinned up, the hand at the crutch missing fingers. A goblin killer, he. Goblins bite.

But it wasn't goblins I was marching toward, and for that, I was strangely relieved.

Even as a slipper who'd never met a living goblin, I knew they'd brewed up plagues to sicken us and kill our horses. I knew the second war, the Threshers' War, went so badly you'd scarcely find a man between thirty and sixty, and the Daughters' War made so many women soldiers you'd hardly find a child between eight and fifteen.

The giants I'd seen in the witness coin were fearsome, and no question, but kynd and goblins were made to kill each other.

7

The Skinny Woman's Bride

———•———

Near midday, I was sitting alone at the Stag and Quiet Drum, a respectable tavern of leaning stone walls braced with beams of straight white pine. The nice thing about the Drum was that, for all the care the owner had taken to make the outside look good, his attic was a mess of unused, rarely disturbed junk, and it was among that junk I made my bed after leaving the Spanth.

Having found the rooms a bit too dear, not for their quality but for the contents of my purse, I had crawled in a high window, found the attic ladder, and gone up. It amused me to no end to sneak out of their stolen attic space and then come in again to pay for a beer, so here I was. I was nicely drunk and doing that thing I do when I think so hard my eyes unfocus and I look simple. Sometimes I even breathe through my mouth. I've been given alms when I do it on the street. They tried to break me of it at the Low School but at last gave up, one master arguing it was a sign of intelligence, another saying it looked more like a symptom of idiocy. The former, a Magus-Reverend, loved me for my skill at languages—the other, an Assassin-at-Rope, scorned me for my affability and the "ease with which I was like to die."

You can't please everyone.

So there I sat, staring into the middle distance, all but drooling while the walls of the Drum shook with a Galtish song in old Holtish. It was a ridiculous song about a magical cat named Bully Boy, and it wasn't worth explaining to them that where I come from it's a children's song to teach Galtish children the Holtish they're obliged to speak.

Still, here in Holt proper, every looming kark with beer on their chin fellows up with all the other twats whenever it's played, and they frog-blurt out what verses they remember of a song nobody from Galtia has sung since they were in knee-pants. Though, admittedly, the chorus does lend itself to drunken blurting.

I was thinking about giants.

As I have said, I come from Galtia, the easternmost of Holt's three kingdoms.

Platha Glurris, to be specific, which means "Shining River" in the language of the Galts, first people to rule Holt, but the real river is underground and made of silver.

My da mined silver, and my best friend's father did, too, until goblins killed the latter in the first battle of the Daughters' War in 1222, when I was twelve. My da came back from the same, unwilling to say more than a sentence at a time, and that rarely. Of course, I only had a year and some to watch him suffer—I was off to the Low School at fourteen, and I doubt he noticed I was gone. I never worked a mine and, gods willing, never will. They slaved like mules in the darkness below the pretty hills eight days of the nine that make a week, but on the last day, Sathsday, they went to church and sang songs. Then they drank hoppy, dark beer until they and their wives were too foggy to remember to unstopper in time, thus increasing the brotherhood of man.

And what god did my father sing to? Not the Galtish holdovers, stag-headed Haros or fox-faced Fothannon. Not Mithrenor, the old Holtish god of the sea. No, my father worshipped the Allgod, represented by a bronze disc in a wood square, or, for the very rich, a gold disc set in a square of iron or lead.

The Allgod, also called Sath, also called Father Sun, was the official god of Holt and its kingdoms. To my eye, the Allgod is the god of compromise and mediocrity, much approved of by the noble class for his gospel of work, obedience, and earning just enough to get by.

Whatever simpleton devised that deity showed a shocking lack of imagination, just walking outside and worshipping the first thing that made him squint. Quite different from the wild-haired, incestuous gods of the Galts. Quite the opposite of the Forbidden God, also called the Upside-Down God, about whom you don't speak in public in Manreach unless you want your tongue split. Old Upside-Downy was rumored to be the true god of my Takers Guild but that only the inner circles of power were schooled in his mystery.

That god might have been real for all I then knew, since he made people so angry, but the Allgod was shyte. He was the kind of god you prayed to for making water wet and fire hot, or for keeping giants out of a land where nobody has seen a giant for a thousand years. He was good at the easy things. I never saw a giant alive in Holt, just the stuffed dead one Bloth the clubfoot used to cart around on two carts lashed together in his Caravan of Sad Wonders and charge a copper shave to look at.

Now the song in the tavern was in full roar. Have you ever noticed how the very sotted delight in drawing out a final vowel? As if it's some kind of contest of breath? And so the Holtish morons of Cadoth sang, making cat noises, in perfect intellectual agreement with the five-year-olds of Platha Glurris.

> Here come a cat at gather week
> Rao rao Bully Boy rao
> A Winney-cat her love to seek
> Rao rao Bully Boy raaaaoooooooooo

Who was I to question anyone's intelligence, though? Streams of refugees would be flooding out of giant-stricken Oustrim even as I made my way toward it.

Now a shape loomed up at me.

"Barkeep?" this one shouted over her shoulder toward the bar while pointing at me.

The barkeep shook her head.

It was my Spanth.

I'd told her where I was staying.

"You're drunk," she said.

"Am not," I said, which is of course the second most frequent lie told in taverns.

She slapped me then, right on my tattoo. Pretty hard.

The brewer's wife was heard to say
She'd cleave the catling's tail in twae
So Bully raoed and ran away
Rao rao Bully Boy raaaaaaaaaaaaoooooooooooo

I opened my mouth, and then remembered I couldn't speak to her unless she spoke. She waited until I shut my mouth.

"Sorry, but you looked like you needed a slap, and I needed a drink."

"You daughter of a—"

"If you talk about my mother, I have to draw blood."

"You shyte. You rank Ispanthian shyte cunny-chin."

"This is acceptable," she said to me, tousling my hair like I was a child, a godsdamn child, and I took it. "My name is Galva," she said. And then she went to the bar to collect her small glass of red wine. Another verse started up, and I was so mad, I had to do something, so I sang it.

I sang the hell out of it.

Rao rao Bully Boy rao.

During the hour or so she sat with me, I learned something about the woman behind the good shield, the quick sword, and the murder-bird.

"Who are you, anyway?" I asked. "Beyond your name, I mean. Galva, you said?"

"Galva."

"Right."

"You don't need to know the rest of my name."

"Very mysterious. Are you famous?"

"Everyone is famous to someone."

"That's a yes."

I waited for her to say more, but she just looked at me over her wineglass like she was waiting for *me* to speak, so I spoke.

"What are you famous for, Galva the Spanth? Famous killer?"

"You have not seen me kill anyone."

She was right, actually.

"There's a good place to start. Why didn't you kill them, the other waylayers, I mean? And me? Are you Galva the Merciful?"

"That day."

"You maimed them to slow down the others. Caring for them."

She raised her glass slightly as if to toast my great insight.

"You fight better than anyone I've seen. I can't think of many people I'd rather have on my side in a pinch than you. And that big, mean, magnificent war corvid. Where is he, by the way?"

"She. Do not ask me about the bird."

"I know they're not strictly legal." I pulled out a Towers deck and shuffled it just to give my hands something to do.

"Not strictly? There's no kingdom in the north that won't torture you for having one," Galva said.

"I haven't studied those statutes. Not my area of lawbreaking, really. What do they do to you in Ispanthia for having a war bird?"

She fixed my eyes and drank before she spoke. "They pull your guts out with a hook and feed them to carrion birds."

"Fitting."

"Our beloved King Kalith has a gift for punishment."

"Here in Holt, they're simple. I wouldn't be surprised if they just hang you."

"No. Here they flip you upside down and saw you through the middle longways."

She demonstrated the sawing with her right hand holding some invisible felon's invisible ankle. I wondered if she were holding the imaginary Holter facing her or facing away.

"I thought that was just for treason," I said. "And incest. We frown on incest here since the reign of Thamrin the Neckless."

"You know what was done with most of these corvids, do you not?"

"I don't know. Big cages in Ispanthia and Gallardia, I guess?"

"That's what they let people think. But the birds were killed. Seven thousand of them. Too dangerous to keep them around in such numbers, the Wise and Dread Kalith decreed. So as we who had learned to love and trust them in the field looked on, Kalith had them fed poisoned meat and burned. This is how he treated the corvids who helped us turn the goblins. Some few of us fought against it. Some more of us went missing long enough to hide our feathered kith somewhere safe and claim they died."

"Where do you hide a beast like that? I mean, they sort of stand out."

She said nothing.

I started dealing us two hands for a round of Towers, but she pushed the cards back at me, so I shuffled them into the deck as smoothly as I could and put them away.

"What's her name?" I said. "Your corvid, I mean."

"Dalgatha."

"What's it mean?"

"'Skinny Woman.'"

"That's your god of death, right? Sort of a skeleton with wings and pretty hair, yah?"　·

She looked at me again. She had a way of looking at you like she was painting the back of your skull with her eyes. "She's your god, too."

"I like them curvy."

"Doesn't matter what you like. That dance is ladies' choice."

There wasn't much I could say to that, so we sat there until, at length, she spoke again.

"You said I was the best fighter you have seen, but you have not seen the fighters I have. And I had some small practice."

"Goblin Wars?"

"Yes."

"Orfay?"

"No, Goltay."

I suppressed a shiver. Goltay was our last big defeat, fought nine years before, in 1224. Also called the Kingsdoom. Everyone knew that name. Everyone knew someone who went there. Very few people knew someone who had returned.

"Bad as they say?" I regretted it as soon as I said it. I wished I could reel it back into my mouth.

"No," she said with disturbing calm. "It was like gathering flowers in the fields. It was so beautiful most of my friends and two of my brothers decided to stay." I couldn't tell if she was angry and being sarcastic or if this was Skinny Woman talk. They weren't supposed to speak ill of death.

She looked away. I found myself scanning her scars to see if any of them looked like bites, but I stopped when her eyes flicked back to me.

"My turn," she said. "This Guild of thieves."

"The Takers."

"Was it worth it? The training they gave you. That is how this works, right? They make you a thief or a killer—"

"Thief, in my case."

"Don't interrupt me."

"Sorry."

"Don't say *sorry*."

I opened and closed my mouth.

"They make you a thief, and you owe them money for the rest of your life, and everybody slaps you for wine."

"Beer, usually; it's just you Spanths and Gallardi that dye your tongues purple. Not the rest of my life unless I die soon. And they only put the open hand on the ones that fall behind on their debt."

"Good incentive."

"It gets more persuasive every day."

"And they make you do things," she said.

"That's one way to pay. The Deed Note."

"Worse things than ambushing strangers?"

"No worse than ambushing you, I hope."

"Why don't you just do something for them, then? Pay your debt off?"

"Most amusing you should say that now. I just spoke to them. I took the deed. They're sending me west."

"To Oustrim."

I nodded and said, "Hrava, specifically. Probably. But yes, Oustrim."

"To do what?"

"I'm supposed to lie now rather than tell you. Can we just pretend I told you a lie?"

"No. Tell me the lie."

"Fine. I'm going there to steal some magical things."

"Good. I go to find a lost princess."

"Perfect."

"Good."

"Maybe I'll help you find her."

"Maybe I will be grateful."

"Fine."

"Good." She drank her wine.

"And to answer your question, it was worth it. The Takers. The Low School."

"What can you do?"

"Extraordinary things."

"This 'talking to animals' I have heard of. Can you do that?" she asked, her dark eyebrows raising just a bit.

"Animal-talking. It's not talking to animals, it's making animal sounds."

"What, *urf-urf,* like a dog?"

I now made exactly the whine of a frightened dog, then turned it into a perfectly credible growl.

"*Bolnu,*" she said, weighing something invisible but pleasing in her supinated hand, a very Ispanthian gesture. "Is it magic?"

"No, just training."

"Do you have magic?" she asked.

"Not much."

"I have a little magic, too. Also not much."

"I didn't think the bird fell out of your arse."

She took a sip of wine and looked at me seriously.

"That would be very dark magic," I said.

She squinted at me, waiting to see where this was going, but not hopeful.

"But not black magic."

She waited.

"Brown," I said.

She searched *brown magic* for any possible meaning besides juvenile scatology. Finding none, she closed her eyes and shook her head in disappointment.

It wouldn't be the last time.

8

Bully Boy

———— • ————

Galva told me she'd made plans for us and that I should meet her by Haros's tower the next morning at sunrise. Unfortunately, not an hour after I left the Stag and Quiet Drum, I got arrested.

It wasn't my fault.

First thing I did, having left my bow and pack stashed in the inn's attic so I could move light on my feet, was make my way to the town square, where the town mouth had cried the coming of giants to Oustrim. Now mouths of a different sort were crying. A group of mummers had come in a wagon all hung with bells and tattered banners and bits of stained or stolen silk. The side of the wagon had folded down and rested on legs to make a small stage, a yard off the ground. Letters on the Wagon spelled DAMS OF LAMNUR, and indeed there didn't seem to be a man in the company.

Several dozen lookie-sees had gathered near, but only about a third of them sat on the benches the players offered—most lingered at the margins, keeping their options open should they grow bored and wish to leave. These would make the easiest prey.

The troop was performing a Crowning Play. These were little farces, half an hour long, meant not only to make laughter but to teach the names of foreign kings and queens. Foreigners were fair game in these shows, but I doubted I'd see the likeness of good King Conmarr of Holt on the boards.

Indeed, the subject of today's mummery was the Mad Princess, the Ispanthian infanta Mireya, played by a comely lass in a red dress. She sported with the pet monkey Mireya had as a girl, the very one she later claimed spoke to her and told her the future. The role of the monkey fell to a lady dwarf very talented at making monkey noises and who capered with great energy.

MIREYA: *Pray, tell me, monkey, what you see!*
MONKEY: *Your uncle comes to shake your tree*
And paint his name with villainy.
MIREYA: *Pray, tell me, monkey, what you think!*
MONKEY: *Your uncle comes to creep and slink*
And kill your da with poisoned drink!

Now a player in an outsized King Kalith mask, complete with foot-long mustachios, sauntered onstage, sloshing a giant goblet of wine. I looked around to see if the Spanth were watching this mockery of her home court, but I did not see her. Kalith splashed wine on the king and queen players, who had been dancing unaware just off the stage. They both sputtered and fell, and Kalith took a large painted crown and set it on his own head.

MIREYA: *Pray, tell me, Uncle, what you chance!*
KALITH: *I stopped them in their foolish dance*
And now I am the king of Spanths!

Mireya cried out while her monkey capered.

MIREYA: *Pray, tell me, Uncle, what you'll do!*
KALITH: *If I would speak and tell it true*
My niece, I have to murder you!
MONKEY: *Help! Help! The villain means to slay her*
Will no one save the fair Mirey-er?

Some had a chuckle at that. The largish woman whose purse I cut with my nip-knife certainly seemed to enjoy it. When Kalith came at Princess Mireya, she held the monkey up before her and claimed the monkey had warned her of Kalith's treachery. At that, the mummer playing the dead Ispanthian king, Mireya's father, stood up long enough to speak. He cautioned his brother, Kalith, that the gods always revenge themselves on those who harm the mad and that nobody in their right mind talked to monkeys. When Mireya heard this, she began to caper about madly with the monkey, even down to throwing pretend feces at the crowd. Most of them howled, including the young lady I bumped into in my own feigned laughing fit and relieved of a silver earring.

Looking back, I'm glad the Spanth wasn't there to see the infanta of her homeland reduced to throwing poo—she'd have likely dry-beat the players with the flat of her *spadín* and caused a brawl. I hadn't heard of the Dams of Lamnur before, but they weren't half-bad. I didn't see the end of the Crowning Play, though. It's best to be away once you've got what you think you can, so I moved on to other quarters. I knew the rest of the play, anyway.

Mireya, her life spared by her feigned madness, was married off to a king sufficiently distant from her home and from the treacherous uncle who meant her ill. Married off to a Gallardian king, who got eaten by goblins at the Kingsdoom. At the close of the farce, all the players would take up little props shaped like goblin heads and bite the Gallard king offstage. It was only in the last year or so that players had the nerve to represent goblins in mummery, and I choose to look at that as a sign of returning strength.

You can't make fun of something everyone's still terrified of.

Manreach was starting to heal.

These mummers supposedly did pretty well for themselves lampooning the woes of our neighbors to the south and east. I later heard the dwarf would swallow any silver or gold coin given to her, which made me wonder if the others let her go alone to the privy.

I wandered next through Sparktown, the old blacksmith's streets just off the river-docks, until I reached the market. Near the eel stalls, I came to notice a gang of cats slinking about like cats do near fish stalls, but one stood out. He was a bone-skinny gray-brown tabby, slower than the rest and he never jumped, but scraped the walls near the bridge with his whiskers, staying out of open spaces. When the old lady'd whack off a fresh eel head, she'd toss it in the gutter, and the other toms would slink over and fight, but not this one. He'd sort of nod in the air, finding the scent, and then amble over in his own good time, content to lick the spot where the head landed after his fellows dragged it off.

He was blind.

That's when the cat-catchers came.

About a dozen years ago, during a round of the plagues the goblins sent us, some old geezer at a Gallardian university worked out that one sickness, the whip-cough, was being carried by cats—so off everyone went drowning, clubbing, and otherwise dispatching anything with pointy ears and a saucy look on its face. Eventually, the plague died out, like all the goblin plagues eventually did, and everyone stopped cat-catching. Except the baron of Cadoth, whose son had died after a cat-bite went sour. Rumor was that the boy had been doing something mean and weird to it—not what you're thinking, weirder than that—and that nobody deserved an unlucky death more than he. Still, the rich hold grudges the poor can't afford, and the baron left the edict in place. Fortunately for cats, inflation made the bounty so small nobody much bothered anymore, and the baron didn't care to adjust it, so cats mostly came back.

Two copper shaves a hide doesn't buy much, but it buys a loaf of bread. It buys a fishhook. It buys three apples. So shoot two cats, that's supper. Cat-catching won't win you any friends, but it might keep you from starving. So here came two of the grubbiest-looking teenaged pricks you'd ever see with sacks on their backs, rag-wrapped sandals, and two cheap but nasty-looking cross-bows. I'd barely worked out who or what they were before they'd both fired bolts.

One bolt chinked on stone and made a spark, but the other took a ginger long-hair through the ribs. All the cats ran but the blind one, who tried to flee but hit a wall, then made false starts in two directions before he just crouched against the wall and shivered. One of the cat-shooting turdlets scooped up and sacked the ginger, while the other hawked and spat, reloading his bow with a rusty bolt he pulled out of his pocket. The blind cat just sat there, staring in this direction and that with wide, useless yellow-green eyes. Most people just looked away, though a couple of shyte kids hooted at the fun. The turdlet with the bow took aim.

"Wait," I said, and gods bless me, I got in between him and the cat.

"Wha, ye knap?" he said, the flower of Holtish charm.

"I'll give you two shaves if you don't shoot Bully Boy."

"Sure," he said, "sure," lowering his bow. I had the unworthy suspicion he intended to shoot it after he got his money, but I couldn't stand on morals—I had no intention of giving him two shaves. Not the sort he meant, anyway.

When I got close to him, I drew a small but very sharp nip-knife from my belt and, quick as a snake, ran its edge up one of his hairy cheeks and down the other, meanwhile slapping his bow down to clatter on the ground. I trip-kicked the other one—the Low School makes expert trippers, blinders, and knockers-down of all its fledglings—and as he fell with a *Faw!* I sprinted at the cat. I grabbed it up by its nape and ran hard as it paddled its back legs in the air.

"My cat!" the ginger-shooter yelled at my back. "That Galtie prigger stole my cat and abused me!"

I really don't know where the chainsdam came from, but I was still a bit drunk from the Drum, and there she was, big, quick, and hard, and me with my hand too full of cat to do anything about her. I saw myself in her steel breastplate, green-eyed and o-mouthed, a squirming blind alley cat in my left hand, and she snapped a manacle on my right wrist before I was fully aware what she was about. She couldn't see my tattoo by daylight, but we weren't in daylight long.

"Guild, eh?" the clerk-justice said in the wobbly candlelight of the gaol. Crutches leaned against the wall behind him.

"Yes, sir."

"The *sirs* won't help you any more than your Guild will, black-tongue. You know what they say about caught thieves, aye?"

"I'm not a thief."

"Yes, and I'll just put the tip in, we know how these things go. What do your masters in the Guild say about caught thieves, boy? Something about branches?"

"Pruned branches feed the tree."

"Mm-hmm."

"So what am I charged with? I didn't steal anything."

"Man says it's his cat."

"I touched it first, doesn't that make it my cat?"

"That's as the law says."

"So can I go?"

"It's like you could if you hadn't pulled a knife on the squire, and I say *squire* with a deep sense of irony."

"You're too smart for this work."

"I could say as much to you, cat-grabber, purse-nipper. Prank. Do you deny tripping the one and abusing the other with a knife?"

"Not a big knife."

"Why do it?"

"Cat's blind. It wasn't sporting."

"Heh. Sporting. There's a word you normally only hear out of rich mouths. You rich, cat-pincher?"

"Do I look it?"

"You look worn and dirty, I grant, but hardly run before the boar. Your split-toed thieving boots are decently made, and that is not a poor man's blade on your belt."

"Then I am rich. I have a hundred gold lions and a thousand silver owlets waiting on my ship in the Hot Sea. I'm going to go find a mermaid with a taste for old plums and a fortune in black pearls up her squinny and send her back to you."

"Mermaids don't have squinnies. T's'what makes 'em a parable for life. Warm and welcoming for the first half, then it gets cold and hard and smells bad. But thank you for not being boring. You know how sick I get of hearing, 'Spare me, Justice, I am inno-cent, I swear by the gods'? I had decided to hang the next squire told me he was innocent, especially if he was."

"Can I keep the cat?"

"Cook him and eat him for all I care. Chainsdam!"

The woman who arrested me stepped forward, the blind cat docile in her fist, a half dozen candles dancing in the darkness reflected by her armor.

"Give him back his love child. Then welcome them both to cell three west."

They didn't even bother taking my knives off me.

9

Fiddle and Famine

─────── • ───────

I sat in the grime and puddled muck of my cell, mulling my chances to find the Spanth again before she set off. They were decent, if I could get out of here. For all that she was trying to be indistinct, that raven knight stood out—for her accent, for her taste in wine, even just for her bearing. When you met her, you felt you'd met someone who mattered. Someone whose thumb would one day rest on the scale.

Me? I was just another Galt in a Holtish gaol. I watched the cat pick his way in the general direction of the high, barred window letting in the last of the sunlight. He felt his path from one dry bit of stone to another. Our cellmate stared over his gathered knees at the far wall, drunk as a pickled fish, bony in that old-man way, like he's easing into his coming skeletonhood.

"Cats are much better at being blind than we are. It's the whiskers," I said.

My cellmate burped and rubbed at his thinly veiled sternum with a knotted fist, still staring wallward.

"No offense meant if you're blind, of course," brought another burp, this one long and whooshy. "Not that I think you are," I said.

He had longish fingernails that looked every bit as sturdy as they were dirty, vying with his teeth and eye-whites for most yellow bits of him.

"You're not in gaol for talking a man to death, are you?" I said.

He produced three fingers and waggled them at me in a way that could only have seemed lewder had he used two. He continued to watch the wall as if it might fall on him if he ceased his vigil.

I also looked at the wall. It was not the first gaol-wall I had seen. The graffiti here was remarkably cosmopolitan, nearly as varied as what you would find in a port city like Pigdenay. Most of it was scrawled or carved in the Holtish I'm using now, of course, but my native Galtish was also well represented. I saw nearly a paragraph of Unthern with its crammed-together, sentence-long words, and a few choice remarks in prancing Ispanthian, best spoken with a mouthful of garlic and hot chilis. Ispanthia and Unther were neighbors of Holt, so it was not surprising that travelers from either land, one east, one west, had run afoul of the chainsmen of the lovely town of Cadoth.

The only exotic language in the scrawl was Keshite, from Kesh, the seat of the old empire, a language we don't share an alphabet with. I could read it, though, and immediately understand it. It said, "Fuck Cadoth in its hairy butt. This is a shithole city full of shit-women worse than goblins. Fuck fuck fuck with the hugest cock of elephants all Cadoth." There was really no faulting the author's sincerity. I could read the slashed, loopy characters not because I had ever been to hot, goblin-conquered Kesh but because of that second birth-gift I mentioned.

I am what is known as a Cipher.

A cipher is, of course, a code, but to say a person is a Cipher means they can read and understand any language without instruction. This often comes as a surprise to a Cipher's parents, and my ma was no exception. When I was a child of five, I found a leaflet some pamphleteer had left in the market, all tread on and muddy, and asked my mother was it true the Forbidden God was the only real god and that he wanted us to please ourselves? She took a moment to understand what I'd said, sounded out the words of the flyer I held in my grubby hand.

"Did you *read* that, boy?" she said. She hadn't taught me to read, she barely could herself.

"I did, Ma," I said.

She slapped me, hard, and told me, as tears welled up in my eyes, "I did that so you'll remember. Never tell anyone but me you can read again, least of all your da. Not while you live under his roof."

I didn't understand the reason for it at the time, but it served me well to hide that gift. I met another Cipher, once. She was pointed out to me at the Low School. She was kept in a comfortable apartment underground, I was told, even allowed to go out into the town with a minder. But most of her days were spent breaking codes, translating texts, or inventing ciphers of her own for the Guild. She was fat as veal and pale as a fish, wanting for nothing but liberty. That was one want too many, as I could see.

Growing up in a mining town, the thought of a shut-in's life made me shudder, still does. Ciphers are infinitely valuable to the Guild, and dangerous—it was rumored we could even read the Murder Alphabet, the language in which the Guild's most powerful corresponded, and in which its true history and most dangerous spells were written, but I was in no hurry to wager my life on that theory.

They were always looking for Ciphers, though. I remember once seeing a sign in a Low School tavern saying, "First beer free tonight. Just ask!" I'd been about to ask when I realized the language was one I'd never seen, probably a dead one. I held my tongue. And I kept alert for other such traps.

I read the graffiti in the gaol cell in brief glances and didn't let myself react to any of it, even though I'd nearly laughed at the thought of all Cadoth being buggered by Keshite elephants. Now the cat had attained the sill beneath the barred window, and he bobbed his head hopefully toward the breeze coming in. A pair of muddy boots strode by at street-level. I thought about using a cantrip to squeeze myself thin enough to slip through the bars, but they were solid iron, and it would take stronger magic than mine to safely work a spell so close to them. If I tried to slip through, I might get the spell snuffed while I was halfway out and crack my sternum between those iron bars.

Iron is to free magic what cold water and laughter are to male arousal. Free magic meaning spells. Caught magic—tattoos, objects imbued with magic—would not be harmed by iron, but it might make the use of those objects less efficient. Steel is nearly as bad, but not quite—you can still toss spells with a sword or knife sheathed on your person, but a suit of chain mail? You'd have to be Fulvir or Knockburr to throw even a cantrip while wearing steel armor. And even those two could likely be damped if you put them in an iron box. Mind, magic can still affect iron, it just has trouble going through or past it. Thus, you could turn a weapon in a knight's hand, but not stop her heart through her breastplate. Colored metals, on the other hand, do not harm spells, and copper even helps. As does formerly living matter, like wood and leather. If you see a fucker coming at you with a copper torque or circlet, watch out. Like as not a magicker. Using cantrips as I do, I wear leather jack and keep Palthra and Angna sheathed in leather-wrapped copper. The arrowheads on me aren't enough to matter.

"Do you want out?" I said to Bully Boy. The cat could have slipped out any time but seemed, for the moment, content to stay. If someone didn't offer us food soon, he was like to go, and I wouldn't try to stop him.

"You're welcome to stay if you like," I told the little blind tabby. He just sat on the sill and bobbed his head wistfully toward the garbagy food smells coming from the street.

As the cat was called by that smell, so was I soon called by music. Someone was playing a fiddle, not terribly well, farther down the gaol in a cell I could not see. It was not the musician's questionable talent that called me—it was that he or she was running a bow across *my* fiddle.

I put an ear to the thick, iron-banded door to the cell and confirmed my suspicions—not only did the fiddle have the same low sweetness as mine, the tune was Galtish, an old, old romance about two men loving the same goat-girl, getting to the point of settling it with knives, then being told she meant to have both or neither one.

That's a blacktongue woman for you—they set the tune, and we dance. I planned never to marry, and if I did, never to marry a Galt. One of us was bad enough. The groom of a blacktongue woman was in for no gentler a ride than the bride of a blacktongue man. Better to take a Galtish girleen for a moon-wife, where you could try it out for a month and see if you'd killed each other by the end of it.

I wanted a look at who was scraping my fiddle. I took the picks hidden in the leather of my belt and had the lock on the cell door open in a few heartbeats. My bony old cellmate watched and burped. I closed the door, locked it behind me and climbed up to the ceiling, bracing myself between ceiling and wall as I'd been taught and trained for, keeping to the shadows.

I followed the music. It led to a larger, open cell, with bars toward the hall. This was more of a general holding area, less secure. I hadn't my cheat-glass with me—that handy folding mirror on a stick was back with my key-press clay, my iron-saw and other tools in my pack, still in the attic of the Stag and Quiet Drum. But the shadows were dark enough to hide me while I watched them. I saw a clutch of sad figures sitting on the dirt floor, listening as a very young man played and a wall-eyed woman sang in Galtish. These two were, of course, the archer brother and sister I had played at banditry with in the Forest of Orphans, the ones who stole the goods I'd left behind at our campsite after the Spanth and her bird ruined us. They had their backs to the bars.

The fellow with the fiddle, Naerfas, was moving side to side with the tune, a few steps left, a few steps right, choking down on the fiddle with chin and shoulder. His leftward drifts took him near the bars. I crept closer, slow as pipe smoke in a still room, knowing the last yard or so I'd be in torchlight. If I could time it right, I might be able to do what I had in mind, but it wouldn't be easy. I felt within myself to see how my luck sat, and it sat high. *Right,* I thought and let the feeling tell me when and how to move. I sprang forward and then dropped. Several of the other prisoners gasped as a shadow fell from the ceiling, but young

Nervous was slow. I scooped my foot in and hooked his ankle out from under him. He fell, still holding the fiddle but dropping the bow. I pulled his foot hard, got him with his bollocks tickling the bars, wrapped my legs around his one and rocked back, bending his leg at a horrible angle. He whimpered.

"My name is Kinch Na Shannack," I said for the benefit of Naerfas's cellmates, "and I declare myself the prior owner of this fiddle." Notice I didn't say *true,* which means nothing to the Guild. "Will you deny my claim?" He did no such thing. His sister snatched at me, but I lay back a little more, and Naerfas howled.

"Don't think I won't break it, Snowcheeks," I said, for the sister was a pale one, and Snowcheeks was easier for Holters to say than her Galtish name, Snochshaeia. She relented. "Now hand me out the fiddle."

She did.

"And the bow."

She didn't, for she didn't have it. A thick woman with a goiter did. "You give me for't?" she said, omitting the *What will you* as northerners do. "It's what I won't give you," a Galtish woman at her side said, cracking her in the ear with a horny fist. Goiter dropped the bow and someone else slid it to me. I let Naerfas go, nodded at him and his sister, who nodded back. The whole thing had been done with proper protocol, and none would likely hold a grudge. I snugged the fiddle with my chin and shoulder, tested the bite of the bow, then finished the song, and far better than fucking Naerfas. Snowcheeks sang the last of it, which translates as something like

> *Full frolicksome the three went on*
> *All the fall and gloaming long*
> *When winter came and sang its song*
> *The goat-girl was with child*

> *Next Lammas when the mowers mowed*
> *And good cheese in its wheels was sold*

A daughter cried out in the cold
Two fathers strong have I

Fuck you, it rhymes in Galtish.

Back in my cell, Skinnybones, still staring at his wall, said, "Yer cat left."

"I thought he might."

"Coulda tied him to summat."

"Why?"

"Inn't he yours?"

"Not really."

"'F'Idda knowd'at, Idda et him."

"That wouldn't have been neighborly."

He waggled the three fingers at me.

At mention of "etting," I felt an uncomfortable but familiar hollowness in my middle. I'd had nothing today but a cold sausage of questionable fillings and beer from the Stag and Quiet Drum.

"They feed us here?" I said.

I got the three fingers again, waggled and bobbed up and down this time.

"I'll stop disturbing you. Clearly, you're working a hole in the blocks with the force of your gaze."

That's when I heard a bell ring three times.

The bone-bag three-fingered at me again, wiping at his mouth with a knobby wrist. A small door opened at the bottom of the larger one and birthed forth a piece of stale, hollowed-out bread with some sort of bean pottage spooned over it. Bony Bonebottom sprang up with surprising speed and took it. I got up, too, meaning to stake my claim to half, but he sneezed all over it, and I sank back down, shaking my head. I thought about thrashing him, but any scratch from those mucky nails of his would be like to go rotten.

"You know, if you had a bit more dignity, you would put me in mind of a rat," I said.

He mantled over his prize and ate until it was gone, then picked crumbs off himself and the floor with great care and ate those as well.

"I really hoped you'd miss the crumb that settled in your chest hair. I thought I might have that one off you while you slept."

He wiped his hands on his shabby pants, then looked at me for the first time. "Bollocks if I'm sleeping here," he said, his grubby Cadothian street-talk traded for a handsome Galtish brogue like mine—only now did I notice his black tongue. And with that, he leapt up to the windowsill, removed two of the bars, and pushed himself out arse-first onto the street. He checked to make sure no one was watching, then he put the bars back.

"This is the Guild's room, isn't it?" I said.

"Thick, aren't you, Prank? Why do you think you were let to keep the knife?" he said. "It's the Guild's fucking gaol." Then he spoke in Galtish, "*Hrai syrft ni'ilenna.*"

I continued, "*Tift se fal coumoch.*"

Then we both said, "*Lic faod kiri dou coumoch!*"

He who leaps at the moon

Into cowshyte falls.

Glory unto cowshyte!

Holy words, those.

"Well done with the fiddle. Now get on yer way—not two days into yer indenture and ye get yerself pinched. Yer not like to follow that Spanth killer far sitting on yer arse in here. Mind ye put the bars back when ye go."

And he scampered off into the new night.

A Galt, like me.

A priest of Fothannon Foxfoot.

And unless I missed my guess, one of the highest orders of thieves—a Famine.

10

The Horsegroom

———•———

The cat found me again soon after I found Galva.

She'd quit the inn where I'd questioned her last night, and I'd missed our meeting at the tower of Haros. I felt sure she wouldn't start off anywhere until the next morning—Spanths like to do things the proper way, and dawn is the best time for a journey's first steps.

After I stopped by the Stag and Quiet Drum to retrieve my goods from the attic, I slipped back down to the main room, where I stuffed greedily and greasily into my face-hole a pie of eel, leek, and mushrooms in a garlicky beer sauce, washing it down with red ale. Watching a Holtish silver shilling, called a knave, turned into four marks, or maids, and two copper shaves hurt, but at least I hadn't needed to wreck an owlet. Gallardia's owlet had the same value as the Holtish knave, but the knave coin pictured a thick fucker on a donkey holding a sheaf of wheat he seemed keen to wipe his arse with. A far inferior coin, one that deserves reduction.

While I chewed my eel and moistened my pie crust with ale, I began to reason out where the Spanth went. I remembered the market had three Ispanthian stalls, one that sold olive oil and dried fish, and two that sold wine. One of these also sold leather and never had a line, so this merchant's wine will have been half-way to vinegar—nothing Galva would suffer. The other merchant barely got to sit down between buyers and had emptied one barrel while I had watched her customers, trying to work out who to nip a purse off of. The stall was shut at night, of course, but a scraped plate, a burp, and a short walk later, my full belly and I were standing in front of the closed wine stall with a cool evening breeze in my hair.

I imagined myself a Spanth chattering away with another from my warm, brown hills. I grabbed my invisible bottle of wine and walked off with that swordfighter's spring the Spanth had, letting my feet take me where I felt hers would. They led me onto Split-bridge Lane and then onto Splitbridge proper, a Y-shaped stone structure lurching across the wide river. The bridge was two hundred years old, the architectural pride of Cadoth more for its beauty than for its sturdiness; packed with handsome stone and timber shops, inns, bookstalls, statues, and even a fountain with water burbling from an ecstatic-looking merman's mouth, it looked to be on the point of a stately collapse into the eel-rich murk of the Caddow.

My eyes were drawn to an unnamed inn two stories tall, green tile roof, granite stones, tiny little windows that looked lockable. When I saw the wooden sign in the bottom window bearing the burned-in legend BATH WITH LODGING, I nodded like a Spanth, said, "*Bolnu, bolnu,*" because it would indeed be good to have a bath, and when you've got a modest budget, you bathe at inns like this one some nights and sleep cheap or free the others.

Ispanthians were notoriously clean generally, and unlike most travelers, Galva managed not to smell like the inside of a hot shoe. This felt right. My luck glowed warm. She was here. Riverside or street-side? Whatever they had, obviously, but I could most easily perch street-side. I sat down in an alley and watched two separate rooms that danced with candlelight. I was in no hurry. After an hour, I saw the leftmost window steam at the tops and decided to have a peek.

After using a gutter pipe to climb, minding the bow, pack, and fiddle on my back, I hung toward the edge of the roof with a small mirror on a folding stick and saw her in the bath, facing the window like a wary guest should, but oblivious to my cheat-glass.

That's when I noticed she had no breasts at all. It wasn't that she was built small, for I had seen that enough times, hadn't I? Rather, her breasts were gone entirely, nipples and all, and in their place sat tattoos, and fine ones. Had she been burned? Born without them? Maimed in the field?

However she'd lost her mammets, afterward she had been expertly inked. A raven tattoo, the birders' mark, was drawn on her scarred, tightly muscled pectorals; a skeleton's hand on her sternum declared her love for Dalgatha; a sword on her arm wreathed in three flowers, one for each year she studied under a certain master. Exactly the tattoos you'd expect to find on an Ispanthian bird knight betrothed to the goddess of death.

Another thing about her—the feel of magic coming off her was stronger without her mail shirt and gorget to smother it.

But ho, what was this?

Now she called to someone at the door. A girleen came in with wine—of course—and a pitcher of piping-hot water to add to the bath should Galva want it warmed. She did. I scrambled up the roof and around to the other side, found an unoccupied room, and let myself in. Got to the hallway and came up to her open door, all this in forty heartbeats. I waited until Galva was occupied, carefully refilling her glass with wine, then slipped behind her shield, where it lay against the wall. Not that it was large enough to cover me entirely, but there are ways to square the body off so the shape tricks the eye.

It was hard not to laugh at the scene that followed—we'll just call it a clash of cultures. The maid used coded language to offer Galva sex for money. The knight clearly didn't understand, so the prostitute/maid got less nuanced, which was already funny because she was from Unther, and their accent is harsh and spitty. When Galva at last understood, she refused so politely the girl thought Galva was interested in sex but not hers, so she asked if the Ispanthian gentledam would like to see a horsegroom, code for boy-whore. Galva lifted her chin, thinking perhaps there was a live horse to be seen, which the maid took to mean yes, so she rang a little bell; but then Galva asked if in truth it was a mare they had here—the goblins' rotten plague magic had killed all the stallions but mares had fought it better, the ones foaling were entirely proof against it, and some few of them still lived.

Galva meant an actual mare, of course. Spanths love horses more than all the other kingdoms put together, but the girl believed she was speaking in code—in the land of Prostitutia, a mare is a whore who's borne children already. The maid said she thought Galva didn't like females, but Galva insisted that she hadn't touched a stallion in many years but would pay to see a mare. The maid thought Galva meant she couldn't afford a male prostitute—far more expensive because of the lack of men generally—but might manage the cost of a slightly older female. The Spanth understood that there was some confusion and tried to set it right by insisting she meant an actual horse, that she loved horses, that in the morning she would pay good coin to see a horse.

I guess the maid didn't get the *in the morning* part, because I next heard the sound of her simple peasant's shift coming off and her knees and palms slapping the floorboards. I peeked around the shield—you would have, too—and saw her with her oat-colored hair, her hanging knaps, and pale, freckly Unthermaid skin, pretending to be a horse. She whinnied, and Galva laughed, and I laughed, and Galva heard me and stopped laughing, but I couldn't, and there she was up out of the bath again dripping wet, swatting the shield aside, picking me up painfully by my nuts and nape and flinging me into the tub, splooshing half the water out. She wouldn't be mad that I'd seen her nakedness—soldiering had taken the shyness out of dams her age—but she beat me with her shield anyway, though not too badly. Not hard. Mainly on the shoulders. I still couldn't stop laughing.

"What is so funny?" she said, her accent making it sound like *fonny*.

"Put your damned pants on first, if you're going to beat me! I'm not here for the mare!"

"Nor I for the horsegroom!" she said.

"Are you sure?" I said and whinnied.

The Unthermaid whinnied, too.

Now Galva was laughing again.

She put the shield down and put her pants on.

I opened the window to let the steam out, and that's when I heard it.

Rao. Riii-ao.

I looked down at the cobbled street.

The blind cat had followed me.

His little blind head bobbing and sniffing toward the window.

11

The Lady of Sourbrine

———— • ————

The next day, the twenty-first of Ashers, we set off west from Cadoth. Before we left that morning, I'd spoken with the cat.

"You don't expect me to believe you're not magicked, do you? Can you speak? No, I don't imagine you'd want to show me all your tricks so soon, even if I am kith to you. That's what cats and dogs are, you know—kith. Not family, nor friends, but something in between. If I take you with me, it means you're like some hairy nephew-friend-dependent, and there'll be a contract between us. I'll keep you only so long as you keep silent; one ill-timed rao could be the end of me, and you, too, just as like, so if you prove a talker, I'll set you on your four feet to preach where you please. Are we clear? Good, don't say anything, that's how I like you. Oh, another thing, on the matter of shyte. I'll feed you when I can, and I know there's nothing goes in a cat that comes out pretty. I'll set you out of your carrying sack every few hours to sow the fields or decorate the cobblestones, but there'll be no shyte in camp, indoors, or on the furniture. One misplaced dab of shyte and it's divorce. I don't know if you're a lad cat or a lass cat, but I'll call you Bully Boy until you advise me different, since a herd of beery morons burbled out that song the day we met. I'm one of those as sees the gods in coincidence. I've oiled my traveling sack to keep the wet off you. My shopping's done, a dozen fresh arrows, a new whetstone, a pint jar of honey, a copper flask of whiskey, a quart of beer. A mess of salt herring you may have the smallest and boniest of. We'll be leaving as soon as that dam says," I said, pointing my nip-knife at Galva, where she sat on the bed, one arm sunk past the elbow in a boot, the other rubbing at it with an oiled rag. She stared at me with the frown and unblinking eyes of someone watching an idiot happily soiling himself.

"We're going west," I told Bully. "I'll bet you've always wanted to see the west. Or smell it, anyway. The bronzesmiths of Molrova. The endless forests of Brayce, the golden wheat fields of Oustrim. The taverns and canals of Middlesea."

Galva stared, shook her head a little.

"What's that?" I said, putting my ear to the cat's mouth. "You're glad we're going west because you don't want to see Ispanthia?"

"Careful," the Spanth said, buffing a boot-toe just that little bit harder.

"The eastern women have mustaches, you say? And woolly armpits?"

"*Baes pu palitru.*"

She hung the first boot half out the window so the weak sun would warm the leather and make it drink the oil. The spring-wood shield, which she'd rubbed with water, she now moved so the window's square of sunlight fell on its wood and gleamed off its storm-faced boss. The wood looked almost new, no mark remaining from the arrows that had struck it in the Forest of Orphans. It really did heal itself. Gods, that shield would buy a manor house.

Who the devils was this Spanth, to carry such a thing?

"*Baes pu palitro,*" I repeated. "She says you're heading for danger, Bully Boy, if I remember my Ispanthian."

"I meant you, not the *chodadu* cat."

"Was that *fucking* you just said?"

"*I* do not talk to cats."

"*Chodadu,* that's *fucking,* right?"

"It is already fucked."

"Fucked?"

"Yes. Anyway, we are not going west yet. North first," Galva said, putting more oil on her rag and starting on the second boot.

I noticed now the boots were quite thick, with articulated horn or bronze plates sewn in to protect the legs. All goblin-fighters put a premium on leg armor.

"Oh? Why would she take us north, Bully?"

"If you talk to me through the cat one more time, I will skin him."

"Why are we going north, Galva?"

"A detour. To meet a witch."

"Is she a famous killer like you?"

"She is a great friend to Dalgatha and has fed her kingdom many souls. Pernalas Mourtas, they call this witch."

"Deadlegs! I've heard of her! Bites her lovers to death, they say. But wait, she's all the way up in Norholt."

"Yes."

"That's a formidable friend. She is your friend, then?"

"I never met her."

"How do you know she'll want to see you?"

"I have a letter."

"What makes you think she'll let you near enough to give her a letter?"

Galva rolled her eyes. "Talk to your *chodadu* cat."

I sharpened my knife—I like keeping Palthra keen enough to shave a Beltian's black, black beard; or keen enough to split the difference between irritating a Spanth and enraging one—and I put oil to my boots, as Galva had done.

It proved a blessing we oiled our leathers. It rained like a bastard as we took the north road toward Norholt, the kind of rain that wets you in no time at all and just keeps at you until there's nothing dry about you. The kind of rain that makes you feel you're just a turd the gods are trying to wash off the road. I had put my bowstring in a pouch around my neck, but it got wet there, anyway.

The cat raoed a time or two, but I forgave him, because water was getting in my pack. Eventually, it slowed to merely a hard rain, and on we marched. The switch north didn't trouble me. As it was nearing fall, we might make better time getting a ship out of Pigdenay, Norholt's big port city, and heading for the far reaches of Middlesea, or maybe even Molrova if we could find a ship willing to put in there.

Molrova was anathema in the east. They were the greediest and most corrupt kingdom in all of Manreach, and the only coastal nobles there who wouldn't let pirates pillage their waters for a price were pirates themselves.

Molrovans also traded with the Horde. Goblin ships came up the Spine River and brought tea and tiger pelts from Urrimad and cinnamon and peppercorns and taback that kynd thralls grew for them on Hordeland manfarms on the grave of Old Kesh.

What's more, and least forgivable of all, was that they had stayed neutral during the wars. Powerful, martial Molrova had kept her axe-guards and cavalry home during thirty years of unimaginable bloodshed, calling the goblin invasions of Gallardia, Ispanthia, Beltia, Istrea, and Kesh "the south's problem." Mind you, the biters hadn't reached the east either, but Holt, Brayce, and the Gunnish archipelago all sent armies to die and navies to drown just the same—so the general feeling was that Molrova was welcome to eat runny shyte with a sharp knife.

And of course, the wars had eventually touched the west.

When the Horde cooked up their wicked magicks, Molrovan horses caught the Stumbles, too. Molrovan Grays, Steppe Ponies, and Rastivan Talls bloated and died the same way eastern horses did, but the Lords of the Lying Lands were making too much money keeping out of the fight. Molrova stayed strong while southern kingdoms fell and eastern kingdoms bled white.

While the Threshers' War fattened worms and buzzards, the karking Molrovans took two Free Cities from Beltia, the Tin Hills from Wostra, and absorbed miles of Sadunther on the Spine River. Molrovan bards wrote as many sad songs about the death

of horses as the Spanths or Gallardians, but nobody outside
Molrova wanted to hear them. Enough about those sealskin-
wearing twats. Suffice it to say that they were bastards, and getting through their cold, deceiving lands would be no skip-hop.

Not that our current trek from Holt to Norholt was a skip-hop
either. It was Ashers, second and last month of Norholt's short
summer, normally a warm month, but not this particular week.
I'll spare you our several days of rain, unseasonable cold, loose
bowels, hunger, talk around fires, and small, weak fires at that.
We passed a hamlet or two, hitched a ride on a vegetable cart
pulled by goats, waded through a mucky flood, got hailed on
and twice nearly struck by lightning. Galva woke up before daylight every day to bend each ear to her straight knees, pull her
chin up past a tree branch as many times as she could, practice
sword forms, do lunges and squat-jumps. Even in the rain. If you
pinched that woman anywhere, you'd hurt your fingers.

My chiefest contribution those dreary days was when I climbed
in some wealthy landlord's window and stole us a roast chicken
right from the pot. Of course, I was criticized by Lady Pull-Me-
Ups for leaving behind the turnips.

The cat raoed and shat and pissed, though always at proper
times and in acceptable places.

The highlight of our journey north was a small army that
passed us, with a wonder in its midst—a baroness sitting on an
old rawboned mare. She had at least a hundred spearwomen and
a dozen teenaged flail-men in wild, patched leathers, as many as
you'd need to protect the treasure that was a mare, especially
a mare still strong enough to bear an armored rider. This one
couldn't have been more than three years old when the Stumbles
came and killed all the stallions and every mare not carrying a
soon-to-be-stillborn foal.

The woman on the horse—Seldra the Fair, Baroness of
Sourbrine—had us stopped and faced with ready blades, though

they were quickly sheathed again when she learned I was about the Guild's business.

I didn't mind being questioned by her as long as I got to fill my nose with the exotic scent of horse sweat, briny, coarse, and real. They were still real. I stole at least ten lungfuls of sweet horse, I burned her soot-gray flanks and fetlocks into the memories I was saving for my unlikely old age. Her every whicker was a song I'd pay an owlet for, but it was the raven knight who got the day's real prize. The baroness, recognizing a fellow goblin-killer in Galva and knowing her for a Spanth, bade her take a handful of oats to let the old mare lip off her bare palm. No one felt the death of horses as sharply as the Spanths. She kissed the baroness's knuckles and turned her face away and walked alone into the rain.

Before I caught up with Galva, I spoke to a young woman with a boar's-tooth helmet and a wicked-looking horn bow.

"So what's this, then, patrolling the border?"

"Yae, ye could say that," she said. "Looking for Hornhead and his lot. You'd do well to get to a town and stay there 'til he's caught, or 'til he quits the barony."

"What's a 'Horn-Head'?" I said.

"Not from here, I hear, nae?"

"Nae," I said, but not mocking. I'm a natural mimic.

"Hornhead's a mixling."

That got my attention. Mixlings could only be made by powerful magic, magic outlawed until some few were licensed to use it to fight the wars. *Making magic,* it's also called, or *bone magic.* The greatest of the bone magi was Knockburr, a Galtish mage who traveled the world looking for exotic beasts to corrupt. Bone magic, making, mixing, that was how we got the corvids. That was Knockburr's doing, mixing ravens with man-high strutting-birds from the plains of Axa and putting giant's blood in them, too. Most mixlings die, but once you get one that's sound, you geld it if you only want one or you breed it if you want more.

Mixing became one of the high arcana, but even those licensed to brew up monsters to fight the goblin Hordes were forbidden to mix kynd. But Fothannon knows there's not a law made won't be tested, and Knockburr was too powerful to be told yae or nae by such drab stuff as kings. It was said his partner Fulvir's library held spellbooks from lost kingdoms; from the mountain-swallowed city of Bhayn as well as the drowned city of Adripur in Old Kesh.

And one of his mixlings was running amok here in Norholt.

"He's got enough bull in him to put horns on his head, but not so much to make him stupid. He's strong as two men and angry as ten. They say he's protected by magic, has some spell tattooed on him makes him proof in battle."

"You said 'his lot.' He's got mates, then."

"Half dozen or so."

"And you've got this whole army looking just for them?"

The lass laughed then.

I cocked an eyebrow at her.

"Friend," she said. "You haven't seen him."

12

The Downward Tower

———— · ————

Ashers month or no, it seemed snow was possible as the road we
had been following clove into the forest known as the Snowless
Wood. It sat ten miles west of the town of Maeth, a dingy little
place known for hangings. It was said the first man ever hanged
was hanged there. Boasting, as far as I'm concerned—hanging's
as old as rope and necks, and I doubt these twats invented either
of those—but that they're proud of dropping noosefruit tells you
all you need to know about Maethmen. Also, the Guild has no
presence there, more from lack of interest than fear. There's little enough to steal anyhow. Another thing—they had more than
their share of war-aged men in Maeth. Clearly, slipping the muster
hadn't been a hanging offense.

"I've already seen that tree," I said.

"What tree? What do you mean?"

I looked again to make sure, but yes, we were passing a tree we
already passed. I recognized its top fork with the very new shoots
like it had been pruned and the one nearly horizontal branch that
would be good for hanging if it were higher but might yet hang a
child. Not that that's done much, even in Maeth.

I pointed to the tree I meant.

"You think we're walking circles?" she said.

"No. When last I saw it, it was near a newly mown barley field,
half in sun. But here it is again in thick woods."

"Maybe it's following us," she said.

"Huh," I said, torn between doubt in my ability to tell trees
apart and jealousy at the strength of magic it would take to set a

tree following someone. I felt my pack jostle and knew Bully Boy was poking his head up to have a listen. I thought that seemed like a good idea, so I strained my ears, too. Several times, I thought I heard singing, but then it became a near brook, then birds. Later, I saw another odd tree, a stone tree for no good reason, like some magicker got offended by an elm and decided to make a statue of it, every leaf and vein faithfully petrified. It was as terrible as it was beautiful. Shortly thereafter, the path ended against a hedge of thorns that looked set to rip us to bits.

"Left or right?" I said. She had told me, during one of our firelit almost-conversations, that she was following directions she had memorized with the help of a witch.

"Always left now," she said.

"But won't that risk to take us in a circle?"

"Not here."

After an hour of fumbling through close-stacked birch trees and rocky ground, we found a path. Gods knew where it came from, but we went left on it. We hadn't been on it the length of a good poo when we saw that we were coming up behind a sort of hunched little fellow pulling a cart, its wheels crunching loose stones, its basket full of tools. All manner of tools, all with the same flaw; a bend or break near where the iron met the wood. Here was a bent saw, there a hoe split near the hoe part, at least two pitchforks thusly awry. The agent pulling the cart, a panting little man with a head that put one in mind of a squash, never deigned to look at us as we overtook him, but his huffing was so fierce you couldn't take insult from it. He was simply trying not to die.

"You'll want to pull over and sit on that hand wagon, man. Have a rest," I said as we skirted him. He ignored us and trudged on, mouth open in that saggy-bag way people who've lost most of their teeth have. "In good faith, man, nobody's waiting for these cocked-up tools. Have a sit-down. You look close to getting piped off, and I'm not being funny."

He didn't even blink at me.

"Well, at least they'll have something to haul you back in."

He might have smiled a bit at that, or he might not have.

In any event, we were soon well past him, and the road gave into a clearing around a hill, at the top of which sat a tower, and an odd tower it was, the stones of it barely visible through the vines that seemed to want to pull it down. Indeed, it seemed ready to fall at a harsh word. It looked well and deeply haunted.

Perfectly fitting a witch called Deadlegs.

That's when I noticed the door. As in there was none, not where a person could reach, anyway. The tower had only one visible entrance, a strong wooden door, oak by the look of it, though it was hard to tell because it sat at the top of the tower, a dozen tall men high.

And not a stair in sight.

It was at that moment Bully Boy slipped the backpack and ran. He ran into a tree, bonked his head with a hearable bonk, put his paw to his nutshell like an old man with a headache, and raoed in a way that sounded very like *Owww*. Then he seemed to remember he was running off somewhere and took back to his little feet.

Galva watched the cat dart and bump his way into the farther trees and out of sight, then shot me a look.

"Will he come back?" she said.

"I'm strung if I know."

"That cat is magicked," she said.

"Do you think?"

"This is sarcasm, yes?"

"Noooo," I said sarcastically.

"I do not enjoy sarcasm."

"Then I tell you, without sarcasm, that tower looks like a very tall grave."

"You are more right than you know."

"I don't think we're wanted here. Are you sure we're wanted here?"

"Towers are not supposed to look inviting."

Fair play.

A raven called then, its harsh voice scratching paint off my soul.

"We have been invited," Galva said, moving forward.

I walked at her heels until we stood beneath the witch's keep. If I had hoped to find cleverly hidden rung-holes carved into the tower's face, I was disappointed.

"What now?" I said.

The raven hawed again.

"Now we climb it," she said.

"I didn't know you had a talent for climbing."

"It was improper for me to say *we*."

"Ah," I said. I couldn't help stealing another glance at the tree line where Bully Boy made his exit. Was he gone? I hoped he wasn't gone. I was suddenly very sad, standing in the cold, foggy air with an irritable Spanth, getting ready to climb, uninvited and unpaid, the tower of a witch known for biting folks to death. Only the ridiculous non sequitur of a blind cat in my pack could have made things seem balanced and proper.

"Never mind the *chodadu* cat, get up there."

I walked to the tree line, hid my pack and fiddle under a bush, then took the hard pattens off my soft leather boots so I could feel with the soles of my feet and get my big toe into it—the boot was split, with a separate sheath for the toe. I could climb simple things with the boiled-leather pattens on, but this would be far from simple. I came back to the tower and tested one of the vines to see if it would hold my weight. It seemed ready to serve, so I pulled myself up, grabbed another vine, started in with my feet, and was halfway up the tower before I could have sung the refrain of a Gallardian trugging song. There was mischief in those vines, though, and I was ready for them to do something unfriendly. Which they did. Every vine on the tower face suddenly went slack. I fell, clutching my length of vine, hoping it would hold, but of course it detached and let me plummet. I skinned my feet and hands raw paddling the wall to brake myself—don't expect to figure that out on your own, the technique is carefully guarded—and I rolled when I hit the ground and came up on my burning feet, hurting where my hard-leather quiver of arrows had pressed itself into my arse.

"Damn those bitch vines, anyway."

"Do you need the vines?"

"If I want to go fast."

"So go slow."

I gave her the world-weary eyes, and she gave me the sleepy-killer eyes, so I took to the wall and made myself flat, light, and hard-handed. I avoided the vines as best as possible, knifing my toes and fingertips between them. The cold stones allowed just enough grip that I didn't have to use any magic to ascend, but I wouldn't be winning a race to the top against a determined ant.

I stopped for a moment.

"What are you doing?" Galva said.

"Just taking a moment to remember why I'm doing this," I said, and it was no lie. I should have been climbing up the side of a rich woman's house to steal her gold and goblin silver and fill my pouches with her hoarded beads of Keshite ivory, but then I'd just have to shovel it over to the Guild, wouldn't I? If not, they'd go tattooing a fist on my cheek instead of an open hand. Or, gods help me, a rose. I'd sooner a noose for my neck than a rose for my cheek.

I spared a look down at the Spanth, who flicked her hand up in a perfectly Ispanthian gesture of impatience and command, and this angered me enough so I climbed angry, thus faster, which was probably her plan.

I was nearly to the top when the vines decided to interfere.

"Oh, bitch, bitch vines!" I said as the damned things now flailed at me. One punched me very much like a sappy fist, and I started to fall, then the same vine snaked around my ankle—I thought to save me at first—but instead it chucked me out a bit so I couldn't use the wall to back-paddle my way to a softer landing this time. I fell from such a height that I was forced to say one of only two break-fall charms I had left, "*Kanst-ma na'haap!*" but it was a big enough drop that even after I landed in a deep frog-squat, I tumbled painfully onto my tailbone and rolled head-bumpingly backward to fall on my stomach in a heap.

The Spanth said the Ispanthian word for hello just then, said it like a Holtish man would have said *hell-oooo* at a pretty girl.

"*Saaaaa-la.*"

I looked up and saw a truly lovely girleen standing on the sill of the door and looking down at us. White moon face, brownish hair, but what got me was her long, pale arm against the door's dark wood. Funny, the thing that hooks you. It's not always the eyes or the wifely parts; sometimes it's just the curve of a well-made arm against dark oak.

"She says you can come up now," the girl said, her words riding the wet air down to hit my ears in a clear, sweet familiar brogue. A Galtish lass, so far west and north? I was suddenly taken with homesick.

"Are you the witch?" I called up.

She winked and smiled, disappeared back into the darkness, but left the door ajar. At just that moment, the wicked vines wove themselves into the nicest stair-ladder you could want. I had gotten to my feet, wiping dirt off my tailbone.

The Spanth looked at me and smirked. Made a cordial gesture to the vine-stairs, and I thought about telling her into which southern port of entry she could cram *that* and to go up first herself, but then I smiled shytefully and went up before her; though of course I waited on the eighth rung or so to make sure she was following close. The only reason I didn't insist she precede me was because I had every intention of falling on her should the need arise. At the Low School, they actually teach you how to use someone else to cushion your fall. Sometimes I miss those bastards.

Sometimes I do.

13

Deadlegs

———— · ————

When I got to the door, which had been left ajar, the girl was nowhere to be found. Some door, too. Oak as I said, and old. Copper studs instead of iron, and copper bracing in the shape of a sideways tree, all gone bluey-green in verdigris. I pushed it all the way in, stepped up to the sill, and saw what looked like a long drop with descending ledges, at the bottom of which, far below, flickered the sort of dim, warm light candles or lamps might give. My hand went to the tattoo on my cheek before I even knew I was doing that. The hairs on the back of my neck and my forearms stood on end.

"Well?" Galva said behind and below me.

"Feels like a trap. Sings with magic."

"A witch's tower? Who would think this?"

"You know that's sarcasm, right?"

"I thought I should try it once."

On the tower's far wall, across from me, a set of inverted stairs starting at the roof descended, but as they were faced the wrong way, you'd have to be upside down to use them. So this is what the ledges were, the bottoms of a topsy-turvy stairwell snaking down. I looked up at the roof of the tower, which suddenly looked very like a floor.

"Jump," the Galtish girl said, her voice full of mirth.

I looked up-down again but couldn't fathom it.

I thought to toss a copper shave down and listen for the clink, but I can't bring myself to waste a coin.

"Jump, you darling. If she meant to kill you, she wouldn't let you hurt your pretty legs."

I wasn't sure I liked the sound of that, but I jumped, meaning to use my last break-fall cantrip if I had to, but I never had time because I only fell two feet. Straight up. And cracked my head doing it. I'm good at taking falls as long as they're down.

"*Hoa!*" Galva cried. I turned to look at her, where she seemed to hang outside the door, staring at me wide-eyed. I looked up at the staircase stretching up to the top (bottom?) of this turret lit here and there by candles in niches.

"Yes, watch that first step," I said. I wanted to offer her a hand, but decided against it and stepped back. Upside-down Galva stepped up to the ledge, jumped, and knowing what to expect, somersaulted to land on her feet beside me. She was very clearly trying not to grin.

"Did you enjoy that?" I asked her. She barely nodded, but she did. Now she went to the stairs and started striding up (down?). I followed behind. It got colder as we went, and at the first landing, I saw a niche full of flickering light. Where I expected to find a candle, however, I saw an upended brick with a bit of burning smudge on it that turned out to be a wasp. Charred black, but very definitely a wasp, and a big one, too. Though it sizzled just a little as it burned, the flame did not consume it. A copper plate, new and well polished, reflected its little light. I looked more closely, fascinated. Then I nearly leapt out of my skin when the creature turned to face me the way wasps do when they're deciding whether or not to sting you. I moved past the thing and took the next few steps by twos to catch up with Galva.

At the top of the stairs, we came into an earthen vault, as big as a minor lord's great hall. I heard a low growl, and a huge gray wolf lying near a hearth to our right bared its fangs at us. We stopped.

Galva's hand topped her sword-hilt. The wolf cut its growl and looked to the far end of the room, where a woman of about fifty with thin, gray-brown hair and a full, beef-eating face sat on a throne of sorts, her hand making a gesture that calmed the wolf and made it lay its head down, licking its chops.

Behind the woman, two inverted torches burned, the smoke falling and pooling on the brick floor. The sconces were of greeny copper like the door bracings. As I looked about, aside from the odd tool, I saw very little dark or silver metal. Even the nailheads in the furnishings were brass.

Deadlegs would have looked like a shabby sort of queen except that her skirts were hoisted up in a most un-queenlike fashion to show bare legs and bare feet that looked like they belonged on a twenty-year-old woman, the sort of woman suitors stabbed each other over whose turn it was to dance with. As we walked up, she crossed those legs at the knee, the toes of the higher foot bobbing, seeming to keep time with our steps.

"Who comes before Guendra Na Galbraeth, Duchess of the Snowless Wood, Lady of the Downward Tower, Marshal of the Greenwood Knights and Supernumerary of the Gibbet?" said the girl from the tower door in her handsome brogue, her purply-black tongue dancing behind her teeth. She stood to the witch's left, leaning on a raw birch staff. So Deadlegs was a Galt as well? My folk had spilled west in no small numbers, it seemed, what with the old Famine I'd met in the Guild's prison and these two spell-cookers. We blacktongues have a knack for rising high in low places.

"Galva of Ispanthia, corvid knight, bride of Dalgatha, and servant of the infanta Mireya."

Something loosened in the old witch's face at the mention of this Mireya. She settled more comfortably into her throne, re-crossed her stunning legs now, and bobbed the toes of the other foot. "Be welcome here," she said. Her voice was not particular in its pitch, the sort of strong, flat edge to it older folk get when they've given up trying to please lovers and have set about getting things done, but it seemed to echo under my breastbone like she was showing me to be a hollow thing before her. "Would you sit?" she said.

"No," Galva said.

"Sit anyway, you've been walking long."

At that, two figures who seemed to be made of dirt shook free from the earthen walls and shambled toward us, then behind us, knotting themselves up and shuddering until they became two simple wooden chairs. When they were done, the spilled dirt from their efforts fell up and joined the dirt of the roof. My unease at sitting on the things came up an inch shorter than my desire not to insult their maker, so I sat, as did Galva. A disembodied leather glove balancing two earthenware cups in its fingers floated to us from I know not where, followed shortly by another glove bearing a ewer. We took the offered vessels, and the ewer poured dark wine into Galva's cup, then amber beer into mine.

"How do I get one of these?" I said, nodding at the magicked vessel.

Galva shot me a look, but the witch seemed to like my spark and smiled, showing very dark teeth. "You become my bond-slave for seven years, and if I'm happy with your service, I might send you off with one, and many other gifts besides."

"And if you're not happy?"

"Then I turn you into a dirt-wight and put you in the ground until one of my guests needs a place to sit."

I hadn't anything to say, so I smiled at her and drank, and the beer was good enough to make me wonder if she was jesting about wanting a servant.

I noticed now her necklace.

Copper and green amber, but if I didn't miss my guess, its centerpiece was a polished and engraved patella.

"I know why you're here," she told Galva.

"Yes."

"May we talk seriously in front of him?" she said, nodding at me.

"I think not yet."

I tried not to look hurt, but I'm sure I failed.

"Then we'll talk pleasantly until I'm ready to send him off. Where are you from, boy?"

The legs recrossed themselves, and the toe bobbed. It looked odd somehow, too similar to the way it happened before.

"Platha Glurris," I said.

"I know of it, between the Shining River and the Tattered Sea. Near the Isle of Ravens. I had the chance to go there once but never did. Does the river truly shine?"

"When the sun's on it, like any river. But people need to feel special about a place, don't they?"

"That they do."

"Where are you from?" I said.

Just then, a noise came from behind us, and we turned to see the squash-headed fellow who'd been killing himself hauling the handcart bounce the thing up the final stair and trudge into the hall. The wolf by the hearth remained docile even at this noise, watched disinterestedly as Squashy dumped the ruined, neck-bent tools, but rather than clattering, they made the sound of a body hitting the floor. That's because a body hit the floor. The tools were gone, and I now understood the neck-bent tools had *been* the body. There never were any tools. A fellow with hairy forearms and legs and, thankfully, a hood over his head tumbled onto the bricks, his noose still attached to him at the base of the hood. The fruit of the famous gallows at Maeth. Now the witch's manservant took a little bronze saw from a pack on his back, and I tried not to grimace as he unpantsed the corpse and set his saw to the place where the leg meets the hip.

"Me? I'm from a pretty little glen hedged round with flowers in the month of Highgrass and with oaks and maples that go yellow in Lammas and Vintners, and not just any yellow. A yellow that makes you weep for the beauty of it. A yellow that, with the light behind the leaves, rivals the proudest panes a master glass-stainer ever turned."

I turned my eyes from the ghastly work of the squash-man, but the *zumpf zumpf zumpf* of his saw stitched under her words all the same.

"The lambs that played in the glen bore the softest wool this side of the gods' own flocks, and the goats gave milk that needed no honey to sweeten it."

Zumpf zumpf zumpf.

"There was a lake there, full of lily pads, and when the sunset shone on the face of the lake, the lake threw back those colors so faithfully there was not a man or maiden born who wouldn't have kissed and agreed to marry at the sight of the heavens and the waters so sweetly attuned."

Zumpf zumpf thump (pant pant huff).

"And fish?" she continued as my eyelids grew weighty.

Zumpf zumpf.

"You had but to lay a basket on the bank, and trout would fight each other for the honor of leaping into it, and when you cut these trout for cooking, you found they had no bone, nor gut, but was all clean, sweet fillet ready for the batter and the butter and the fire."

Zumpf zumpf zumpf.

"Wouldn't you like to have been born in such a place as that?"

I nodded, just on the edge of a hard nap.

Zumpf . . . zumpf.

"The sweet darling, I think he's getting tired."

ZUMPF thump.

The last thing I saw before I fell asleep was the sort of thing one could easily mistake for a dream. Guendra Na Galbraeth unhooked herself from the hoisted-up skirt and sex-nymph legs that carried on crossing and recrossing themselves at regular intervals without her. Dragging her legless hips behind her, she used her very muscular, overlong arms to walk like an Urrimad mountain-ape over to where her girl had laid out the hanged man's severed legs. The manservant was gone, but a small pile of early fall gourds and melons spilled out of his clothes where he had finally exhausted himself and broken the spell that held him together.

"Now to business," I heard the witch say.

I passed into a dream where I suckled honey directly from a goat's teat and was happy to do it.

14

Witchling

———— · ————

I awoke on a torn and burned stretch of sheet, probably an old horse-blanket from the days of horses, with a pile of straw packed under it—my circumstances were not yet so poor that I would have called it a bed. A bit of flame provided the only light, but it was moving around so, at first I thought of a child circling me, moving a candle up and down, but as my head cleared, I saw that it was one of the smudge-wasps like those that lit the stairwell. Such a clever bit of magic! The Low School had lamps enchanted to burn brighter but weirdly cool (this to spare danger to the precious books we read), but that was little more than a cantrip, and you had to fill them with whale oil like any other lamp. But a wasp? I wondered, did they come when called? Within fifty heartbeats, I had figured out they responded to Galtish, ignored Holtish, and had burned myself a good one telling it to come before I figured out how to make it go.

Now it stopped responding to me and started butting up against the door, smoke curling from wee black spots where it touched. It wanted out. I let it out, and it flew into the hallway but waited for me. I was being summoned.

It led me through ever narrower earthen tunnels until we went down a ladder, at the bottom of which lay a trapdoor. The wasp butted against it until I lifted the door and let it through. Weak light flooded up, and the creature went down. The door seemed to open to a long drop up into dark gray sky shot with holes of distant, lighter gray. I risked a leg, then two, hanging straight-armed now from the ladder's bottom rung, at eye level with a ceiling of inverted grass, where an upside-down squirrel chittered at me, then ran down a tree. I heard laughter and smelled food.

"Let go, you feeble babe. Do you fear to fall into the sun? For Norholt hasn't any."

I let go, and as the world flipped, I was ready for it this time, and landed on my feet. I heard Galva laughing and looked to see her sitting astride a sort of bucking horse made from wicker and twisted wood, its head a carved horse's head that looked to have been a ship's prow from the seas, its overlarge eyes painted white and wide as if in killing wrath.

The witch stood near, holding the automaton-horse's reins, tall in long skirts hiding the borrowed corpse's legs that would carry her for a few days until the smell made her quit them. I guessed she hadn't yet sorted out how to stop them rotting. She was grinning a broad, froggy grin to see the Spanth so happy. Not that it was only happiness, I guess. To feel that counterfeit horse so near to what the real thing felt like beneath her must have thrilled her and grieved her both, as it thrilled and grieved me to see the half-forgotten shape we once took for granted, woman on horse. By the ears of Fothannon, the thing moved like a real horse, too. I wanted to touch it but also didn't, because the feeling of dry reeds instead of the moist bite of sweaty hide would break my heart.

The witch let drop the reins, and off they galloped, Galva now standing in the stirrups over a small jump, now hugging its neck to duck low branches, all the birds in the trees chattering their displeasure with the commotion. All at once, I wanted to be on the back of the thing, to go fast like that. That's what the goblins took from us, our speed. Our beautiful, noble, deadly speed.

Now the only way to go so fast as a horse would carry you was to sail on the sea or fall from a height, and both would end in tears. I hated goblins even then, though I had never yet seen a live one. I hated what they had done to us, and all the things we'd done to them didn't seem enough to pay for this great four-legged hole in us. Only when a cloud of gnats flew into my mouth did I realize I'd been standing with it open in a child's simple grin. I wiped my tongue off on my sleeve and spat, and when I looked up, here came Galva and scooped me up around the hip, swinging me into place behind her.

We tore around the clearing in great circles, both of us laughing, until Deadlegs said, "That's enough. You've only an hour on it, and we've drained a twelfth of that. Maybe more, since that mail shirt you wear is doubtless sapping it." At that, the Spanth reined the clockwork beast and brought it to a trot and then a stop. We slid off, and no sooner had we than it shuddered and folded into itself until it became a walking-staff of ash, with a small horse's head for a top-knob and a grip of roan horsehide under that.

"You've a Spanth's touch for riding, and no mistake," Deadlegs said. "I think you've all got a drop of horse blood in you."

"All my blood misses them. And this . . . ," Galva said, looking at the staff in awe. "A general could do much with a hundred knights riding these. She could turn a battle."

"Yes, she could. She could also half kill a hundred witches of my strength making them, but there's the problem. There aren't ten in the world who can do this, and for a moon's worth of work, you get an hour. Just one hour. Use it well."

Galva nodded and turned to walk off, but Deadlegs wasn't done with her.

"And use my great-niece well, or I'll hear of it, and you've been such a friend to us, we'll both rue that day."

Before we left the Snowless Wood and the Downward Tower, we sat at outdoor tables in a grove, the tables covered with white linen and wildflowers, and we were feasted with berries, bread, and game. Several folks I didn't know, folks who had the look of farmers, ate at the witch's table, too, wishing her health and praising her kitchen, which was nowhere to be seen. I had no idea how Deadlegs prepared the lot, but I would have been surprised if it involved stoves and pans. This witch spent so much magic on animating servants and preserving her upside-down tower, it would be a wonder if she had any left to do battle. And yet a wonder she was, and I had no doubt of it.

What gave me pause was the thought of what she might be capable of if she let all this go and simply went to war. Pity the king or legion on the wrong side of that. Deadlegs was one of the great magickers who had spurned the Magickers Guild, in the same category as that infamous mixer of ravens and beasts, Knockburr, Fulvir, and maybe six or seven others of their caliber. Deadlegs made the Arcane Masters at the Low School, and their more pretentious cousins in the Magickers Guild, look like dockside swindlers. At least the ones I had met.

The food was the best I'd had since I don't know when. The witch's girl, whose name I learned was Norrigal, said the trees had snared the game for us—mostly rabbits, squirrels, and pigeons, but one young roebuck, too.

"The roebuck never would have been taken, but it stopped and barked at one of the trees, and the tree didn't like that, so it ran a branch through him. It was too heavy for the trees to pass us by branch, so the squash-man had to fetch him, after he finished his rest. But here he is at table, peppered and salted and with a good crust of garlic. It angers Haros to waste deer flesh."

"That it does," I said, feeling it sounded lecherous even though that wasn't how I meant it. The thought of Haros with his stag's horns and his permanently hard deer-cock pointing up was putting notions in my head. Norrigal blinked slow, and I didn't know what that meant, but it gave me time to see she had tattoos on her eyelids, faint reddy brown like mine. Tattoos of eyes. This girl would have magicked sight of some kind, whether for distance or darkness or catching lies. Another reason to feel nervous around her, as if I needed one. Nothing I said to Norrigal sounded the way I wanted it to. If my token for her was her white arm perfect against a dark door, her thought for me will have been a dog pissing fast against a tree, or so I felt when I spoke to her. Well, if I sounded leering, she was the one who brought Haros into it.

"Anyway, roebucks have an ugly bark. Like old men yelling," I said, trying to get Haros out from between us.

After the feast, Deadlegs strode over on those legs borrowed from the hanged man. I could smell them already—at this rate, they wouldn't last her more than another day or so before they became too foul to use, no matter what she rubbed on to preserve them. It was an impractical matter, grafting corpse's legs beneath her, but the act inspired awe, as it was meant to. These Norholt peasants she'd fed looked at her like half a god, and I can't swear she wasn't.

She fixed my eyes with hers and presented me a sharp, curved knife with a bone handle and golden runes etched into the copper blade, runes promising to send whatever blood fell on them straight to the gods. Deadlegs saw me looking at them, said, "Do you believe that?"

The runes were in an old Galtish tongue I shouldn't have known. I bit back my answer.

"You think I don't know what you are?" she said. "That you have the gift for reading? Now tell me, do you believe in sacrifice?"

"I do."

Norrigal walked up and joined us.

"You'll offer something to Solgrannon, then," said Deadlegs, meaning Solgrannon the wolf, the blood-muzzled Galtish god of war and manhood. I looked about and noticed a number of Galtish gods represented by statues in the grove, even Fothannon the Fox. No sooner had I seen the altar-stone with the wooden wolf near it than she took my shoulder in her strong, old hand and steered me there.

"You've something to learn I can't teach you with words." At that, she made a gesture with her thumb, and a young rabbit leapt through the grass and into her hand. She took it by its hind legs and held it over the stone, looking at me.

"Learn?" I said. "I've killed a rabbit before."

"Stop your mouth. Think of a wolf now and give this rabbit doe to Solgrannon against the troubles to come. I know you'll want to serve the lord of foxes by farting on the butter or the like, but I think he's fond enough of you already. You'll need the blood-muzzled wolf for iron and bite."

I'm not squeamish, and if I'm a little sentimental, it's not so much I can't kill an animal for food or magic. Still, I stayed my hand, just looking at the rabbit. It looked smarter than it should. It turned, upside down as it was, and looked at me, its nose a-quiver. To my great surprise it now batted a forepaw at my knife-hand. I opened my mouth a little, and it did it again. It *wanted* me to kill it.

"Kinch Na Shannack," she said, "turn your thoughts to Solgrannon and cut the sweet doe's throat before ill befalls us."

I did it.

I grabbed the little thing's ears and stretched it taut while the witch held its feet, and then I cut its throat. We laid it on the altar as it twitched and bled, and that's when it happened. It twitched harder and harder and became a wolf, the big gray wolf from the hearth.

It shook its coat like a wet dog and now licked my forehead, and I swear its big, hot tongue almost knocked me over.

"The blessings of Solgrannon go with you," she said. "For I've more than half an idea you'll need him." Now she dabbed blood on my forehead, and her own, and on Norrigal for good measure.

Galva joined us after the sacrifice. The four of us walked together and spoke, and I was glad to be included. Norrigal was coming with us all the way west, I learned. Whatever Galva was heading to do in the giantlands, these witches were in full support of it. Then the great witch turned to me, wobbling as the hanged man's knee beneath her buckled.

"I've had a look through that head of yours," Deadlegs said to me, "and it's clear to me the Guild hasn't entrusted you with what business they'll want you to do in Oustrim."

"That's right."

Now a rabbit jumped across our path. I was pretty sure it was the same doe whose throat I just cut, which told me something important about that spell.

"I also saw that you're loyal to my Ispanthian friend, in your way. You'll do your best to keep Galva safe so long as she does the same for you."

I nodded, feeling uneasy. What else had she seen? Did she have any inkling how infatuated I was with Norrigal?

"More than an inkling," she said, though I'd not spoken to her, and she winked. "That's her business."

"Hey," I said. "That's not neighborly, poking about in my thoughts."

"It's necessary."

"Well, you found what you wanted, so get out of it."

"Make me."

"Fair point."

"Just know this, Kinch Na Shannack—though I haven't the legs to go with you, my arm is long to reach you. Your Guild is worse than you know. It's the water drives the wheel. It's why we who tap magic's deep drafts live on the margins, that we wouldn't bow to them and won't. Your Guild magickers are shyte, all smokepuffs and powdered faces and weak fire, all informers against the ones who mix bones, and swivel, and make stone men move. Their Guild, like your own for purse-nips and killers, is half a racket to bend lads and lasses into debt. Oh, they've got some few strong magickers, but only passing strong. I could use the best of them for a soup spoon."

I opened my mouth and shut it again. I had suspected the Magickers Guild was run by the Takers Guild, but I'd never heard it said by one so like to know. And if my thief-masters at the Takers had the Magickers Guild by the hair, were there others? Were the yellow-garbed adolescents of the Runners Guild, or the dark-handed women at the Dyers' vats also beholden to my beloved/hated Guild? If so, the scope of their true power would be dizzying.

"And what of you?" this true witch said, looking at me with such intent, her gaze burned cold. "They're still taking your measure, I'd say. They've not got you so firm as they think. There's more to you than they know, much more, and I've some hope you'll turn away from them, and a thorn to them you'll surely be if you do. But make no error—if a time comes when the Guild's business turns you against these two, I'll deal with you as though I'd never met you."

"If our paths diverge," I said, "I'll go my way in peace and friendship."

"I believe in that event you'll do so . . . if you're able to. So *you'll keep your pretty skin today, and take my blessing on your way.*"

I had the feeling that last was from an old Braycish bard's poem, but I couldn't remember which one or if it ended happily.

Most of them didn't.

15

The Charcoal Makers

———— · ————

Norrigal walked out of the Snowless Wood with us, carrying a pack that looked half again too large for her but doing so without complaint. We passed a section of forest where a copse of young-ish trees stood near the road, and I noticed old bronze swords planted near many of them, greening where they stood.

My first thought was that swords, even old swords, were like to be stolen, left out in the trees like this, especially in poor country where most folks defended their sheepcotes with axe and pitchfork. Then I remembered the farmer folk at the table, and it occurred to me the witch was a sort of duchess or countess here— the lord on the hill, the queen in the Downward Tower. People knew her; some loved and feared her, doubtless some hated and feared her, but they would no more pluck an old sword from this wood than the people of Cadoth would pry the gold lion coin off the Takers Guild sign. There are things worse and more vigilant than worldly justice.

"Are those grave markers?" I said to Norrigal.

"Maybe. But not for anybody yet dead."

The hairs on my nape had been standing up so constantly I wasn't noticing anymore. Strong, strong magic here. The stron-gest I'd been near in my life.

Galva had been silent this whole time. I think it had something to do with the girl—the Spanths had been among the last to start to recognize female property rights and to allow the practice of arms by women. They hadn't liked sharing, those manly horse-breakers lording over their serfs and vineyards on their proud brown hills. When the horses went and the battles turned to slaughters, though, the only way to keep the goblin Horde from marching all the way to the capital was to breed up corvids and teach their girls the sword.

Women of Galva's age would've had it hard, proving themselves first to their swordmasters, then to the white-bearded old horselords, and then down in the mud of Gallardia with the biters, as they call the goblins. Now, here was a girleen of twenty years who took it as her birthright to go on quest with us, trudging a pack half the size of her, walking so hard and fast we had to step long to keep pace with her. Norrigal fair reeked of confidence and privilege. It wasn't that Galva disapproved of her, I suspected, but I don't think she knew quite what to make of her or how to speak to her, so she kept her peace.

That there was more to Norrigal than met the eye was clear, but that was true of all of us. Knowing what Galva's horse-staff could do made me wonder what the piece of birch Norrigal carried was capable of, but I doubted she would betray its secrets to me at this early stage of our acquaintance.

All I know is we were a quiet bunch as we came to the glorified oxpath they called the Salmon Road. This road led through cold pine forests and a few river hamlets known for good salmon, and then joined up with a branch of the White Road that made for Pigdenay, the big port town on the northwest corner of Holt.

It was near the end of the first day's march that we found the bodies.

We saw a marker telling us we were coming up on a village, so we left the road, looking for a place near the river to spend the night, maybe catch a fish in the morning. We saw smoke coming from a copse near where we'd hoped to camp ourselves, so Galva sent me to have a quiet look at who our neighbors might be. I kept to the long shadows and stepped even and quiet, but it turned out there was no need for stealth.

The boy and two women by the fire wouldn't be hearing anything but the pipes of Samnyr Na Gurth, the god who leads souls to the cold wood. The boy had his head the wrong way round, and the women had kissed swords or axes, it was a terrible mess. The fire they were tending wasn't just a fire—it was a charcoal mound, and they had been about the dull, days-long business of watching it smolder, which would take three days. The mound was about my height, and still smoking proper. A smaller fire near at hand still smoked a bit but had been out an hour or more. Near it, a turned-over cookpot that still smelled of chicken soup and mushroom. One woman clutched an ancient, graying wooden bowl. A piece of bread too badly muddied for eating sat near the dead man's boot.

They had just been trying to eat their supper, and they were killed for their food—not proper at all in a wood so full of fish, game, and berries.

Just next to the backward-head charcoal-lad, I saw a mash of footprints, some of which were as long as my hand and forearm together. When I brought the others to see it, I asked Galva, "Are you thinking what I'm thinking?"

She made a fist with the two outside fingers sticking up like horns.

She *was* thinking what I was thinking.

"And what exactly is that?" asked Norrigal.

I told her about the baroness on the mare, about her hundred speardams, and about their quarry.

"Hornhead," she repeated when I said his name. "I imagine there'll be quite a reward for whoever takes him."

"As there should be," I said, looking at that head twisted as easily as a robin's.

"And if it is him?" Galva said.

I thought about the great, jingling bag of coins we'd likely have if we could get his mixling's head off him, then consulted my luck. My heart felt bathed in warm water. I didn't particularly want to fight the beastie, nor his mates, but they were the sort to kill peaceful people, it seemed, and I could almost see the glow of the money, feel the gold queenings and silver knaves in my hands. This money wouldn't have to go to the Guild, as I was paying them with service. My share of any reward would be mine to keep. A few good takes like that, and I could build a fine house on a cliff and fill it with books and money.

"It's Hornhead," I said. "And I think we can pull that big bull down."

Tracking them was an easy matter at first, what with that heavy bastard's foot making a baby's grave with every step, but, as I suspected, the tracks soon disappeared. They had some magic to hide them. Whatever it was, was too faint for me to detect—but not too faint for Norrigal, who from the depths of her rucksack produced a sort of false nose of wood she fastened around her face with a leather cord. She looked ridiculous, but the thing worked.

"This magic smells like salt and shoe leather. I'll bet he's got sandals charmed not to leave a mark so long as he steps light. Light for him, anyway."

"You look like a fucking heron," I said, trying not to laugh. I also managed not to squawk when she pinched me.

We followed halfway through the night. They were keeping just west of the Salmon Road to stay hidden, making for the port of Pigdenay, second biggest city in all the Holtlands, but with a deeper harbor than Lamnur, the capital. Convenient for us, as that was our destination as well, but I doubted the bull-man wanted to be seen in any city. They would double back or cross west to lay in ambush on the road.

Exhausted at day's end, we made camp. We chose a knobby hillock with more trees atop it than skirting it and settled in there, Galva watching little yellow birds, finches maybe, fly about the top branches. She wore the closest thing to a smile I'd seen on her face in some time.

We made no fire. I hadn't any cantrips for making warmth, but Norrigal did. She pulled an acorn from one of her bewildering array of pouches and breathed on it and rubbed it, saying words I didn't recognize over it until it began to warm noticeably. It built up heat until it was very like a piece of coal, then a whole brazier, though it only gave off the faintest glow.

"Nice, that," I whispered, though she paid me no mind.

Soon, we three lay down near the fire-nut, which Norrigal set on a rock, and Galva said, "I'll watch first, then I'll wake you." I guessed she volunteered to watch because she was rationing her wine and wouldn't sleep well, if at all. Not that I was like to sleep any better with the neck-twisting soup thief about. Still, my watch was coming, and I had to try.

I lay there and counted girls I'd kissed, but that didn't take long and only provoked an uncomfortable physical condition in myself I hadn't the privacy to attend to. I started cataloging all the girls I wished I'd kissed and got morose thinking if they had a battle with the ones I had done, they would have rolled over them in an utter, humiliating rout. Not least because the ones who'd turned me down thought better of themselves than the ones who consented, with one or two exceptions, and self-esteem is very important in a fight. That began to ease the condition I mentioned, and the condition went away entirely when I realized my blanket was on fire.

"Foth Fuckannon!" I said in a hoarse whisper, throwing dirt on it, but the flames were magicked and wouldn't easily go out. Galva tried to help, stamping at it, to little effect. Norrigal awoke then, saying, "Shyte! Shyte!" to see how badly she'd managed, and searched her pouches for some remedy. By now my poor blanket was half a torch and starting to touch the trees near us, but Norrigal found a bag of frost sand and scattered two pinches of it, dousing the flames, yes, but setting the hillock a notch colder than it had been when first we sat down shivering. Galva looked at the witchlet and shook her head. Abashed, Norrigal sat and looked at her hands, which lay in her lap like dead birds.

"Could be worse," I said. They both looked at me now, the witch hopeful, the knight weary. "We could have been on a ship. Carrying a load of hay."

"No ship carries hay," Galva said, disgusted.

"It does if it's got livestock aboard."

"Then you say the ship is carrying animals. The hay is . . ." She searched for the word. "Incidental. No ship carries only hay."

"What are their cows eating now, I wonder, in hayless countries," I said, and the girleen laughed, which was what I wanted, and to hell with ten grouchy Spanths.

Now Galva seemed to remember herself and where she was.

"We are leaving this hill now," she said, her normally decent Holtish faltering with the force of her anger, "since this *pruxilta* made a *fadoran* of it."

"Witch, lighthouse," I translated.

"I understood her," Norrigal said, and we gathered our goods and filed down the hill into the now profound darkness.

It was not an hour later that we found our quarry.

Or rather, that our quarry found us.

We walked north and west, following the sound of the river the Salmon Road skirted, and even crossed that road twice. I had asked Norrigal if I might use the magic-sniffing false nose, and she was tired of the cord chafing her, so now I had the ungainly thing on. That salty-leathery-bully smell, with just a hint of some sort of herb, suddenly gave out. I looked for tracks and saw nothing.

"Damn it," I said. "They're onto us. They've retraced their steps somewhere."

"So they are at our rear now?" Galva said. "How close?"

"How should I know?"

"How many?"

"Two, maybe," I said. "More if they're good in the woods. I think they're good in the woods."

I then noticed Norrigal drawing something on the palm of her hand with a bit of waxy black stump. I moved closer to it and looked at it.

"The fuck's that?" I whispered.

"S'an ear. Now quiet. I haven't used this spell before. Not when it counts."

She whispered some words into her hand, then her eyes got wide. She pulled us both by our shirts to stop. Pointed behind to our right and held up one finger. She pointed behind us and held up three, shook her head, held up four, then shrugged as if she weren't sure of that. She tilted her head, listening. Then she whispered to us, cupping her hand over her ear, wincing a little as she spoke.

"The one to our right is fast. Doesn't mind the dark, near running, getting in front of us. The ones behind are slower. Our bull's back there, one or two of em's large."

"How do you know?"

"Stop shouting."

"I'm not."

Galva pointed left, where the river was, and we moved toward it. We were hemmed in, but at least they couldn't surround us. I took my bow out, but it was dark enough I wondered what good it would do. One shot, then maybe I'd drop it and pluck out Palthra. Have I mentioned I'm good with a knife? Once we got to the river and put it at our backs, Galva stripped off her shield and pack, then her shirt, then her chain mail.

I looked at her as if to question her sanity, but she couldn't see me in the dark. She took back up her shield and put her hand on the *spadín*'s hilt.

"The fast one's just there," Norrigal whispered, nodding at the trees to our left. "Walking now."

I put myself behind a knobby young pine tree that painted my shirtsleeve sticky with sap while I unstrapped my fiddle and nocked an arrow. I remembered the charcoal makers wrecked and murdered on the ground.

"Someone's about to tell a lie," Norrigal said with eyes half-mad.

"Friends," a reedy voice said from the dark between the trees. The witch winced at the voice.

We kept quiet, watched as a thin, dirty, straw-haired woman in deerskins with an axe at her belt seemed to form from the very night. Just enough moon and starlight shone on her so I could see she was smiling. I kept an eye to our right, where I thought the others might come from—she was the distraction. I'd have used her the same way; she had a good smile.

"Would you have any food with you?" Deerpants said.

I remembered the soup bowl in the dead woman's hand and got a shiver. These were the killers, and no question. I cut my eyes to Galva, but she just knelt there, shield ready, watching.

"We have only enough for ourselves," I said. "Now in the name of peace, go on your way."

"Peace?" she said. "Who speaks of peace thinks of blows. Do you mean me harm?" She was moving closer. I remembered what the witch said about how fast this one was, shifted slightly so my first arrow would go at her.

"I don't," I lied. Poor Norrigal's teeth gritted against the noise of my words—our sound was beating her brains.

I watched the blond woman with the axe and the sharp smile.

"I don't mean you harm, but I don't want you closer," I said. "Stop walking."

She didn't. "Are you so scared of a lone lass in a forest?"

"Many tales start just so and end in blood," I said. "And you're not alone. Now stop walking."

"I'm stopping," she said, but she wasn't.

"Fucking stop."

"I have. Why are you so scared? You who put yourselves in our way. You who followed us."

She hadn't stopped. She kept walking like she was creeping up on a sleeping babe.

I was going to have to feather her. I didn't want to, even though that's why we were here, and she knew it and was using it against me. I was good enough in a fight, but it was hard for me to start one. The Guild had tried to beat that out of me and had mostly succeeded.

Mostly.

One more step and I'd do it.

I would.

Fothannon, steal some courage for me.

Norrigal, still gritting her teeth, pointed at the trees to the right now.

Everything happened at once.

16

Hornhead

———— • ————

I shot at Deerpants. If you were raised inside a castle's walls, you'd prefer I told you she struck first; but if you grew up in the real world, you'll know that would have been too late. The true attack was coming from the right side, and I couldn't have her flinging that axe at us from the left.

I needed her down.

So I loosed.

It was a good shot, aimed right for the middle of her. I've handled the bent tree long enough so I need no aiming, just up and shoot, fast as you like. But she was faster. The arrow flew a Gallard's nose behind her, and she sprinted to flank us. At the same time, a great noise came from my right, and I glanced just in time to see a spear the size of a sapling wobbling at my head, having glanced off the Spanth's shield.

I ducked and set another arrow, loosed it at the shapes breaking from the tree line, then dropped the bow and turned to deal with Deerpants, my hand skinning Palthra from my belt, my left foot already launching me at the woman.

Norrigal had barked in pain at the sound of the spear on the shield and at that moment threw her staff in the air. It whipped in front of me like a thing alive and knocked down the thrown axe I hadn't seen in the darkness—the deer girl was too fast for me, but not for that wonderful staff. Now she was running at me, pulling another axe from her belt even as her first axe disappeared in the river. I crouched with Palthra in hand, ready to meet her, not at all confident it would go well, but the staff wheeled forward and cracked the woman full in the mouth. She yelped and buckled down to all fours, spitting a tooth and moaning, her weapon dropped in the dark. The staff kept beating her.

I turned and saw too much to understand all at one glance. There was the mixling, Hornhead. A huge man with a flat, bovine nose and nubby horns on the sides of his head rushing at Galva, swinging overhead a flanged bronze mace I doubted I could pick up with both hands. His armor was nothing more than a leather girdle, but the tattoos on him thrummed with magic.

I recognized my arrow sticking out of the root of a horn, but he didn't seem to mind it. Two more brigands, one a stout man with a proper battle-axe, shield, and brass ring mail, one a woman with a short sword in one hand and a flail in the other, were fighting for their lives against the same war corvid that had shredded my onetime companions in the Forest of Orphans. Where the fuck had it come from? The woman with the sword and flail, we'll call her Flail, whipped her weapon at the bird, but it shivered its wings and warded the blow. The bird then bit off her nose and part of her cheek, and Flail fell screaming.

Hornhead, meanwhile, had grabbed the Spanth's shield and was simultaneously flinging her about and trying to hit her with the mace. He probably could have crushed the shield with it, but he *wanted* that shield with its pretty, living, unburnable wood. Everyone wanted that shield. Galva licked at his legs with her short sword, and though it looked like she hit skin, the blade left no mark—it looked wrong.

Now I came behind him to try and cut a hamstring. The beast saw me, though, and back-kicked me in the chest so hard I felt my breath leave me even as my feet left the ground, keeping hold of my knife only because the Guild had trained that into me; you did *not* drop a knife at the Low School. I landed in the middle of the other fight.

The man with the axe, we'll call him Axe, warded the corvid's beak with the shield, spun, and aimed a dirty chop at my head.

I rolled away from it, came up to my bow, sheathed Palthra, and picked the bow up. And there was Deerpants, and she had her fight back. She had lost her axe, but now she grabbed the bow I had just picked up and tugged for all she was worth, which was a lot.

Norrigal was out, lying on the ground, the staff inert beside her. The flail-woman's scream must have wrecked her, with her hearing being magicked still, and I only hoped Deerpants hadn't found a knife to plunge into her as well.

I pulled the bow, but Deerskins yanked harder, and was about to get it away from me. I suddenly let it go, and she fell on her side in the sand. If I pulled my dagger, I'd lose a beat, but a dropped arrow lay beside me, so I grabbed that and followed her, fluid as a snake, jamming it hard in her side. Not deep enough to kill her, though. Fuck, she was tough.

She kicked me in the side of the head so hard I started to black out, and she got on top of me, drooling blood from her wrecked mouth all over my face, straddling me so I couldn't reach my knives. Her backup knife came out now, a small skinner, and she jabbed at my neck with it, but I writhed up under her and hunched so she only got my shoulder. The fight with the bird and the armored man had wobbled closer, though, and the bird now grabbed Deerskins by her hair and wrenched her up off me. It didn't have time to do more than that before the axe-man was after it again, but that was enough.

I pushed to my feet, and Palthra came out now, Deerskins and I circling each other. Behind her, I could make out the bull-man and the Spanth still at it, Galva still refusing to let go of her shield, still untouched by the great mace, but tiring. It wouldn't go much longer. She angled a vicious backhand cut at Hornhead's arm and her wicked-sharp sword did nothing to it. But now I knew why—a tattoo on the thing's arm lit up like coal embers. That tattoo was a spell to keep the creature safe.

I had to get closer and read it.

I broke from Deerpants, who I gambled wouldn't be so fast with my arrow in her side, and ran for Hornhead. He had to be killed. The only reason these thieves were fighting to the death was because they feared him more than us. As long as he fought, they would, but when he fell, they'd likely run. He should have quit and pulled them back when he saw they were well matched, but he was too proud. He should have splintered that shield and the arm behind it, but he was too greedy.

And he thought magic would keep him safe.

I saw the tattoo as I ran at him.

Old Kesh letters.

True Hand Turns.

Also a pictograph of a shield.

I didn't get it yet.

"Marrus!" Deerpants yelled at Hornhead to warn him.

Closer to me, Flail, who was on all fours, sobbing and blind with her own blood, was in just the right place to serve me for a vault-horse—I leapt on her back and launched myself at Galva, gambling she was about to get jerked in another quarter turn. I gambled right. Quick as clapping, Hornhead had his flank to me. I wanted the jugular, couldn't reach it at my angle, so fetched him what should have been a brutal cut from the corner of his eye to the back of his head, just under one of his awful bits of horn.

He swung at me as I went by, tangling up my legs a bit, so I touched the ground with my hand but still landed running. I glanced back to see what I'd done to him, but I'd not even nicked him. Fuck! A pretty move like that and I hadn't hurt him—it had felt like my blade had pressed hard air and got knocked at a bad angle to cut.

True Hand Turns.

Now I understood.

"Galva!" I yelled. "Cut him with your other hand!"

The bull-man, who hadn't much cared about me running a knife over his head now glanced wide-eyed at me, and Galva understood. She let go the shield and ducked a mace-blow that never came, simultaneously tossing her blade into her off hand, then lunging forward and up the monster's mail skirt, putting the bullnutter to its true use.

"*No!*" Deerpants screamed, but stopped as the Spanth wheeled from the stricken Hornhead to face her. The corvid had Axe flipped on his back now. His weapon was down, and he had his mailed arms covering his face, but the bird was breaking him apart with rib-splintering pecks to his body. He was already coughing wet, dying coughs, though he said "Caelm!" and "Bretha!" and I thought it might be another language, but I knew they were names when he wheezed out a Holtish "Please" and "Help." For all his armor, I knew him then not to be a knight— they don't use those words.

I came up behind Hornhead, or Marrus, where he knelt groaning, my arrow jutting out of his bony head like a panache. I was just able to reach his great neck as he was on his knees, so I traded Palthra into my right hand and cut his cords in a great wash of blood. His hands never left his crotch while I did it. I heard an animal sound and looked where Deerpants bared her teeth at me. She wanted to run at me but knew she'd never make it past Galva. A good fighter, her. Wish she were on our side, but she'd let a bull-man turn her evil. We all make our choices.

Deerpants screamed, wild with hate, and hobble-ran off into the darkness. The bird looked at the Spanth, and Galva shook her head. She let Deerpants go, which was folly—her ideas about honor, if that's what stayed her hand, were going to get her killed. On the other hand, it was exactly that sense of fair play that caused her to spare me when I tried to rob her in the Forest of Orphans, so who was I to complain?

I couldn't resist shouting a proper goodbye at the brigand as she went.

"Hope you enjoyed your chicken stew, you murdering bitch!"

I noticed something queer about Galva now, as she limped

toward Norrigal, her naked, flat chest and muscly shoulders steaming in the cold.

One of her two inked ravens was gone, and the spot where it had been was a bloody mess.

Hornhead wasn't the only one using enchanted tattoos in battle.

That beautiful, killing bird was a *sleeper;* a magicked tattoo. The chain mail Galva wore over it damped it so it was harder to detect. It also meant she'd have to remove the armor to free the bird or put it back. By all the hoary, whoring gods, the Spanth hid a war corvid on her chest.

17

Spoils of Battle

———— • ————

I spent the next moments spitting on my shirt and rubbing the ear sigil from Norrigal's palm. She was breathing, and when she came to, I spoke to her quietly. She didn't remember what happened at first, but it soon came back.

"I'm such a fool. Mistress is always telling me I try to do too much too soon and that it'll be the death of me."

"Hard to argue with. You burned the shyte out of us and knocked yourself out with noise. But if your staff hadn't busted the teeth out of that axe-woman, she'd have had the top of my head off and then took the birder in the back. We'd have all gone to the worming vaults instead of those three had you not acted. It was a near thing, and you played your part. I suspect you've got more surprises in you yet."

She took my hand then and said, "Maybe I do," in a way that could have meant several things. I decided not to get my hopes up and realized they were up already. For a heartbeat, I felt bad even thinking about all that on a killing ground, but how's that gather-song go?

Where Samnyr pipes one man away
A bastard's gotten in the hay

Samnyr wasn't done playing yet; Galva was finishing off the face-bit flail-woman now. She spoke to her first, though.

"Kiss her hand, and thank her for her favor, to take you in battle. So go her most beloved."

"No, please!"

"I cannot refuse you this gift."

"Wait! Wait!"

"Quiet now."

It was just about then my stabbed shoulder started to ache, though it was nothing next to the way it would feel the following day—I'd been hurt enough to know pain's calendar. When she'd come back to herself, Norrigal ministered to me, packing my stab with yarrow and rubbing at the edges of it with ointment. Aside from bruises and the bird-hole in her chest, the Spanth was un-hurt, which seemed ridiculous.

"Didn't even bite your damn lip, did you?"

She shook her head.

"You shouldn't be so lucky," I said. "You're stealing it from the rest of us."

"You shouldn't be so slow. The gods favor the quick."

"Slow? Did you see that bitch move?"

"Better than you saw her."

I had no rejoinder, so I switched subjects.

"And did you ever think about selling that shield? That spring-wood's worth twice its weight in gold. And worth our heads to some as well," I added, recalling that Pagran's desire for that shield is what got me in this mess to start with.

"It was my grandfather's shield. And gold never stopped an arrow."

"Well, a shield never kept you from starving, or bought you passage on a boat, or attracted a lover to you, or put wine in your flask, and if gold also brings thieves, that's only if you don't hide it. There's no hiding that shield."

"With an arrow in your heart, you're not hungry, and they throw you off the boat."

"For fuck's sake," I said, but she wasn't done.

"And your lover marries your brother, and the wine leaks out of the hole in you."

The witchlet shook her head at us.

"This is the most ridiculous argument I ever heard," she said, but she was laughing as she did, and since she was done stuffing and smearing my knife-hole, I set about my favorite after-battle chore, raiding the pouches of the slain.

Only there were more slain than I thought.

"Where the spiny devils did these come from?" I said.

Two more of Hornhead's party never made it to the fray, a stout woman in a breastplate, a broadsword near her, and a girl-een with a bow that might have turned the fight. Hell, a wet sneeze might have turned that fight, so close it was. The stout woman was purple in the face with bugged eyes and a lolling tongue, clearly strangled. The bow-girl had fallen clutching her chest, but I saw no wound on her. It was possible her heart burst, it's been known to happen, but her youth argued otherwise. Poison seemed more likely.

"Hey, witch," I said.

"Yah," said Norrigal.

When she was closer, I said, "You kill these two?"

"You know I didn't."

"I know nothing. Least of all who killed Chopper and Plucker here. And if the killer were trying to do us a favor, why'd they take these two and not that great, thick stream of piss of a bull?"

"Maybe they were trying to even things up, not hand it to us."

"Yeah, and maybe they're listening right now."

"Could well be."

"Hey!" I said, louder. "I just want to say thanks. That's all."

Silence was the only answer I expected, and that's the one I got. Not that it meant anything.

When listening for danger, one must never mistake silence for safety.

The most curious thing about the aftermath was the bird, Dalgatha, and the way she got on with the Spanth. Woman and corvid were like woman and horse or woman and dog—but also something else entirely. She followed the knight's commands like those other animals, and with great discipline. I had heard corvids weren't allowed to feed on kynd, for it wouldn't be wise to encourage the habit in them, and so she stayed away from the dead even though she walked near Galva and croaked the Spanth word for food, "*Nourid.*"

Galva gave her the last of the grilled meats we had taken from the feast at the Downward Tower, including a haunch of roebuck I coveted, though we still had some smoked squirrel and rabbit. That done, the great, lethal bird rolled in the field near the corpses and kicked her feet up in the air, very like a horse or a dog in the grass. Galva knelt behind her head and scratched at the hackles of her neck and rubbed the top of her wicked-sharp beak. Dalgatha stretched her wings out one at a time for the woman to rub her pinion feathers, then she play-beat Galva with them, and put her cheek to hers, making contented clicking sounds, blinking her great, black eyes.

The fucking bird loved that Spanth.

And I loved *my* birds.

The man-bull had three silver owlets in his blood-stiff pouch, as well as a good Holtish duchess—a handsome coin, that, with a wee slender lady holding her hand to her mouth as if to blow a kiss or stop herself making sick—and no shortage of silver knights, knaves, and maids. Into my pouch they all went after I had a good smell of the metal in each one. It was too dark yet to really see them in their beauty, but silver and gold have their own nose, and I drank this from each coin, diluted though they were by the stink of the hide.

The creature known as Marrus carried divers other odd bits as well—ivory buttons, rune stones, a needle and thread I couldn't imagine his fat fingers pinching, pewter pins from hats, a deer-bone whistle. That I kept as well. You never know. Neither did I know if the filthy cloth poppet he carried was a minder from his own mewling calfhood or a trophy from the murder of some farmer's child. There's nothing so opaque as the heart of a stranger.

Nor so heavy as that bastard's head. I picked it up by a horn twice to gauge it, and by the feel of it, it was mostly bone in there. I got my knife ready, wondering if I should use my off hand, but deciding not to. Most magical tattoos stop working when the owner dies, and this beastie was straight dead. I rolled my sleeve up.

"Ho!" Galva said. "What are you doing, thief?"

"Thought I'd shave him so his mother's not embarrassed at the funeral."

She actually paused for a moment to work out if I meant it, then said, "Do not cut his head off."

"Would you mind telling me how we're supposed to collect the reward if I don't?"

"Take the horn."

"They'll say it's a drowned cow."

"Not if I say it."

"Why, because you come from the holy land of holy fucking truth-tellers? They'll call you a liar, and someone else'll take the head in."

She considered this. "*Bolnu,* then we make a, what's the word for it, like a sled?"

"A sled."

"Travois," said Norrigal from somewhere I couldn't see.

I said, "Are you seriously proposing we try to scoot this heavy, dead cow all the way to Pigdenay? We're cutting his head off."

"I am against this."

"For fuck's sake, why?"

"Taking heads is goblin-sport. They have a game they play with heads and spears. Are you a goblin?"

"You're saying that because I'm short."

"No, *jilnaedu,* because you are about to cut a warrior's head off."

"What's *jilnaedu?*"

"It is like idiot, but with meanness. The idiot cannot help himself."

"I like that."

"Give me your knife."

"So I could say *jilnaedu chodadu* and that's 'fucking mean idiot'?"

"Put them reversed."

"I thought you Spanths did that already."

"Most of the time. Not for commands or insults."

"So *chodadu jilnaedu.*"

"Yes. Perfect."

Now she took Palthra and walked away with her.

"Hey, come back with that."

She just kept walking.

When I was about to catch up with her, she drove the knife into a tree, hard, and kept walking.

"Hey, I had a good edge on that!" I said. I was glad she didn't look back. I wouldn't have wanted her to see me have to use both hands and even brace my foot to get the blade out of the tree, though the bird watched. Scary how quiet they can be. It bobbed its head at me, and I couldn't help thinking that's how they laugh.

By the time I got the sap off my knife and walked back to Marrus, Norrigal was red to her elbows and had the head in a sack, holes cut out for the horns. Galva shook her head, but Norrigal didn't give the Spanth the pleasure of looking back at her. She looked at me, though.

"Men like you always find something to argue about when there's nasty work to do."

"That's not fair," I said. "I was going to—"

"Shut your cake-hole," she said, brushing her hair away from her eye and leaving a bloody streak on her forehead.

We traveled by the river now. When we settled, we set watches against the possible return of the deerskin girl, and, after I whetstoned my knife, I slept. My sleep was better now, exhaustion playing the largest part in that, but also better for the wrong of the charcoal makers' deaths having been righted. I know, a thief who wags his tail at justice, there's a sorry creature. Especially one who can hardly bear to start a fight.

Sometime while I slept, Dalgatha slept as well, for when I woke in the morning, the Spanth must have had her tattoo back on her, shirted and chain mailed over, for we heard the bird's croaks and clicks no more. I hesitate to say it, but I almost missed them, for I knew we'd be a hard bunch to tussle with where she stalked, but without her, we were one sword, one knife, and a powerful but green witchling as like to hurt friend as foe.

Bully found me again. It *looked* like I found him, because he was yowling in the dirt road near the fishmonger's in the last hamlet before Norholt's capital, just about to earn a clout from the fishmonger's broom-wielding wife, when I scooped him up. No sooner had I than he purred blind in my arms. After that, he was all lazy yawns and calm licks of his bunger, as if we hadn't met a witch who walked on corpse's legs and fought a half bull for our lives since last he abandoned me.

"Please tell me that is not the same cat," Galva said.

"It's not the same cat," I said and plunked him in my pack.

18

Pigdenay

———— • ————

Pigdenay, city of warships, city of armorers, city where the first sick horses clomped ashore, let me weave a garland of wishes for you.

O city of gray-brown bricks and mud-brown swans, city of small green windows and mean gray eyes looking out, may your salt-rubbed rotting timbers stand another year, may the anvils of your hundred smithies bang forever in the hungover skulls of King Conmarr's wodka-drunk, lad-mad sailors. May the greasy fishpies you are famed for never cool so much one can taste the earthworms ground for filler, nor may your dungeons ever want for Galtish bards who mocked your huge, fat duke.

Pigdenay, city of rain and ashes, Pigdenay, city of whores and rashes, capital of kidnaps and ambergris, cradle of half the world's soot, I praise your cobbled promenade, where the whale's blubber and the kraken's tentacle are grilled and sold across from the hall of lost sailors, mostly killed by whales and krakens.

I sing of the heart you were born without, and of the twice-sized belly you got instead. You're a cold city, Pigdenay, but I'll forgive you your faults as you forgive mine, for your beer is never warm, and I'm never short a stolen copper shave to buy it.

"Give us a ship stout enough to carry us, and a captain fool enough to take us west, for my feet are tired of walking and I'm keen to clear my debts."

This last I said aloud in a sort of Allgod prayer as the city came to view.

"Let it be so," said Norrigal, and *rao* said Bully Boy from his pack, for the little bastard felt quite at home there again. Now we three, or four if you count the cat, or five if you count the murder-bird sleeping flat on the Spanth's scarred chest, looked west down the Cumber Road that led to the city's east gate.

"First, to the harbor to find an inn," Galva said, "I need a bath." And in we went through the main gate, no bother given to us, nor to any who paid the entry toll.

We pushed through the swell of ox and donkey carts, past servants quick-quicking off to do their masters' errands, past beggars comparing takes, and almost into a procession for the god of the sea. A wild-haired man with a mirrored, seaweed-bearded mask and a whip capered, clearing a path, beating his hip-drum like thunder, whipping the sky like lightning, making children laugh for joy or cry, as they will at storms. Following him came a dozen stiff-necked priests to Mithrenor bearing headdresses with silver bowls of seawater at their tops, water they dared not let spill out. At the street-corners stood cabriolet pullers offering to tug their gaudy two-wheeled carriages to the harbor, or to the university, or to the covered market hall, which was the best one outside Gallardia.

I knew this city well. I studied here three years, at the Low School, which was a True School of the Takers Guild and not a straw farm. Or at least I think it was.

We passed the Greenglass Library, a private library that rented books for copying or reading, and where copper-scholars scribbled furious notes under threat of an hourglass. It held the best collection in Holt, which I know in part because I stole nine books for them that year, two from burghers' houses in Pigdenay, five from other towns, and two from visiting ships.

An assassin had come calling for me once, sent as a test for her and me. She'd have had me, too, but she poisoned my beer, and I fed it to a stray dog because Fothannon says giving animals booze is such pure mischief it's like feeding him directly. Me it would have sickened, but the poor, small dog died in my sight. I shudder to think how her Assassin-Masters punished her for her failure, but I found a silver Gallardian owlet in my bed that night for my good luck. The Low School likes luck, so it liked me, until I fell into arrears.

Though I'd acquitted myself well that time, assassins scare the hell out of me, and would scare you, too, if you'd met one. The Killers Wing of the Low School has a whole building full of them, chuckling over monkshood and lethal mushrooms and castor beans, brewing stillheart and thieves' dew in vats, practicing strangles and stabs and bathtub bleedings, swimming underwater without needing to breathe, chucking knives and blowing silent darts, magicking themselves invisible or silent, or putting on false faces.

This is important because I was about to meet an assassin again, only this one wasn't sent to kill me.

Not yet, anyway.

Norrigal failed to sell Hornhead's noggin to the duke's men, who'd scarcely heard of him and didn't think much of head-sellers. There was a carnival in town, though, and carnival people are always in the market for a curiosity. Besides which, they know more than soldiers. They have to.

Once the head was sold and the coin collected, Norrigal, Galva, and I set out on an even more challenging task—to try to find a cheap westbound ship whose crew wouldn't kidnap, rob, or rape us, or sell us for goblin-meat, or any combination of the above.

19

The Spigot and the Noose

———— • ————

The Spigot wasn't as rough as you'd imagine a whale-city's busiest port tavern to be. It was rougher. I saw two women get in a fight that made you sick to look at, and the fellow who tried to break them up had one eye thumbed out of its socket and wandered to a polished brass mirror on the wall, yelling and trying to get it back in.

The fellow at the table nearest the mirror didn't like this yelling and beat his head against the brassheet until he knocked him out and the whole thing fell on him. The women fought on. One of them at last succumbed, thrashed bloody with some iron thing, I think a fireplace instrument to judge from the soot stripes whacked on her. She got dragged out the door by the hair and she was saying, "Bitch! Bitch! Bitch!" all the while, which wasn't going to help her much when the victor got her outside. The alley, by the way, was called Cutpipe Alley, and unlike most city street names, this one left no mystery as to why it was called so. Who drinks in a place like that, anyway, aside from those looking to settle feuds or start new ones? Sailors, that's who. Pirates, whalers, dreadnought salts. Patchy-haired, waxy old goblin drowners carrying their burns without a word to say.

We were there because the half-respectable ships were full and the respectable ones didn't go to Molrova.

We were there because we had been unlucky.

As we walked across the gray, worm-tunneled floorboards, ripped no doubt from some ship that had spent time in warmer waters, and into the press of bodies at the Spigot, I wished I had been born a few inches closer to ceilings. It was hard to get a look around. They grow them tall up north, so here in Pigdenay even the Spanth was mostly looking at noses in the press, where Norrigal and I had a whole gallery of armpits and chest hair to enjoy. We wriggled to an almost-corner at the far side of the Spigot. The corner proper was held by a swarthy, tiny-eyed man with a bandolier of throwing knives and a tattoo of a cunny on his forehead, and none of us felt inclined to ask him to move. He sipped at a tall glass of what smelled like a paint-removing agent and stared in the middle distance, sometimes moving his lips a bit as if spellcasting. No wizard, he, just bugshyte mad.

A group of Sornian women sat at the table to our left, recognizable by the grapevine torques they wore. Sornia was a Beltian goddess always pictured as conjoined twins, one hand pouring wine from a pitcher into a goblet held by another. She had been a minor goddess of wine in Beltia before the Goblin Wars, but since the death of men and horses, she had been elevated as a symbol of women given to loving women. Her followers were found throughout Manreach, from Holt to the borders of Kesh.

Sornians were famous for violently resisting royal decrees to marry and reproduce—such decrees being popular after the Threshers' War. You might think such a movement would be easily suppressed, but many of its adherents were birders and other warriors, and knew how to fight, both singly and in formation. One Sornian poet was arrested in Unther, but her captors never made it to gaol with her, as they were drubbed by a phalanx of her sisters using tentpoles as pikes. The group near us had the words *As We Will* tattooed in Beltian on arms or napes and were armed with short swords and truncheons.

Starting on opposite sides of the Sornian table, two youths were casing the place to steal. They were using a crossing pattern, coming near each other, then separating, which did nothing particularly useful except to alert professional thieves that amateurs were in the house. Poor lads who signed away their financial well-being for parlor tricks at a straw farm. One caught a look at my tattoo. I shook my head at him. *Don't even think about it.* He would have guessed I was at least a Prank, and he was clearly scared he'd be wearing the tattoo himself soon. They didn't claim the Guild's pint—it went to an Untherian soldier-for-hire in bright striped stockings. I was so civil about it she didn't even lean in, and tipped her bright red hat at me after she got her ale, half of which she shared with a ship's captain she seemed keen on.

You could tell ship captains by their medals of command, issued by the Seafarers Guild. The medals varied between nations but usually included a pearl for merchants and a shark's tooth for privateers. They wore these about their necks or on hat or lapel even when they were out drinking, just in case people like us should approach them with a need to be separated from our money.

The first captain we interviewed, and by *we* I mean *I*, was a black woman from Axa—an unallied island kingdom that had somehow managed to stave off the goblins quickly and alone. The secrets of their campaign they shared with no one, though it was rumored they had a sort of wall of mirrors on the cliffs near the capital and could burn a ship like a bratling with a hand lens burns ants. I would have liked a look at the Axaene fastrunner this captain owned—the clever riggings of Axa's sails were poorly copied in many places—but I could barely get her to speak to me, as it was clear a galley oar would do more pulling of me than me of it.

The next commander, a woman from Istrea, had captaincy of a sleek merchant sailrunner and was looking for fancy men to keep her crew happy. I could tell she was Istrean not only by her habit of humming *mmm* to stall while she thought of the Holtish word but by the fly-veil on her belt. Flies in hot, marshy Istrea carried the fearful Smiling Sickness, and the disease had been getting worse. In the summer months, Istreans went veiled, and they tented their beds with fine nets.

I spoke to her longer than I should have just because I was hypnotized by her liquid brown eyes and her captain's pendant, a coral dolphin clutching a tear-shaped pearl in its mouth. I didn't say I *wasn't* a fancy man. I asked where they were headed, what the quarters were like, and so on, staring at her the while. Foolish, but I couldn't help myself. When she saw I was playing coy, she leaned close and said, with her trotting, weirdly musical accent, smiling all the while, "My time is valuable and you steal it. If your cock is not for pleasure, I will hook it for *mmm* bait." I got off my stool like it was a hot stove, and her bodyguard, a woman with a hat made from sea-snake skins and a short, wicked bull-nutter much like *my* bodyguard's, kicked me in the shank with her square-toed boot as I went. I don't say this as a matter of complaint. As with most of my suffering, I richly deserved it.

The boat we did ship on was a whaler. I hadn't wanted a whaler because they tended to be more large than fast, and I needed to get us west in haste—we'd already passed fifteen of the fiftyish days the Guild had given me to arrive in Oustrim.

I made a point of asking if the crew would be hunting on the way to Molrova, and the captain, a Molrovan himself, wearing a baby kraken's beak as big as a fist around his neck, made a point of making me feel stupid for asking that. He licked beer foam from his waxed, lethal-looking mustachios, and said, "No. We will sail through the Gunnish sea as quickly as possible. If a red or a spotted fatling or a square-head biter should spout near us, we will say, 'Nim, whale. Go your ways. We have important passengers paying not one hundredth part of your value, and they do not wish to smell your burning fat.'"

"But we won't be expected to hunt. We're just passengers. Is that clear?"

"Perfect-clear. You will rest in your corner of the hold, and you will be dry and well fed."

That's what he said.

That Molrovans lie and boast of lying was well known to me.

Where a Galt may lie for the sake of poetry, a Molrovan sees poetry in the lie itself. I let myself believe him because he didn't lie
about whaling on the journey, or at least, he lied in such a way
that he told the truth. I trusted in his words because I wanted to.
I was an accomplice to the lie because it was a comfort. To communicate with a Molrovan, you have to understand their culture.
When two of them marry, they say, "I have never loved before
you, and I will never love again," and their oath-rings are made
of wood. The first thing a Molrovan midwife tells a baby is, "You
will live forever!" This is not a blessing, and it is not a wish. It is a
lie, and the midwife laughs after she says it.

Before we shipped out, I thought I'd get a bit more silver in my
purse, so I worked a hanging at the Marspur Commons, otherwise known as Noosefruit Square, where the duke's justice was
done.

   The day was cold, and a fine, misty rain was falling, the
sort of rain that took its time wetting you because it knew you
weren't going anywhere. Beggars had arrayed themselves near a
new fountain featuring Cassa, the goddess of mercy, who must
have despaired at finding herself in a place so bereft of mercy as
Marspur. I recognized the statue—Cassa looked a good bit like
a dancer who'd broken the city's heart by dying young last summer. I knew her, too, when I was in my studies here, and she was
as sweet as the summer day was long. The artist clearly had her
in mind when he took up his chisel. There were her cheekbones,
her wee nose, her beautiful legs, now marble, shown to good advantage by her short Norholtish dancer's skirt. Gone forever were
her pale blue eyes, like sunshine through ice, and there's a pity.

   Two of the beggars leaning against the fountain were sharing
a sort of greasy tarp to keep the wind and rain off of them while
one gnawed a bit of hard-looking bread. Holding up the tarp was
no easy matter, though, as they hadn't a thumb between them.

These were likely not goblin fighters but failed thieves who'd run afoul of the Guild and been unthumbed. They sat atop a sort of crushed and sodden carpet of wildflowers offered either to Cassa or to the woman whose likeness she bore. I watched a rich dam throw a flower into the water, mutter a prayer, and go her way, seeming inconvenienced by the mendicants. And there's humanity in a glimpse—we've always got a copper for a stone idol, but none for the beggar in its shadow.

I'm no better.

I gave them nothing but a second look, and they'd be buying no pies with that.

The gallows were freshly built, the whitish pine standing out against the red-brown bricks behind them. The square was only half-full, which was perfect because I'd have room to move around. They were dangling three of them; a thief who'd robbed a runner from the Runners Guild, a killer, and a bard who'd written a vicious ode about the duke's male member, suggesting it hadn't reached normal size because nothing grows well in the shade. She'd slandered him before and been flogged for it, but hadn't learned. I wondered if she was a Galt, that sounds like one of us. Drannigat himself sat on a huge blackwood chair on the dais, pale-faced and puffy, watching because he couldn't resist revenge. They hanged the disrespecter of the ducal knob first as if to say she wasn't as important as a thief.

Drannigat's young wife sat next to him on a smaller throne and watched the proceedings, with the duke's thick, ringy hand on her lap and a smile that never touched her eyes nailed to her face. She looked fine in her sage silk dress with her diadem of moonstone. I got close enough to grin up at her, but never caught her eye. I wondered what she'd be like to tumble. I wondered how much I'd get for that diadem. It occurred to me that I'd be hanged myself if I said half of that out loud, and I hoped the poor lass on the gallows at least got a good, long laugh for the verse that cost her neck a stretch. What a fabulous kingdom the mind is, and you the emperor of all of it. You can bed the duke's wife and have the duke strangled in your mind. A crippled man can think himself a dancer, and an idiot can fool himself wise. The day a magicker peeks into the thoughts of commoners for some thin-skinned duke or king will be a bad day. Those with callused hands will rise on that day, for a man will only toil in a mine so long as he can dream of sunny fields, and he'll only kneel for a tyrant if he can secretly cut that tyrant's throat in the close theater of his bowed head.

Even as the tool-impugner apologized to save her family, and gods bless her, she made it sound just as insincere as it was, I got a shabby leather purse off a chainsdam.

Truth be told, it was too easy stealing here—people were so cowstruck watching souls quit their bodies, they were like simpletons. So I challenged myself to do something harder. I started stalking a merchant's fancy boy for his gold boot-anklet, trying to work out how to kneel down without being noticed, but then they led the killer onto the gibbet, and my breath caught in my throat.

It was Deerpants from the fight in the woods, the straw-haired bitch who'd nearly done for me with an axe. I was close to the platform at that point, close enough to see the carved bone fox pendant around her neck, just below the noose—were it ivory, a chainsman would have had it. When asked if she wanted to speak, she shook her head. I doubted she could have spoken out of that mouth, swollen up and missing teeth as it was from the beating Norrigal's staff had given it.

They asked if she wanted a hood, and she was about to nod, I think, when she saw me. She actually laughed. She shook off the hood. The hangman tightened the noose, went to yank her standing-block, and she fixed me with her eyes. I should have looked away but didn't. Her gaze wasn't hateful. I know I'm reading into it, but it seemed her eyes were telling me lots of things at once—she forgave me for stabbing her; she forgave me for killing her man-bull; she couldn't believe her not-so-long life was ending in this rainy place; she'd like one more mug of beer; she'd have that beer with me if she could; she hoped the life after was better than this one, and if not, she'd rather it was nothing at all. Just nothing. She looked at me and seemed to be asking me not to look away because I would help her more than some mumbling Allgod priest wagging a bronze sun on a stick, or even more than her own folk, who'd be ashamed of what she was. So I stayed there with her, another fool in thrall to the fox god and like to find his own noose.

I held my hand up in kinship, and her elbow moved, so I think she would have held her palm to me as well were she not manacled. When the hangdam yanked the block, she said *ah* as she fell, and that *ah* before her neck broke seemed the realest thing I'd ever heard said. Her voice as expressed in just that one syllable was perfect, not the deceiver's purr she'd used before the fight or the harpy's cry in the fray, but it was her essence; killer, lover, thief, daughter, all of it together with something of the divine as well. I loved her for that *ah*. I wanted to leave then, but I felt I needed to do something for her, so I removed my pattens and toed off that fucking fancy boy's anklet as if she were still watching me, and I can't swear that she wasn't.

But I wasn't done in Marspur yet—I had one last holy duty to see to. I waited until the duke's young wife had a good snootful of mead, then cantripped a right, juicy, snotty sneeze out of her, all over Drannigat. Oh, the big man raged, near fit to split his two-cow belt, and seethed while a steward wiped him down. By the time he thought to have a magicker dowse for whomever tossed that spell, I was down an alley and bound for the sea.

20

A Knife in the Mouth

———— • ————

The whaler was called the *Suepka Buryey,* or "Pig-Lady of the Tempest" or just "Storm Sow." *Suepka* was a versatile word, meaning "sow," but also meaning "female bastard," or basically anything you don't like that has tits on it. But like many of the world's best insults, it could be a grudging honorific. Like, that woman's a real *suepka* with a knife. Not that I speak much Molrovan, but as you may have noticed, I collect vulgarisms.

We had taken a look at the ship, bobbing against the pull of her ropes, casting shadows on a smaller oar-ship beside her. No oars on the *Suepka,* she was too big for that, but had two huge mainmasts and a smaller lateen mizzenmast at the back, this sitting on the square, flat aft castle. Two oar-boats sat at her sides, ready to be lowered down for the whale-chase, and a trio of ballistas on her forecastle showed she thought herself ready to fend off or reel in whatever the foamy sea would throw at her. Her wood was so dark as to be almost black, and her shape was round and piglike. An exotic and diverse crust of barnacles peeped at me from below her waterline. The smell of old whale fat hung about the ship like perfume in a whore's drapes.

Two members of the crew, greasy-looking women, surly to have been left aboard while others tried their land-legs, glared down at us, so I looked back down at the barnacles, but not before one of them, a barrel-shaped tan woman with sun-bleached hair slicked against her head, sucked her little finger at me. While I was puzzling out whether that was an insult, a proposition, or both, Galva said, "I think you're going to find a bride on this boat."

Norrigal snorted.

I looked away. It occurred to me that walking the several hundred miles to Molrova might be a better idea than climbing on that roll-bellied fatburner of a whale ship to be dandled by Lady Suck-Finger and coated in oil and filth, but if I didn't get to Oustrim in a timely fashion, I'd have the Guild to answer to, and they were more frightening to me than the sea. Or so I thought.

I hadn't put to sea yet.

I went back to the inn one final time to pack and ready for the voyage.

I had a goodbye to say.

The Spanth was off to market buying wine—too proud to let me haggle for her—and Norrigal had gone in search of peppercorn and other ingredients for some seasick-spell she had in mind to cast upon those of us who'd need it.

I watched Bully Boy paw his way to and fro in our room at the Heads-Up Penny, wondering how he'd get on in Pigdenay without me. Just as he'd gotten on in Cadoth, I imagined, until his luck failed him. Same as the rest of us.

"Come here, you little weed," I said and scooped him up by the nape. He stuck his paws out in front of him like they do, and I spoke right into his face, looked him in his useless, pretty eyes.

"Bully Boy," I said, "time has come to part ways. There's no place for you on the ship."

He raoed.

"I know. It's sad, but the world's made of sadness, if you hadn't noticed, great gray bricks of it and mortared all together with pain and obligation. For kynd, at least. No obligations for you, my kith. Precious little power or choice, but nobody expects a damned thing of you, and there's a worthy birthright. I wish you uncountable pans of milk, a bit of cheese and fish, and fewer kicks than you deserve, and I know you'd want the same for me. We'll part as friends, then."

I put him on the bed and petted the length of him so he pushed up with his back and curled his tail, but he wouldn't purr as he normally did. I dug in my pack and went to feed him one last bony flake of salt herring, but he turned his nose up at it.

"What's that, taking it hard? Eat the damn thing, you're too skinny as it is," I said, tickling his nose with it, but he wasn't having any. "Fine," I said.

I tossed the fish on the floor and swung my legs on the straw mat to lie down for a moment. It occurred to me that this was going to be the most comfortable bed at my disposal for untold months, so I might as well enjoy it. Bully went under the frame of the bed, ignoring the fish, and he proceeded to cough and hack as if to deliver one of his charming little hair-pellets onto the floor beneath me.

"You know, trying to make me feel bad won't work. I said I'm going, and going I am, at first light tomorrow. Hack as you will, that's an end to it."

I felt my hairs stand up a bit on end.

I mistook that feeling for a pang of sadness to lose Bully Boy, who had a handsome little face on him and wasn't bad as cats go, but by the time I realized it was magic, it was too late.

Bully ran out from under the cot and thumped his head properly against the wall and sat there panting, looking sightlessly back under the bed, where something much heavier and faster than a cat was moving.

I was reaching for my knife when a tattooed leg swung out from under the bed and a nude woman followed it. Just as Palthra cleared its sheath, she had me by the arm and vaulted toward the wall, kicking off it in such a way as to wrench me backward by the arm so I did a full turn and fell off the bed with her. If I weren't a fast bastard myself, that particular move would have dislocated my shoulder, but I went with her to save the joint. Like she knew I would. When we hit the floorboards, she ended up on top of me, her legs spidered out so there was no leveraging her off and her pressing my knife arm against me with the weight of her so I couldn't use it.

Now, quick as you like, she did something where she wrenched my arm back and briefly almost straddled my face. I glimpsed her right in her lady parts, but to be perfectly honest, I couldn't have been less interested in them. Or so I thought. But when her knee dug hard into my biceps, I did get less interested. I bucked up and tried to knee her off me, but I didn't even manage to annoy her. Then she worked my wrist the wrong way just shy of breaking it and plucked my knife. *I'm done for,* I thought. This was an Assassin-Adept, one of the Guild's best, and I had no more chance against her than a blind cat would have.

The knife appeared and settled under my nose like the world's most unwelcome mustache. I regretted how sharp I kept it.

"Open your mouth," she said at just above a whisper. When I hesitated, she pressed the keen edge of it up so that it was clear she could cut my nose right off me if she liked, and I mean shave my face as flat as a plate. So I opened my mouth, but just a little.

"Wider," she said, applying just a bit more pressure, just so I felt the skin between my lip and nose starting to separate. I pulled my chin farther down. Now she put the knife in my mouth, depressed my tongue with the flat of it. "You'll hold still now. I wanted to make sure you listen rather than talk. I come from the Guild with instructions for you. *Don't* nod. Blink twice."

I aborted the nod, a stupid gesture when you've got a knife in your mouth, and blinked twice. I recognized her now. I had seen her in Cadoth, the one who took my money away in a sack back at the Takers Guild Hall. All the tattoos on her. I grew less afraid, relaxed a bit, not because I was sure she wouldn't kill me but because I was so very lamblike helpless there wasn't much to do about it, and there's a freedom there.

"Kinch Na Shannack, I am going to help you discharge your debt to the Guild. Your real mission is not to bring magic articles back with you; your actual task is to get me to Oustrim in the company of that humorless Spanth. Once there, I'll tell you what's next; you're to help me do something, but what that is you don't need to know yet. Just know that this comes from the Full Shadow of Holt and, by his command, your success or failure will bring you gratitude and wealth, or pain and death. Blink twice if you understand."

There were only eleven Full Shadows in the Guild, who ruled their secret realms like upside-down monarchs; to say the Full Shadow of Holt was as if to say *the hidden king of Holt*.

I blinked twice.

"Good. I had to make myself known to you so you wouldn't leave the cat behind. Leave the cat behind, you leave me behind. Let the cat drown, you let me drown. If I die, Kinch Na Shannack, the Guild will know immediately, and you'll die in such a way as to envy me. I'm going to take the knife out. If you have any questions, ask them, but please know that I don't like questions."

"I have one," I said, when the knife was clear, the taste of the metal thick on my tongue. She just looked at me. "Is the cat just a cat?"

"Yes, the cat is just a cat. But mind, I use his eyes and ears and steer him when I want to."

"I thought he was blind."

"He is. But I'm not."

"So you've seen me at times I thought myself alone except for a blind cat."

"I have."

"I'll try not to think about that too much."

"Same here."

She stood then, in all her runed and scripted glory, and flicked the knife up so it stuck in the ceiling.

"You're a frightening woman," I said.

"You haven't the slightest idea."

I studied the tattoos on her. As I'd first noticed at the Hanger's House, her arms were solid black, from fingertips to shoulders, and I had no idea what magic that brought, nor knew I anything about the clockface tattooed on her sternum. I saw a few words in different languages, most I couldn't identify even though I understood them all. *Up. Horse's Kick. Bottle-of-Breath.* I caught those in glimpses, dared not read longer lest she divine I was a Cipher. No one could ever know that unless I wished to live out my years squinting and fat in a pillowed cell.

"Did you get an eyeful?" she asked, thinking I was intrigued with her nakedness. I let her think it.

"Yeah. S'not bad."

"Not bad? Fitter than you'll ever touch, Prank."

"What's your name?"

"I murdered it."

"What will I call you?"

"Sesta."

"Istrean for *six*?"

"Aren't *you* proud of yourself. It's how old I was when I first killed."

"What, a bug?"

"My sister."

"Must've been hard on your mum."

"I'm revisiting the idea of shaving your nose off. Have you got anything else to say?"

I shook my head.

"Good."

Now she stuck her finger down her throat and vomited up a leather pack. She got clothes out of this, dressed herself.

"Do you have any food?" she said. I showed her where it was, and she ate it all, looking at me the whole time. She even ate

Galva's and Norrigal's food. Then she made me give her money for more food, and she went to the market. Apparently, being in a cat for a month makes you hungry.

When she had gone out, as quiet and fluid as the shadow of a cloud, I looked at Bully Boy. He yawned and rolled his tongue. Then he sauntered over and ate the dried bit of herring on the floor.

"Thank you very much for bringing *that* into my fucking life."

21

Old Friends

———— • ————

We left Pigdenay on a calm sea, a cool gray sky above us filled with gulls wheeling and taunting and diving. The *Suepka Buryey* felt as sturdy as land while still in harbor, and I allowed myself to hope the voyage wouldn't be too bad. The captain, Yevar Boltch, had given us barely a nod when we boarded. He stood on the aft castle to confer with his first mate, a fellow Molrovan named Korkala, a brutal-looking dam who'd cut her iron-gray hair so close to her head you could see the map of scars on her scalp. She's the one who got things done on the *Suepka*.

Just before we pushed off, I watched her pay the Seafarers Guild's man, a thin swaggerer in filthy woolens. Korkala also handled discipline on the ship, and I would soon find out she liked her work. She carried a baton with a hurtful bronze fist on the end of it, not so large you'd call it a mace, but not so small you'd soon forget a sharp blow from it, even through the greasy leathers and fur these northern sailors wore.

As we put out of the harbor and Pigdenay receded to a sort of fat, handsome pile of bricks in the distance, the captain spotted the three of us above decks and nodded at Korkala.

She approached us and said, in barely understandable Holtish, "We cannot safe-keep you on decks. Ropes move, beams move, hit boys, waves take land-walkers below water, very cold. Is better below most times, with others, yes? Yes. Is good now, say good gladness to city while in harbor, but when city gone below sea, you below deck, out of way with others. Deck not safe. Remember I warn you this."

"Thank you," the Spanth said. "We will be very careful with ourselves. We will not be in your way," and I never heard her accent sound so mild. Next to this bronze-fisty-carrying western whale-butcher, she sounded like a Holtish scholar. Korkala nodded at Galva, and me, and Norrigal, and that's when the captain spoke to us for the first time since the Spigot.

"You," he said to me. "Again, where in Galtia you from, black-tongue?"

"Platha Glurris," I said.

He grunted and nodded, winking at me like he'd heard the name before, though at the time I thought this was shyte, the way you say "Ah," in false recognition when you ask a foreigner their hometown and they mumble some unpronounceable syllables. Now the captain considered us as a group.

"You ready for sea-voyage?" he said, smiling just that little bit, as if he were already relishing the sight of some or all of us casting up our accounts over the railing at the first touch of rough weather.

"All packed and pretty and eager to break a wave," I said.

"*Good!*" he blustered over my last word, clapping my shoulder and moving away. He didn't give a kark and didn't mind letting us know it.

Maybe it wouldn't be so bad, though.

We were supposed to be in Molrova in two to four weeks, depending on the whale-hunting. Never mind the cool feeling in my stomach that told me my luck was running low. I had no choice but to see things through. I'd gotten past periods of bad luck before, hadn't I?

We had been given a small stall in the hold, near the big, empty barrels that would later slosh with rendered blubber and, if a squarehead or red whale were caught, spermaceti. We had hammocks to sleep in, a shared trunk for our goods, and a little graywood table for playing Towers or dice. Other crew members slept in their own hammocks, all in a common part of the hold practically on top of each other, save the first mate and the captain, who had their own cabins. I was just starting to think I could do this for a month when I heard a familiar voice.

"Did someone say Platha Glurris?"

Oh shyte, I thought, not sure at first why the voice was bad. Normally, I'd have put my head down and moved away just to be safe, but there was no place to run and no place to hide. I looked up and met the eyes of a strong man of thirty, missing two fingers, his face marked with a half-moon scar that was clearly a goblin bite. He was oiling up the wicked-sharp, barbed head of a harpoon. He smiled when he saw me, and a stranger would have thought it a friendly smile unless he'd seen a snake about to eat a mouse. They smile just like he did then. With his Galtish black tongue like tar behind his teeth.

He knew me.

He'd known me all my life.

And he hated me.

22

A Blind Cat's Luck

In the summer of 1224, while the crowned heads of Manreach were feeding kynd to goblins near Goltay at the Kingsdoom, the last wave of youngsters were mustered off for training. That training would take a whole, hard year of shield walls, spear drills, archery, and fast marching.

Manreach had learned during its second war with goblins—the Threshers' War—that the Horde easily killed green peasants armed only with clubs and pitchforks, no matter how many they numbered. During the Threshers' War, 1210 through 1217 Marked, we'd lost nine men in ten.

I was born in the first year of that calamity.

So I was fourteen when the muster came to Platha Glurris.

The war raging then was being called the Daughters' War, for it was mostly daughters left to fight it. Lads my age were the oldest to be found in numbers, and eventually went with their sisters and mothers and aunts into huge armies allied against the goblin Horde. This newest group of Unthermen, Holtishmen, Braycish, Gallards, Spanths, Gunns, Middlers, Wostrans, and tributes from the Odd Cities in Istrea and Beltia called itself the Glorious League, and the gods hate that sort of thing. They like to decide whose the glory is, and so they did. The worms got the glory.

Even that last wave who, with the help of the corvids and the unburnable springwood ships, finally pushed the goblins back to their homelands in this Daughters' War mostly didn't come back. Goblins fought with poison, you see. They fought with great mole-blind, moon-white ghalls they'd bred up from manslaves underground and pain-mad boars the size of ponies, with spikes inside their armor as well as out. They fought with rolling palisades and a hail of bolts.

They fought with illness.

They fought with fear.

King Conmarr of Holt sent letters bearing his seal to all the towns in all his three lands; Holt proper (also called Westholt), Norholt, and Galtia. Platha Glurris got such a letter, and it empowered the duke to set mustermen—these had the responsibility of recruiting soldiers, and if a musterman named you, it was treason not to go. If you slipped town, the musterman paid a fine. He was never a noble. He would be one of the townsfolk, someone known and well liked, like a reeve. Someone wealthy enough to have something to lose, but not so wealthy the fine wouldn't hurt him.

A month before the last muster, the Takers Guild had sent a musterman of its own to Platha Glurris. He said his name was Cavanmeer, and no one ever so ennobled greed, disloyalty, and desertion. Listen, here's his solicitation, as near as I remember it:

> This war is not for you, Kinch, not you. It isn't that I don't want us to beat those evil buggers, I'm kynd like you, aren't I? It's just that the gods give us each our gifts, and those gifts are not the same. Take your Coldfoot guards, the cream of Galtish infantry. Kynd so hard they wear no shoes, not on frost nor rocks. Finest spearmen in Manreach, yes? That's their gift, by the gods, their strength and warlike prowess. They were shaped in the womb to hold a spear, their lungs are made for yelling the wolfish howl of your Solgrannon Bloodmuzzle, god of war. But you. You're a Foxfoot man, aren't you? Called by Fothannon to the subtle arts? I thought so. I know your brother went to the mints for stealing, there to be deafened and maimed. And what did he steal? Don't tell me, I already know. We already know. To be maimed for a bit of dyed cloth is a poor boy's lot, if that boy lets things fall that way. And now he's off to war himself. You don't have to let things fall that way.

You don't have to answer the muster, go to some Goltay or Orfay to die unfucked and unsung for King Conmarr, whose tongue's as pink as mine. Look at you, you Galtish wonder. Blood of dead elves runs in you mad cunnies they say, for those who believe in elves. I don't, but if I did, I'd say they shot their seed in Galtia. A lutist's fingers on you, a fiddler's fingers, fine fucking fingers. Your fingers were made for coaxing locks on doors, locks on trunks, the locks of a maiden's hair. Not being bitten off by some goblin's fish-toothed mouth. You were made for scaling bankers' walls to raid their silver bars, not to crouch behind a cheaply made shield, and a heavy one, too, and with shaking arms try to hold it steady, imagine it, while an armored war boar, see it in your mind, heaves his quarter ton at you and goblins poke unclosable holes in your pretty legs with their three-sided spike-spears. It insults the gods themselves to spend such rare coin as you to buy, what, another dead soldier in the mud? Trampled under mud, I say, all but his sad, dead face wet in the rain. Or worse, carted off to hang in a Hordelands butcher-hole until they can salt his thighs and eat them off the bone with the foul mushrooms that help them dream their formless smudge-smoke god alive. And shit you into a ditch. Is that what your mother would want? You to be shit out a goblin's arsehole in far Gallardia? What did a Gallard ever do for you? Right. Nothing. Now ask what your good aunts and uncles in the Guild will do for you. What are you, seventeen? Only fourteen! Big for fourteen. Not big really, but big for a small lad, big for a small, clever lad of just fourteen. Would you like a copper shave right now? Here it is, I don't give a toss, we don't give a toss, we're rich as Old Kesh, aren't we, as full of gold as Adripur of old. You like coins, I can tell. Ever see a trounce? Gold all the way through, here's one, three ounces of paradise, just a peek. Oooh! How'd it get behind your ear? That's fasthands work, don't worry, we'll teach you that the first day. Let the Coldfoot guards poke with the spear, let the farmers thrash with the flail, they've been practicing on the wheat, haven't they? You'll serve another way, sure as Oathday follows Ringday with Widdersdy behind. But you'll know your dys and days, a smart lad like you. You know they use our assassins and thieves in the army, yes? We lend a hand, not cheaply, mind, but crowns can pay. You might end up doing that, sniping goblin chiefs from far away, sneaking into goblin camps to free our brave prisoners. Someday, later, with skills to keep you alive and useful. Who knows? You know that lad Fullen from the next village? He's coming with me. He's already gone, or I wouldn't have told you. He'll be rich, I promise you. He made his choice, same choice you've got— march onto a troopmule next month and die a bad death, or leave with me this week and live a good life. I can see in your eyes you know who you are. Not sure if we'll take you to Lamnur or Pigdenay, we have a school in each, but either way you'll still be by the sea. Where a river meets the sea, that's the place to be. Meet me tomorrow and we'll talk again—speak a word of my visit and I'll be smoke in the leaves. But you're much too smart for that! This time next year, we'll both be thieves.

After our talk, I walked the several miles to the Tattered Sea and borrowed a rowboat, which I took to the Isle of Ravens, called so for the colonies of huge, brave bastards that roost in the salt-sickened trees there. No land for farming, that, all rocks and marsh. A perfect place to take a girleen or hide out with a pack of mates. A perfect place to weigh a life-changing decision.

What did I think of thieves back then, anyway?

Well, to be very clear, the first thing I had wanted to be was a magicker. All the river towns, Platha Glurris, Brith Minnon, all the way out to the sea, had rung with tales of the time Fulvir Lightning-Binder and Knockburr the Galt had come to the Isle of Ravens to find the birds they'd later breed the corvids from. It was said they had enchanted fences to come to life and box the taxman's ears; or turned the moon pale green to celebrate Summerdawn; or made two seagulls sing, one in Galtish, one in Molrovan, with a beautiful curly-haired woman to judge which bird sang better. These stories made the pair of warlocks out to be almost demigods, bending nature and matter to their wills, and with such panache and good humor I wanted to be as they were. But I knew magic came from books, and though I could read anything you set before me, I would never have the means for such luxuries.

And I never saw these wizards for myself.

Thieves I had seen.

My oldest brother, Pettrec—actually, only my stepbrother, for I was the eldest of my mum's—was a thief of sorts but hadn't a talent for it. He never went the Guild's way. He'd been caught hooking a shirt off a drying-line one hamlet over, and he'd been drubbed soundly by the neighbors—people in little towns watch over each other.

That should have been the end of it, but it was a fine, plum-colored shirt belonging to the reeve. The reeve complained to the lord, and Pettrec got sentenced to work in the king's mint. Sounds foolish, eh, putting a thief near all that silver? Well, the penalty for stealing from the mint was death, so no one much tried. The sentences were short, too. Three months was all he got, but he'd have been better off taking a year in gaol.

The real punishment isn't the time—it's the work. Mint-vassals hold the blank steady while the striker works the hammer. If you get a good striker, you'll just go deaf. Takes about a week. Unless you plug your ears with wax, but you're not allowed to bring your own plugs—they check your ears. You have to buy them, and they cost three shaves each; they should be fine candles for so much. You have to buy new ones each day. You see how this goes. The dishonest poor go deaf.

Also, you have to pay to choose your striker. The older, sure ones cost two shaves a day to work under. The new ones are free, until they crush you a finger because they miss, and then they cost a finger. Too bad, right? Shouldn't be a thief, right? That's not how I took it. The ones in charge are thieves, that's what I gleaned from Pettrec's crippled fingers and loud conversation. "Don't get caught" is what I learned. Get in with the Guild.

Pettrec went with the muster that should have taken me as well, and he fought goblins. They killed him in some Gallardian mudflat, and him probably shouting "What!" the whole time.

The island was pretty that afternoon, the air cool, the trees full of the hoarse shouts of ravens. I found one proud, night-black bastard on a branch, throwing blue highlights off his feathers, and asked him should I slip the muster, but he had no opinion beyond *craaark,* which I knew I might interpret as I pleased. So I sat on the cold, rocky strand, and I watched the waves roll in like they'd done before thieves or soldiers, thinking, *What's any of it matter?* and then, *A boy does as he's told, a man does as he pleases,* and then, *Soldiers get beers bought for them,* then, *Dead soldiers get none.*

I tried a prayer to Fothannon for the first time, told him to show me if he wanted me for one of his own or should I take up a spear.

When I got back to the mainland, the fisherman whose boat I'd borrowed cuffed me about and named me a thief. I saw one hand on him was nothing but thumb and one finger, and he had an ear off him, too. Bit of the king's ribbon on his straw hat to show him a soldier. And here he was wrestling cold cod out of the water with a boat needing paint and a pincer for a hand.

I made a little fox out of river-clay that night and declared myself his servant.

I left town with Cavanmeer two nights later, off to Pigdenay, leaving the musterman who named me to pay a fine. That man was Coel Na Brannyck, father to Malk Na Brannyck, both of them Coldfoot Spears, both of them blessings to their friends and devils to their foes. The father died in Orfay, in Gallardia, hacked and bitten down by goblins, the son saw it happen.

And here he stood before me on the ship I was to call home.

Malk Na Brannyck.

Older, goblin-bitten, sun-leathered, and, it seems, one of the toughest hands on the *Suepka Buryey*'s deck.

"Welcome, fucking Kinch. Welcome to my fucking ship."

"Thank you, fucking Malk. I'll try to make the fucking best of it," is what I should have said, but what came out of my mouth was some weak little grunt. You see, while Malk was a man to reckon with, fear wasn't what muzzled me. It was shame. No one can still your tongue like somebody who knew you at your worst. Of course, I'm not confident I was worse when I was younger. I may be the worst I ever was now, ethically speaking, but I know now how not to *look* so bad. We don't usually know that when we're young, so our worst traits are on full display. One of many reasons not to trust a traveler is that he may not be wanted by those who know him best.

"Aye," he said, "best not let's say too much now. We'll have time to talk later. I just can't believe my good luck seeing you here." Once again, you'd have to be paying attention to see how hateful that was, how what looked like warmth in his eyes was actually a frost so cold it burned. Then, in Galtish, he said, "*Ec sa imfalth margas beidh.*"

It is smart to have a dog.

That's a Galtish way of saying, "Watch yourself." One response to that was, "*Me saf math margas fleyn.*" *I am my own dog.* Meaning, "I won't be caught sleeping, and I know how to bite." Of course, what I actually said was, "*Me edgh bein i catet tull.*"

I have a blind cat's luck.

When it croaked out of my mouth, I meant it as statement of fact, but looking back, it sounded perfectly weird, ambiguous, and off-putting, so it was just the right thing. Or as right as anything else. What I said wasn't going to matter to Malk. My chances of dying on this voyage had just gone from decent to excellent.

23

The God I'll Take Today

———— • ————

The first few days weren't so bad. Ashers burned to ashes. Lammas month came in, and with it autumn. The full moon rode high and bright over the sea, Norrigal singing to it over the rail.

The crew mostly left us be, except to offer us the pot-scrapings of the oats they ate and to sell us wodka. The Spanth drank from her barrel of wine and looked so murderously at any of the crew who watched her tapping it that the watcher went on and never peeked our way again. They swabbed around us and shouted and called above. On the second of Lammas, the *Suepka* hit a windy patch, and she pitched and rolled and even seemed to scoot sideways at times, and this made both Norrigal and me so sick it strained our guts. We moaned like the dying and hugged such vessels as we could find to receive our offerings. I only had a hat. After she'd near filled a pitcher with hour-old oats and wodka, she wristed vomit-tears out of her eyes and looked at me.

"Your seasick spell's not working," I said,

"Brilliant one, you are," she said, spitting out some of her own damp hair. "I couldn't find an ingredient."

"Which?"

"Turmeric."

"The fuck's that?"

"Keshite spice," she said. "It's . . . it's yellow." I was glad I'd never had any, because I guess the thought of it's what made her heave into her pitcher again. I considered the hat in my lap and wondered how long before it would soak through or if I could find the strength to stand up and empty it in the slop bucket.

I couldn't.

"Fuck this shyte, karking knobhole of a trip," I said and heaved dry, on the point of crying but didn't, or won't tell you if I did.

But that was the worst of the first four days.

The rest were tolerable.

Bully roamed the lower hold, but either the cat or what was inside the cat knew to keep him close to me most times. Also, and thankfully, he was good enough to piss and poo in the same place so I could find it and rag it up before anyone else complained about it.

Malk Na Brannyck came below to sleep in his hammock six hours a night, I know because I slept by day so I could pretend to sleep at night and watch him. He was like the rain in Pigdenay; he knew I wasn't going anywhere. I thought about telling Galva about him, but that would mean telling her I had slipped the muster, and I couldn't. I just couldn't.

I had some few talks with Norrigal, though, those first days.

"What gods do you worship?" I asked one afternoon when we were close enough to some island to draw gulls.

"All of them," she said, looking at the sea a-twinkle and cleaning her teeth with a splinter from the *Suepka*'s rail.

"But which particularly?"

"*Whichever suits the present spell . . .*"

"*Or keeps me out of any hell,*" I continued, quoting Kellan Na Falth, a Galtish bard known for doggerel.

We finished together:

> That's the god I'll take today,
> I had another yesterday.

Funny part about that poem, "A Song for the Allgod," is that it makes us blacktongues seem faithless. Rarely does any Holter stop to think it rhymes in Holtish; it's no translation. The poem in Galtish, with much the same rhythm, praises each of the Galtish gods, but especially the fox. The Holtish version is such shyte as we answer Holters with when they come telling us to squint at the sun and call it our lord. The Galtish title isn't "A Song for the Allgod" but "A Dirge for the Allgod."

Kellan Na Falth was hanged in Lamnur during the Upstart Wars, his work forgotten outside Galtia. We're overdue for another rebellion, but you won't see one while we've all got the goblins to hate together.

"The Bright Moon," she said in Galtish, her black tongue dancing behind her teeth. "She's my mistress."

Cael Ilenna.

"Fits a witch," I said.

"As your fox fits you. Why do you expect things to be other than they seem, or hold them smaller when they are? Are the facts of the world laid out only for your amusement or contempt?"

"They are," I said, turning to look at her and leaning back on my elbows, hoping I looked a proper rake.

"Then this should serve both," she said and flicked her tooth-cleaning splinter at me and walked away.

A pity she didn't see the result of her toss. Her toothpick should have missed or bounced off my shirt, but it hit me right in the forehead. And stuck there.

"Thanks for that," I said, less to her than to Fothannon, but he had mischief enough yet in store.

It was on the fifth day out, the fourth of Lammas, that I heard the crew shout "*Keleet, keleet!*"

I'll bet you know what that meant.

The whale was a small one, but a red. Red whales are related to squarehead cachalots and black-and-white orcas, just between the two in size but colored rusty orange and twice as mean as the squares. Their spermaceti isn't as plentiful, but there's enough to make them worth the fight, and they are twice as likely to have ambergris in their guts. You need more hands to take a red. And that's how we became whale-hunters, Galva and I.

Korkala came to us in our stall and said, "Guest of *Suepka Buryey*. Now is time hunt in whale-chase. You stay here, you pay double fare. You hunt whale, you get some money, better food, we let cat live. Some of crew, those from Albyed steppes, want eating cat, I say no, is friend of guest, but Albyedoi love meat of cat, *lya*? But by ship rules, spear-mate have, how you say for small animal not good for nothing but feed and clean shit?"

"That's a pet," I said.

"*Lya*, pet. You hunt whale, not say no, you have by law of ship, pet. You say no . . ." Here she shrugged the shrug of a woman trying to be coy about cutting the throat of a cat hiding an assassin whose death would bring another assassin to kill me horribly and, as I've heard can happen, poison my family back in Platha Glurris. I cut my eyes to Bully and saw him sitting, staring at me. I'd never seen a cat grin before, but he was grinning, which I think was meant to be a snarl. It must be hard to make a cat's face do things from inside him, but I hope never to find out about that.

"The captain said—" the Spanth started, but I spoke over her.

"*Yes!* I'll go."

"Is good," the Molrovan harpy said.

Galva spoke up. "He can go if he cares so much about this *chodadu* cat, but I will not go."

"Yes, she will," I said.

Galva looked at me like a bull looks at you when you swing a leg over its fence.

"*No*," she said. "We paid for the right to transport. We did not agree to help you hunt whales; in fact, your captain told us in specific it is not for us to do. We have important business in the west we cannot do if we drown chasing your *chodadu* whale."

"Ah," said Korkala. "Sorry, am not realizing we have aboard ship Ispanthnoi princess. Sorry, princess, not to have velvet for bedsheet and incense pot to cover smell of crew working."

Galva grunted. As you no doubt remember, Spanths don't care for sarcasm. Or lies. If Molrova and Ispanthia didn't have seven nations between them, they would have fought to the death of one or the other centuries ago.

"But," Korkala went on, "captain tell you about ship's charter for wodka, wine, other liquor?"

Galva's eyes got flintier still.

"Is charter rule captain control all liquor on ship. Is to prevent mutiny. Is unusual, but captain *can* say no hand have private good wine while others drink shit-water, keep all equal, friendly. Maybe if princess no help with whale, when brave whale crew come back, is for celebrate captain give them expensive wine of princess, *lya*?"

Galva's hand moved slowly down to her belt. She didn't touch her sword. But she put her hand so close to it the meaning was hard to miss. Korkala was unimpressed.

"If you defend wine, maybe ship's poisoner put something in it to make you sick. Maybe worse. Princess look like fighter, maybe Calar Bajat fighter. Is good! Ispanthnoi sword make must-respect. But . . . ," she said, raising one finger *almost* too close to Galva's nose, "even if princess kill whole crew, save wine for herself . . . who sail ship?"

24

The Whale

---·---

We were in the first of two boats.

Galva got the oar opposite mine, right up front. We were to row while three harpooners did the bloody work up front by us, Malk, the Coldfoot guard, being the chief of the spear-crew. Just my tossing luck. "Row! . . . Row! . . . Row!" he called, practically spitting on me, and it was all I could do to keep up.

"Rudderdam, adjust! Why's the right side dragging? Oh, I see why, the front oar's being pulled by a high-nut boy. Pull harder, boy! Pull like it'll keep you out of the *aaar*my!"

Galva shot me a look, but I managed an eye-roll that said, *Don't listen to him.* I tangled my oar with that of the woman in front of me, who was actually behind me boat-wise because rowers face backward, and she cursed at me in Untheric. Apparently, I'm something one finds in one's poo that one does not remember having eaten. They've actually got a word for that in Unther.

Tangled oars were soon forgotten as we drew up on the red. I saw a spout then, we were getting that close. The creature was just getting the idea something unpleasant was happening, and I think he was thinking, *Dive,* or, *Fight.* Reds often choose *fight.* He put his fluke up, a great plane of red muscle with water sluicing off of it, warning whatever little kynd-fish were hoping to challenge him to think twice. It worked on me. I thought twice and three times. Now we were wheeling about. I did what I could to hang on to the oar with my weeping blisters—my hands had a bit of callus from the bow and climbing, but not the sort you need to fight an oar for an hour.

"Fothannon Foxfoot, help your child make mischief," I said under my breath, and I know it's dangerous to call on old Foxfoot directly—he likes to help as little as possible, then muck about with the results. Looking at uncountable pounds of about-to-be-furious whale, I was prepared to take my chances with him. Mithrenor's the proper god of the sea, and I hoped I didn't anger him, but we barely knew each other, so maybe he'd understand.

I could see the whale's eye now. I didn't like how smart it was. It seemed to be saying, *Don't let's do this. We're all going to hate this.* It's bad business when you have more in common with a fish than your shipmates. It was about to dive, and I hoped it did so quickly.

Now one of the oarmen, some minor Magickers Guild mage, cast a spell at the whale, and it slowly closed its big, black eye. A drowse cantrip, not unlike the one I'd set on the pawnbroker's fat thug back in Cadoth. Shyte, that red wasn't going anywhere. It was having a nap and about to wake up in a fight.

A fight it was, too. I couldn't tell you much about it past the first stroke, which Malk threw, trying to slice behind its flipper and skewer its sheep-sized heart. Whether he did or not, I couldn't say, they don't always die quickly, nor did this one. What followed was a thrashing confusion of seawater, tangled oars, spinning boat, a blinding bump on my head, more seawater, an unearthly rage-filled bellow of the beast as it realized, I think, that it couldn't save its life but might help some later whale by drowning a boatful of whale-killers.

It came at us pig and palisades. It managed to capsize the second boat, sailors bobbing, their faces pink with water and whale blood, and it bit one sad-eyed Molrovan harpooner right off our boat, crushed her legs while she squealed piglike and then went under to die of pain, blood loss, seawater, or all three together. Then, like blowing out a lamp, the beast lost his fight. He went slack and drifted. The fight was over, and I'm not sure the best man won.

25

The Kraken

———— · ————

The first order of business was righting the turned boat, which we managed with lines and hooks and another cantrip from the mariner-mage, whose magic I now had to allow might be a bit stronger than mine. But he was going bald, so I had that over him.

Now came the hard, long business of rowing the dead whale back toward the *Suepka,* which was tacking against the wind to meet us. But the good news, and the bad news, the mixed gift of my mischievous god, was that we wouldn't have to row this particular whale all the way back to the ship. Another player was about to enter the game.

"Row! . . . Row! . . . Row!" Malk Na Brannyck called mostly to me, angrier than he'd started for the loss of his harpooner, and he'd started pretty angry. The ship was getting closer, smoke from the fires under the render-pots further darkening the mizzen sails. Then the prow of our boat raised up as we came to a stop—the dead whale was dragging us. Malk Na Brannyck said, "*Moch!*" and he had good reason to. "Watch! Watch!" he said, hoping what he suspected wasn't true. There was a word he needed to yell, but it couldn't be yelled falsely. He had to be sure.

"Watch, hands, watch!"

All were quiet now, the only sound the water lapping and gurgling on the boats.

"Tentacle!" a woman from the other boat said, pointing now where a black, oily rope of suckered muscle had wrapped itself around the red's tail. It yanked the tail, and we were all pulled backward, which was the way we faced, anyway.

"*Moch!*" I said, and then, as if I had to translate for my oar-
mates, "Shyte! *Shyte!* What the sixteen ways to fuck a fuck is
that?"

But I knew.

Malk yelled it now in his rich Galtish baritone.

"*Kraken!*"

Now it showed itself to us, raising its mantle out of the sea and
rolling one big weird plate-sized eye at us.

It did that to frighten us.

And it worked.

If you've never had the pleasure of meeting a kraken, I'll tell you
that they're not squids, and that can be confusing because most
people call both beasties krakens. They are to squids what kynd
are to monkeys. They're bigger than most squids, they're smarter
than all squids, and they eat squids for supper. They are, in short,
the emperors of the sea, and if we had met a mature one instead
of a juvenile, you never would have learned my name.

After I realized I'd shat myself, I had a moment to feel bad for
Malk. Sure, he's a proper bastard, but he had a horrible choice
now. Did he turn the whale loose, a whale with a head full of fatty
white gold, and save his sailors? Or did he fight the clever beast
and spill our blood for the fortune we had in tow, a fortune any
captain would be willing to sacrifice a hand or three to get? Malk
loved his crew. Malk was loyal. Part of the reason he hated me
so much was because he'd watched friends die in what he saw as
my place. Also, he was scared. I could see Malk had no fear for
man or whale, and he'd gotten through it with the goblins, but a
kraken? You'll no doubt think less of me for soiling myself, but
until *you* see one from a small boat in the middle of the sea and
keep your linens fresh, I suggest you reserve judgment.

The Spanth leaned to the woman in front of her, an old Holter,
and said, "This kraken, how do you fight it?"

"Stab its brains to kill it, cut its arms to chase it off. Neither's easy."

"Harder to kill than a whale?"

"Some. And it's much better at killing us."

Malk now looked back to the *Suepka Buryey*, hoping to see some sign from his captain that he might release the whale, but the captain pointed his finger at the big, red carcass so that it was clear he meant to have it, whatever the cost in our lives.

"Bring us up!" Malk said, and gods help us, we rowed closer to the whale and the thing that meant to poach it. "Blades!" he said. "And watch for its arms, they'll come up on all sides!" So saying, he drew his cutlass and aimed a hard chop at the tentacle around the whale's tail. A great gash in it split, and the beast loosed the whale, the tentacle slithering down into the brine.

Now the kraken's head, visible under just a yard or so of water, puffed up, then threw itself, arms trailing, just past our rowboat. Its arms were longer than the body and seemed to go forever as it rushed by, and it put itself behind us, between us and the ship, the way the oarsmen were facing. Now the sea seemed to boil as three, four, five tentacles climbed into the sky, raining water. "Brace!" Malk said, but he didn't have to tell me. My hands were white on my oar from holding it.

The tentacles fell like whips, and we in the boat gave a common shout. The boat didn't break, but it was a near thing. The shout turned to a mix of yelps and screams as more than one rower was ruined by the great, falling arms—leg bones or necks broken just by the weight of them, among them the balding magicker who'd sent the whale to sleep. The Untherdam near me got caught under one of these falling black treelike arms, and though it didn't crush her, it latched onto her and sucker-bit her, then ripped away, opening great holes in her. She screamed and launched herself off her bench, landing on my legs and pinning me with her yelling, bleeding bulk. Now the Spanth and Malk were up, side by side, and started in chopping at the arms as they fell. They managed to cut one off the thing, but the other arms were doing bloody work on the oarsmen, who were mostly too close pressed to swing such blades as they had, which were too few regardless.

A huge tentacle darkened the sky as it fell toward me, and I got under the Untherdam, who'd stopped her yelling, and I squealed as it latched her. The suckers bit her, lifted her up off me, then dropped her heavily on me again. I had a weird moment of feeling at least I wasn't cold, but that's because the poor half-skinned woman had bled all over me. I got Palthra out and waited to feel the thing's arm chop again. When it did, I curled around from under the Untherdam and gave it three hard, deep cuts, but I couldn't help thinking I was a kitten pawing at a wolf.

The woman was suckered up into the air and dropped on me again, knocking the breath from me. The noise from the injured and dying was awful. The stink was awful. Feeling helpless was worst of all, so as soon as I could suck enough air into me to move, I quit the shelter of the Untherdam and squirmed in the blood-slick boat to get to my feet.

The fight had shifted now. The other boat had rowed up to one side of the sea-beast, and the harpooners were trying for its brains. They heaved and threw, and stuck it, but not deep enough; the creature plucked the spears from itself then lashed out at that boat, giving them what it had just given us. The *Suepka Buryey* was closer now, close enough for the ballistas to shoot, and so they did, the great sharp bolts flying up and then plunging down, the lines of them uncoiling behind. One missed entirely, one stabbed deep into the awful fish and hooked it with its rearward barbs, and the last one crunched through the hull of the other boat, bringing a fresh yell from some unlucky salt. The kraken was hurt, and the *Suepka* was about to use her cruelest arts.

A clay pot the size of a head arced into the sky and fell on the water near the thing, breaking open with a pop and a flash like a piece of the sun had found its way to the sea. I thought it would dive away from the hurtful fire spreading on the water and catching on it, but what it did was to run a tentacle up the rope attaching a ballista harpoon to it, a rope now hot with flames, to get the measure of where the threat was coming from. It gave the other rowboat one more thrash, then puffed and rushed under the surface toward the *Suepka*. Cries went up in Molrovan. It closed distance fast. I had heard tales of krakens wrapping up whole ships and dragging them under, but this one had no hope of doing that; it wasn't a fifth the size of the big, piggy whale-taking ship.

What it did was to sucker-climb its way up the starboard side of her and spill itself onto the deck, where it became a typhoon of whipping arms, catching sailors and sending them off into the water. It was very hard to see exactly what was going on, but one thing I'll never forget; it overturned one of the render pots and used a tentacle to beat at the hot coals beneath, spraying them on its adversaries like, "Burn me, will you, you cunny-monkeys? Have some of your own."

Now the mighty ballistas had been recharged; one of them shot, caught a glancing blow, cutting a groove in the monster before impaling a short sailor against the mizzenmast. I liked that girl. She spoke not a word of Holtish, but she told Molrovan jokes in the hold to make the others laugh in their hammocks before sleep. Before the other great bows could shoot, the thing must have decided it was pushing its luck.

It grabbed the biggest sailor in one horrid arm and then spun like a wheel across the deck, diving off the side of the ship and out of my sight. The ballistas fired after it uselessly, sailors yelled at it and discharged their bows, the ones on the ship around me moaned and writhed. Malk said, "Those who can still pull an oar, to me!" The other whale boat was sinking now, its hull pierced by the ballistas and cracked by the terrible fish. The dead were pushed over to make room for the living from the other boat, and we started toward the *Suepka*. Galva, bending at her oar, saw the Untherdam's blood all over me and said, "Are you hurt?"

"No," I said, "I don't think so."

Her talking turned to hissing now. "Then where were you while we fought that thing? Did you hide?"

"No," I said, "I . . ." But I didn't have anything else to say, and I felt her anger smoking under her skin.

This sea voyage was turning into utter shyte, and fast. The captain came to the rails then and glared down at Malk. Malk took a breath and then said, with no small bitterness, "All right, hands, let's go get the captain his redfish."

26

Catch the Lady

———•———

Of the *Suepka*'s crew of eighty, she lost one to the whale and sixteen to the kraken. A further ten were too badly injured to resume their duties at first, so we soon found ourselves pressed into service. The captain himself had come to me, saying, "Our ship's magicker said he thought you maybe have some magic to you. You or girl. Is true?"

"I have a little," I said. "Very little."

"What about her?"

"Less," I lied.

"Here is situation. You make spellwork for ship, work like crew, you keep separate quarters, wine, cat."

"So we're to pay for the privilege of working while the crew gets paid for working."

"No. You pay for privilege of transport on ship in separate cabins, but now you must work, too, because crew is short. I pay you back what I pay rest of crew if work is good. You make magic for me when I need this?"

"Yes."

"Good! First thing you do, get in whale's head, get whale-wax out with bucket."

"Wait, why me?"

"Because kraken-bastard killed funny girl who used to do it." Actually, it was the ship's ballista that killed her, but now wasn't the time. "And you are small. Pays good, and is very pleasant work. You will smell like best perfume on best whores in Gallardia."

* * *

I've never been to Gallardia, but I've smelled their perfumes on the whores of Pigdenay, and I'll tell you now that while spermaceti isn't as unpleasant as the other smells coming out of a whale, I never want to smell it again. Not after wearing it from crown to heel. I went down beside the ship where the whale was lashed and bucketed that white waxy goo out of the beast's head, crawling into the bony part of the red that was too hard to saw through and better to send a short person or child to bucket out. They hoped to sell this in Molrova since you'll not find a better lubricant for clock gears or, properly scented, the arts of love. While I did that, cheers came up from the blubber-strippers, because a woman found a big, black mess of ambergris in the guts of the redfish, and that stuff goes for ten owlets an ounce. Between the spermaceti and the ambergris from this one whale, the captain would be able to hire all the hands he needed to replace those the kraken killed.

But the worst was to come. First, once the blubber had been hauled up to the ship in long strips, it had to be cut—and there were the Spanth and Norrigal stabbing down with big half-moon blubber spades, trying not to part their toes from their feet, trimming the huge rolls of whale fat to manageable sizes. Then the blubber-rendering started, and when the copper cookpots got going, they didn't stop for days. The whole of the *Suepka Buryey* was presently coated in the rankest grease you'll ever meet.

After the first day, I sat below with Norrigal while she wrung oil from her hair with a look on her face that, well, I probably had, too.

For my part, I was thinking that I had almost died for real and ever. Just the memory of the kraken brought a shudder, and still does, even with all I've seen since.

I could still smell the briny, punk smell of that squid-lord, and I would never forget it; not the sight of its rending suckers squeezing out water on the bottoms of its tree-thick tentacles, nor the sound of sailors yelling for their lovers and mothers while it stripped the skin off their backs or plunged them into the brine. That single peril had nearly ended me, and for what? So I could follow a surly Ispanthian into giantlands and only *then* find out why? So I could bounce unlikely grandchildren on my knee and tell them, "You know your grandfather saw a kraken once? That's right! Stay the *fuck* on dry land."

I was wondering what it would look like if, the next time we took to harbor, I simply jumped on some fast ship headed gods-care-where and left the whole mess behind. I could go where the Guild was weaker. Oustrim was the only kingdom so far to forbid the Guild entirely, and it's said the Guild had made no inroads in the vast island of Axa, which was a kingdom unto itself.

There were so many thieves in the Odd Cities down south, pretty Istrea and rocky Beltia, that some local Upright Men and Dams had kept their independence. Might a fallen Prank of the Guild find work enough to scrape by below the notice of the Problems, Worries, and Shadows he once quaked to think of?

And yet I knew these were fancies. The Guild's arm was as long as sails could haul and feet could run, and I had a family besides.

Also, Beltia, like its neighbor Istrea, was full of the Smiling Sickness these days, and you didn't want that.

I looked at Norrigal.

She always looked just on the point of laughing, and I liked that about her. She seemed made of uncountable secrets and layered mirth, a sweet onion of many skins.

"You got a family, witchling?" I said. "Besides your famous great-aunt?"

"None I care to name," she said. "I've a few with some of the same blood, but none that would spill a drop of it on my account. Why do you ask?"

"I don't know. Just to hear something besides the ship creaking, I suppose."

"There's worse things than a ship creaking," she said, as if to suggest I was one of them, but she grinned when she said it and never meant it, for we talked another hour down. She told me about a doe she'd befriended and taught several words to, and a place in the Snowless Wood where the mists imposed a silence you couldn't break with a shout. She told me her mistress, Deadlegs, professed to hate bairns but had enchanted a wool blanket so it would comfort any crying babe and given it to a new-married maid in Maeth who'd left her flowers every new moon. Norrigal said she couldn't wait to take her studies up again with Deadlegs, for whom she'd cadged a bit of ambergris from the *Suepka*'s take. Ambergris, it seems, was highly prized in spells. Ironically, I was summoned away from exactly this conversation to discuss magic with the captain.

I did the best I could not to look disappointed at having traded Norrigal's heart-shaped, fay face for the mustached, sun-whipped leather beak and chops that Yevar Boltch steered above his neck. He had brought me before him to measure my worth as a magicker now that his was drowned.

"What can you do, little magicker?" he said. "Can you bring luck to a hunt?"

"Yes."

"Raise a wind?"

"No."

"Right a capsized boat?"

"No."

"Can you make ship's mast strong to hull? Is already done for now, no wind, no stone will break mast, but spell must be done again every moon or two."

"He could actually do that? That's big. Are you sure he really did that?"

"So . . . no?"

"No."

He wiped his beard with his hand like there was something disgusting in it, which there probably was. "Are you sure about the luck?"

I nodded. He knew I was lying, but he didn't hold my lie against me. If anything, it made him like me better.

After another few moments of this interview, he finally discovered something I could do that interested him. I had my fiddle and could play it decently. The only other fiddler on the ship had been the Molrovan harpooner bitten half-sized by the red whale. So fiddle I did, facing the corner of the cabin, while captain Yevar Boltch and Korkala had violent-sounding sexual relations. Having picked out a few words in Molrovan, I gather she did something unsavory to him with that bronze-headed baton she carries around, but it could have been worse for him had we not been sailing with a treasury of world-class lubricants.

While I spent evenings scraping away at my fiddle, accompanied by the nastiest grunts, oaths, and imperatives east of Molrova, trying to pretend I was in a fine house full of magic books and owlets, the Spanth and Malk Na Brannyck were becoming fast friends. They shared a love for Catch the Lady, a card game very popular with soldiers too poor or smart to play Towers, which needed money and eventually blood. They shared Galva's wine, though she wouldn't drink his whiskey. She told him as she had told me when I offered her a pull from my own copper flask that it made her evil. He had a laugh at that and said, "That's the fucking point of it."

She laughed, too.

She almost never laughed.

They talked about goblins and horses, great blind ghalls and how to kill them, and, like as not, they talked about what a pathetic coward was Kinch Na Shannack.

The next few days were mostly shyte. I would say that I worked like an ox except that an ox's field is much cleaner and more pleasant than a whale ship. As much as I hated the work, I feared a lull in it because that would be when Malk would strike, if strike he meant to. While the crew was short, and while I slaved away with them, I was too valuable to hurt. So I worked.

The only bright points of the whole voyage came from the time I spent with Norrigal. Following the days of cooking down the sheets of whale fat, she and I had the indescribable pleasure of helping scrub the deck with a nose-burning, eye-watering blend of ash and human urine—yes, we shat for ourselves, but we pissed for the *Suepka Buryey*—which meant a lot of kneeling and brushing on our hands and knees together. You'll think this mad, but the smell of stale piss, when it catches me unawares, makes me oddly nostalgic for that knee-bruising, back-wearying labor, and all because of Norrigal. Mind, she was greasy and she stank, but I doubt there would have been a general hoisting of skirts at the sight of myself coated in filth and half crying from disgust.

She told me about her home, a hamlet near a glen in Galtish Estholt, and about chasing her brothers with spells that sounded like wolf-howls, or spells that brought ground-wasps up to sting their arses. She said she did that to stop her brothers beating her and wrestling her down, which it did for a time, until the bastards reported her to the baron's chainsmen and she had to renounce magic in front of three villages.

"I'll never forget it," she said. "It was a fall day and the trees were that brilliant yellow they get to be, and everyone I ever knew and loved was standing with strangers against me, looking at me like I was a fell thing, their breaths steaming in the cold. Ravens cawing in the trees. It was then I knew I had more love for magic than family, and it more love for me.

"'Norrigal Na Galbraeth,' the baron's Holtish Allgod priest said, 'as you stand accused of mischievous sorcery, and as we have no cause to doubt the source of those accusations, you are required to abandon the hidden arts for the rest of your minority. Will you abide by the judgment, which accords with the will of your family, the standards of the village, the edict of the baron, and the pleasure of the king, and will you turn your back now and until your nineteenth year on the false advantages procured by unnatural entanglements?'

"But magic seemed to me the best way to get ahead in this world, and here they all were asking me to give it up—that or they'd send me off to the mines near your town and fine my father into lower poverty than he already knew. He was a shepherd and hadn't a lamb to spare. So I did what all those with a gift for 'unnatural entanglements' have always done. I lied. I let them put the iron manacles on me to damp me, but then went to the blacksmith one town over and became his lover so he'd take them off. As soon as they were, I gave the smith his promised night and then marched straight back to the old magicker who'd been teaching me and begged him to carry on with my education. He was just an old lakeside net-man and bear-tamer, singing fish up to the bank and giving old husbands charms to stiffen the branch, and though he gave me my start in the arts, he hadn't the nerve to defy the baron and risk his own license. So I practiced what I already knew on my own, in secret, until my seventeenth year, then set off and went to find my way with Deadlegs."

"Your seventeenth year can't be far behind you."

"Far enough, you faithless flatterer."

And so it went.

We slept near enough so I heard her night-breathing and she mine, and Bully took a liking to her. He purred with great energy when she came near and once even dropped from the foot of my

hammock to climb up to hers, and she comforted him quietly, in
the dark, and though I couldn't make out what she was saying,
it cheered me to hear her affection. Quite without meaning to, I
imagined Norrigal holding a bairn to her bosom, my bairn, and
talking thusly to it, and my eyes opened wide in the darkness. I
had never thought of putting a nut in the shell with anything but
raw terror, and here I was fondly musing on my own perpetual
servitude. "What the Foxannon Fuckfoot is wrong with me?" I
said in the darkness.

"How's that?" Norrigal whispered.

"Nothing, nurse the cat."

"What?"

"I mean pet him. He likes that."

"You're a nutter," she said and fell silent.

I heard the cat drop to the boards and slink off, and the moment was done.

27

That Bitch Death's Cunny

—— • ——

The next day was a day for paying debts.

I was on deck, and I got a hard biscuit from the quartermaster, which, like every hard biscuit on this ship, was shiny with whale blubber. I was just biting into it, hoping today wasn't the day I'd lose a front tooth, when I saw Malk making hard eyes at me. Galva leaned against the rail near, frowning over her biscuit and sipping wine from her skin to soften the crumbs she'd chiseled off into her mouth. I knew from the look on her face it was just starting to sour—the merchant who sold her it in Pigdenay will have lied about its freshness, but there was no surprise. Sailors likely to return got the fresh wine, while unknown travelers and passers-through got the soon-to-sour. She should have asked me to haggle for her, I could have charmed the sweetest barrel the merchant had off of her, and gotten her a discount besides, but she insisted on going on her own because, of course, as a Spanth, it was her birthright to know every tossing thing about wine. Point is, she wasn't paying attention when Malk moved in.

I knew it was coming.

The captain and Korkala were getting bored with each other and had no need of a fiddle. The whale was stowed in barrels, its teeth carved for scrimshaw, the mess of its butchery and meltdown as near to cleaned as it would ever be. The winds had stopped, and we were calmed and idle, anchored to keep us off the rocks near a barren island by the southern tip of the Gunnish

Islands. Now was the time when the crew's grudges would bob up, and Malk's was not the least of them.

When he saw his staring was getting nothing but blank billy goat eyes in return, he said, "Are you staring at me, Kinch Na Shannack?"

"Nah," I said. "You're standing in front of what I'm staring at. Would you please move?" Several of the crew laughed at that, which of course did nothing to soothe Malk's humor, but I'm a religious man, and my little ginger god demands mischief.

"Funny one, you are," he said. "I remember that about you. I remember the great joke you had on us all when you were called to war and others went in your place."

"Well, you won, didn't you? You think my feeble attempts to heft a flail would've helped you?"

"You're no brute, I'll give you that, but I've seen stronger than me die and weaker than you live," he said. An Ispanthian standing near him, a short, black-haired man with a badger pelt and a wild look in his eye, raised his chin at that, which I took to mean, *I agree with my friend that you can go fuck yourself.* Spanths are gifted at nonverbal aggression. And this fellow was no one to trifle with—the pelt likely meant that *he* had been a Badger, one of the poor, mad bastards they sent into abandoned goblin hives to make sure they were actually abandoned.

"Besides," Malk continued, "your bow might have saved me this," he said, showing me a missing finger, "or this," he said, pointing at a bite-scar on his forearm, "or you might even have saved my father getting piped off by Samnyr Na Gurth."

"I wasn't good with the bow yet. I'd have shot your da by mistake," I said, but I knew how weak and flippant it sounded. I knew where this was going. I'd had a look at that ship's charter you've heard about. Any sailor can call out another to duel if he's willing to do that sailor's duties in the event of death. In the event of his own death, his goods become the captain's property. If I waited for him to call me out, I could choose the weapons, but I couldn't stand his goading much more. Both had to agree if it was to be first blood—if either said *death,* to the death it was. Death didn't really scare me that much. Besides, it occurred to me, if he killed me, I wouldn't have to deal with the Takers Guild again.

"Maybe yes and maybe no," Malk said. "We'll never know, will we? Nor will we know how many men got thrown into that bitch Death's cunny for want of one more to stand with us. I saw the hand tattoo on your cheek. Crawled off to thieves college. Couldn't even keep your promises to that den of snakes, could you? And now every Jon-salt in every kingdom in the world gets to slap you like the whore you are, and you never raise a hand."

At that, Bully, who had made an unprecedented trip up to the deck, raoed and did that creepy smile again. Malk ignored him. He was building up to it. Think what you will of the Galtish, we'll never be accused of leaving our feelings a mystery.

"A thief, of all things. A crawler in windows and a stabber by night. Your sort might enjoy the protection of the all-feared Guild of sneaky cocksuckers on dry land"—Bully raoed again at that—"but out here it's two-tailed Mithrenor who rules, and he likes strength."

I saw that Galva was paying attention now, staring stony-faced at Malk. Malk waited here. He wanted me to challenge him so he could pick his own weapon. He knew "our sort" were often deadly with a small blade and, for all his bluster, wouldn't want to throw me the advantage of engaging me knife to knife. I could choose knife against his spear or cutlass, but good luck to me if I gave away that much reach to a trained fighter. What would he pick? Spear, of course, being a Coldfoot guard—he'd been drilling with poles and long, sharp sticks since a boy, trained by his da. If he didn't want to seem too much advantaged with the spear—for a public duel is theater and the quality of the show affects reputation—he might just nod to his new life as a sailor by choosing cutlass. Something he could get his muscles into and beat me down with. He needed to goad me again to make me challenge or attack him. He needed to find a sore spot.

"What would your own father say to see you brought so low? If your father he was, for he seemed an honorable man."

"He was honorable," I said. "But your comment suggests otherwise about my mother. You want to know what my da would have said? He would have said, 'Whatever mistakes you make, son, let no man call you a coward.' And he would have said, 'However poor a supper you put on your table, let no man you can make answer speak ill of your family.' You have done both, Malk Na Brannyck, and you'll answer for it with your blood."

I was a better fighter than Malk thought, but I wasn't at all sure I could beat him at cutlass—that's a weapon for strong arms and tall men, which I haven't and I'm not. And if he said spear, I might as well impale myself on one and save everyone the trouble.

But.

My eyes cut to Galva, because her face had changed.

Her mouth turned down at the corners as her eyebrows jumped up, an expression of appreciation I'd seen her make many times. She even nodded, barely perceptibly, assessing me not as a fighter, I think, but as a man.

Malk said, "Is that a formal challenge?"

Before I could say yes, the Spanth spoke up.

"I formally challenge you, Malk Na Brannyck, to fight me to the death with the weapon of your choice."

I almost brayed out a laugh. I couldn't let myself, because people would have thought I was laughing to see my hide saved, but really, it was just because Spanths can't say Galtish names. Well, "Malluk Na Braneek" looked very put out indeed to have matters so complicated for him. He couldn't challenge me without answering Galva. But he could seek clarification first.

"What?" he said. "Whatever's your grievance with me?"

The Spanth said, "I am proud to take ship with another who

fought in the south, and I enjoy to play cards with you. But this man is my companion, and we have important work to do, more important than my affection for you. I did not wish to help him if he was a coward, which I began to wonder, but his offering himself to death against a strong man has satisfied me."

"That little wanker knew you'd help him."

"No, he did not, but still he did right. It is right to answer an insult to family, which you have unfortunately made, with blood. But even if I did not know this man, I would have called you to answer, for you have insulted Death, and she is my most beautiful and serene mistress."

28

Practical Experience with Poison

———— • ————

They decided on Malk's spear versus the Spanth's bullnutter—you can choose a smaller weapon than whatever the challenged party picks, but not larger—and I truly wondered who would prevail. Coldfoot guards could whip those spears around with blinding speed, now battering with the butt, now sweeping out the legs, now stabbing through the liver. He was larger and stronger in the arm, as well. But against an Ispanthian birder, schooled from girlhood in the art of Calar Bajat? The earliest the duel could be set was tomorrow at dawn, this rule in the charter so combatants would have time to reconsider their profound stupidity, and I was certain none of us would sleep, except maybe Galva.

I was right.

Several of the friendlier crew came up to Galva as she drank on the deck, watching the moon. Some wished her luck. Some confessed their dislike for Malk. The Ispanthian with the badger pelt even sang with her; a song to Dalgatha, the Skinny Woman, the Mistress of Death. Then he joined her in toasts to the health of the infanta Mireya, and, upon reflection, I'm sure it was this treacherous bastard that poisoned her.

Our Spanth soon came down to join Norrigal and me, holding her head in her palms. "Your head hurt?" I asked her. She shrugged, which is Galvese for *Yes, a lot.* I should have been watching her, not only for her own sake but because my life, and probably Norrigal's, depended on her.

I knew what had happened immediately, but finding out what was in her and how to help her was another matter. Norrigal had no shortage of potions and herbs but little practical experience with poison. I sat Galva on the floor, myself on one side of her, Norrigal on the other, opening her case to see if there was something to help the Spanth.

Bully sat himself near, past both of them where only I could see him, and tried to look nonchalant while he licked his paw. Norrigal made Galva tell us exactly what she was feeling, which was head-split and drowsy, and I made her tell me who'd been near her. The poison hadn't been in her long and didn't seem to be one of the stronger sort, which was to our advantage.

"Do you think we should make her vomit?" I asked Norrigal.

"How the devils should I know?" she said.

Past her, the cat nodded.

"Let's make her vomit," I said.

With the help of an evil-smelling herb Norrigal made Galva chew, we got her to sick up in one of the seasick-buckets left from our miserable first days on the water. The winey, tart smell of it filled the close space, and now Galva swooned and slumped deathlike into Norrigal's arms.

"Shyte, she's dying. Is she dying?" I said.

"I don't know!" Norrigal said, fishing wide-eyed in her potion box.

The cat shook his head, as in, *She's not dying.*

Probably we'd gotten enough of it out of her.

"What, then?"

The cat put his paws together on the floor, yawned, and put his head on them.

"I think she's just sleeping," I said. "I wonder how long."

"'Til you're dead, like as not. That's surely the idea."

The cat scratched his neck.

I stared at the cat, not getting it.

Norrigal turned to see what I was looking at, and the cat looked in the other direction.

"What's so interesting about the cat with your friend full of poison?"

"Nothing," I said.

The cat moved a little closer and scratched his neck again, this time idiot-slow so I realized he was counting.

"Twelve."

"Twelve what?"

"Hours?"

The cat nodded hard.

"Hours," I said. "She'll sleep twelve hours. I heard of this poison."

"What's it called?"

I looked at the cat, but he just stared at me like, *What am I supposed to do, spell it?*

Norrigal laid the Spanth down, giving her a wool wrap for a pillow. The cat wandered over, sniffed Norrigal's case, then rested his paw on a vial of milky white liquid. He pulled it away fast when she looked back at him.

"Cat," she said, "get out of that!" She shooed him away, and he hissed at her—I'd never seen him hiss—then retreated. He padded farther off and sat with his back to us, a perfectly catlike gesture.

"Try this one," I said, picking up the vial he'd indicated.

"Moonweed? You sure? That's for lady pains."

"Good. Give her a lot."

She did, then wiped the corner of Galva's mouth with her skirt.

"Will it wake her?" she said.

Bully shook his head, still facing away.

"No."

"What'll it do?"

The cat licked himself intimately.

"Make her feel better."

"But it won't wake her up?"

"No."

"What'll you do, then?"

Bully lay down with his paws up in a deathlike posture.

"Exactly what the gods want. I'll be well and truly fucked."

The Spanth mumbled, "*Chodadu*," in her half sleep and then snored.

"It surely looks that way," Norrigal said.

An hour later, Malk came down the steps to the hold with a small mob behind him and formally challenged me. He didn't want to miss his chance. He thought I'd choose dagger, but I chose to face him with both of us stripped to the waist and unarmed.

"Truly?" he said.

"Truly."

"That's surprising," he said, "a little fellow like you. You know we're not just boxing. You know it's to the death, right?"

The Ispanthian Badger stood among the small, gloating crowd behind Malk. The Spanth oarsman who'd sung with Galva about Dalgatha. The one who'd surely poisoned her.

"It shouldn't be surprising," I said. "A dagger fight would be over too quickly. This way I can bugger you, too."

He nodded. "That's it, then. Enjoy your profanities. You haven't many left."

He turned away, then he turned back, the way very angry people do when they think of one more awful thing to say or one more bit of harm they might do. Before Bully could react, Malk grabbed the cat by the neck and went upstairs. The cat started to cough, but it had taken a few coughs to get the assassin out of him under my bed, and I didn't think she'd be able to get free in time. I went to follow Malk, grabbing Palthra, but a dozen men drew their swords and deck-axes and waited for me, many of them smiling. They were hoping I'd do it. Norrigal grabbed my arm.

"Let him go, Kinch! It's just a cat!"

"No," I said. "It isn't." But I stopped pulling. I had only been half pulling, anyway. It was hopeless. The bastards went upstairs.

A cheer came from the top of the ship.

"Swim, swim!" they started to chant.

I lay down and stared at the boards of the hold's ceiling, trying to focus on this or that nail, sorry a ship's hold was to be my last home. Though I could have done worse for company.

Norrigal took my hand and held it as more laughter came from the deck and someone started playing a drum and hornpipe.

"Shyte, you're ugly," I said, meaning the opposite.

"Yeah," she said. "You, too."

Then she kissed me.

29

The Tooth of the Vine

———— • ————

Dawn wasn't much to speak of, what with all the clouds. You couldn't really pick a moment when you could say, there it is, the sun's up now. Choosing to fight a man with my shirt off was an easy enough decision to make when my blood was up and my leather was on, but now I saw the cold in this godsforsaken place was like to make me shiver. If I had to die, and there seemed little remedy against it, I didn't want to do it in such a way as to confirm the legend of my cowardice.

"Norrigal," I said, and she turned her fair face to me, the face I'd spent the night kissing warmly, wetly in the dark since sleep was unlike to come. "You wouldn't have something to make a man stop shivering."

"I would, but it'll make you slow."

"Keep it, then."

Malk with his shirt off was no more encouraging than Malk with a shirt full of muscles. I still believed the Spanth could have beaten him at weapons-play, but doubted she'd do any better than me against this bruiser at fists. Speed be with me. Luck be with me. Let me do that bastard mischief. I wrapped my fists in strips of hide to keep the bones together, though if the bones of my head held together, I'd count myself happy.

"What do you think, sprumlet?" Malk said, cheerful as any man about to get tested at his favorite sport. "Shall we say it's dawn?"

"Since we're as like to see the moon next as the sun, yeah. Dawn. Let's get on with it."

I'd said my goodbyes to the Spanth, who inclined her head to me and moved her lips, though whether she was speaking in this world or a dream, I had no way to know. Either way, I thought she was hours from standing, and things would surely be settled by then.

I winked at Norrigal, and she gave a sad little wave with her hand. The decks near the mainmast had been cleared, and the crew stood above us on fore-and-aft castle. Captain Boltch sat on a sort of throne with Korkala at his shoulder. He'd taken not the slightest interest in this matter as a question of discipline, but seemed very keen on it as entertainment. He was making bets like the rest of them. Some very few had bet on me, thanks to the tempting odds, which I believe stood at twelve to one. I wasn't so like to lose at that, but I'd have scarcely called it even.

The captain took the little bronze fist from Korkala—I wrinkled my nose to think of what adventures that artifact had been on while I fiddled—and raised it up. When he dropped it, the beatings and chokings would commence. It was nice, that moment with the baton aloft. A man who can pitch a tent and live in a valley three heartbeats wide is a happy man. I heard a seagull call, I heard a gurgle and a churn in the water as some tide or other rushed against the hull. It wasn't so bad, that instant.

The baton fell.

Half an hour later, I was still alive but in an exhausted, nauseous sort of hell. I had Malk from behind, my legs wrapped around his waist, and I'd been pressed against him like that for almost the whole long, weary struggle. This style of fighting was called *li denchēct di lian*, the tooth of the vine, or just *the vine,* and it was Gallardian. They have some of the best open-hand arts in the world, and the tooth of the vine was the most useful. Oh, it wasn't much to look at. No beautiful kicks, no breathtaking throws. Just a studied approach at finding what the body doesn't do well, then trying to make your opponent's body do that.

They teach the vine in the Low School, of course—it's embraced by thieves as warmly as the army takes to boxing and the navy takes to buggery. It's the best way for a small lad or lass not to be murdered by a larger one, and thieves run small. So there I was, alternately burning and freezing, coated in cold sweat, my left eye swollen shut, a tooth loose, a rib likely broken. But I was still alive, and my man was getting tired. Countless times had he kicked me glancing blows, punched me with poor leverage, headbutted me at bad angles, but he had only hurt me twice, and neither time with his fist. Twice he'd made it to his feet even with me tangling him and flung us deckward, me taking the worst of it. For my part, I had broken a small finger on his off hand, slapped the piss out of his ears, and thumbed his eyes a time or two. But here we still were, muscles on fire, lungs full of razors, the noble tree and its cowardly kark of a vine. Still any man's fight. The crew didn't like it.

"Are you going to fight him or breed him?"

"Fight like a man!"

"Stop it, Captain, pull them apart!"

"It's witchcraft, you know he's got arts!"

"Coward!"

"Coward!"

"Slipper!"

Those were the things I heard in Holtish. The Molrovan, Untheric, and Ispanthian were worse. Boos, however, have no country. The malcontented mob of salts booed, hooed, and grunted at me, though, to be honest, they'd been doing it worse toward the middle, and now they were used to my tactics. Just lately, they'd been throwing things, and that was a worry. So far just bottle corks and scraps of whalebone, somebody's dirty stocking. But it was only a matter of time 'til something wood or metal clonked me hard enough to stun me and loosen my grip.

Malk was working his way to his feet again, drooling all over my arm and breathing like he needed a midwife. I was tangling my feet around his and digging at his kidneys with my knees when I could, because when he stood again, he would dive us back at the hard, hard deck and me on the bottom. He was up on one knee, wrestling my cross-arm with one hand, the other arm tangled up under mine to save his neck a goodnight-squeeze. Though his chin was tucked, I hope painfully, under my arm, he managed to talk. Where he got the wind for it I don't know, but he started shaming me again.

"I . . . should have known . . . you'd fight like this . . . It's fit for goblins . . . no honor . . . never had it."

"Never claimed it," I said.

"Coward."

Guilty.

"Slipper."

As in, slipped the muster. Guilty.

"Fucking biter."

That meant *goblin*, I know that's what he meant, but in my pain and exhaustion, it struck me angry, because I'd passed up more than one opportunity to bite him. I could have had his nose off or an ear or a chunk of his neck a dozen times. So, to hell with him, I bit him. I bit the shyte out of him. He yelled and drooled more, started biting my arm in return.

A belaying pin flew out of the gray and hit me right near the corner of my eye. I can't say I blamed the thrower, it was a disgraceful display all around. I looked in that direction to see if more were coming, but that was my slit-shut eye. I looked the other way and saw Norrigal. The woozy, barely standing Spanth was leaning on her, holding the horse-headed staff the witch had given her. I should have known that Skinny Woman's bride would heal fast—Death wasn't done letting Galva's sword feed her kingdom. But the Spanth wouldn't interfere in my fight now, and I wouldn't want her to. Her for honor's sake, me to stop the crew cooking and eating us.

The third time I bit Malk, he should have thanked me, because apparently the pain gave him the strength to stand. He bulled up on that wobbly leg and pitched me off him so I hit the deck and rolled sideways like a lumpy branch. The next thing I knew, he hit the deck and rolled as well, and someone yelled and fell off the forecastle. Everyone was yelling. The sea seemed at the wrong angle to the ship. And then I saw it. The tentacle.

The kraken had returned.

30

The Pig in the Drink

———————•———————

Funny how an attack by a sea monster makes everyone less interested in a duel. It certainly diminished my enthusiasm. I grabbed
Norrigal by the elbow, and we hobble-ran to my side of the main
deck, opposite where the thing was climbing up, and toward the
forecastle, where the oar-boat hung near the ballistas. Captain
Boltch started yelling in Molrovan, giving orders about shooting the monster, I think, and abusing one panicked sailor who'd
started toward the firepots.

The kraken spilled itself up on deck now with a sound like
tons of wet muscle hitting wood. It tossed our anchor up on deck.
When I saw that, I realized the shore was farther off than it had
been—the beast had pulled us quietly, slowly out from the island
without our knowledge, the better to sink us deep. I'd heard that
krakens were vengeful, but it had never occurred to me that the
one we burned and speared might have followed us, intent on
making us pay for hurting it and taking its whale.

I was sure it was the same one, though, the same size and color,
missing the tips of the same three tentacles from its fight with us.
The most disturbing thing about the creature wasn't its appear-
ance; rather, I was discouraged by how smart it was, how clever
in its destructiveness, how like us. It didn't bother trying to shred
the kynd-fish poking and cutting at it this time; rather, it reached
its great ropy arms up to the mainmast boom and climbed it like
a tree. The ballistas discharged at it, but two missed, and one only
hit a tentacle, pinning it to the mast.

The kraken detached the tentacle and left it hanging, climbing ever higher. Malk stood near me, just as horrified and enraptured as I was, just as unmindful of the fact we'd been trying to kill each other moments before. The kraken was near the top of the mainmast now. Malk's eyes went wider yet as the creature's likely intentions became clear. I still hadn't caught on. I went below to see where Galva had gone and found her trying to strap her shield to her back.

"Help me," she said, and I did, buckling her sword belt on for her, too, working fast. I gathered my scant belongings in my pack, put it on my back along with bow and quiver, thought about taking my fiddle, but then grabbed Norrigal's potion case instead.

As if to confirm our unspoken conviction that the ship was doomed, it rocked then, nearly knocking the wobbly Spanth off her feet. I wasn't so steady myself, having very little strength left in any part of me. We got our gear to the top as the ship lurched to the other side. Sailors were yelling and pointing; they were shooting bows and throwing spears, all futile. A number of arrows hung limp in the mainsail, near stains where the thing's blackish blood had spotted the fabric. The monster was at the top of the mainmast now, moving itself back and forth, rocking the ship with its weight, gently at first so as not to topple the mast and tumble into the sea. Frightening things, krakens. It had followed us, working on the problem of how to sink such a big ship, and it had come up with a solution.

It meant to capsize us.

And it would.

Now only the captain and a handful of optimists continued trying to shoot the kraken where it rocked the ship from the top of the masts. I say *optimists* because it was clear the captain still hoped to save his barnacled old pig of a ship—Korkala, less sentimental about Boltch's vessel and brandishing a long bronze knife, led a trio of realists who managed to cut one of the thick rope stays keeping the mast up, hoping that even with the old magicker's strengthening spell, the mast might break or come loose with that monster on it. Better to lose a mast or two and float than capsize—had the whole crew moved as one to that end, they might have prevailed, but alas, the kraken spotted them before the ropes could all be cut. The wicked black thing broke off part of the crosstree and whipped that down at Korkala, breaking her head and scattering the rest of them. It now draped itself out to embrace the mizzenmast as well, not wanting to crack the mainmast with its full weight, and it swung between them and rained water like the worst laundry ever.

Most of the crew who were able to pressed toward the single remaining oar-boat, hoping to launch it before the *Suepka* went belly-up, but they were too busy fighting each other to get much done. Now Galva, still sick with poison, did something unexpected and damned smart of her. She knew she was too weak to fight her way onto the oar-boat, so she decided to borrow her strength from another source. She rapped that staff of Deadlegs's on the deck, and it turned into the clockwork branch-horse I had seen and ridden in the witch's yards. She was up on that now, and though it skidded and slid back and forth as the doomed boat pitched and yawed, she made a zigzag course for the press near the rowboat, and though I could barely walk, I followed after her.

If the last thing the crew had expected was to see a kraken rocking their ship toward a capsize, the second to last thing might have been a cavalry charge, but that was exactly what those killing each other for access to the oar-boat suffered. Galva set on them in a flurry of stone hooves and wooden legs. The witch's nag even bit at them with that ship's prow head, and had soon scattered them well enough that Norrigal and I could press forward. Galva dismounted, turning the horse back to a staff, and drew her *spadín*.

The ship lurched and slid us all away from the oar-boat like beer-mugs across a bar. I grabbed an iron ring on the deck and held myself in the middle of the ship 'til it lurched the other way, and I let myself slide on my rump for the oar-boat. I got over and in at the same time as two others—Malk and the Ispanthian who'd likely poisoned Galva. The latter came toward me with a knife but, instead of trying to fight him, I said, "Help me launch this bastard and kill me after."

A flailing tentacle nearly decapitated him, and the ship's next lurch, which put us near sideways and spilled water on the deck, convinced him. Now Galva and Norrigal had made the boat, along with a harpooner. We freed our vessel and crashed down to the sea even as the *Suepka Buryey*, for all its piglike strength, squealed and tipped into the drink, its masts at last breaking, its men and women screaming, and that awful black prince of squidkind slipping into the water and wreckage with us.

"Row!" Malk said, which was little surprise, as that was his favorite word, and row we did. Just ahead of us, Captain Boltch, clinging to a piece of the mizzen yard, loosed the clasp of the waterlogged whitefox cape that threatened to drag him under, let go of the yard, and swam for us. The harpooner helped him clamber in, whereupon he sputtered and swore, but Malk slapped him and said, "Grab an oar!" and that's what he did. We pulled for our lives. The shoddy rockpile of an island seemed a summer, fall, and gloaming away, but it was our only hope. I looked back toward the thing in the water, and I shouldn't have done, because what I saw made me want to piss myself. I just lied. It did make me piss myself. It was floating almost leisurely amid the debris, shoveling my former shipmates toward its awful beaklike mouth, where it had made a sort of gurgling, bloody whirlpool. I hadn't thought I had any strength left, but I found some and rowed yet harder.

"I've an idea," Norrigal said and put her oar down to start fishing in her pack and potion case. "Row, girleen!" Malk yelled. "I don't know where you think you are, you silly cow, but row!"

"Cow yourself," I told him. "She's a witch and a strong one. Let her work!" I didn't know how strong she was, but some part of me was hoping saying it would make it true.

The kraken had run out of sailors to eat and, after swiveling one huge, too-smart eye in our direction, was floating toward us now.

"Oh, for fuck's sake," I said, sorry I had no more piss to run down my leg.

It came up to the boat. Three tentacles reached into the sky, water sluicing down them.

"Weapons!" Malk cried, but he had none. I drew my dagger, feeling I'd do just as well to wave my manhood at it, had that not already shrunk itself as far in my body as it could go. Galva's sword was out, and Norrigal fumbled with some bottles. The thing looked at all of us the way a fat man considers which cherry he first wants the pleasure of popping in his mouth, but the eye stopped on Yevar Boltch.

The captain drew a bronze knife and bared his teeth, and I saw the thing's eye go from yellow to a fiery orange. Its gaze had locked on the captain's neckchain. Of course.

He carried a silver-gilded beak on that chain around his neck.

A juvenile kraken's beak.

And the monster knew what it was.

If it could have shrieked it would have, but what it did was to whip its arms about in fury, all but the three in the air, boiling the water around us white. The tentacles in the air, which I thought might pluck us one by one or thrash the boat as it had after the fight with the whale, now all reached for the captain at once, one grabbing an arm, one grabbing his head and the last yanking him up by both legs. It hoisted him aloft above us, and ripped him in pieces as he yelled, chucking the head like a ball and thrashing the water with the parts of him it still held.

We stood agape, transfixed by its power and fury, and by the awful end of Yevar Boltch. All but Norrigal. When it had tossed the scraps of the captain away, it set that fiery eye upon us again and readied another brace of tentacles. Norrigal pulled a cork out with her teeth and let the bottle fly. It turned over and over, spilling its cargo of silvery powder into the air as it went. I knew that powder and wrapped an arm over my eyes. She shouted, "Cover your eyes!" as an afterthought, too late for the others. I heard the thing thrash again, and this time, it dove with such force the wake nearly did for us, tossing us against one another. The others groaned and swore, one in Galtish, two in Ispanthian, and I saw why they were so troubled.

They were blind.

"Ha!" Norrigal said, still looking where the killing fish had slipped into the deep. "Ha!"

"Well done!" I said. "Brilliant!"

She went "Ha!" again, and I said, "Ha yourself! Now row, you magnificent witch! And you blind shytes row with me!"

They grabbed for the oars.

But I thought we could do with one rower less.

Norrigal's eyes popped wide when I crammed my arm in the mouth of the Spanth Badger and stabbed him deep in the chest with the rondel dagger eight or nine times before he could comment. I grabbed his legs and dumped him twitching into the water. Norrigal pursed her lips and nodded at the rough justice of it—the treacherous knob *had* poisoned my friend, his own countrydam. I thought about killing Malk as well, but couldn't bring myself to it. There he was, *my* countryman, rowing like a bastard, blind and faithful. Like he'd been his whole life. I didn't know if any of us would make it alive to the shabby pile of rocks off in the gray distance, but I didn't want my last act to be unceremoniously stabbing a man I'd just spent half an hour trying to kill bare-handed.

I can't explain, but it made sense to me at the time.

31

A Galtish Love Song

———— • ————

The island we came to, if it deserves the name, was little more than a tilted pile of rocks, scabbed over with green moss and mad with seabirds. The breadth of it could be walked in a quarter hour, the length in twice that, though you'd want your worst shoes as nearly every hand-span of it had been shat upon by the many seabirds who nested there. Some walked and cried at us, some ignored us and flew off when we got too close, a few mock-dove at us when we came to their nests, but, as we later found out, could only summon the heart to shout when we stole their eggs and cracked them down our throats.

Puffins, which Galts and Norholters call *cliff-chickens,* were most numerous. Funny birds, puffins, fat little black-and-white things with orange beaks and sad, tiny eyes. There must have been two thousand of them on the island, but terns, gulls, and others I can't put a name to had their own neighborhoods as well. That so many birds of different shapes agreed to share these windblown rocks told me we were far from land and this the only place to lay a foot for many miles. The tentacle-beaten oar-boat, which we had tucked in the shadow between two rocks, was in no shape for a long journey. In other words, we were well and truly buggered.

Myself especially. Reminded me of an old poem about lovers separated by war. She asks, he answers.

Conath bit tua caeums abaeun?
How will you be coming back home?

Sthi clae, sthi ešca, sthi tann nar braeun.
By earth, by water, by fire or crow.

Meaning, not at all. They'll bury me in a grave, dump me off the boat, burn me on a pyre, or leave me for carrion. It seemed to fit my present state, only I had no lover at home to ask. Only siblings, a mother, and a niece to suffer for my failure. And there were no crows to eat me here. Only fucking puffins.

I should have gone to war. Goblins would have killed me, sure, but they wouldn't have gone to Platha Glurris to punish those I loved. The cat was drowned, and the killer he carried, and all my hopes with the twain.

It was already eleven days into Lammas month, I was supposed to get to Hrava by the first of Vintners—just shy of three weeks' marking—and here I was with my feet nailed to a shyte-bedabbed island in the middle of the kraken-haunted Gunnish Sea.

"Fothannon help me," I said with a glum face before I could stop myself.

I felt something on my chest and looked down to find a fine streak of gull shyte from my tit to my hip.

It was my own fault—you don't ask that bastard for anything wearing a frown.

When Galva and the harpooner, an old Pigdenish named Gormalin, got their sight back, the first thing they did was engage in a lively argument about whether it was time for everyone to start drinking their own piss.

"I don't care what the rest of ye do," Gormalin said, "I'll not wait 'til I am half a skeleton from thirst, for then's too late, and ye might as well drink seawater and die of it. Ye start drinkin' yer piss now, ye can keep alive a fair while."

"Life is not so precious as to be bought at any price," Galva said. "To drink my own piss is too expensive."

"That's as ye say now, woman. There'll come a time ye'll wish ye'd not been so proud."

"This time will never come."

Five heartbeats fell.

"May I borrow your mug?"

"No!"

"I'll rinse it with seawater after."

"There is not enough water in the sea."

"Be reasonable."

"Do not mention this unclean thing to me again."

"As ye say."

"If you touch my mug, I will kill you."

"It's yerself ye kill with pride." The harpooner got to his feet and shuffled a few steps before stopping to take off a shoe.

"If you are going to do something bestial, please do it out of my sight."

Gormalin grumbled and shuffled farther on, behind a stand of man-high rocks.

"We haven't even checked the island for fresh water," Norrigal said.

"Some people just want an excuse to be filthy," Galva said, clearly still disgusted by the proposed violation of her wine-vessel.

It occurred to me to wonder if the harpooner had been ship-wrecked before and if it had made a cannibal of him. I knew that was a bit of a reach, but it was just a feeling I got. I resolved to sleep lightly. On the subject of cannibals, I had a look at the bite-marks I'd put on Malk. I hadn't given him anything disfiguring; my heart wasn't really in biting anybody. He looked to be coming out of his blindness now, as Norrigal had assured him he would, and I thought about getting up so I wouldn't be the first thing he saw, but I was too tired. He pinched his eyes and rubbed them with his thumbs, shaking his head, and finally, he squinted at me. I looked back at him impassively.

"You killed Menrigo, didn't you?"

"He the poisoner?"

"I suppose you could say that of him."

"Then I suppose you could say I killed him."

"Why not me?"

"Seemed a waste."

He nodded, staring at me the while, the blues of his eyes adrift in a sea of angry, insulted pink.

"So what do we do?" I said to him.

"You know as well as I what's owed."

"Well, as I see it, the charter of the *Suepka Buryey* is dissolved. We owe each other no duel."

"That doesn't pay for cunny-all."

"I'm not saying it does. I'm only suggesting we suspend our hostilities until we make proper land in a proper country."

"My quarrel with you is not finished."

"My quarrel with *you* is not finished," Galva said, pointing at Malk.

"Screw you sideways, you Spanth . . . nutter."

Galva didn't need to put her hand on her sword to show how close things were. It showed on her face. Malk had likely saved his own life by choosing *nutter* instead of the *bitch* that his lips had pursed to utter.

"You sound like a pack of jackasses," Norrigal said. "Fighting over who's to kill who when thirst and hunger are like to do for us all. We could be a year on this rock."

"She's got a point," I said and was ignored.

Galva said, "The only way to end our quarrel is for you to swear not to harm my companion. And to apologize."

"I don't apologize to no man nor dam," Malk said.

"Hee-haw, hee-haw," said Norrigal.

"I need no apology for myself," said Galva.

"What the spiny devils are you talking about?"

"I'm for making the old man captain," Norrigal said. "The lot of you ought to piss in your shoes and drink it, that makes more sense than this karkery."

Galva said, "Malk Na Brannyck, you will apologize to Death."

Malluk Na Braneek was how it sounded, and if you know how not to laugh at that, please let me know, too; I'm the fellow sniggering behind his fist.

Malk peeped open an eye.

"Apologize to fucking *Death*? You're serious?"

"I have never been so serious in my life."

One thing a killer's good at is knowing when he's talking to another killer, and also knowing when killing is close. "Fine, you mad Spanth shyte-pot. I'm sorry if I offended Death, though you can go fuck yourself."

"This is acceptable," Galva said.

Nice bit of whale boat diplomacy, that; my fellow Galt did what the Spanth asked and saved face at the same time. And so a vulgar little truce was hammered out where it might have been us killing Malk and wanting his arm on an oar if the boat was our only way out, which it likely was. Such is the grease that keeps the wheels of civilization turning. And here came the old man waving his foul shoe at us and wiping his lips with his sleeve as if to show us how much smarter he was, and maybe he was.

We did find fresh water; rainfall had collected in a sort of rock bowl not too far from a gnarled tree. It was a bit mucky, which the embarrassed harpooner was more than eager to point out, but Norrigal assured us it would serve if we could find something to boil it in. I couldn't restrain myself from saying, "Of course, those of us who prefer drinking urine are under no obligation to stop." That earned me a loveless sideways glance from old Gormalin, but Norrigal's snort more than made up for that.

Our next discovery was a queer one. Norrigal and I had gotten off by ourselves to scout the sunward side of the island. Up in the rocks, in a cleft between two greenish-gray boulders that offered some shelter from the wind, I noticed what looked like a bit of rusty old metal. If the sun, what there was of it, had not been shining at just the right angle into the fissure, I never would have seen it. I four-legged down between the boulders into a sort of loose cave and started pulling weeds and smaller rocks away from the metal.

Soon, I uncovered a helmet belonging to a head belonging to a dead man. Not that we had suffered from any shortage of those—three crewmembers from the *Suepka* had washed up since the wreck, one of them the treacherous Menrigo—but this man was dead of long vintage. Just a bearded skeleton, really, decorated here and there with arrows.

These waters were Gunnish, and though there were still enough of the fierce northern raiders to trouble shipping, they held just a shadow of their former strength. I'd read that ancient Gunns loved spirals, and this musty old corpse had three of them etched into his rusty steel breastplate. Should have spent the etcher's money on three more inches of plate, because the arrow that lunged him looked to have missed the armor by the breadth of a finger. Whether he'd crawled down here to hide or die, he'd done both—he still had silver in his pouch, which I relieved him of. I wondered whose arrows were in him. Probably other Gunns'.

Every once in a while, the northern clans banded together under some great king and came south, as they'd done when they conquered what would become Oustrim, the giant-ridden land we were currently trooping toward, but it was said they never fought southerners with quite the fury and passion they saved for one another. In order for a great king to rise in Gunnland, he has to kill an astonishing number of lesser ones. Really, to be a Gunnish king was no great distinction. Beardy-bones here was probably the third holy king of cliff-chicken island, the gods watch his soul. One thing about the Gunns, though, they threw in on the Goblin Wars with every ship they had and wrecked their strength doing it. Now the Molrovans held the greatest northern fleet, though Holt was rising fast.

"Thanks for the silver," I said.

Norrigal looked down the hole at me, her eyes bright in the sun.

"Who's your friend?" she said.

"It's my brother," I said. "No wonder we haven't had a letter. Want to meet him?"

"You just want a snog," she said, making me smile to think of our warm kissing in the dark before my duel.

"Sure, and I do," I said. "Maybe more."

"What, with him watching?" she said, nodding once at the dead fellow.

I stripped my shirt off and flung it over the dead man's head, lying back and smiling as sweet a virgin-killing smile as I had in my quiver.

She laughed and said, "You're a cad. You get your way despite your ill manners, not because of them. It's that sweet head above your neck and nothing more."

"Something more," I said, knowing full well the salt's what brought the thirst. "Come down here with us."

"Cad," she said, laughing. "You'll not have more than a snog, and you'll not have it now."

"If you know a beach-side inn, I'll pay," I said.

"I know a beach."

We settled on a meeting that night, on the far beach from the camp, after the harpooner started to snore. He was always the last one to snore, but he meant it more than the rest. Galva wasn't sleeping much, but she'd not care what the girleen and I were about. She would watch the fire and think her goblin-haunted thoughts or maybe imagine herself dying at last and running with her skinny woman to far beaches crashed on by waves of black Ispanthian wine.

It would be a long day waiting for that night to come, what with the promise of Norrigal's lips and not unpleasant young-dog breath. She was a smart one, and I suspected even smarter than she let on. I was more than half-sure she saw through my rakish nonchalance; the truth was I was growing fond of that greening witchlet, and if she knew her dance steps, she'd soon be binding me round whatever finger she chose. And the harder I tried not to be glad of it, the gladder I was.

Now that we had water, it turned out filling our stomachs wasn't so hard. We had eaten our eggs raw before I found the dead man's cleft, but now I built a little fire and fried some gull eggs on the breastplate of the dead northerner, whose conical helmet also served as a boiling pot for water. Galva seemed uncomfortable dishonoring the tools of war with such mundane treatment, but I did notice she ate her eggs hot like the rest of us.

As our second day on the island turned to night, I listened to the cries of birds, and to the hush of the surf, and I listened to Malk and the harpooner under their little driftwood lean-to, talking about this port town and that, laughing gruffly in a way particular to soldiers and sailors. Together, they had caught a fish in the shallows, a big, handsome silvery devil that they'd gutted, cleaned, and cut, setting on sticks to slow-cook over the fire all night and which we were all looking forward to eating for our breakfast. The clouds had gone and given way to a rare splay of stars, bright and cold as ice chips in the black. I thought, not for the last time, how good it would be to play a slow, sweet reel on my drowned fiddle just then. Old Gormalin must have felt me wanting music, for he wandered over next to us and said, quite out of the blue, "Hey, lassie, why don't you sing us a Galtish love song." Malk followed after him and sat. Galva sat a bit off, but well in earshot.

"Oh, I'm for singing love songs, am I?"

"Better you than me. A maiden singing love songs is cheery. From old men, it's for tears."

"Gods and you've convinced me. Here's as cheery a song as ever you'll hear this maiden sing."

She cleared her throat with some ceremony, then began, in her sweet, high voice.

My five Upstart sons are all bloody and brave
I've got one on the gallows, and two in the grave
One is your prisoner, and none is your slave

"Pish," said Gormalin. "That's a war song!"

I've got one in the hills that you never have met
And though he is young, he will murder you yet
For the hour is coming you'll answer your debt

"That song's *illegal!*" he protested, and right he was. It's the very song that got Kellan na Falth hanged. "You can't sing about men killing men since the Goblin Wars! Especially not a song against a proper king of Holt, even an old, bad king!"

Now, of course, I joined in.

My five Upstart sons have declared against you
Their tongues are as black as their promise is true
And they'll call you to answer whatever you do!

No Coldfoot guard was going to be left out of an illegal Galtish rebel song, so Malk picked up the next verse with us, his strong, confident baritone suddenly making the whole insurrection seem credible.

The crown you so love sits but light on your head
The castle you stole has a cold, stony bed
And though I am old, I will yet see you dead

You've hundreds of men with long swords and long knives
But you've lain with near half of their fair Galtish wives
And none of them love you to lay down their lives

Abandon your tower and open your gate
No silver-bought army can alter your fate
If all my five perish, my neighbor has eight

Our ten thousand sons have declared against you
Their tongues are as black as their promise is true
And they're coming, they're coming, whatever you do

The silence that followed was only broken when Galva said, "This is a good song."

Another hour passed before sleep stole upon the camp. When at last I saw Malk curl up facing away from us and heard the thick breathing of the harpooner give way to fatty snores, I checked on Galva. We hadn't set formal watches, because she normally kept vigil most of the night, stealing her sleep back from the day in pieces, so I was surprised and a little put off to see her chin against her chest. I poked Norrigal with a stick of driftwood, meaning to point out the drowsy Spanth to her, but damned if she wasn't sleeping as cozy a sleep as the rest. Well, I'd be doing neither Fothannon no mischief nor Haros no rutting this cold night. I sighed and settled in to a sleep I was glad to have after all.

I woke to the sound of shells.

32

Spiders Out of String

———— . ————

Not seashells, but eggshells.

Some creature or other was moving about in the pile of eggshells near our camp, and I hadn't an idea what it might be. My first thought was a dog, but I had seen not so much as a rat here, birds and crabs being the largest things to walk the beach besides us, though when it was birds and crabs at the same time, the crabs were usually in a bit of a hurry. I sat up, seeing a small, dark shape in the shell-heap. It bobbed its head as if to sniff the air and then mewed a tiny mew at me. I had no more thought the words, *It's a cat,* and then, *Is it Bully Boy?* when the latter was confirmed by the arrival of Bully's deadly passenger, announced with hard fingers at my trachea.

I knew better than to speak. I looked around and saw a dark silhouette, as if a feminine and muscly shape had been cut out of the stars to show the black behind them. As my eyes adjusted, I saw pale skin like mapped streets around the strange black architecture of her tattoos, her glyphs and wards.

Sesta.

My Assassin-Adept.

She motioned for me to follow and also for me to bring the cat, so I hung the little bastard around the back of my neck like a stole and followed the shadow-woman up the rocky hillock into a congregation of stars like far candles the wind couldn't snuff.

"Are you going to kill me?" I said.

We sat in the cave made by the rock-cleft next to my Gunnish friend, who looked much frailer without his helmet and breastplate.

"The cat getting tossed wasn't your fault," she said, "so you live. Congratulations."

"Thanks," I said. "Would you like my blanket, from the beach?" I said. She was naked as a bride, and I was shivering in my leathers and hemp. She barely shook her head, then raised an arm, pointing at a faintly glowing rune tattooed near her ribs. It said *Hearth* in some language I didn't recognize. I now noticed that what little warmth there was in our little grotto was coming off her. She was making about the same amount of heat as the coals of the nearly dead fire had been.

"That's how you stayed alive in the water. Kept the cat alive with it, too."

She just looked at me.

"So you shake your head for *no*, but contemptful silence, that's a *yes*. Yes?" She just looked at me. "Right, got it."

"Tell me everything you did and saw after they pitched me off," she said, and I told her the shortest version I thought I could get away with. She watched impassively through most of it, but her eyes lit up when I told her about stabbing the Ispanthian poisoner. When I finished, she just kept looking at me, sitting nearly as still as the armored old duffer next to her.

"So what's the plan?" I said.

"That depends on how you get off the island, but it's more or less the same. If you're picked up, you take the cat. If no one comes in the next few days, row for it. If you row for it, you take the cat. I'll improvise from there. Most importantly, don't you dare delay getting us to Oustrim."

"Wouldn't dream of it," I said.

"Also, make up whatever story you like to explain the cat's reappearance, but anyone you tell about me I might have to kill."

"No need to tell a thing. I'll quietly continue in my fondness for feline companionship."

"Good."

Bully raoed.

We sat there awkwardly for a moment.

Then the killer cocked her head like a listening dog.

I thought, *What is it?* but didn't have time to whisper it before Sesta was crawling backward and flattening herself against the rocks. I won't say she disappeared, but I will say it got difficult to see her—I couldn't tell which of her many magical sigils allowed that particular feat, but it was impressive. I barely had time to think, *Someone's coming, I hope it isn't Norrigal,* before Norrigal's head appeared in front of the stars, looking down at me.

"Did you forget me?" she said. "I thought we had a date."

I could feel the invisible eyes of the assassin drilling me.

"No!" I said.

"No?"

"I mean, you fell asleep, and me, too. We slept."

"Have you never shaken a girl awake before?"

"Not without consequences."

Fothannon had a bit of mischief with me as the thought of shaking Norrigal awake to snog her produced a state of excitement. I saw her notice it.

"Perhaps you prefer to be by yourself."

"No, nothing like that."

"You needn't fib, I understand, I had brothers."

I supposed wanking was as good an excuse for my departure as any.

"I didn't want to trouble you."

Her eyes darted left, and I followed them to the cat, who was looking nowhere in particular as blind cats will, but here it made him look like a guilty party feigning innocence.

Her eyebrow raised.

"At least three questions occur to me, but I'm afraid to ask any of them."

"The cat didn't drown, because he's magicked."

"Two to go."

"I'm the one magicked him, with a protection spell."

"Now the weird one."

"I came here to be alone, and he followed me. I only just noticed him. It's got nothing to do with him."

"That's a relief."

I nodded at the skeleton now. "Or him."

She smiled. "You telling me that's all for me, then?"

I smiled at her as if to say yes, but dared not say it. And then she started to climb down in the cleft with me.

"Wait!" I said.

"What for?"

I couldn't think of a plausible reason why she should wait.

"What, you want to be alone with your cat and your corpse?"

"It's dirty down here."

"Perhaps you've noticed the whole island's covered in shyte." She kept climbing. "Besides, it's cold up there, and you'll not be hogging the only pocket out of the wind. It's almost warm in here."

She was down with me now, about to settle herself right where the adept had been.

"Stay still!" I said.

"What?" she said, exasperated.

The assassin had shifted so she was actually upside down over me, stuck buglike on the bottom of the rock.

"Thought I saw a spider, but it was just a shadow."

"I don't know what sort of girleens you're used to, but witches aren't scared of spiders. I can make them out of string."

Now she sat, so close to the deadly shadow it could have reached down and flicked the bottom of her nose. So close to me I could feel the warmth of her leg on my leg. I could feel the adept hating the interruption, hating me for not putting a stop to it. I hated her right back for wrecking what could have been a night of real pleasure after months of drudgery and peril. Prudence should have made me send Norrigal off, but I don't worship the god of prudence. The Galts don't have a god of prudence. My god is as much fox as man and gives luck to the brave and clever. He doesn't want to be praised so much as amused, and it's said that if your death makes him laugh, he'll let you into his sacred wood in the afterlife to run naked and rut and steal honey on the comb until you get tired of it. What happens then, I don't know, but I'm sure it's a good laugh—Fothannon is generous to all but the cautious.

"Spiders out of string, is it?" I said. "What more could a man want from a woman?" Now I don't know a very great deal about women, but I know they don't follow boys they don't fancy into filthy caves at midnight and sit right up against them. Doesn't mean they'll sell the whole horse to you, but a whinny and a kiss is more likely than not. I bent to kiss her, and she leaned to me, but I just brushed her lips. Damned if I was putting on a show for the world's most lethal hairball.

"Not here," I said. "Let's go to the far beach."

"What, the cold one, away from the fire?"

"I'll keep you warm."

"And why not here?" she said.

I nodded at the Gunnish warrior.

"Oh, you'll have a wank in front of him, but snogging a girl, that's disrespectful?"

Fine logic, really.

"Nah, it's more like I don't want to share you. We're going to kiss like lovers tonight. In no hurry. I'm going to remember it a long time, and I don't want anything gruesome looking on."

"I like that answer." She got up.

"You run along, and I'll be right behind you."

"As you say," she said, smiling at me in a way I'm sorry if you've never seen, and she left.

Bully followed her out.

When they were gone, I felt a stony hand tangle its fingers up in my hair and pull hard.

"*Gruesome,* is it? That was rude," the upside-down assassin said.

"Yah, well. I thought it was important you know I'm my own man. I'll do the Guild's business and do it as well as I can. You can pull my hair if that's thrilling for you, but if you mark me, the others'll see, if you hurt me, the others'll know, and whether or not you really need my help out west, the Guild wants me there, and you serve them as much as I do. So kill me if you like, but I doubt they'll be happy if you hadn't a good reason."

The hand loosened in my hair and let go.

I didn't even look at her.

"Another thing. If any harm comes to the witch I'm about to snog, please know that despite my affection for the wee cat, I'll wring his neck with iron and throw him on the hottest fire I can find, and you with him."

A low, gravelly chuckle came from the rocks above me.

"You know," she said, "I'm actually starting to like you."

"Maybe one day it'll be mutual."

"Well, you've earned yourself a treat. Go to the beach and fuck that girl."

"Nah, not tonight," I said, standing up. "Some things are worth waiting for."

I'd like to say that was the end of it, but the killer got the last word. Yes, I had a joyous, teasing, tempting night shivering on a cold beach with Norrigal, kissing her full lips and tasting her black, black tongue with mine 'til light bled into the clouds and we walked hand in hand back, dropping hands just as we rounded the cliffside and came to camp. We were met with evil stares from all three of our fellow castaways—not because we'd been dallying together. It was because that tattooed bitch went and ate Malk and Gormalin's fish. All of it. And left the bones where we'd been sleeping.

There was some arguing and grief about that, you can believe it. But it ended up not being so important in the long of it.

The goblins came two days later.

33

Fucking Unmarriageable

---·---

In case nobody's bothered to tell you, and in case you haven't seen one, goblins are ugly. Not like your odd cousin with too many freckles, no neck, and sausagy fingers; that's plain homeliness. Someone will marry him if he can push a plow or brew beer. Goblins are fucking unmarriageable. Something deep in us knows they're our blood enemies and reviles the sight of them, like a shark or a biteworm. They're not like an ape, which you can look at and say it's not so different from a man. But goblins? Something else again. Nobody knows where they came from. No record of them before the Knock, and scholars mostly think it was that same cataclysm that brought them over from some worse world or up from the ground. They look like they came from the ground.

This was the first time I saw one close. Actually, there were eighteen of them on the ship that came to our remote little island. They like numbers divisible by nine. That's because they have nine fingers. What should have been a finger on their off hand became a hook they can sheathe like a cat's claw, and they'll drive that in and hang off you, trip your feet up, bite. On some it's right, on most it's left. The right-handers are held in higher regard, thought to have been blessed by their weird little god, who looks like nothing so much as a smudge if you see their praying-boards.

But the hook. That hook-hand is smaller and weaker than the weapon hand, and that arm is shorter, and maybe that's why they don't care for symmetry. One of our generals said the reason they tear the corners off buildings in kynd cities and collapse parts of houses is because straight lines make them queasy. They find our most beautiful monuments noisome and brutish, an affront to nature, with all the math and right angles. Goblin structures are equally bewildering to us, and the same is true of their ships.

I had been bow-hunting for cliff-chickens, having failed to catch a fish to make up for Malk's, which I had to confess to eating, though I hadn't had a fin of it. I was well aware that the traditional way to hunt puffins involved dangling from a cliff face and whacking at them in midair with a net on a long pole, but having no such net, no such pole, and little urge to dangle, I used cruder methods. I already had two wee birdies strung to my belt, and I was covered in puffin-shyte the high winds had whipped into me. I was just having an argument with a puffin hen who had watched me shoot her mate when I saw the sail. A green goblin-sail on the very blue water near the horizon. A gray plume of smoke dragged behind the ship, almost white against the dark gray, fast-moving clouds.

I loosed my cliff-chickens and ran, ducking behind a lift of rocks and making for the beach where we'd made camp. I knew from talking to soldiers that the handcant for goblin was to make a fist and stick the two smallest fingers out, curving them in the semblance of that hook, so that's what I did. Galva began stripping out of her clothes, presumably to let her war bird loose. Malk took up his sabre.

"Wait," the harpooner said. "What color was the sail? Green?" he said.

I nodded. It was green, sort of a gray-green like sage.

"That's good," he said. "That means they're honoring the treaty. That's the color of their blood. Red means our blood and they're hunting."

"They're always hunting," Malk said. "They only show the red when they've got numbers, and that to frighten us."

"What's happening?" Norrigal said.

I told her.

"Shyte," she said, her eyes widening. "Shyte, shyte."

"Yeah, that's the word for it," Malk said.

"So we fight?" I said.

"We fight," Galva said at the same time Gormalin said, "Depends on the numbers."

She shot the harpooner a look.

"They might not even land," Malk said. Galva hesitated now. If she pulled that screaming bird off her chest, there'd be no hiding. "Come on, Spanth, help me scatter this lean-to." Norrigal kicked sand over our fire pit and gave it all a brush with a leafy branch from the island's unique tree. She sprinkled a powder that amplified a faint rotten fish smell already in the air so it would gobble up our scent. Malk went up the rockpile to have a peek, and I went with him.

"What are they even doing so far north?" I said. "They're supposed to hate the cold."

"They do," Malk said. "But they come up the South Spine River, take the old Kesh High Canal over to the Spine River proper, up to hunt seals and trade. They like seals almost as much as kynd. It's the fat. And they take the fur off the young."

I joined him at the top of the rocks now.

"See that smoke?" he said. I nodded. "That'll be steam-pots. They burn coal belowdecks and splash water on it, make it hot and damp down there like their islands. Solgrannon, I know you like blood, but just don't let them land."

"Why wouldn't they land?" I asked, raising my voice just a tiny bit to be heard over crying gulls wheeling above us.

"They hate birds," Galva said.

I'd heard that and forgotten it. Now the use of the corvids against them took on another layer. Kill our horses? Fine. Here's a host of giant murder-birds fit to shred half you little pricks and give the rest nightmares in your hives.

"They probably saw debris from the *Suepka.* If they figure it was a kraken, they won't expect survivors, they may just sweep the beach for valuables. If we can stay out of sight up in the rocks . . . Oh, for fuck's sake," he said.

"What?"

"The bodies."

We ran back down the rocks toward the three dead bodies that had washed up yesterday. We'd covered them in seaweed but had decided not to burn them because we couldn't spare the wood. They were lined up neat as you please, orderly, the way we kynd like it. The way no bodies ever washed up randomly on any shore.

"What?" said the harpooner.

"Hide them!" Malk said, pointing at the corpses.

"Where?" said Norrigal.

"Up the rocks."

What followed was a desperate race to tug, hoist, and carry three nasty, waterlogged dead whalers up the loose, shyte-bedabbed rocks and into crags sufficiently deep to keep them from sight. We hadn't a quarter hour before the ship might wheel about and see the blind side of the beach. We'd just managed to haul the last body, the mortal and stinking remains of the tan, barrel-shaped woman who'd leered at me from the deck that first day, onto a kind of saddle and pile smaller stones and birds' nests on her, and Norrigal had just gotten the drag-marks broomed over when she remembered her case of vials and potions.

"Leave it!" I snapped.

"If they find us, we'll need it!" she hissed back, and I let go her arm. Shouldn't have done. Oh, she got the case and smashed herself down next to me flat as shoe leather, but she was in a bad place. Not comfortable. Had to hold herself up with a braced leg at a bad angle. The goblin's sails had only just come into view when she began to shake. We both knew she was in danger of starting the mother of all rockslides if she fell.

"You hold on," I told her.

"I am," she said.

"You're light as a vine," I said.

"And you're thick as shyte. Leave me be, I'll manage."

"You will," I said.

"Shut your hole now."

"Both a yas shut both yer holes," Malk hissed.

The goblin ship was closer now. Peering through a veil of twigs from a nest, I watched it. In a way, it was beautiful in its weirdness. The mainmast was straight enough to do its job, but they had left burls in it, and it seemed to twist. Did they grow tortured trees on purpose to suit their tastes? The lateen sail wasn't so different in function than what you'd see on a kynd-built ship, except that it was more a severe trapezoid than a triangle and had a patchwork of different shades of green sewn into it to further break its lines. The prow of the ship, where kynd ships would have had a winged goddess or a serpent or a wolf, displayed a goblin hand in greened-over copper, pointing with three fingers, the thumb holding the smaller finger tucked. The wind filled the sail, pushing the goblin ship fast through the water.

I saw one of them now, standing just behind the prow. My first goblin. I couldn't make it out well, but I could already see that they were cunny-ugly, just like I'd heard.

Of course they came ashore, six of them at first, two of them holding torches they eagerly waved if a bird happened near. If you squinted, they looked almost like hunched, gray-skinned children with furs and leather on, and it was better to squint. If you stopped, you'd notice they had no noses or chins to speak of, and their elbows were in the wrong place.

They loped as much as walked, and they wore their gray-brown hair in complicated braids that said much about their station. Bits of their speech came up to me. It was a raspy, hissing business I knew humans had great pain to imitate. They had at least two consonants and one vowel that kynd could only approximate, partly because their tongues were armored against the sharpness of their teeth, the sort of teeth you'd expect to find in a river fish. So rasps, rattles, and an annoying sort of throat whistle. Not a language built for poetry, at least none I'd care for. I had a look at Galva, and she seemed to be trying to follow it.

"You speak that shyte?" I whispered.

She waggled her head, the Ispanthian signal for *maybe* or, in this context, *a little*. Then she put two fingers to her lips, pointed to the beasties, pointed to her ear, and made a one-handed weighing gesture that she used when she saw a beautiful woman or when food or music was particularly good. Right. *Shut up. They. Hear. Good.* Soldier's cant and Guild cant weren't always so different.

The biters were troubled by the birds and clearly disgusted with their shyte, so much so that their cursory walk through what had been our camp raised no suspicion with them, and they didn't walk so far down the beach as to put them close to where we'd tucked the oar-boat away. Things looked hopeful. Then, for a bad half moment, it seemed as if one of them wanted to come up our hill, and there went Galva starting to sneak out of her mail shirt again. Then a second one talked the first one out of it. I resolved to buy the reluctant one a drink in the unlikely event we found ourselves in a tavern that would serve us both.

The discussion grew less heated, and soon, the pack of them went loping back to the wee, weird boat they rowed back to the larger weird boat. Poor Norrigal had switched positions three or four times, once spilling a fine rush of gravel that made us all clench our backsides—perhaps I shouldn't speak for the others, but I know my own arse could have cracked a walnut. Now she was shaking like a cold dog, trying to hold herself up again, and I grabbed her belt and pulled a bit to take some of the weight off of her awkwardly braced legs. The things had made it to their ship now, and they hoisted up the anchor and caught the wind with their sails.

Thank you thank you thank you, I breathed to Fothannon, and the tosser said, *You're welcome,* and here's how he said it: I sneezed. A hard one. The kind that makes your body jerk. And when I jerked, my foot slipped off the rock it was braced on, and I kicked Norrigal. Not hard, but enough. Norrigal lost her grip on the potion case. Three little bottles and some moss or other flora went over and broke with a tinkle on an almost-flat rock below us. She gasped but then made a small sound of relief, apparently because those bottles ought not be mixed and hadn't been. But you remember when I said the rock was *almost* flat? Right. Little rivulets of the potions started flowing down the rock's surface, first toward each other.

"Oh!"

Then away.

"Ah."

Then decisively toward.

"Shyte! Shyte!" she hissed, and a second hiss came from where a bead of brown liquid had crashed into a rivulet of pearly-clear goop.

"Shyte!" I echoed. "Should I look away?"

"Doesn't matter, sneezer," she said, and now a bit of fire sizzled on the rock, and soon a fine, thick plume of white smoke rose up.

"Maybe they won't see it?" I said.

Nobody else said anything.

"Maybe they'll think it's, I don't know, a geyser?"

Galva grunted.

"A volcano, then," I said.

The goblin ship turned.

We readied ourselves to fight.

34

A Shiver of Her Wings

———— • ————

Hours later, at sea, I had occasion to think through the battle many times, and I really found no winning scenario for us, given that they had a wizard. Goblins have magic, too, you see, different from ours but just as strong.

"Would you mind moving your foot? Take it out from under my arm and put it over my shoulder. I'll help you. Thanks." Malk got his foot over my shoulder. He was hurt, but not so bad as the harpooner, who was not hurt so bad as Galva. Norrigal was scratched up a bit, but that was just from how rough they dragged her. She had also caught a poisoned bolt, but it was a three-pronged drugger for pricking, not a bodkin point for punching through. Me, I had a cut from nipple to hip that I was sure would go sour, and that's what Malk's foot had just been touching, lighting on fire with every twitch. It had been no easy matter for him to get his leg shifted, given the dimensions of the kynd-cage we'd been crammed in.

Our strategy had been brilliant, or so I thought. Norrigal up in the rocks calling a wind against them to make it too hard to shoot arrows or bolts, the rest of us to rush them as they came ashore, before they could get on land and use their speed. It was going all right. The same six from before had just got out of their smaller boat, three with crossbows, the rest with their awful spears. The main ship had pulled as close as it dared, their crossbowmen crowding the shoreward side. Norrigal put the wind against them, so hard their boat started drifting back to the main ship. They quit the boat then and swam for it, the crossbowmen holding their weapons up out of the water with one arm while they paddled sideways, half drowning for the waves.

When they were too far to make shore easily and too close to go back, Galva said, "Now!" and we ran at them. Their archers shot bolts at us, but the wind caught under the fletchings and lifted them hopelessly up or pitifully wide, and not a one hit us. They started making a sound between a bark and a monkey's call, a panicked sound, and that's because they saw the corvid. The big, beautiful, awful corvid.

The swimmers, catching sight of it, lost their courage and started back for the ship, but it was too late for one of them. The corvid, thrashing its wings up over the water, caught it by the leg and plucked it back toward the beach. It didn't waste its time with that one, just tossed it back for Galva, who easily cut it to pieces. The goblins were wearing no armor, dressed for landing as they were.

I had only my bow and knives, so I stayed at the waterline and tried an arrow at one of the ship-goblins; with Norrigal's wind behind it, it went hard but left. I adjusted and shot again, scoring one's arm so he howled and dropped his weapon. Then I shot a swimmer. Got him square between the shoulder blades, and he seized up and sunk in the foam.

Then the karking wizard came from below and stood on the deck of the ship. Makes sense they had a wizard on a ship. Hard to take one with an army since all that metal and iron armor in one place dampens free magic, but sailors don't wear armor because it would sink them. These beasties had naught but leather and horn to armor them, none of which impeded magic.

Their magicker was shorter than the rest, and old, but his hair made him taller. His white, stringy hair had been done up in a sort of tower of braids that Norrigal's wind played havoc with in a most undignified fashion. A choker of pure, shiny copper shone at his throat. If that was my first clue what he was, Galva soon delivered the second. She held up a severed goblin leg with her shield arm, pointed with it, and yelled in Ispanthian.

"Tirau sul magauru!"

Which of course meant "Shoot the wizard!" as I understood upon later reflection, as I also later understood that seeing the biters had swept her back to the Daughters' War, when she waded in blood with her countrymen. But at the time, I couldn't understand that any more than she could understand that she was shouting Ispanthian at a Galtish Holter. She said it twice. By that time the two remaining swimmers had made it back to the ship, and their bolts were coming nearer even through the wind as they learned to adjust, so we went back to regroup. The old one took a stone on a string and started swinging it over his head. It made a whining sound I could hear even through the wind, and I knew then what he was, and what Galva had been saying. I nocked another arrow, shot, and missed. I nocked again even as we reached the shore, but it was too late.

The wind had turned.

It was wretched hot down in the hold.

An old goblin tended a coal-pot, ladling seawater over it from time to time and growling raspy commands at the several crewmen sleeping or warming up down here, not letting them get too cozy in the steamy belly of the ship. It also served as their mess hall, which was convenient, as we were in the pantry. They hadn't butchered any of us yet, but it was coming—they'd pinched and sniffed at us, and one of them had indicated the harpooner, whom they'd taken out to a second cage and washed with seawater, putting him in a sealskin diaper so he wouldn't shyte and piss all over himself. To his credit, when he wasn't crying, he was telling them to go fuck themselves.

"If I could just get at my potion case," Norrigal said. "Or what's left of it." She said it funny because her cheek was smashed up against the flat bars of the cage, and because she was still drugged from the bolt she'd taken, but I understood her. I was a bit woozy, too. All our worldly goods sat in a long trough-box on the starboard side of the hold, with Galva's horse-staff and Norrigal's staff of thumping lying against the wall. They hadn't even bothered going through it yet; Malk said they would sell what they could when they put in to a kynd city or a hidden goblin colony.

"They have those?" I asked. "Up here?"

"Aye, they do," he said.

"Where?"

"They're hidden, aren't they? But I've heard they'll take a little island like the one we just quit and dig tunnels like in their hives in the archipelago or on Urrimad. But now that the king of Molrova's their best friend, they do all right in Molrovan cities. Grevitsa and Rastiva have whole quarters for them, though most of the people with means have left Grevitsa. It's just goblins, thieves, and whalers there now. And the odd lace-maker."

"What's the king get out of it?"

"What do you think?"

"Goblin silver."

"Aye, that."

"No war on his southern border."

"Aye, that, too," Malk said. "Besides a ready supply of scapegoats for any foul deeds he undertakes. The people bear it because they know what the Threshers' and Daughters' did to the rest of us, and they've chosen ignoble peace over brutal war. And they get rich. You know the price of tea."

"So they're occupied."

"No, the king's strong. He doesn't let so many biters in he couldn't kill the lot at will. But if that day comes, the biters'd do the same to the Molrovan kynd trading in the Hordelands. Though death is a fair wage for those as choose to live among those fuckers, I say. But if the killing begins again, Molrova'd have no more peppercorns, cinnamon, and tiger pelts to sell, and the Horde would lose their seal meat, cheap iron ore, and amber. The pricks love amber. They use it like gold. Besides the kynd-meat they steal on the seas."

I was about to ask him where they get that, but the answer was perfectly obvious.

"Does our king know?" I asked. "Conmarr's no lover of goblins."

"Sure, but what's he going to do? Link arms with Ispanthia and their prick of a king, Kalith? No offense."

Galva groaned, then whispered, "None taken."

"Our Conmarr's in no hurry to cull his land of sons and mothers now that it finally has a few again," Malk continued. "Unther's got less to give than we, and Gallardia's just pretending nothing's wrong, selling pretty paintings and teaching everyone to dance. But make no mistake. War's coming again. It's just a question of which side first feels itself sufficiently recovered from the last round to start hitting again. Probably them—they breed faster. And whether Molrova will remain neutral this time or actually throw in with the goblins."

Malk told me more about Molrovans and goblins. How Molrovans who go to live in the Hordelands are called *black-hands* because they tattoo one hand black so goblins know they're not to be touched. They send good fighters there so goblins will think all Molrovans are that hard. I'd heard of Grevitsa, the infamous Molrovan island city. It was the sort of place you associate with kidnappings and killers for hire and, weirdly, lace. In gentler times, it was a capital of lace-making, and now Grevitsani wore a bit of lace on their cuffs or collars to let you know where they were from and that they weren't to be trifled with.

"Well," I said, "here's hoping we put in at Rastiva and not a biter colony."

"Hope?" said Malk. "They'll not put in to a kynd-city with us lot in the hold. They'll break this cage down and store it or claim it's for seal pups or goats. And you can guess where we'll be by then."

"If there's no hope, why are you telling me all this?"

"Me? I'm just running my mouth to keep me from thinking and you from crying."

"I'm not crying," I said.

"You will be."

"I haven't cried since your mother left the whorehouse in Platha Glurris."

Malk said, "Platha's too small to have a whorehouse."

"I know you didn't call it that. You just called it *home*."

He let slip a gravelly chuckle.

"I do not understand you Holters with your jokes of mothers and fathers," Galva said. "You do not love your mothers?"

"We're Galts before Holters," Malk said, and I said, "We love each other's mothers."

"And fathers," I added.

Galva grunted, and Norrigal muttered into her iron bar, "Both your fathers had bigger berries than twigs. And your mothers had too conservative a policy on infanticide."

She laughed at her own joke. Her stomach moving moved Galva's head, and *she* laughed, which made Malk chuckle, and I did, too. And the poor harpooner laughed even though he knew he was the next calf on the block. I even kept laughing when I saw a trickle of someone's blood roll on the floor, not knowing whose it was. Through it all, I thought I heard the yipping of a fox.

When the wizard started whirling his magic-stone, he tricked Norrigal's wind into listening to him, and now their bolts had it behind them. We were on shore by then, running for the rocks, hoping to make a stand on high ground. If Norrigal could keep alive, she might have another trick to keep their crossbows off us—we hadn't enough armor to take it otherwise, and the thing about a bow against a crossbow is that the bow's faster with the second shot, but not as good for ducking around rocks and such.

You have to draw, then release, too slow for a peeker. Crossbow's a better siege weapon, just a lever-pull and all that stored force goes *whack*. What's more, goblin bows are stronger than you'd think because they have a stirrup on the shooting end and a claw on their belt, so they step, squat, hook, and stand, using all the strength in their legs to cock the weapon. We were bollocksed. I had a moment to wonder where my cat had got to, but I couldn't see him. With this development, I wouldn't be a whit surprised if the assassin hid the little beastie 'til they scooped us off the island, and then waited for a better chance.

The next thing the biters did was go after the corvid. They tried shooting it with bolts, but Galva turned course away from the rocks and jumped in front of it with her shield. Meantime, it fluttered its wings over itself—a tactic called *shivering*—so it got its wings stuck through a few times, but nothing was hitting it to kill. They'd have to close with it. They didn't want to close with it. The wizard made sure they didn't have to. He whirled that stone at a different angle, and the wind died. Nine of the goblins had got to shore now, four with bows, five with spears. The old wizard was on the ship, a good eighty yards out. I couldn't hit him from the rocks, but I might have a shot from the beach, and I knew a path to get down there without being seen, so off I ran.

By the time I got there, Malk and the harpooner had run down to join Galva, Malk with his cutlass, Gormalin swinging the old Gunnish warrior's ancient rusty sword over his head like he hadn't the first clue what to do with it. He had a bolt in his leg I don't think he'd noticed yet, and Malk had been grazed once or twice. Galva was shielding them both as best she could, but it had cost her—she'd been hit in the shoulder, and the bird was stuck in the body more than once. What the wizard on the goblin ship was doing, I didn't know. What Norrigal was doing, I didn't know. I just ran. I got all the way to the waterline before they saw me—I found out later it was because Norrigal had masked me. She knew better than any of us that me hitting that wizard was our only chance, and I had a good shot, seventy yards from the waterline. A long way with a short bow, but I had a chance. To shave the distance, I splashed another fifteen yards into the water so it was up to my thighs.

"Don't miss!" I heard Norrigal yell.

But my luck was out, I felt its absence under my breastbone like an old lover's rebuke.

I missed.

I was still correcting as I had been when the wind was blowing, so the shaft went far left. I shouldn't have, of course, but you don't think right in a real fight, or at least I don't. If you can keep perfectly calm and logical with biters swarming at you, good for you, but I couldn't then and can't now. Fighting means making mistakes and just trying not to make the last one. Luckily, the wizard didn't see my arrow whiz by over his pile of braided hair. He was just at the end of his spell, and now he caught that magic-stone he'd been twirling in one hand and shook it twice. A piece of the cliff over Galva and the rest chunked off and tumbled with a great noise. I nocked an arrow. Goblins splashed through the water at me. A goblin-bolt from the beach tickled the back of my head. I fired my arrow at the geezer on the boat. After I loosed, I pulled a third arrow and glanced over my shoulder at the beach. The biter who shot at me was just at the tide, starting to step and claw for a reload, much impeded by wet sand and gravel and bothered by the sound of agitated gulls crying.

Past him, Galva and Malk and the corvid, Dalgatha, had killed two goblins, but more had ringed them. That didn't matter, though. A boulder the size of a cow had crushed Dalgatha. I peeked right and saw the wizard bending over, my arrow in his guts, another helping him. I had my arrow nocked now and shot the crossbow-squatting prick in the face just as he stood and loaded it. Galva now bent and grabbed a feather from the great, awful corvid even as it shuddered.

It was important that she grab that feather before the bird

died. So important, she turned her back on her attackers even as they speared and shot her. She broke the feather, and the bird caught fire under the rock and pitched black smoke into the sky.

Her chest smoked, too, and she cried out—one of the only times I've heard her do that—and fell to her knees.

Now two goblins came running after me, so I ran back up the rocks toward Norrigal, who was down, curled around a quarrel in her belly. One of the biters shot me a grazing hit in the shoulder, and that put enough poison in me so I would soon fall down. They were thrashing Galva and Malk with the shaft-ends of their twisted, dark spears now, the harpooner lying senseless next to them. The goblins wanted them alive. They wanted us alive. And that's how they got every one of us.

"So did he die?" I asked the old biter ladling seawater onto the coals. "Your crusty old rock-breaking wizard. Did he go to meet the great smudgy kark in the sky—or under the ground, more like—you pricks worship?" If he understood, he made no sign of it, just worked his grayish lips around his river-fish teeth and brought another gout of steam from the coals. Norrigal was sleeping again; she got more of their drug in her with the solid hit she'd taken in the belly than the two grazes I took.

Of course, had they known they would absorb such losses they might not have tried us—on the other hand, it might have been worth seven sailors and a wizard just to take down the corvid and eat two veteran biter-killers. They hated corvids worse than they hated us, and who could blame them? The great black birds had turned the war around, them and springwood ships.

The springwood was all but gone, but thanks to the likes of Knockburr the Bone-Mixer and the Molrovan Fulvir Lightning-Binder, we'd mastered the art of making corvids. Normally, I felt a pang of guilt saying *we* about what the armies of Manreach had accomplished, but I'd killed goblins now, too. I didn't go to the wars, but I'd fought, however belatedly. Killing a goblin mage, if I'd done that, was no small feat. If I were to be filleted and eaten, Malk's forgiveness would be small balm, but at just this moment, lying in the cage with his foot in my face as we bled all over each other, I managed to convince myself it mattered.

"Hey, Spanth," I said.

She tilted her head to show she was listening, her eyes barely open.

"Might as well tell us why we were really going to Oustrim. I mean, I'll take the secret to the grave."

"And soon," Norrigal said.

"You tell him, *pruxilta*. I . . . do not wish to talk."

"Wait a moment," I said. "She fucking knows and I don't?"

"You're Guildron, aren't you?" Norrigal said. "But you're maybe something else as well."

"What's that?" I said.

"Pork shank for a biter," Malk said.

"Deadlegs thinks you're exactly as your name. A *kinch*. The tangle in the Takers' web," said Norrigal. "I don't want to go bothering your fond head with things that might or might not be true. What is true is that we were going to Oustrim to put a witch on a throne."

35

The Bright Thing in the Grave

———— • ————

Once and long ago, for that's how fables start, there was a king-
dom by the sea. It was full of handsome, brave men and beautiful,
clever women. The realm was called Ispanthia. Of course, all king-
doms were full of the brave and beautiful if you asked somebody
from that place. Nobody says, "My country's full of craven karks
and reeky old fishwives," not in a fable, anyway.

But of course, the goblins came again as they had once before,
and half the brave warriors in Ispanthia went south to fight them.
But the horses that once helped them win the Knights' War had all
died of the Stumbles, and the warriors didn't fight so well on foot
as they had ahorse.

So the goblins ate those warriors.

And came closer.

The goblins said, "We're hungry."

So the kingdom sent half of the brave warriors they still had and
all their farmers and shepherds and miners and even the little rag-
picker boy with no teeth who played with himself in public.

But the goblins ate them, too.

And came closer.

And there they stayed.

Now in the kingdom of Ispanthia, there was a good and brave
king, and he went to the wars and fought. But fighting goblins
wrecked his head and made his dreams all shyte, and he didn't care
to rule anymore. He just wanted to dance. He didn't care to bother
with his daughter, a sweet child named Mireya, so he bought her a

menagerie full of animals. And he danced, and he danced, and he danced and gave away his lands.

The thing about a crown, though—if you lay it down too long, someone else'll pick it up.

Like your brother.

Now the brother, a sly, handsome bastard named Kalith, asked the peers if they thought the king was mad, but they said no, because the king was handing out lands and titles like a river-child hands out mudpies. So Kalith came and poisoned the king and queen and blamed it on the fool. He tried to poison the daughter as well, but her monkey told her not to eat her soup that night. So the fool was burned alive while the little girl cried.

The uncle petted her hair and smiled at her and said, "There, there."

She was next to be queen.

Kalith smiled and smiled at her.

The monkey told Mireya the uncle would kill her before she could be crowned and that her only chance was to make herself harmless.

So being a particularly clever child, Mireya talked to the monkey in public.

And stopped washing.

And started howling at the stars and moon.

So the peers declared her mad.

Now in this kingdom, the mad are thought to be favorites of the gods, so even the uncle dared not harm her lest the people cast him down. For the people had winked at the murder of the king who danced while the country fell to ruin, but they loved the infanta Mireya and pitied her for her madness.

The mad may not rule, but they marry well enough, so the uncle, now king, sent his niece to marry a lord in the kingdom of Gallardia. He wasn't handsome—they called him the Toad Earl of Orfay—but he was brave and good to his mad lady, Mireya, who wasn't so mad anymore once she got out of Ispanthia.

Now the goblins came closer.

They said, "We're hungry."

So the kingdoms gathered all the brave men who were left, but it wasn't enough. And so the clever women became warriors, but it wasn't enough.

Mireya wasn't so mad, but she was dangerous. Turns out she could talk to animals. And bring rain. And make waters run uphill. When her husband, the king, went off to fight the goblins and never returned, the Gallards who were left decided they didn't care for witches and sent Mireya off to marry the king of Oustrim, far away.

And there she stayed.

Now back in Ispanthia and Gallardia, the kingdoms bred up big war corvids to go into battle with the very last of their men and half their remaining women.

And it turns out goblins are scared of birds.

And the corvids bit the legs from them, and the daughters whacked their arms off.

So they said, "Fuck those birds, we're not hungry anymore," and went back home to their shyte tunnels and manfarms and mushroom gardens.

With the goblin tide turned, Mireya, now queen of Oustrim, set about cleaning house. The king loved her and did all she said, so she cast out the Takers Guild. They sent Assassin-Adepts to kill her, but she always knew they were coming because animals told her. And the Guild was driven underground. But she'd used up so much magic laying the Guild low, she didn't hear the animals when they tried to warn her about the giants. For the kingdoms of Manreach were unlucky, and now that goblins had drained the lands of strength, the giants were come and took the westernmost city.

A cold city in a vale between two sets of mountains.

And no one knew where the queen went.

But her old friend was coming to find her.

A warrior who fought with birds and drove the goblins out.

And who now meant to restore Mireya to Ispanthia's throne.
With the help of two witches.
And maybe a Coldfoot guard.
And a thief who hated his Guild.

That was the story Norrigal told me, if not in so many words.

After the story, I nearly slept.

I was going to die, but not with bastards, and on a failed but worthy quest.

Would I really have been ready to betray the Guild and work against their interests?

I didn't know.

But the bright thing in the grave was, as things stood now with us in cages and bound for goblin bellies, I didn't have to know.

I only had to die.

Relieved of such a burden, I managed to keep a sense of calm and dignity about me, even when the old steam-geezer came near me and showed me a little gadget with a crank. Gods, he smelled putrid. But I kept from heaving even as he held his clawed little hand up and showed me the crank. Invited me to turn it. When I didn't respond, he took my hand out through the bar and made me turn it. I watched as a fine spill of white crystals fell out one end. He spread these on my arm and then licked it, his awful, armored little tongue, something between a cat's tongue and boiled leather. One of his teeth cut me just the tiniest bit, and he rubbed salt grains in the little bit of blood that came out, fingered it up, and went back to his steam-making, licking that finger like it was the best finger in the world. Fuck him, fuck all goblins forever, and fuck any who make peace with them. If you don't yet understand why, heed the next bit. Heed it and know it to be true.

36

A Death of Seagulls

———— • ————

"Just look at me," I said to Norrigal later. Maybe an hour, maybe half a day, time makes no sense when you're miserably uncomfortable and waiting to die. Weird lanterns burned in the walls of the hold, it might have been night. She locked her eyes on mine. They were going to butcher the harpooner in plain sight of our cage; I saw one who seemed to be the captain come in and speak to the old steam-maker, and they both took up cleavers and rope and started for the harpooner's cage.

I didn't want any of that in my dreams, should I chance to sleep again before dying, so I kept my eyes turned away and thought Norrigal might want to do the same. She did.

Now the old man started whimpering, he couldn't help himself, and neither could I blame him. It was a horrible sound to have to hear yourself making, so I started singing a song I had learned during my time in Pigdenay, a song called "Lovely, Fit, and Gay," also known as the Pigdenay Round, for that was how it was often sung. I broke out my best tenor, and I sang against the dark thing about to happen. I sang it loud. It may have been the best I ever sung, for I wanted the poor old bastard to leave the world hearing a song of his own city, and I wanted to do it right.

O, you are lovely, fit, and gay
And though your troubles seem today
A few too many to be borne
You'll none remember come the morn

Malk knew the song as well and sang it with me, loud and baritone.

Embrace each hour you are young
For soon enough a time will come

Norrigal joined in, blending a high and nasal alto as best she could with her face against the bar.

When all your friends both fair and bold
Will lose their beauty and grow old

The harpooner started to sing with us, but they didn't like that, and so they hit him in the head and like killed him there, which would have been a blessing. They started on him proper then, but on we three sang.

That time, my love, has not come yet
So don't you worry, neither fret
To you and yours belongs this day
For you are lovely, fit, and gay

I've never seen, nor do I know
On rocky cliff or strand below
From yesterday or anywhile
A cheek to break a sweeter smile

So smile to show me that you've heard
And listened to my every word
These cares of yours can never stay
For you are lovely, fit, and gay

We sang the whole thing again three more times before they were done with him, and we never looked over there, not one of us. Not even when the crew came in to eat. There was no singing over that, not over the sound of the cutting or the working of the salt grinder, and whether I passed out from my injuries or from pure horror is beyond my guessing. I know I wasn't the only one, for when I woke again in the steamy darkness of the goblins' hold, I was the only one conscious.

The first thing that struck me was the warmth under my breast-bone—my luck was back in. The second thing I noticed was that the old steam-maker was gone. The third was that the ship was quiet. Where we had heard the sound of the crew barking and throat-whistling through their duties tacking into the wind and working the rudder, now I heard only the crying of seabirds. That struck me funny, too, for they chased gulls and terns away with whip and fire, so badly did they hate them. The crying of gulls still comforts me to this day. I noticed we were rolling a bit more than normal, and a goblin ship rolls a fair amount because they don't build their ships with much of a keel to them. They like being able to come up in shallow waters. On one of the larger rolls, I saw the salt grinder go skittering across the floorboards, and it stopped when it hit the foot of the steam-geezer, who was down.

I wanted to say something, but I didn't know what. I was bewildered. I touched the cage door and found that it opened when I pushed. I opened it slow. I looked back to confirm that Norrigal, Malk, and Galva were all out, and they were, hurt Galva snoring almost enough to call the poor Gormalin to mind.

I padded out and made my way to the bench-chest where our goods were kept, watching both the plank that led up to the deck and the still form of our goblin gaoler, who I now noticed was lying near a heap of his own awful vomit. I found my knives and belt. My bow and a quiver with a few arrows remained—I took those. I prodded Malk, but he slept on, looking very pale. Norrigal began to stir. I put my hand over her mouth. Her eyes went wide as she remembered who and where she was. I helped her to her wobbly legs and to the chest, where she found her staff of head-busting. I motioned for her to try to wake the others and that I was going to creep above deck and see what was happening.

I slunk up the plank with an arrow ready, and I came upon a scene of great carnage. The goblins lay in postures of tortured death, bloody heaps of their vomit all over the deck. One still lived, holding to the side and emptying his guts over horribly. It was the wizard. He looked up at me, drool trailing from his sharp-toothed mouth in the wind.

"Clever," he said. "You know we eat weak one first. Clever. I congratulate you. I—"

One thing I know about wizards is don't let them talk. As impressed as I was with his ability to speak Holtish and as curious as I was about what he might have to say, I didn't want him charming me, putting me to sleep, or making a spar fall on me, so I shot him. I shot that prick, right in the head, I hung a wee skinny horn on him, say it how you will, but the short version is he won't be turning any more witch winds around, he won't be bringing cliffs down on any more war corvids, he won't be diddling with his stone on a string, and when you invite him to dine with you on leg of harpooner, he'll have to say, "No thank you." He bared his sharp teeth in pain and grabbed the arrow, then he bled out of one eye and one of the two holes where a nose should have been, he tottered three steps, then he sat down and died sitting.

And no part of me felt bad about it.

It's a much easier thing to kill a goblin than a man.

Seagulls wheeled overhead. One gull walked the deck near the back of the ship, making his way to a goblin corpse he'd like to have a peck at. Two more fought on the spar, a fat, mouthy one driving off another with mocking shouts. A whole pack of them pecked at a fresh pile of sick. And one mottled brownish gull lay dead near a similar pile of sick, his feathers blowing slightly in the considerable wind.

I congratulate you.

Poison.

The lot of them had been poisoned.

The ship rolled under my feet. Thunder rolled overhead. A storm was coming in now, and me on a ship full of dead biters without the first idea how to sail it.

"Fothannon, Lord of Mischief, this is your day," I said into the rising wind. "I praise your hand in this, as I see it clear. I offer you no tears, for you hate them. I ask for no blessings, for you scorn supplication and always take more than you offer. Instead, I give you the sound that's dearest your heart, and mine, you incorrigible old groper. I congratulate you."

And I looked at the chaos around me and listened to the wind and the crying of the poisoned gulls, and I laughed into that wind.

I laughed tears onto my own cheeks.

I laughed straight until Norrigal called me back belowdecks.

"What the five flying fucks is the cat doing here?" she said.

Bully sat near the dead goblin steam-maker, licking a paw as though none of this held the least concern for him. Norrigal held her own hand.

"I don't know," I said. "What's wrong with your hand?"

"The little bastard clawed me."

"Did you try to touch the salt grinder?"

"And how would you know *that*?"

"Don't touch the salt grinder. It's full of poison."

I didn't envy whoever would have to explain the cat's reappearance on the ship to Malk and Galva, and I envied him even less when I remembered it was going to have to be me. I told her what I saw up on the deck.

"I don't know if you properly understood everything you discovered in the service of your underground witch, but a lot of it seemed mysterious and wonderful to me. Can we just say that something mysterious and wonderful has happened for us at last? Can we just say we're glad the cat's here? Without looking too far down his throat, I mean?"

After a moment's consideration of both myself and the cat, she said, "We can."

"And might we just say you got out and poisoned the lot of them? And that Bully here had just stowed away in my pack, unbeknownst to us and our gentle hosts?"

"We might," she said, looking at me hard.

Bully now leapt into the pack and pulled its flap shut over himself.

"You've got to be fucking kidding me," Norrigal said.

Malk wasn't in the best shape, but there was enough of him to direct us when the storm hit and, our luck in for once, we only caught the very tail of it before it howled off west with a quiver of lightning for the ships of Molrova. By the second day, Galva was trying to help us, but we made her lay lie down. We kept the goblin vessel afloat, the three of us, and even managed to steer it toward the south by day. Our biggest problem was water. Goblins can drink seawater, you see. The solitary barrel of fresh water on the boat, the one they'd been watering us with, had been vomited in by a dying goblin with a misplaced sense of discretion. If only we had thought to put out vessels during the storm, but we'd had other matters on our mind. By the first night, we had ignominiously slurped up all the rainwater that could be gathered from wringing out sailcloth.

Norrigal and I were too throat-raw to talk much, but we sat and held each other for the comfort of it, looking at the stars in their great numbers. There's nothing like the stars far out at sea, with no torch nor lantern to argue their majesty with them. We dared a dry kiss or two, but no more. This was still more funeral barge than pleasure raft, and though we had grown somewhat used to goblin-stink, it is no aphrodisiac.

"Deadlegs could have kept us off this ship," she croaked at one point.

"You don't know that," I said, my voice a husk of itself.

"Oh, I do."

"Then you don't know that would have helped us. We'd still be on the island. Anyway, the old girleen couldn't have made the journey. That's why she sent you."

She nodded, her eyes sad.

"I wasn't ready," she said. "Three more years of study, maybe I would have been so. But as it is, I've botched as much as I've sorted out."

"No," I said, "you're just being a Galt. There's no tongue speaks against itself so harshly as a black tongue."

I was looking in her pretty gray eyes so close and hard I could see stars in them. You'll not believe this, but I saw a shooting star reflected in her eye. Her eye widened a bit.

"You saw it?" I said.

She nodded a tiny nod.

Grinned just a bit when she realized I must have seen it in her eye.

The eye moistened then, just at the edge, but Norrigal was too dry to make a tear.

By the second day, we were all of us well on our way to thirst-madness.

Happily, that's when we saw the sails.

"Whose ship is that?" I asked Malk, who was giving himself a headache trying to look through a goblin farglass. "Is it Molrovan?"

"No," he said. "They're flying the three white dragons of Middlesea."

"That's lucky!" Norrigal said.

Middlesea was Holt's closest ally, grown from Holtish conquests half a hundred years ago when Holt and her knights controlled everything on the north half of the mainland from Ispanthia to Molrova. As with the kingdom of Brayce, Middlers speak the language almost as we do. Not sharing a border with Holt, as Brayce did, made things more cordial. Middlesea was a strange, flat, horseshoe-shaped nation, ringing Deepbelly Bay and best known for cold-weather flowers, beer, and warships.

"Normally, a Middler fireship would be lucky," Malk said. "If we were flying Holtish banners, it would be lucky. But they think we're goblins."

"Aren't they under treaty?"

"Of course they are. As were these pricks when they found us on the island. You know the saying—*Waves have nor ears nor tongues.*"

"Actually, I don't know that saying."

"What happens on the sea stays on the sea," he said. Then he said, "Oh shyte."

"Please don't say that. 'Oh shyte' what?"

"You see that smoke?"

"You're the one with the glass. But I think so, yes. Does that mean . . . ?"

"Yes."

They were readying firedarts.

Balls to the treaty.

We were goblins.

And our good friends from Middlesea meant to burn us.

37

The Fourth Woman

————•————

The fireship bore down on us, her sails full and the foam white at her waterline. The dragons on her sails were white, too, faint against the sun-bleached blue of her sailcloth, like the ghosts of dragons. This ship, a fine old fireship that had doubtless seen action in the Hot Sea, had one ballista capable of firing head-on, and they used it. That first dart arced up and plunged down wide, leaving a thrilling spiral of smoke behind it. It would have been beautiful, with its little pot of oil jelly, its wick of burning fast-punk and its gull-feather fletching, were it not so lethal. It plished harmlessly into the sea.

They readied another, these misguided allies of ours, and prepared to try for our lives again. I could see them working on the deck in their white Middlesea tunics and foxfur caps. I waved at them madly, but they ignored me—we could be Molrovans serving as larder-boys for the biters, and Malk's ship-clothes did have a hint of Molrova about them. I shouted, but we were still just too far out.

The second dart missed as well, but the third launched true, coming square at us, set to stick deep in the wood; its clay pot would crunch, splashing oil jelly through burning fast-punk to spit unquenchable fire pools on our deck. This was how our fleets narrowly won the battle of Hammerhead Bay, which opened the shores of the Hordelands to us. It was said we burned so many goblin ships in that rocky bay the sun set red for three nights because of all the smoke. I had always wondered what naval combat really looked like, and here was my curiosity good and settled.

I was unenthusiastic about dying, however historically, so I was glad to see Norrigal loose her staff at this new, true dart. Bless that staff, and bless Deadlegs for making it, if she did. Norrigal cast it like a spear, and it flew straight, whirling at the last instant to bat the dart off starboard, hanging and waiting for its next challenge. It wasn't easy for her keeping that staff in the air with the boat tossing on the waves and the friendly enemy boat coming straight at us. She had an adorable sweat-mustache even in the cold spray as the staff swatted the next dart.

It struck this dart in the worst possible place, crunching its jelly-pot and igniting the Axaene firejelly all over itself. The staff must have had half a mind of its own, for it seemed to go mad when struck ablaze. It whirled furiously, trying to get the awful stuff off of it, but it was no use. It dunked itself in the sea, but I knew enough to know that wouldn't help—Axaene jelly burned under the waves as hotly as above them. I almost felt bad for the thing until it shook a spray of burning fuel at us, catching Malk on the arm and setting a few candle-sized fires on the deck that, thankfully, had not enough fuel to burn long.

The blazing staff flew up in the air and separated into several pieces, making quite an end of itself. And making an end of us, like as not. The Middlesea ship turned now, preparing to show us its side, where most of its ballistas waited.

"Get down!" Malk yelled, and he did, and Norrigal and Galva, too. I stayed standing now, driven by some intuition that told me ducking wouldn't be enough. As the fireship turned, I saw the battery of six ballistas, all stoked and smoking. I saw the boat's first mate with her baton raised, ready to lower it and torch us as bright as a low sun. I yelled, not sure what words I would say. I would like to report that I said something like, "We sons of Holt send our compliments to the three kings of Middlesea, long may they live, and long may our nations trample the goblin Horde! See what prize we bring for the honor of our good and noble king, Conmarr!"

What I actually said was:

"*Shyte*, don't! I'm a Holter! Hold your fire, for the love of fuck, *friend! Friend!* May the gods save *Middlesea,* we're your *friends!* Fuck! Don't!"

As it turns out, it worked. Mostly. I watched the first mate's arm, the one holding the baton, start to fall but catch itself, like a standing sentry starting to sleep but catching himself straight again. One eager ballisteer pulled the trigger-bolt. I watched the dart come, watched it get larger almost slowly in that queer way missiles have when they're aimed exactly at you and your heart's beating so fast time slows down. While my mind began to work on the problem of whether to duck or jump, my body acted on its own and I leapt hard and high. I felt my hands reaching for the spar well above my head, grabbing oddly twisted wood and hemp; I felt my legs parting as my feet kicked up on opposite sides of me. The dart, six feet long if an inch, sizzled by beneath me, so slowly, it seemed, I could see it wobble as it went, though in truth it flew as fast as every arrow did.

I heard Norrigal gasp and Malk say *Ah* and Galva say *Ay!* And then my legs were closing again where I hung from the spar. Last was the smoke-trail, which wafted up to make my eyes sting, and would have brought tears if I had so much moisture in me as that.

A stunned moment passed, and then a cheer went up from the Middlesea fireship. Before I knew it, they'd boarded us and lifted me up over their heads and spun me round like I was their pet now, and I was happy not to have been drowned or burned or eaten, so I bore it laughing, and they laughed, too, but then my laughs turned into coughs and they put me down and gave me water and I said, "How many darts do I have to leap to get a whiskey?" and they laughed piss-hard, and I had to declare it a good day after all.

38

The First Daughter

———•———

The third most important woman in the port city of Edth sat
before us in a very large chair in a very large room on the third
landing of a tower that leaned just a little over the harbor as if
listening. A cool wind blew through the window she kept open
to justify the fire that crackled in an open hearth in the room's
middle. We four sat on our cowhide stools and drank our good
Middlesea lager, listening. She was the harbormistress of Edth,
and she was telling us our options. All the while I had the feeling
we weren't the first to hear some version of what she said.

"I have heard some of the words you have spoken to the captain of the *Fourth Woman*, the ship that nearly roasted you. It is
my suspicion you have spoken them in delirium."

Middlesea Holtish wasn't exactly the same as Holtish proper,
but you could get it easy enough. She spoke to us in our version
of the language, else it would have been more like, *I haert somme
fall of the werts thoost spook wards the capitan,* you get it. Point
is, she was a canny old cunny, and she knew what she was about.

She was a fat dam, too, dressed in good Gallardian velvet.
Her golden chain of office featured dragons chasing stars, with
diamonds for stars, real stars presumably being just beyond the
reach of Middlesea's deep coffers.

"We have before us a series of ifs, and you may think of those
ifs as axles upon which great wheels may turn." She said *turn* in
a way that was both delicious and threatening, drawing it like a
knife coming out of a roast.

"If goblins attacked you on the island, as you may have mistakenly said, it means they have violated the treaty. This would be a matter of the most grave import. It would be necessary for you to prove that the crew attacked you and imprisoned you and ate of kynd-flesh. You will be required to testify before at least three sovereigns of Manreach and convince them that your story is true. You shall need to convince them despite their great interest in keeping the peace, and you will need to stay alive on the roads between the kingdoms hoping no actors in Manreach, or beyond, find your story so inconvenient as to move them to hire blades in the night against you. It should be noted that two expeditions have set out this year hoping to prove goblin aggression on northern seas. One made it as far as Brayce, where a bridge collapsed into a river, drowning the lot. The other disappeared in Gallardia enough months ago that we despair of finding them."

She stopped there to let that sink in and to give her underneck a moment to stop wobbling. She took a sip of mead. She was drinking mead. We got beer. I prefer beer, but bugger her, she didn't know that.

"If you did manage to give testimony in three courts, the goblin ambassadors may manage to prove that the goblins were merely exploring the island and that you struck at them first."

"They were—" Malk started to say, but the harbormistress spoke over him, using the muscles in her belly the way actors and town mouths do to get louder without shouting.

"*Please* do not say anything I do not wish to hear and which you would not wish me to hear. May I continue?"

Malk nodded.

"Some crowned heads of Manreach will be eager to maintain peaceful accommodation with our foe, however fragile, so the odds of them accepting the goblins' version of events are not small. In that case, you will be denounced as traitors to the peace and publicly hanged right back here in Middlesea, under my hand. Or worse, since you count a Spanth among your number, turned over to the Ispanthian army that recently passed near who will torture you to death as bearers of false witness in matters touching war."

She met our eyes, each of us in turn.

"If you did manage to survive the perils of the road and to convince reluctant monarchs of your story's truth, the League would have no choice but to accuse the Horde of breaking the treaty. If the Horde kings denounced their lost crew as independent actors and traitors to the peace, the matter should be closed. Goblins do not admit fault, however, and their language contains even fewer expressions of apology than Ispanthian. The truth is that they know we destroy their northern ships as they destroy our southern ones. The goblin Horde would be insulted that we did not simply burn their ship and let it sink with no evidence of its existence, something they would consider just and fair, something the captain of the *Fourth Woman* was on the point of doing until you good citizens of Manreach were espied; something she perhaps should have done, anyway. The result of public accusation instead of discreet disposal may very well be a resumption of the wars which I think two of you may have been too young to enjoy, but about which the other two might be able to instruct you."

At this, she crossed her hands on the table so we could plainly see the left one had two fingers gone. Heavy gold rings on the other one.

"There is also the matter of the ship itself," she went on. Even if she used exactly our words, there was no hiding her accent. If you've met a Middler, you'll be able to hear them stretching those words out, as if trying to load extra vowels into each sound. *Maater of the shiyep itseyulf.* "If you mean to claim the goblins attacked you and that you killed them in self-defense, the ship will be seized by the crown as evidence."

"And if otherwise?" I said.

She smiled for the first time.

"If, for example, you rowed your little boat out to find the goblins already dead, their ship adrift, and you were apprehended while sailing it to Edth as a gift to the crowns of Middlesea, you would receive some small token of our gratitude. A few gold duchesses each, perhaps a whole quarter trounce. Unless, of course, one of you were nobility," she said, laughing, "then you'd be entitled to 10 percent of the goblin ship's value. But . . ." She trailed off, waving her maimy-hand dismissively while she sipped at her mead. "So which is it? Trials, death, and maybe a war? Or a week in feather beds?" She looked at the Spanth now. "With hot baths besides?"

Before Malk could start the fucking war, I said, "We rowed the boat out and found the poor darlings dead. We wept and wept for the loss of their sweet little lives, then determined to bring the ship into your fair harbor."

"Excellent," the harbormistress said, motioning a near steward to bring more beer for us and mead for her, as well as an ink pen and several papers. "There'll be oath-writs to sign, assuming you're literate; if not, make whatever mark you may. We'll all have a cool beer and keep the peace. And you'll each have—yes, I think His Majesty would approve my generosity here—you'll each have a quarter trounce of Middlesea gold and our king's thanks for being reasonable gents and dams."

I signed.

Norrigal snorted and signed.

Malk shook his head and signed.

Galva did not sign, but looked at the harbormistress as if deciding something.

"No," Galva said at last.

"No, *what*?" the harbormistress said wearily.

Galva pushed her cup away. "I will not have beer, I will have wine. Good wine."

The harbormistress stared at her, then sighed and nodded at her steward, who brought the mead-bottle for her.

"And I will not have a quarter trounce for the goblin ship to pass to your hand."

"I do not know where you think you are, my Ispanthian friend, but this is not an auction-house, and I have already told you how much the king offers."

"Yes, you have. And you will keep your word."

"Indeed," she said, "a quarter trounce, and not a shave more."

"No," Galva said and stood up.

The halberd-bearers by the door stepped near now. They had already taken our weapons to hold, but Galva, though skinny, weary, and injured, was clearly a serious dam.

She reached slowly into her pouch, the one she carried on a strap beneath her arm, and pulled out a golden seal in a leather case. The seal of Ispanthia.

"I am the first daughter of the Duke of Braga," Galva said in Holtish. "You may keep your feather bed, but I will have a bath, and I will have 10 percent of the value of the goblin ship to further my envoy to Oustrim."

What little conversation remained was conducted in Ispanthian.

39

The Moon-Wife

---•---

"Well, your ladyship, I wish I'd known I was traveling in the company of Ispanthian fucking nobility. Were you planning on telling me you were highborn?" I said to Galva back at the inn.

Galva had just had her bath, and I swear the woman looked an inch taller since she'd let slip she'd a duke for a father, and a famous duke at that, one known outside his country. Even I knew Rodricu Braga lost half his fortune on dead horses but still had more wealth than any but the king's family. Braga had the finest pasturelands in Ispanthia, which means the finest in Manreach, and they'd been mounted knights going back five hundred years. The Braga crest, as you may know, is a horse rearing over a skeleton. Ironic. And how sad for the duke to lose his horses and all his sons and to see his daughter and heir in love with death. Fit for a troubadour to sing about on a warm Sathsday in the month of Flora with a maiden's head in her lap.

That the Guild had attached me to her now took on new meaning. Galva was after the supposedly mad infanta, the Spanth princess who'd been married off to the king of Oustrim. Galva had said she was going to rescue a princess, and being a liar myself, I assumed it a lie. But now it seemed a certainty. What was the Guild's interest in Mireya, who had led Oustrim to outlaw the Guild? Kill her? That made sense, but the Guild was greedy, and a queen was a valuable thing. Kill the birder and ransom Mireya? That rang true. But you never knew with those fuckers. My head was reeling.

"Why should I have told you who I was?" Galva said.

"I'd have picked my nose less often and pissed farther off in the trees."

"No. You have would jested about my family and forced me to hurt you. That my brothers have died and left me heir to my father's title is not meat for your japes, but you would have japed all the same. You cannot help yourself. Your mouth is like an old man's bladder."

"That's just mean. There's no reason for you to be mean."

She grunted and poured wine for herself.

"It's the middle of the afternoon. You're going to die the yellow death from that," I said, pointing at her cup.

"My death will be red, like my wine, or so I pray. Now tell me what you really know about that *chodadu* cat."

"Other than that he's good luck?" I said.

"Do not be evasive."

"What do you want me to say?"

"I want you to tell me the reason he is trying to open my side-pack."

"Did you leave any cheese in there? He loves cheese."

"There is no *chodadu* cheese in my pack. What does he want? He wants something."

"Probably love."

"He will find no love in my pouches."

"Maybe he thinks your heart fell in there. You look so harshly at him. Why don't you give his ears a scratch and make friends?"

She made a disgusted sound and left the room, leaving me alone with Bully Boy. Malk was prowling seaside taverns, looking for another ship, or a fight, or both. Norrigal had gone to the magic quarter to see how she might replace what she'd lost from her cases.

I looked at Bully Boy.

"What the hell were you doing rooting through her gear? You want her to wring your neck?"

Bully raoed like a simple cat, his face pointing three-quarters of the way toward me.

"Are you even in there?" I said. "Hoa, killer, are you there?"

The cat just sat. I didn't know if Sesta was out of him or just sleeping, if she did sleep, I didn't know much about harboring. But I was pretty confident she was gone, out roaming the city of Edth, filling the great hollow of her belly. So I picked Bully up by the nape and put him in my lap and scratched his ears, making him close his blind eyes and purr so hard, in and out, in and out, he might have been a busted bellows. "This is just for you, then," I said. "This is just between us."

Edth was a beautiful city. Three-hundred-year-old canals of greenish water cut through streets of white-gray brick, while terraced stone pyramids planted with frost roses, tulips and juniper, bear's breath, plumvine, and goldenberry stood at crossroads. The Queen's Trees defined the borders of the neighborhoods, witched to regrow picked fruit overnight. Any Edther could take a pear or apple at will, but taking two would earn a clout from the Queen's Cudgels, who enforced the law here as chainsdams did in Holt.

Edth's strong, pale lager and honey-sweet cider were shipped to Brayce and Holt and carted as far south as Beltia. *To sell an Untherman beer* was an expression for pulling off a real coup, and that's exactly what Edth did. It was said Untherkind would only drink the beers of Unther and Edth and declare the rest not fit to piss in. Edthers drank Unther beer as well, and Gallard and Ispanthian wine, as well as Braycish mead and cider, Istrean grappa and whiskey from Norholt and Galtia—every sailor gladdened to learn their ship would dock at Edthport, for Edth had more and lovelier taverns than churches.

These taverns also had the best names—the Sotted Bear, Her Lover's Poem, the Hook and Goad, Your Father's Belt, the

Quartered Sun, the Feathered Scold. This last was named for the Middlesea queen who upbraided parliament, saying donkeys were made to pull, not sit and bray. Five of those old men had her seized and covered her with glue and feathers, saying hens were for laying eggs, not singing. She became the lover of a great general, got the knights on her side, and disbanded parliament. She told the geezers she'd outmaneuvered that hens and donkeys had gone to war and that hens had won. The Hen and Donkey tavern is on Water Street. She then had the five who had feathered her lashed to a cart and made them pull her around Edth for all to see. The Five Men Bridled is on Castle Street, and that's where I met Norrigal for supper.

"I was thinking," she said, looking at me over her cider-cup and her plate of plummed quail and rosemary-bread, her eyes merrier than I'd ever seen them, "that you might fit for a time."

"Fit what?" I said.

"Me."

I've never been a blusher, but I'm fairly sure I colored.

I pulled a rabbit's leg out of my stew and sucked the gravy off, trying for all the world to look like I was thinking only of gravy.

"We might make a moon-vow together, with all that means, but only if you agree to certain conditions."

She tore her roast bird's tiny wing and stripped the flesh off it with her teeth, sucking the bone in a way that somehow seemed more natural than lewd, though of course it meant what it meant.

Her lover for a month. Her husband, of a sort, for a month. This was old Galtish business, Haros business, older than Holt, older than the White Road and the Knock. It sang to my blood, and not just because I was young and full of want for her.

"I'm listening," I said, smiling my best half smile at her.

"I'll bet you are, you fond man. First, rub a bit of this on your cheek. *That* cheek," she said, pointing at my tattoo and handing me a five-sided bottle of some coppery unguent. "Ask me what it is and I'll take it back."

I nodded. I rubbed a bit in, and it was warm. I was hoping it wouldn't take the thing off—if I were spotted in some place or other without my penalty-mark and my debt not timely, I'd be in for trouble. The Guild might make it a fist rather than an open hand. They might have one of my thumbs. But I trusted her. Fothannon protect me, I trusted Norrigal Na Galbraeth.

"You know about magic tattoos, then?"

"More than a little."

"Can you make them?"

"I can."

"That's proper strong magic. You never told me you could do that." I stole a bite of blue carrot and onion out of my stew.

"And when did you ask? Now do you want to hear my conditions, or shall I find some other fellow? The new moon's tonight, you know."

I did know, but not for spell craft. Knowing how dark a night was going to be was a thief's business.

I touched an ear.

I'm listening.

"First, you'll do as I say to keep my belly flat. I'm not for making bairns to raise. I serve my craft and my kynd, and I'll not do that so well with my knap in a pup's mouth. This besides the world being no fit place to live."

I remembered my fancy on the whale ship of breeding with her and released it. She watched me do that before she moved on.

"Second, you'll not tell me your secrets nor I yours, none that you don't want to share. We're making a month together, not a life, and even life-wives have locked a door or two in their hearts."

"Agreed," said I, mindful of and grateful for the way she hadn't pressed me on the matter of the cat.

"Last and most," she said, "you'll not change your manner with me. You've never been less than a friend to me, and you'll not start when I share your bed, or I'll regret it. If a man looks upon me, even a fair man, you'll know he's got at least a month to wait, and probably forever. And I'll know the same of you with the girleens."

"Agreed."

"Oh, and there's one more thing."

"What?"

"I don't do that one bit."

I looked around to be double sure we weren't listened to and dropped my voice. "And what bit's that?"

"You know."

"Sure and I don't. There's lot of bits. Some don't do some bits, and others think nothing of it. But those second bits the first ones do might shock the second ones who prefer to do the first bits."

"Right, I forgot what an expert you are. But I know you know the bit I mean, you kark."

"Killing crotch fleas with lamp oil?" I whispered.

She put her hand over her mouth and giggled at that, and it was her turn to color.

"Well," she said, looking at me over her mug again. "Will you have me? Will you stand under the blind moon with me tonight and say some binding words?"

Before I could answer, my margin-eye noticed a shape coming up on my right, a weaving, drunken sort of shape.

"Barkeep!" he said.

Oh shyte, here it came. And a drunkie, too. The drunk ones were the worst, not only because half the time they'd miss and cuff your ear, but because it was twice as galling being cuffed about by someone you could thrash without trying. My luck felt chill. This wouldn't be good. I ate my rabbit fast.

"Barkeep!" he said again, and this time the barkeep looked. "Anyone claim the mark on this one?"

I chewed and chewed.

"He's minding his business, Johash," she said. "Why don't you mind yours? It's not like you need another."

Those at the bar laughed good-naturedly. Have I mentioned that I like Middlesea? Maybe being ringed in by larger, dangerous neighbors makes a nation smarter and kinder. They're smarter and kinder there. Except for this twat, Johash, I mean. Nineteen years old if a day, big as life and dumb as bricks.

"Well, I claim him."

Bite.

Chew chew chew chew.

He staggered close now.

Swallow.

"Will you stand up, or do you want it sitting?" he said as if he were offering to shine my boots for me. I noticed his barely grown-in mustache was damp, and I was disgusted.

"Just get it over with," I said, mortified that my talk with Norrigal had to be cheapened by this shyte. I thought about taking another bite of stew and spitting it on his face when he struck, but the Guild wouldn't have that. Made them look bad. I just had to take it—I knew it was a risk coming to a tavern.

But still, a cullion like this paddling me.

He upped his sleeve with some ceremony. He nodded at Norrigal—a gentleman to the last. She winked at him, I couldn't guess why at the time. He swung his meaty hand at me, and it hit me, and it stung and rung my ear. A big, heavy stack of *coumoch*, that Johash.

But he wasn't done hitting. The same hand that hit me now swung up and Johash slapped himself across the cheek, harder than he'd hit me.

I barked a laugh before I could stop myself.

"Uh!" he said, too drunk to know what was happening. He backhanded himself now for good measure, and said *Ow* more quietly than the blow deserved.

I looked at Norrigal.

She shrugged.

"Haw!" a girleen near him said, amused by the spectacle. The hand of Johash immediately reached out and slapped that lass, though Johash hadn't even been looking at her. That woman's friend put an arm on Johash's shoulder, saying, "See here, now," so the hand of Johash fetched her a mighty slap, too, wrenching Johash around. I think it hurt his shoulder, because he went *Ow* again. Now the first woman punched Johash, Johash kicked at her, the hand of Johash slapped another woman, that woman elbowed Johash hard like a soldier, and he staggered, and pretty soon Johash was on his knees getting the shyte beaten and kicked out of him.

Norrigal took my chin in her hand and wheeled my face back around to make me look at her. "You never answered my question," she said.

"Yes. Of course it's yes."

"Good. First, I'll have you wear this," she said, hanging a cord around my neck. From that cord dangled a pretty, pearly-gray half of a stone that had been cleaved in twain. It was small, just about the size of half a plum pit. She put the other half around her own neck.

"What is this?" I asked.

"A clovenstone."

It was a delight to behold. It had been split right where a brown flaw winked like a tiny eye. Her half had a speck of the flaw in it, too.

"Feels like it's got magic in it."

"Oh, it does."

"What's it do?"

"Lets me call you, or you me."

She didn't get to show me how yet, though.

Now a man yelled, "Johash is witched! That one there witched him!" he pointed at Norrigal. Hard gazes fell on us.

"That's right, I witched him," Norrigal said, standing. "I am the handmaid of Guendra Na Galbraeth of Galt, Queen of the Snowless Wood, called Deadlegs, the witch of the Downward Tower. I enjoy her protection as this man enjoys mine."

That paused the crowd, but irked the barkeep.

"She's away in Holt," she said, coming from around the bar with a truncheon, "and this is my tavern. Out with you." She pointed the truncheon.

I grabbed what was left of my stew.

"Leave the bowl."

I turned it up into my mouth and slurped what gravy I could, taking what remained of the rabbit leg in my hand. It had cost me two pretty Middlesea maids, finer than the marks they minted in Holt, and I wasn't losing my whole supper just because karking Johash wanted a karking free lager.

Norrigal turned with some dignity and walked slowly for the door. I set the stew-bowl down, wiped my face with my sleeve, and went with her, but didn't turn my back, as I rightly suspected the crowd was against us. Several of them came, but not to do us injury, just to toss us out the faster. We were roughly grabbed and jostled, myself more roughly, for they fancied themselves gentlefolk and were scared of Norrigal besides, and we soon found ourselves facedown in the mudded wheel ruts outside the Five Men Bridled, the rabbit leg in the mud as well, an alley dog now making bold to snatch it and run back.

"Better him than the potwash boy," I said, laughing, and she laughed, too. We sat up like children making mudcakes and laced our fingers together, looking up into the black, cloudless sky, looking toward the gray-black disk that was the blinded moon.

She took my face in her hand, and I took hers in mine as was the custom.

"Kinch Na Shannack, as the new moon is your witness, will you take me as your moon-wife and do me one month's good in bed and out of it?"

"I will. Norrigal Na Galbraeth, will you do the same by me?"

"You know I will."

And we sat in the mud and kissed dirty, cold, and careless, her tasting the beer and rabbit of my mouth and me tasting plum and cider on hers, this until an oxcart rumbled up and we stood to walk together. She ran ahead of me, then turned to face me, putting the clovenstone in her mouth.

"What's it, a whistle?" I asked.

"*Zust wed*," she said, meaning, *Just wait.* One of the marks of loving somebody must be that you can understand them with their mouth full.

"Wait for what?" I said.

"*Zgudda morm op.*" *Gotta warm up.*

She kept walking backward, looking at me. In just a moment, my stone lifted like an iron slug toward a magnet, floating up on its cord, which tugged gently at the back of my neck.

"Stay still," she commanded. I did so. She now ran around to my right, and the stone followed her. She made a circuit of me, and so did the stone. She spat it out of her mouth then. An instant later, the stone began to drift down, slowly, in pulses, like a man's pillock after a tumble.

Which wasn't far from my mind, between her kisses and watching her mouth that stone.

"Will it do that if you put it anywhere else?"

She smiled, open-mouthed, said, "Anywhere that'll warm it up."

We all but ran to the public baths.

40

The Baths of Edth

———·———

Norrigal. Norrigal. Sweet-bitter Norrigal. Norrigal the frail and mighty, smelling of clove and beeswax, cider, and the quick, animal scent of a doe. I conjure you to appear for me again as you were in Edth, if only for this too-brief train of words.

I conjure the white, perfect spar of your arm, the one I saw from far below when you leaned from the witch's tower and etched your name where I will never be smooth again. I call you and your dark-honey hair into the sunlight of memory to stand on your two good legs; I enjoin you to sing, and if you will not sing, only speak. Speak to me as you did in the baths of Edth, doubled in echo, with the drip-drap dropping of water to bejewel your voice; tell me in my ear which of your perishable wifely duties you mean to bestow, and demand what husband-gift of me you will, for in this moment, you are mine again as you were mine in Edth, your skin a coin that shone by moonlight and beneath candles, a coin mine to spend but never save.

What hunger I stoppered in you and what thirst I slaked, another might have done so well, but Haros tangled up our roads together in a braid, so your eyes and hands and laughter fell on me. I will remember until I grin in the soil how you crowned me, and how you beggared me, and I will call none your better.

The Stone Baths in Edth were a wonder of architecture and engineering, the destination of pilgrims from all of Manreach. Hot springs fed them, so they never needed stoking. The waters poured into huge stone pools carved with benches here and niches there, mosaics of trees and fish, and a hippogriff cleverly inlaid on the walls. On the roof, the most artfully wrought stained glass skylight outside Gallardia, and the size of a longship besides, showed Sath, the sun, in amber, with blue sky around him, and leaves and branches for a frame. The rock walls were alive with figures ten feet tall; lovers entwined, their backs and haunches, their pleasured and pleasing faces coming smooth out of the rough rock as if unfinished. On the pool's floor, visible through the clean, greenish water, a mosaic of old Mithrenor himself, his twin fish tails bent beneath him, his right hand whipping a storm and the left one dandling a nymph. The pools were public, and man and woman young and old bathed there without shame, priestesses of Mithrenor keeping two hundred oil lamps lit, skylights letting shafts of sun spear down through steam. For those who wished less public discourse, a trough led the waters past horned and hermed caryatids of old Haros and into a honeycomb of private limestone cells they say half the bastards in Edth got their start in.

Bathers usually wore nothing but a pouch around the neck for coins. Lutists for hire wandered the baths, strumming slowly for lovers in nooks as readily as singing known ballads in the common pools. For a copper shave, handmaids would strew the waters with wildflowers. Vendors sold chilled mead or lammasgrape or cider, or hazelnuts or little bags of cooked snails. A knot of Sornian women, naked but for their torques, sat packed as close as grapes on the vine with no weapons near to hand. Bankers with the great houses of Hellernock, the financial capital of Manreach, sat nude next to oysterwives and goatherds; knights shared benches with cardsharps and chandlers. The waters were a leveler. The waters were safe.

Norrigal had just left me alone in the baths, this after our fourth bout of lovemaking under a small waterfall almost too hot to bear, when I let my feet hang in the warm deeps of the largest pool. My skin was covered in scratches and love-bites—Norrigal was expert in biting just when the pleasure was greatest so the pain only followed after. The hot water salved it all and pulled the ache out of the rarely used muscles I'd strained or tensed at love-play.

I thought nothing of the middle-aged man who frog-swam toward me, his froggy mouth opening and closing froggily as he made his way to me slowly, so slowly, his every double kick pushing his chin an inch or two closer and sending weak little waves before him. When at last he flopped from the deep water on to the tiled bench next to me, he said, "They keep it good and hot here, don't they?"

Normally, I wouldn't have minded such a platitude, but it was lethal to the afterglow, so I favored him with the sort of grunt that acknowledged having heard a comment but gave no encouragement to another.

And yet another came.

"I hear they had a murder here this year."

Now I had to pay attention to him, damn him. Murder talk from strangers is best not ignored.

"What, in the baths?"

"Aye, in this pool."

"Were you the killer, then?"

"No, not I," he said.

"You're quite sure?"

"I am."

"So why are you telling me?" I said.

"Just by way of being friendly."

"Telling me where they make the best fish stew, that's friendly. Warning me off a tavern where they water down the wine, that's friendly. Blurting out an anecdote about murder while I'm remembering a moment of earthly bliss, that's not friendly at all. I'd call that macabre at best and threatening at worst."

"Well, how was I supposed to know what you were thinking about?"

"You weren't. I might have been sleeping for all you knew. But up you swam anyway to blarp at me with the trumpet of your mouth."

"I just thought you'd like to know—"

"Well, I wouldn't, and I didn't, so whatever's next, don't."

"I thought you'd like to know—"

"For fuck's sake, man." I closed my eyes, hoping he'd go away.

"That you're going to keep following the Spanth."

I opened my eyes again because the voice was different. It wasn't the froggy-man's voice anymore. It was the voice of the assassin in the cat.

Sesta.

I looked, and there she was, tattooed and lethal, her eyes flat and dead after Norrigal's eyes so gay and full of pleasure. Her tattooed-black lower lip almost in a pout, her solid arms black as pig iron out before her as she clutched the stone edge of the pool.

"Well, why wouldn't I follow her?"

"Because you're a married fucking man now, aren't you?"

"Just for a month."

"A month too many."

"What business is that of the Guild's?" I asked, though I already knew. Emotional entanglements were greatly suspect. The Guild had been known to kill objects of too-great affection when said objects threatened to distract Guild assets or began to turn their loyalty. The Takers Guild was none too fond of the great independent magickers like Deadlegs and Knockburr, Fulvir, and the others who wouldn't bend the knee to the Magickers Guild, which everyone knew was cousined to the Takers.

She let the silence do her work.

"Just make sure you don't get any ideas about romantic flight. You go where the Spanth goes, full stop. And you stay sharp, little Kinch, and remember your place. We believe the Spanth is in search of the infanta Mireya, the niece of Ispanthia's king. We had her in hand, but we've lost her, and we believe the Ispanthian birder may be able to find her. You are a tick on that Spanth's arse, and the moment you fall off, you risk to get stepped on."

"So the cat is a flea on the tick. And you a turd in the flea."

She huffed a half laugh before she could stop herself.

"Clever. Before you get too clever, look at this."

She pointed at a tattoo near her breast, just left of the clock; a tattoo of a heart with Keshite writing near it that said *Heart, Drum,* and a word that meant both "call" and "report."

"Keep looking at it."

After a moment, I could see that it was beating. And that it glowed, in a very subtle way, despite the blackness of the ink.

"What's it do?" I asked.

"It keeps you alive. Because it means I'm alive. If I die and this winks out, a matching tattoo in Pigdenay winks out. When it does, they'll send a spoilsport after you and yours. I know I've told you before, I just wanted to show this to you so you knew it was real. We need you to know you're ours. Think on that before you go renewing your heathen Galtish moon-vow, should you both live the month out."

I hated her then. I hated the Guild. I wished I'd gone to the Goblin Wars even if I'd died or lost my hands.

"You're jealous," I said.

"Of what?"

Out of nowhere, I said "Happiness," and the word stopped her short. Though she recovered quickly enough, I'd hit the quick.

"What do you know about it, Prank? What you call happiness is just the breeze you feel falling off a cliff. I'm here to catch you. This is the Guild's business now. You've endangered that girl with your love-oaths, and I'd hoped you'd know better."

"I told you what I'd do if you threatened her."

"Right. Kill the cat when I'm in him. Wring his neck with iron and so on."

"Do you think I won't?"

"I think you've stopped thinking. I think the ground has

crumbled under your feet and you've been too distracted to notice."

"If you harm her—"

"Plug your hole and listen, Kinch á Glurris Na Filleen."

Saying my real name got me to shut up. Kinch from the River, line of Filleen.

She continued.

"Your family house in Platha Glurris sits at the bottom of a hill not far from the banks of the Shining River. When your mother works the butter-churn, she looks at the water and she sings. The song she sings most often is one about a girl who drowns and then comes back as a frog to sing under her lover's window. Do you know the words?"

I tried to burn holes in her with my eyes, but it didn't work.

"Yes, I thought you did. Anyway, every ninth day, she walks two hours to the next town over to visit your sister and their children. Your niece has developed a stutter. You wouldn't know that, but I do. Think about that before you deceive yourself."

I opened my mouth, then closed it.

"I know. You're furious. But we shouldn't quarrel, being two loyal servants of the Guild. Shall we kiss and make up?"

She pouted her tattooed lower lip at me, which I was sure was full of poison.

"I'd sooner fuck a badger," I said.

"So noted. I know just where I can find you one," she said and smiled. And her smile morphed as her flesh sagged, and her hair retreated from her head and turned grayish, and she turned back into the froggy man and frog-swam away, enjoying how powerless I was to do anything but watch her leave.

41

The Quartered Sun

———— • ————

The next day, the four of us from the *Suepka* met in the Quartered Sun, a tavern known for Gallardian wine. Of course, this was Galva's idea, and she had set herself up in a corner chair with a fresh burgundy shirt on her, making her look young and vital, even comely, against the peeling sage-green paint on the bricks behind her, as she dove hips-deep into a carafe of rubyish Gallard lammasgrape. She probably could have gotten the black wine she preferred at the Quarrelsome Spanth, but I believe it would have hurt her pride to go there.

Once the three of us had joined her and filled our cups, we weren't long in knocking them together.

"To death," Galva said in a toast.

"To fallen comrades," said Malk.

"To that right cullion Gormalin," said Norrigal about the poor old Pigdenish harpooner the goblins had eaten on their hellish ship.

"May his cup be always full," Malk offered.

"But only with beer," I said before I could stop myself, getting a look from the soldier and the sailor and a swallowed snort from Norrigal. But then Malk and Galva also smiled despite themselves.

"*Jilnaedu*," Galva said, then raised her cup to me, drained it, and filled it again.

"I have brought you here to formally invite the three of you to continue with me on my path," she said. "I will leave to cross Molrova, into Oustrim, where I will see to the safety of Queen

Mireya, the infanta of Ispanthia. Oustrim has fallen to the giants and its king is dead, but the queen is believed to be alive and in hiding."

This declaration wrenched me back to the steaming hold of the goblin ship, when, with Malk bleeding all over me and me thinking we'd be stew for the biters, Norrigal had told me such a story. What Galva sought to do was a thing almost unthinkable outside fables—to put a witch-queen on the throne of Ispanthia. Such a frank invitation meant we must have earned her trust, and an Ispanthian's trust was priceless coin.

"But I go first to meet the army of my country," she continued, "which is marching to aid Oustrim in its fight against the giants. One of Ispanthia camped with this army will join me. This is my instructor of sword, who taught me for three years, and whom I am very eager to see."

"If the army is heading for Oustrim, why should we?" I asked.

"To conquer a kingdom, a thousand is not enough. To free a prisoner, ten is too many," Galva said. "The army goes to fight the giants, to push them back to their mountains. We will find the infanta and set her on her way home. Our journey will be hard, for we will march with long steps and rest little. The sinking of the ship delayed us many days, and we must tarry here no longer. We leave in the morning, and we do not stay two nights in any place again. All of those who aid me in this endeavor shall have rich rewards and the thanks of the sovereign of Ispanthia."

"You didn't say Kalith," I said, winking at her.

"Lower your voice," Norrigal told me.

"An oversight," Galva said, smiling a little, waving her hand in dismissal. "The crown of Ispanthia is generous, and the return of the infanta to her rightful place will serve the good of Ispanthia and all of Manreach."

"If there's money to be earned, I'm in," Malk said. While we served on the ship, I hadn't noticed Malk's mercenary side—the work was so bloody and greasy there was no point in wearing fine things, but since he'd gotten his share of the goblin-ship money, he had availed himself of the best Edth had to offer.

His jerkin of leather sewn with bronze rings would turn a knife and most swords. He'd gotten himself a longsword as well, Istrean steel if I were not mistaken, head and shoulders better than the battered cutlass that served him on the *Suepka*. He looked a man to be reckoned with, and he'd even found a Galtish hammered-gold torque to put around his neck as if he were a prince's son and not just a Platha Glurris soldier's brat. His hair cut, his stubble shaved, Malk had doubtless turned the heads of half the daughters of Edth on his way to the Quartered Sun.

Another thing—while Norrigal and I played at moon-marriage, Malk and Galva had taken up again the close friendship they'd cut short over whether I was to be murdered or not. I wondered had they gone shopping together like two gossips gone to market, Galva showing off her fine burgundy shirt to her skainsmate, Malk saying, "Which torque do you think shows off my jawline to better advantage?"

I chuckled.

"What?" Galva said.

"Nothing," I said. "I was just . . . admiring your shirt."

"Why are you always laughing?" Galva said. "You laugh when you should be silent, you speak when you should listen. And this shirt was made by an Ispanthian tailor of great renown, it is not for mocking."

"My god demands it of me. You still want me to help you find the infanta?"

She blinked twice, presumably blinking away the words she'd have rather said. "Yes."

"Good! This border rendezvous, is it anywhere near Grevitsa?"

"Why do you speak of Grevitsa?"

"It's a Molrovan city."

"I know this. Why do you say it?"

"No reason. I hear they have good lace."

"Lace?"

"In Grevitsa."

"What are you wanting with lace?"

"I thought you might want a bit of lace. For your fine shirt."

She reached across the table and fetched me a slap, but that just made me laugh harder.

"I deserved it," I said, getting up, still laughing. "You just sit there. I'll fetch your next carafe of wine for you. It's on the Guild."

42

The Goddess of Second Chances

———— • ————

That night, I left Bully in the room and took Norrigal to the oldest part of Edth, near the harbor and the low, round fortress they call the Merman's Tower. We dangled our feet over the seawall, listening to the creaks and gentle thuds of the ships, the gurgle of the water, the cries of night birds.

A huge statue of Cassa, goddess of mercy and Mithrenor's wife, stood with one open hand cupped toward the sea in supplication, the other on her breast. It was to her all prayers for lost sailors were directed. She stayed faithful to Mithrenor no matter how many nymphs and daughters of man he put bastards in, and her only price was that sometimes, just sometimes, he was to show mercy and be kind. If she had to trick him, it wasn't beneath her. *Would you drown your own flesh?* Cassa would say, taking hold of his whip-hand as he was on the verge of capsizing some stricken vessel. *What trick is this,* he would ask, *for my flesh is divine and cannot drown?* To which she would answer *Do you not remember the black-haired maiden who loved you on this shore not thirty years agone? Her issue went beneath the sails and on this very ship cleaves to his life.* Mithrenor would say, *Which is he, then? Show me him, and I will pluck him off and drown the rest.* To which the clever Cassa would reply, *Why, he is the most handsome, the most like you.* And while Mithrenor scanned the boat and tried to determine which sailor most resembled him, Cassa would calm the wind and still the sea, and Mithrenor, unable to see himself more reflected in one sailor's face than other, yet seeing something of himself in every one, would let the vessel go.

That's how the myth goes, at least, but you know how the gods are when you need them.

To look close at the statue of Cassa, you'd see her pretty feet are pocked where grieving wives, sons, and mothers have gouged her with hammer, pick, or rock for not saving their most dear ones. Her feet were stained, as well, where some had cut a thumb to bleed on her in protest. It is to be noted they attack the goddess of second chances because she's a safe outlet for their grief—Cassa will never take vengeance. Mithrenor's statue, just on the other side of the fortress, that's a different matter. Everyone's afraid of that bastard. His twin tail fins had not a mark on them, even though he's the one with the whip. He's the ship-killer. People don't *really* believe he'll send a giant wave to drown the city if his statue is desecrated, but better safe than sorry. Sweet Cassa gets the chisel and the weepy bleeders while Mithrenor does as he pleases. You see? You really can learn something from the gods.

I looked about and saw nobody near enough to hear us.

Cassa, I thought as hard as I could, *don't let Norrigal stab me or curse me or blind me with a powder when I say what I must. If she needs to hit me, I understand, but let it not be in the parts, or the throat, or with a rock larger than would easily fit in her hand.*

"There's an assassin in my cat," I said.

"What?" she said.

"You heard me. And not just an assassin. An Assassin-Adept."

"What's that? The worst possible kind of assassin, then?"

"Yah. She's got about a hundred magic tattoos, one of them's got her heartbeat in it so the Guild'll know if she dies. Her name's Sesta. She's fairly horrible. Wasn't sure if I should tell you her name, but she knows yours, so it only seems fair. Especially since I doubt that's her real name, just her killer's name, 'cause that's how old she was when she killed someone. The first time, I mean. *Sesta* means 'six.' In Istrean. So I guess she's from Istrea. Though she's not got much accent, but they train them out of that."

Norrigal fetched me a cuff on the crown, fairly hard. But just one. Then she licked her hand and smoothed what must have been a proud flag of hair she'd slapped standing.

Wasn't so bad. Thanks, Cassa. You're a plum.

"You babble like an old man when you're nervous, do you know that?"

"Yah, but I learned to control it. Except around you."

"You're a right wanker."

"Do you hate me?"

"What's to hate about you? We all serve our masters. The situation, though, that's to be hated. They've really got your carrot in the goat's mouth, haven't they?"

"I've never heard that expression."

"I invented it."

I sighed and looked at Deepbelly Bay, where the lanterns from the huge, round Merman's Tower's walls reflected in the water.

"Even if I could, I'm disinclined to kill the cat," I said.

"Your soft heart's going to be your undoing. Sometimes you've got to cut a throat."

I remembered the bull-man in the forest and shuddered. There was one throat I'd cut, and no pleasant business.

"I know. But killing the cat's not an option, is it?" I said.

"It wouldn't be prudent. The life-rune she showed you, that's strong magic. Not flashy, but sure."

"So the cat can't die."

"No."

"And that assassin will find me no matter how I try to throw her off—besides reporting me to the Guild."

"Hmm."

"I know that *hmm.* You've got something, haven't you?"

She stood then and stood me up with her. She got behind me and put my arm in the same pose as Cassa, held out to the sea. She put my hand on my own breast, and in that posture, she held me from behind and whispered in my ear, "Light a candle to sweet Cassa tonight; the notion she put in my head may yet show you great mercy."

To make a good magical tattoo, you need to have an understanding of flesh in general, but also the flesh of the one you're going to mark. There are many types of these tattoos; the assassin Sesta was covered in skin-runes and glyphs, each a sort of stored spell or ward. She was a walking grimoire. She had much of the power of a magicker, but the power was borrowed from others—all she had to learn to do was use it, not make it, which left her free to train her body into the fearsome thing it was.

My tattoo, a penalty mark, disappears in all but firelight. That sort's easy. The one who put it on me had been a lover of mine, which made it go fast.

One tattoo the Guild was famous for was a telling-mouth. Some mouths bore messages and would disappear when those messages had been discharged. Some translated languages, though these were hard to make and notoriously mischievous—it was said one had intentionally started a war. The most coveted sort, however, was a tattler; one of these mouths, paired with an eye and an ear, would report all you did and said and with whom you spent your time.

Of course, the key words were carefully guarded, but a good wizard could coax a telling-mouth to speak, so the Guild never put them on its own. As these things work out, many a jealous old dodderer had herself ruined when her pennygroom turned out to be a spy, witting or unwitting, and the same tattoo that reassured her of his fidelity sang her banking secrets away or disclosed enough about her to get her blackmailed or twinned by a mimic.

Of all our traits, the gods most hate jealousy because it makes us like them.

The hardest tattoos to make were sleepers, and that's what Galva bore. The corvid that leapt from her chest when she needed it existed in a sort of sleep-time, never aging, but drawing a certain amount of life from its bearer. Calling it forth hurt her, reabsorbing it hurt her; if it were injured, she could heal it by putting it back, though she would suffer some of its pain, which was what nearly undid her, absorbing some of the crushed bird's hurt on the goblin ship. I didn't know a very great deal about the art, but I knew enough to be impressed that Norrigal had nearly mastered it. For all her occasional bungles, she was already a damned impressive magicker at a young, young age. Little doubt she'd be a match for Deadlegs if she lived so long.

We stole upon the cat while he seemed to be sleeping, though it was hard to tell because the little bastard slept wide-eyed. Norrigal had taken a circle of leather and written charms on it; she sunk a drawstring in it to make a hood and fixed iron on it to bind. It was mine to approach the cat using the hood, but not to bring the hood out until I was ready to act. We came home near the night's exact middle. Malk and Galva were laughing drunkenly in the next room. The cat was perched under a table in the room I shared with Norrigal, seeming to keep vigil. If it were just the cat, he couldn't see a damned thing, but how was I to know? The Assassin-Adept *had* to be in him for our plan to work. Best to test him.

Norrigal lay down on the bed, feigning exhaustion, while I approached the cat.

"Hey-ho, Bully," I said and took out a fine, plump Middlesea snail I'd saved him, letting him smell it. He raoed his interest in it, and I used it to lead him from under the table. Tossing it against the far wall would have guaranteed his back was to me, but if the bitch were looking out his eyes, it would have seemed too suspicious. I had to do something *a little* suspicious. Right, the middle of the room it was. The snail landed with a fat plop. Bully bobbed his head snakelike, sniffing, then started for it, feeling his way along with each step. A change came over him as I watched him, and he stopped. He looked over at me. There was the sign I was looking for—the Assassin-Adept was moving him. Had I turned away from his gaze and pretended to occupy myself with something else, that would have looked too suspicious. But if I watched him placidly, perhaps lost in thought, that was just *a little* suspicious, and so I did. Norrigal lay as if on the verge of passing out.

Bully looked back at the snail and, instead of feeling his blind way there, slunk quickly to fetch it, then went under the bed. I listened for hacking but heard none. The assassin wasn't alarmed; she was letting him eat his prize. We knew from the way the sailors had nabbed Bully and tossed him over on the *Suepka Buryey* that he could be moved against swiftly, so now Norrigal, who had seemed halfway to sleep, sprang alert and alive and grabbed wee Bully by the tail.

Friends and lovers, this was a fight. I'll not describe the fury of clawing and biting that followed except to say that the better half of it was Norrigal's. In the end, she flailed poor Bully on the bed like she was trying to break him, getting her hips into it and all, and she managed to stun him and the evil thing he was hosting enough for me to get the hood on. The sleep-drugs she had crumbled up in the nose of it soon did their work, and Bully snored in his leather-and-iron hood while Norrigal bled and breathed hard. Her hair was a fright.

"Do you think he broke his back?" I said, picking up one of Bully's paws.

"Do you think I care?"

"I thought we agreed not to hurt him," I said.

She wiped a bit of blood off her scratched cheek and said, "We'll play a little game now. I'll pretend you didn't say that, and you pretend you're grateful you haven't a new knot on your head."

The door opened now, and Galva rushed in with her shield down and her *spadín* cocked over it. "*Quei chodaderias bain elchi?*" Her Holtish always suffered when she was drunk or agitated, and just now she was both.

What fuckery goes on here?

"Nothing," I said.

She looked at the hooded cat, then looked at Norrigal bleeding and panting. She saw her horrent elf-locks. The witch saw what she was looking at, spit in her hand, and smoothed down her hair. Galva shook her head and left, meeting Malk in the hallway. Malk asked what was going on.

"They commit some act with the cat in a mask; it is not my concern. I am going to bed."

The sound of a tattoo needle tapping is a particular sound, one that you won't forget, especially when you have to look at the reminder each day. The cat went on my arm, my left arm, between the elbow and the armpit. I could hide him as I pleased and look at him when I needed. If anything went wrong, and a lot could go wrong, better it was on a limb I could lose than close to my heart or other necessaries. Not that I relished the thought of spending my remaining days a beggar, which was what a one-armed thief could expect, but where there's life, there's pain. Or hope. I'm terrible at keeping my sayings in order.

Norrigal tap-tap-tapped that cat onto me in the space of about half a day, sweating over me the while despite the cold air. She mixed the ink with ash made from burned fur and clipped claws, along with other things she'd got in the magic quarter. A bit of caterpillar ichor (I don't know if it's really called *ichor*—she called it *goo*, but that hardly sounds thaumaturgic, does it?), kraken's ink for power, iron filings for binding. She spoke her spells in the language of the old Galts, a bit different from what we speak at home, but the best possible idiom for change magic.

When she started in with the ink and the tapping on her thorn, the magic feeling in the air got strong, and I saw a wondrous thing; it looked as though she'd caught a thread from the cat, who lay sleeping near me, and hooked that onto the thorn, and as she made the image, the real cat unraveled like wool. I watched it happen. She didn't outline the tattoo of the cat and fill in—she drew it entire starting at his tail and ending at the tip of his nose, and when she was halfway through, half a cat lay on the table near, still snoring his snore in his hood. When he was down to just a head, off came the hood, but she left sleep-herbs crumbled near his wee nose. He was breathing, I could see and feel his illustrated chest rising and falling on my biceps, and yet the air came and went from the head on the table where his whiskers moved and his eyes, closed at last, twitched under his lids. A fantastical business, magic—it's easy enough to see how it drives some mad.

Norrigal explained it all to me when the cat was gone to ink.

"You've not killed the killer. Whatever's in the cat exists now just as it did, only stilled and silent. Your living heart should power that rune of hers and make her seem alive to those who watch. Have a care, though—you may rouse the sleeper if you speak the cat's true name or the killer's."

"I don't know either."

"Then let's hope they're not so simple you say them accidental."

"How else might the spell come loose?"

"A witch could peel it off you and rouse it. A lightning storm could rouse it, no one knows why except that lightning comes from the hands of the gods direct, and they're with us when it sparks. If you die, it could die with you, or it could spring from you living, no one knows which. Careful of your dreams—the Spanth sleeps easy with her bird because it's not got a human mind in it and because it loves her. You've a hostile intelligence within you, and it may try to worm its way into your mind. Dreams would be the best way, because we're the least guarded then. If you sense yourself having a nightmare about the tattoo coming off you, especially if you bleed, wake yourself up, because it might be tearing itself off you to spill that killing bitch into your bed. But for now? They shouldn't have the first clue where she went. You've hid the killer twice. Once in a cat and the cat in you. She's as good as disappeared. When you're ready to kill her, you can. But no mistake; you'll need to kill her one day or the next. She's in your blood, and you in hers. If she gets out of you, she'll be able to find you wherever you go. Just by dreaming."

That night, I lay in my cold bed considering my options. I still had the Guild to answer to, and the first of Vintners was coming fast.

Try to make Hrava by the first of Vintners, two bright moons hence.

New moon had been the night before.

Just shy of two weeks left in the month.

Seventeen days.

Not enough time to get so far, I thought.

How late would I be?

A week?

Two?

The word *try* was encouraging, with its suggestion the Guild understood unforeseen events. Like a kraken taking a whaler. But how much grace would they afford me, with their assassin gone silent? How often did she normally communicate with them, if she did?

And what day would trigger my own unseen, unheard, but soon felt punishment?

The bastard of it was that I had no way to know.

Every day past the first of the month was dice rolled with ever worsening odds, and all that I loved on the table.

Trapping their assassin in my flesh would, for the moment, save my Norrigal getting killed, for I was sure that was Sesta's intention. If I left Galva, Malk, and Norrigal to their plan and went my own way, another Guildron would likely catch their trail and follow. The most obvious thing the Guild was after in sending me with Galva was getting their assassin near Queen Mireya, probably to kill her, but possibly to catch her. I had foiled this, though it would take them a while to figure it out.

My best chance was to help Galva do what she planned, for Norrigal was bound by Deadlegs to help the Spanth. Then I would take such money as I could to aid my flight. I couldn't lie to myself. I was utterly bollocksed. One way or the other, the Guild would find out what I did and make an example of me. Unless I disappeared. If they knew I betrayed them, my family would come to grief. But if I were simply gone, and the assassin with me? Any number of misfortunes might have befallen us, and they wouldn't waste time harming my kin when I might not have been at fault.

As for my chances to disappear, they increased with every step I took west. The Takers' power was greatest in the east; Ispanthia, Gallardia, and Holt—they were still formidable in the central nations of Middlesea, Istrea, Sadunther, and Unther—but Molrova, Wostra, and Beltia, in the west, were mere outposts.

Brayce, between Holt and Middlesea in the north, was another possibility, as it was nearly uninterrupted forest from end to end. The Guild had no interest in taming the wild Braycish clans, and less in the trading of deer skins and lumber. What good was a thief in a kingdom of hunters, woodsmen, and war chiefs, whose strange timber capital, Door, was not so populous as the third largest city in Holt? Unless I wanted to take up long-axe and bow and live in a fucking treehouse hung with antlers and the hacked-off arms of my enemies, I'd best keep west.

It was known the kingdom of Oustrim, where we were now heading, had outlawed the Guild and driven them underground. I would say exiled them, but there's no getting rid of the Takers— they just go into hiding, and there's nobody better at that, but their presence would be much diminished in Oustrim, and a careful man, particularly one with a witchlet's help, could likely slip their notice.

The problem with going west was that Oustrim was said to be full of giants and Molrova full of Molrovans. Still, disappearing takes luck and money, and the more of one you have, the less of the other you need. My best chance was to continue with Galva away from civilization and toward possible wealth.

Also, there was the very small matter of my being hopelessly enamored with Norrigal Na Galbraeth.

All roadsigns, every last one, pointed west.

43

The Ispanthian Army

---•---

We left Edth on donkeys we bought at great expense; four for us
to ride, one for baggage, and a sixth for the mysterious Spanth
Galva hoped for us to acquire when we met her army. Even with
the beasts, it was a cold, miserable business getting to the western edge of Middlesea. We stayed on the White Road laid by the
Kesh, this in the last flat part of the country, where oxen, asses,
and, on the poorest farms, packs of muddy children strained at
plows to plant the year's last roots and onions. When the land
turned rocky, we were glad for the donkeys, who proved sure-
footed if occasionally ill-tempered. I was bitten on the arm by
my foul mount in a misunderstanding over a radish, and nobody
would trade me donkeys.

We soon found ourselves in the Shorn Hills, through which
the pewter-colored Vornd River cut. The best meal of the journey
was had in those hills, a merry little goat who was good enough
to accept my arrow through both lungs near a patch of wild mint.
The worst was a bunch of green apples that puckered our mouths
up miserable but didn't afflict us with the squats, gods bless their
Cassine mercy. We all stored some of these away for later.

On the sixth day out of Edth, we saw smoke and banners
near the river, just near the Beaten Man, a rocky tor said to have
been cursed. It looked cursed. It looked exactly like its name, all
hunched shoulders and spilled rocks like an abstraction of tears.
Galva brightened when she saw the smoke, then brightened further when she saw the banners bore the bull of Ispanthia, not the
cornered eight-point star of Holt.

Tents in scarlet and silver littered the banks, tents of gold at the hilltop, where the largest banner flew. It was very near dusk, and the light of the failing sun was pretty on the river, though not so pretty as the smell of garlic and olive oil coming from the cookfires of the Ispanthian army. A party of scouts sprinted down from the hilltop to meet us, two lads and a lass with black hair and disapproving eyebrows very much like Galva's, bullnutters at their belts and shields at their backs.

One look at Galva's seal and they bowed proper, the challenge in their approach traded for camaraderie as they led us toward the tent of the commander. Someone was playing an Ispanthian cornemuse, the pipes high and sweet, and a woman sang with it, though too softly to be heard even had I known her words, which I didn't.

Glad faces loomed up for a look at Galva, and many a warm embrace slowed her, though she could not have insulted the waiting general by stopping. We three foreigners were suffered to come with her at least to the guarded perimeter. After some negotiation, we ascended to the tent, its flap folded open to show a haven of candlelight alive with the smell of roast meat. A quartet of women who resembled Galva in passing, though far taller and broader through the chest and more stoutly armored, assured the entrance, and two of them followed us in. We were not made to surrender our weapons. Ispanthians were too proud for a practical measure like that—Galva was known, and we were her responsibility, however rough we looked after nine days in the field.

And so, with a brief announcement, I was let into a tent of cloth-of-gold, an opulent tent containing an opulent man, the Count Marevan da Codorezh en Nadan, general of the Fourth Wing, the head of six thousand Spanth light infantry and eight hundred archers. My chief concern upon entering was how to discreetly get a stubborn bit of sheepshyte off my boot, and I think I managed all right by sort of scraping it up against the other boot and tramping a bit on the grass. If anyone noticed, they were too polite to make it obvious.

This wasn't my first time seeing a general, but it was my first of the Ispanthian sort. The count was a small-boned man with a withering gaze he often shifted forward in his seat to deliver. He was old, too, of an age to have fought in the Knights' War. That was the first of the three Goblin Wars—the one we were so proud to have won, not knowing how much worse their second go at us would be. Anyway, this geezer will have been one of those still crying in his wine for the feel of a horse between his legs and looking down his nose at the younger bunch who'd damned near lost half the continent. I didn't know how many battles he'd won, but his tailor and armorer couldn't be faulted. A steel breastplate etched with lions rearing up to fight each other embraced a slate-gray velvet doublet with a high collar, his sleeves studded with buttons alternating copper and gold.

Though he was cordial to us, he held his conversation with Galva in Ispanthian so formal and rapid I only snared a half dozen words. *Giants, mountains, war, honor, quail,* and *wine.* We ate quail and drank wine. Giants, war, and mountains were on their way. If honor decided to attend our adventures, I only hoped I'd recognize her; she'd been pointed out to me a few times, but we'd never really gotten acquainted.

The second tent I followed Galva to was spun of crude hemp, not silk or cloth-of-gold. Dinner here had not been quail but mutton, and the smoke the opening flap released was not incense but taback, a foul but stimulating plant smoked in the south and east. There were no guards here but the lone occupant.

Galva's swordmaster, or Calar Saram, was a far more interesting person than the count. I had the impression the count and Galva, though bound to civility, were neutral to one another at best, Galva's father having been the man's rival for this or that post. Not so with the instructor at sword, who was a short, thick-middled tree trunk of fifty, missing teeth and scarred like the last gourd in the market. She smoked her taback not in a pipe but in a rolled stump that glowed hot at the end when she sucked on it.

"*Corme seu dalgatha,*" she said when she saw Galva.

She hit her in the chops with a meaty hand and blew smoke out the side of her mouth. She looked at we three behind her and quickly took our measure. "*Holteshi?*"

"*Galtesi,*" I said, but something about the way I said it made her squint and switch to Holtish. Mostly.

"You three are skinny also. You starve with my Galva? Hey? *Vosu cravit nourid?* You want food?"

"We ate," I said.

"Then smoke," she said and stuck her wet stump of taback in my mouth. I'd had it before; I didn't care for it. But I sucked on it and half retched but wouldn't let myself cough.

"Good!" she said. "You cough, you are weak testicles."

"Have," Galva corrected.

"*Ai, os,* you cough, you are half-testicles. Now give me this back; it is not for finishing to you."

I liked her.

I wished I spoke Ispanthian just so I wouldn't have to hear her Holtish, but I liked her.

We spoke friendly for half an hour. Nadalle Seri-Orbez, called Yorbez, the swordmaster, smoked and laughed and switched between Ispanthian and Holtish, sometimes speaking a mix of the two. She shared around a ball-shaped flask of Braycish liquor made from pears, though it was more burning than sweet, and she asked us about ourselves. She seemed to care about the answers. I saw nothing obvious to indicate she was a fighter, except perhaps a ropiness of the forearms and a way of moving that wasted no motion. At first glance, anyone who did not know that Galva called her master would take her for a sort of cook or innkeeper. A sword belt and sword hung from a hook on a wooden stand, and when she saw me looking at it, she said, "You know how to use that?"

"I'm better with a knife," I said.

"You have to be much better with the knife if your adversity have the sword."

"I prefer peaceful negotiations."

She laughed and slapped me good-naturedly in the jaw in such a way that actually hurt. "Os? This work with the goblin, this talk?"

"I've spoken with one," I said.

"It go well?"

"I lived."

"Because you stab him while you talk?"

"Actually, I shot him with an arrow." I thought about this, then corrected. "Two arrows."

"Good. Is the best talk for them."

She and Galva exchanged a few sentences in Ispanthian, looking at me and the others in such a way I was sure they were deciding whether to ask us to excuse ourselves. In the end, she settled her eyes on Malk. Galva said to him, "Do not take offense at this please, but she would like you to go outside and away for a short time."

"Bugger me, then," he said jovially enough, and got to his feet. "I'll just find a Towers game to lose my new shirt at." Out the tent flap he went, whistling so we could hear he was gone.

The woman looked at me and at Norrigal.

Then back at me.

"Right," I said and got to my feet.

"No," Galva said, and I sat down again.

"Why?" I said.

"I explained to her that you are married to the witch now."

"Only for a month."

"Three weeks left," Norrigal said.

"And she would tell him, anyway."

"Depends what it was," I said.

"That's right," Norrigal said, "I can keep a secret from the likes of him."

"It's true," I said. "She doesn't tell me a damn thing. Should I go?"

"Is true you are with the Grabbers?" Yorbez asked.

"Takers."

"Yes, I see the hand on your face for the hitting."

"I more often feel it."

She took a moment to process this, then went "Ha!" hitting me with her heavy hand-heel again. I'd have to remember to joke with her less.

"No," she said, "you stay. You stay for this. Soon we will go to Grevitsa to meet with another thief, also once with your Grabbers. She have for us a map we need."

"After that," Galva said, "we will see a magicker in the Bittern Mountains. These magickers are with us, not with your Guild, and with the queen."

And then they planned their treason against King Kalith.

I learned much I hadn't known about that mustachioed bastard.

For example, nobody was allowed in his inner rooms with their own clothes or jewelry on; they were all given beautiful but light linen gowns or shirts to wear, and they were escorted by *gailus du cuth,* or knife-boys. These were orphan lads who were utterly loyal to the king in the way only twelve-year-olds can be, trained from toddlerhood in the mysteries of knife-fighting. When you went to see the king, one of these escorted you, walking in your blind spot, steering you by the belt. One look from Kalith, and quick as clapping, you'd be hamstrung or kidneyed by the wee darling behind you.

Galva said she'd heard of a rare Axaene brassworm kept in a

labyrinth below the palace, and that's where servants who failed in their duties would go as Kalith watched their scalding and eating from above. Kalith was a darling of the Guilds, and assassins were at his beckon, as well as magickers. He had a forty-year-old mare these wizards kept alive at great expense, and he rode her out on state occasions, though she clearly suffered and barely held him.

The last conspirators against him had been found out by means no one ever learned. It's said their bones were liquefied and they were sealed undying in glass amphorae he visits from time to time, reading poetry to.

By the time I heard an evening's worth about Kalith, I was practically an Ispanthian rebel without benefit of being fucking Ispanthian.

I thought about Mireya, growing up with this villain for an uncle, talking to monkeys and yelling at the sky to stay alive.

Some home life.

After this sort of talk, of course I dreamed dark dreams.

44

A Bone in the Throat

———•———

I was home. My mother had just served a roast hen and a pottage of peas and barley, the top shiny with drippings from the bird. It was a luxury, eating a bird. We smeared the stew on our trenchers and took small bits of the chicken, there being eight of us, my father first, mother next, three brothers, me, two sisters, and the one orphan boy we'd taken in who'd run away after only a year. Geals, his name was.

My da was moving slow from his bad joints, drinking beer so fast he'd have to go out and piss loudly against the wall before the meal was over, and before long at all, he'd get to telling us how this was his house and we'd best show him some respect. The little orphan lad was showing us his food while my mother rebuked him for it. She had curly hair, my mother, and it never behaved. She'd try to tie it up out of her face, and a strand would always come untucked and she'd blow at it while my little sister went on about how the goat deviled her or were clouds made of wool or she didn't ever want a husband unless it was a boy with blond hair because she fancied blond hair.

Then my sister stopped jabbering and said to me, very serious, "You'll watch the bones now, Kinch. Mother said this hen's bad for bones."

I said, "The hell you say. All hens are boned alike, it's the beauty of 'em. You can go anywhere in the world and open up a hen, and they've put bones in the same place, just like home."

"Mother said this one's boned particular."

"Boned particular," I said back to let her know how that sounded coming out of her, and I swallowed a bite of the wing. What do you know, but I felt a tickle in my throat now, a sharp tickle, and I wanted to say, "Godsdamn it all, I've a bone in my throat," but that's the chief embarrassment of choking; there's no talking. I coughed, though, which means I wasn't choking proper.

I coughed horrible and painful and bloody, and now everyone was staring at me, except da, who kept eating because, screw you, he works in the silver mine all day so someone else can deal with the ungrateful blood-cougher. Now it felt as though the bone was actually poking through my throat, so I bugged my eyes and clutched at it—my throat, I mean—so the bone stuck my hand.

My sister, Shavoen, said, "You see, Mother, I told him about this hen."

"Boned particular," she agreed and blew a lock of hair out of her eyes.

"He doesn't listen."

Then I realized it wasn't a bone poking me at all but a knife. A knifepoint was stabbing out of my throat, and I tried to remember the handcant for *My throat's being cut open from the inside out,* but I'd honestly never had to use that before.

"You'll be in the shyte for making a mess now," Shavoen said, and I tried to tell her how she shouldn't swear, especially at the table, but all I could do was wheeze blood all over the chicken.

"What?!" my dead, deaf stepbrother shouted. He was wearing the reeve's shirt he'd stolen.

Now a voice from my throat said, "Take me to the looking-brass," so up I went to the sheet of polished brass on the wall near mother's clothes-trunk and had a look at myself. I looked all right except for a pint or so of blood all over my shirt and a cut in my throat and a knife poking out of the cut and a pair of eyes behind it. Now a mouth appeared in the cut in my throat and spoke out of it.

"See here," she said, because of course it was the Assassin-Adept, "you're going to let me out of you, or I'll cut my way out and kill those cunnies at the table."

"You'll kill my moon-wife if I free you," I said, and I almost said something about how we were supposed to go and find Mireya so she could be queen of Ispanthia and fuck the Guild over, then remembered that would be bad.

"You were going to say something?" she said.

"No," I said.

"You sure?"

"Yes."

"Where were we?"

"You said you'd kill my family."

"Right," she said. "Would you rather I kill the witchlet or your family?"

And I said, "You'll do neither," which angered her and she cut me open, throat to navel, like a fish. She put a booted foot through my stomach like she was going to step out of me onto the floor, and I remember being angry that normally she went everywhere barefoot and nude but for her tattoos, but she had worn big, heavy boots today just for the pleasure of stepping all over my guts. The pain was breathtaking, and I coughed and choked and sputtered and woke up sputtering hot blood in my mouth.

Only it wasn't blood, just awful bile from the pear liquor of Yorbez.

Malk groaned his annoyance at having been awakened and hit me with a boot. I didn't want to see a boot at all, as you'll imagine, so I gathered up my leather jerkin, which I'd been sleeping on, and headed out from the strange tent into the night to look west at the stars over Molrova, which seemed no better or worse than the stars behind me over Middlesea.

The plan was to leave in the morning and ride our donkeys hard toward the land of pretty lies.

45

Blood to Milk

———— · ————

If I had any worry that one of Yorbez's age might hold us up, they were put to rest watching the industry with which she conducted her morning exercise just before dawn. First, she ran to the top of the hill and back to get her blood up. Then she tied a rope between two trees and did a sort of dance around and under it, ducking, then striking up with sword and shield, ducking, then striking up. Made me tired just to watch.

Then she and Galva sparred with several students, including Malk, using wooden swords, and that was a brutal business. Malk did all right for himself against most, but he was easily outclassed by both Galva and her mistress. I wonder if he got a chill to think back on the duel he'd nearly fought with Galva—it was pretty clear from the sparring that it wouldn't have gone well for him.

I confess I hadn't thought much of Yorbez to look at her, but when it comes to fighting, it isn't always the most fit-looking geezer that wins. Yorbez was only fast when she had to be, and then it was blinding. When she fought Malk and the younger Spanths, she ducked, reversed directions, cracked knees, got behind her adversary, all while never seeming terribly bothered. You couldn't put your finger on *why* each exchange ended with the other eating wood; it looked like luck, but of course, it wasn't. She just seemed to casually fall into place where she was supposed to be and feed the other one a sword or a heel or an elbow.

Her tough wooden bullnutter whacked one girl in the chest so hard she gritted her teeth and dropped her sword, which earned her a crack across the back of the knee that dropped her to the ground. Yorbez, hot from the fight, stripped off her shirt. I was standing near Galva at the time and couldn't stop myself from saying:

"Why are you and Yorbez *both* missing your tits?"

Galva flicked me an eaglish side-eye, then went back to watching the sparring field. Malk was stepping up for another round with Yorbez. "We took the cut of Dalgatha."

"You mean . . ."

She nodded and chopped over each of her own pectorals to illustrate.

"By the crooked pricks of goblins all. I thought you were injured in the war or the like."

Galva shook her head. "I took the cut when I was twenty, before I marched to Gallardia. The Skinny Woman loves a dam who prefers blood to milk."

As if to illustrate how very loved by Dalgatha she was, Yorbez kicked Malk's leg out from under him and landed heavily on his chest with a squat, grinning and tickling his neck with the wooden point of the bullnutter.

She let Malk up and motioned for Galva, saying something in Ispanthian that made the rest laugh. All but Malk, that is, who brushed himself off and limped over to me, saying, "You want to give the old bird a go?"

"Fuck if I will," I said.

"Fuck if I should have. It's got to be magic."

"I didn't see any magic," I said.

"It's the only explanation," he said.

"Is it?" I said. "I saw her run up and down a hill for breakfast while you were lying in, sorting out whether to pick your arse or scratch your nuts."

"Magic," he said, and spat, and limped off.

He missed a hell of a show.

Galva and Yorbez fought so pretty with their deerlike Calar Bajat leaps, whip-turns, skip-lunges, and the lightning-fast leg-sweeps that dropped soldiers of every nation on their arse, I'm not even sure who won.

We broke camp soon after and crossed the border into Molrova.

46

City of Lace

———— • ————

In the country, we met priests of dark gods, bounty hunters, rabbit-skinners, Angrani tribeswomen who'd made their wild hair tall with dried mud, root farmers, lake-fishers, cidermen who drank too much of their work, and too-jovial woodcutters who cast covetous eyes on our donkeys.

I can't speak for the others, but a tour of rural Molrova left me ready for a bed and a hot meal in a city.

Shame that city was fucking Grevitsa.

The plan was to meet with a thief there who'd sell us a map of Oustrim's giant-sacked capital, Hrava. But not just any map—this one was supposed to chart the city's maze of sewers.

And with Hrava invested by giants, knowing how to skitter under the streets could be the difference between life and that other thing. If it were accurate, this map would be worth our weight in gold.

Maybe even worth going to this rotten little hole of a town.

Grevitsa sat on an island in the Spine River with five bridges across one side and two across the other. The island was such a good natural fortress, it was said to be two thousand years old. It's a good thing most people only live to be about sixty, because nobody'd want to spend two thousand years with those twats.

The whole town was the color of cheerful mud, sort of gray-brown shot through with bits of red or the odd flower pot. The most carefully made and delicate lace in Manreach lay displayed like the webs of divine spiders in shops that fronted on streets patrolled by garbage-eating pigs who'd nip at you if you came too close.

The pigs had earrings or brands to indicate their ownership, and if you carved a slice of bacon off one, you'd answer to the swineherd, most of them tough ex-soldiers who'd received pigs as part of their twenty-year retirement. Remember, Molrova stayed clear of the Goblin Wars, so if these men knew less of killing goblins than Spanths or Gallards did, they had fought enough feudal actions against one another in the meantime that they were no strangers to killing kynd.

Molrova was also known for amber, exquisite faceted teardrops of which hung from the throats of ladies while unworked hunks of it made belts for laundresses and tavern maids.

The real arsehole of Grevitsa, though, was the fact that biters lived there. As in, the vile, sharp-toothed, hook-armed, man-butchering, horse-killing, high-nut horrors that made the last forty years hell for all kynd everywhere were allowed to buy *property* here.

The Goblin Quarter stood near the harbor.

Its boundaries were marked with chains and warning signs in three languages; neither the king's law nor the Horde's would save those who left their own quarter. Such goblins as killed men behind their boundary faced only Horde law. Such goblins as wandered into the streets of Manreach did so at their peril. And yet risk weighs itself against profit, and there was profit to be made in dealing with the enemy.

Good profit indeed.

We found an inn, stabled our donkeys, and got to business.

The thief we had come to meet was an expatriate Spanth who now *lived with* goblins, in their quarter, an expert in their rasping, high speech. She met us in a Molrovan Tavern called Barana Morzhaxh, which meant, as near as I can tell, "the Man-Faced Ram," because such was the image on the sign that swung over the iron-studded door, which had a smaller, goblin-sized door set within it. The windows were grated with iron, and skulls both goblin and kynd hung on the wall behind the bar below a rusty Molrovan long-axe. Busted skulls. Words weren't really needed, but if you insist, *All transgressors beaten equally* seemed to be the moral.

One thing I couldn't help noticing in the tavern was the abundance of men. And not just whelps of twenty-two or less—these were shipwrights, soldiers, smiths, all out drinking and dicing with beer-sogged beards, making the walls rumble with their low voices and their bellicose laughter. These were not veterans, not of the Goblin Wars, at least. Molrova had sent no levies to the second or third musters, so those levies had not been bitten, poisoned, stabbed, tusked by boars, cloven in two by blind ghalls, their stripped bones left in the dirt of Gallardia and Ispanthia or sewn onto goblin banners. I did not stand out, with my twenty-three years and my full complement of fingers.

I was in a whole country of slippers.

Molrovans were a bunch of selfish karks, just like me.

The Ispanthian thief told us her name was Chedadra, or Ched, which meant something like "rough fucker." Rough Fucker had cheekbones that could cut glass, a war axe on her belt, horse's teeth sewn into her dreadlocked hair, and a badly painted false eye. She was also missing the tip of her nose, which meant some Spanth or other had caught her stealing.

Fucker's street Ispanthian was so clipped and rapid that Galva seemed barely able to follow her, let alone myself, but she gave Ched a fair bag of silver, which she weighed approvingly, and a piece of hexagonal amber with an ant lion in it. This the thief pressed against her cheek and neck with such gratitude I thought Galva might be in for a rough fuck, and she seemed to think so, too, from the way she crossed her legs toward the door and scooted her chair back.

Rather than a lesson in how illiterate killers show their Sornian love for raven knights, what Galva got for us was, as promised, a map of Oustrim's capital, Hrava, which indeed included the sewers, as well as a bonus—the name of a non-Guild thief who might help us when we got there, if said thief had not yet been found and pulped by giants.

Ürmehen.

The Upright Man, or king of thieves.

I let my attention drift out the grated window of the Man-Faced Ram and toward the goblin quarter. Night was coming on, and the biters lit no lanterns, for they needed none to see, but I could still make out their warped, irregular buildings. I espied one or two of the nasties going about their business, moving in their arrhythmic but strangely graceful way. It gave you a headache to look at. I understood that half of Goblintown was likely underground, for they were fond of tunnels, and I could only imagine how bewildering those must have been. I was torn between a thief's curiosity to see them and a very human desire not to go where I'm like to be eaten.

Little wonder that Ched was mad; whether her madness made her tolerant of life with the Horde or whether it came to her as a result of it was anybody's guess, but nobody sane chooses to live with creatures who spend half their time thinking about how delicious your thigh meat would be served raw with a bowl of poison mushrooms.

I looked away from the confusion of Goblintown, and my eyes lighted on the barman, a big fellow with a greasy lace collar. His face looked recently smelted, and his hand had been tattooed black. He had lived among the biters, too, then, with them in their Hordelands. He looked at me, and I nodded. He just kept looking, and I thought about winking at him, but disappointed the god of mischief by turning my gaze away. Mischief wasn't chief god here. Here they worshipped murder, and murder wore fine lace.

With the other business concluded, Ched surprised the lot of us by offering to sell us a magical ring. Galva waved her off at first, but Ched insisted that the other Spanth translate for us.

"What's it do?" Norrigal and I asked in unison.

Ched spoke, then Galva said, "She says it fires lightning. Just one bolt, but deadly."

I looked closely at it. White gold with a sort of iron trench down the middle, probably sky-iron from a fellstone. Runes in it from the Gunnish Islands promising Wolthan's vengeance.

"Why get rid of it?" Norrigal said. "A thing like that could save your life, if it works." But Norrigal was looking at it the same way I was—neither one of us had any question that it did *something*. It prickled the hairs on both our necks.

"She says she needs money more than to have her life saved. She is in debt to a goblin priest. One lightning strike won't protect her from that."

The price she asked seemed low for magic on that order.

Norrigal and I looked at each other.

I was thinking maybe Rough Fucker was not sensitive to magic and wasn't sure it worked. But she wouldn't want us to *know* she didn't know, so she asked the highest price she thought she could actually get at a negotiation in a tavern. Which was still a bargain for what it probably was.

"How'd you get it?" Norrigal said, but I grabbed Galva's arm and shook my head at her before she translated. That's not something you ask a thief.

Norrigal handed over a gold queening and two silver knights in Middlesea coin, which was the same as Holt used.

Rough Fucker tasted the money, then made it disappear.

She handed the ring to Norrigal, who found it too large for any finger but her thumb, so that's where she wore it.

We left the bar, happy with the way the evening had gone so far, Norrigal admiring the magical ring from time to time on the sly. I was admiring Norrigal from time to time on the sly.

Galva kept her eyes open, her hand never too far from her wicked sword. Yorbez smoked her taback stub. Malk was walking in a way particular to young bravos, but perfected nowhere so well as in the Galtish lands of Holt. There's a way a blacktongue tough sometimes walks, each step a small kick, so that the torso sways just a little. The word *swagger* nearly embraces that walk, but misses an element of boredom, mischief, a hope for something out of the ordinary to please happen whatever the cost.

It's like a small, dark physical prayer.

Such prayers rarely go unanswered.

47

The Pull

———— • ————

We skirted the chain dividing the goblin quarter from Grevitsa proper, not because we wanted to be so near the biters but because that was the easiest way to find our guesthouse near the bakery again.

But we weren't home smelling mutton pasties yet.

We were still following the chain by the goblin quarter with a different smell entirely in our noses. If you haven't smelled goblins, I can't tell you what it's like, because it's like nothing else from our world. We'll just say you might gag the first half dozen times, and you'll never forget it.

One of the things to know about Malk is that he *looks* like he fought in the Goblin Wars. It's not just his fingers and his age. It's in his eyes and in the way he moves. People can tell. And so can goblins. As we skirted the chain, the smell of the biters doubtless stirring memories for him and Galva, a goblin began walking along with us on its side of the chain, keeping pace with us. It was a larger one, more than four feet tall, its gray-brown hide scarred and puckered as if by fire. It seemed at first to be minding its own business or, rather, like it wanted us to think so.

A Molrovan called something to us from his window, motioned at us. Clearly a warning to move away. Seemed like a good idea to me.

"Maybe we should get farther away from the chain," I said.

"Why, 'cause a' him?" Malk said. "Fuck him."

He walked a little closer.

So did the biter.

"Get away from that thing, you idiot," Norrigal said.

"Nobody's telling you where to walk," Malk said.

"You're right," said she and crossed the muck in the middle of the street to walk in the dryer bit on the other side.

I wanted to cross with her only slightly less than I wanted not to seem like I had her ring in my nose, so I kept walking near Malk, but I said to Galva, "You think this is a good idea?"

She shook her head but kept walking on the chain side of the street. I noticed that other shapes were stirring on the goblin side, some two or three of them now keeping pace, but a bit farther off.

Now it spoke. It didn't look at us, but said, "*Molroviniy?*"

Were we Molrovan.

When we didn't answer it said, "*Untheriy?*"

Were we from Unther.

"I'm from 'go fuck yourself, biter.' Where are *you* from?"

It said, "Holt. You Holt man, blondie."

"Don't talk to it!" Norrigal said.

"Galtia. What's it to you?"

"I know you. From war."

"I doubt it."

"This is enough," Yorbez said, tugging at Malk's elbow, but he shook her off. She shrugged and crossed to walk near Norrigal.

Several Molrovans had gathered on our side and were speaking to us, clearly calling us away, but there was one laughing and pointing us toward the chain. I wanted to cross the street but knew damned well Malk wouldn't.

"What are they saying?" I asked him.

"Warning me I'm going to get in a *pull.*"

"What's a *pull*? And would you please get on the less stupid side of the road over here with me, please?

"Fuck that biter if he thinks I'm crossing a road on his account," he said and glared at the goblin, which still wasn't looking at him. If it had pockets, its hands would have been in them, such was the air of nonchalance it was trying to cultivate.

"Yes," it rasped. "You. Friend. I eat. I eat you friend, blondie." It showed him its teeth.

Malk reached for his sword now, but two of the shapes on the goblin side stepped forward with their wicked little crossbows. Several more showed they had knives. They appeared quickly. Galva pulled her *spadín*. Yorbez was crossing the street back toward us now.

But the goblin by the chain seemed unconcerned.

"No weapon," it said. "No bite. You want, you *pull*."

Still without looking at us, it raised its arm over the chain.

Malk let go his sword.

"Don't do it, you idiot," Norrigal said, though she knew good and well he would.

"Pull. Coward. I kill you like friend," the thing said. "I think you scream. Friend scream. Pull. Pull!"

Now Malk grabbed its arm.

It grabbed Malk's forearm with its other arm, sinking the hooklike talon on the left forearm in.

Malk yelled and pulled it off its feet, like a father yanking up a naughty child. He got it over the chain, but then it tangled up its feet in the chain, anchoring it. Now three or four goblins ran up, fast, they were so fast, grabbing the legs of their compatriot. They heaved and pulled it back half its body length. Malk lost his balance and headed for the chain. We all grabbed him just as the chain caught him in the thighs, and started pulling him back. But more goblins came. Now five, now six were yanking on their friend, and he wasn't letting go of Malk's arm for all the mushrooms in Urrimad.

Norrigal piled on, as well as some Molrovan who smelled of fish and had scales on his apron. Molrovans were coming from their houses and from the many taverns on the street. Women appeared in windows, banging pots with wooden spoons, and the alarm was taken up on other blocks. Some smaller Grevitsani held bows at the ready, making me wish I hadn't left mine in my room, but none shot. I later learned it was death by hanging to fire a missile into Goblintown unprovoked, or to strike first with a weapon over the chain, or at any biter who had some part of his body on the other side of it. It was all very formal. This happened several times a year. Not everybody was good-hearted enough to warn foreigners about it—Grevitsani liked a good pull. It was far more entertaining than their other favorite sport, batting a dead, frozen dog around with a stick.

Malk was beginning to suffer now. Only the one goblin was allowed to touch him, and it couldn't bite, but the stress on his back and shoulders was building. The Grevitsani did their best to share the torque around by pulling on his belt, his hair, getting under him and grabbing him by the waist. He was horizontal now, and so was the biter. The goblins had been faster piling on and were winning—Malk's head and shoulders were over, and the one who had him by the arms grinned sharp teeth at him, even opened its mouth to waggle its rude, armored little tongue at him.

The Coldfoot guard grunted and sweated. Grevitsani had poured on now, bigger, stronger folk taking the place of the less powerful. Like me. I was roughly pried off him by a bald, beardy fellow with black teeth and upper arms the size of my thighs. I did as others did and grabbed *his* belt even as someone grabbed mine. Galva still had Malk by one boot. Norrigal and Yorbez had been pushed off entirely. Malk had a nosebleed. His hands on the thing's arms had gone white. It was yelling in its own language at its fellows because now *it* was halfway over the chain. They were losing. If we could get the goblin wholly past the chain, we could do with it as we pleased, and nothing would please this lot more than pulling this biter's head off. A cheer went up from our side as the creature's knees passed the chain.

That's when things went sour. Another goblin, a very long-armed one, slid under the chain so only its feet were on the other side, and it grabbed the arm of the boy under Malk, sinking its hook in. The boy yelled and let go of Malk, and a wave went through the goblin Horde as some of them left off pulling Malk's goblin and started tugging the second one. This was now a two-front fight, and that was terrible news for Malk. All the mighty Molrovans who had been yanking him from his doom now left off him and grabbed the beefy lad being pulled under the chain, some of them saying his name.

I rushed for Malk's receding legs but was blocked by others rushing to save their own. I saw Norrigal reaching for a vial of something or other, but a woman who had been beating on her pot with a spoon now hit Norrigal with that pot and knocked her down, yelling at her in Molrovan and pointing at the chain. Apparently, magic was illegal in these matters as well.

Malk yelled as his knees crossed the chain. Galva had hold of Malk's ankle, but now a goblin unhusked Malk's foot from his boot. As Malk slipped away, a big Molrovan man grabbed Galva by the waist and pulled her back. She screamed and flailed him with the empty boot until he was forced to let her go.

Closer to me, the Grevitsani pullers had managed to yank their boy back, without his pants, which had torn completely off him. The goblin who had grabbed him was now clear of the chain; his fellows left him to his fate and all joined in on Malk.

Galva chucked the boot at the man who had grabbed her, drew her sword now, and plunged for the chain, but she was tackled and disarmed by more massive Grevitsani, who held her until it was clearly too late. To their credit, they gave her the sword back. To hers, she didn't kill the lot of them with it. When she swore at them in Ispanthian, they just swore back in Molrovan and went laughing to help dismember the hapless goblin.

What the men did to the goblin was no better than what the goblins did to Malk. In fact, it was worse. Malk they valued as meat. The goblin was less than shyte to men.

I gathered up Norrigal, whose head was bleeding, and Yorbez led Galva off as she sheathed the sword that had been no use to her and said a prayer of praise to her Skinny Woman. Galva was smiling. This angered me at first until I remembered that she was really a believer—she believed life was a kind of virginity, to be defended until the wedding day, then joyfully given over. Our friend Malk had been married now, and he and Dalgatha were celebrating as intimately and pleasantly as any young bride and groom. That or, if the Galts were right, he was being piped off by Samnyr, Lord of the Gloaming, to run in the Cold Forest, as free from right and wrong as any deer.

That or he was just gone.

It looked to me like he was gone.

I glanced back one more time at the scene of the fight, which was rapidly emptying. One thing you won't know about big fights unless you've seen one is what a great litter they leave on the ground. Two young girls were sharing a torch, looking for the wink of silver or copper in the street, and gleaning such other items as people dropped or had torn from them. I saw one fellow, covered in goblin blood, reel the snake of his belt up from the street's turned earth and wrap it around his muddied, bloodied pants. The meaty lad who'd been saved was now headed off to tavern with what looked like his uncles mussing his hair and laughing that he'd pissed himself.

I hated Grevitsa, and I hated goblins worse, and I hated the rashness of men that let wars and waste cull us so. I'd have liked to report that Malk died bravely saving Galva's infanta, but no. On the thirty-third day of Lammas, 1233 Years Marked Since the Knock, Malk Na Brannyck died in a stupid bit of bloodsport in a muddy Molrovan alley, and none but us mourned him because a goblin's death was more entertaining than a stranger's life. Selfish Grevitsa, ugly for all your lace and amber. Stupid, witless, dear Malk; he had but thirty years behind him, and thirty more might have been purchased for the price of crossing the street.

As far as I knew, his mother was living; she'd had him at fourteen. If I ever got back to Platha Glurris, sure and I'd see her. Would I even tell her I'd met up with him again, knowing the story led here? No. He'd died on the wreck of the *Suepka Buryey*, which I'd heard about but not seen. That's what I'd tell her. Better her boy drowned than got fed to biters seven years after the wars. A sorry, godsawful business either way.

It wasn't until we got back to our lodgings that I realized I was holding Malk's boot.

I didn't remember picking it up.

We left Grevitsa the next day.

48

The Bitterns

———•———

We took a sail-raft from Grevitsa to Rastiva, and it was a good thing Galva had a fat purse from the sale of the goblin ship in Edth, because we had to hire the whole boat to get the donkeys on. It saved us time, though, and both Galva and I had cause to hurry. It only took us two days and a night to get to the capital of Molrova, which sat where the Spine River met the Gunnish Sea.

Rastiva. We pulled up to her docks on the thirty-sixth and last of Lammas. I was supposed to be in Hrava tomorrow, but the way the false girleen at the Hanger's House had said it, it sounded more like a goal than a command. With luck, the Takers wouldn't be after my blood just yet.

As with all capitals, there was no other city just like Rastiva, but those who prefer cities will find it more familiar than any small village back home. The official color of Rastivan nobility was blue, so all the houses up the hill were painted some shade of it, the newer ones darker, but most of them proudly faded to a handsome robin's-egg hue.

The skies were so full of slate-gray clouds and the high houses such a brilliant, pale blue, I remember thinking the city looked upside down. Under the three hills of Rastiva, the elegance of the people thereon diminishing with altitude, the lesser city roiled with noise and color.

In lower Rastiva, we met cardsharps and courtesans, embittered clowns and bear baiters; we had pointed out to us two of the king's rumored hundred bastard sons, these two apparently older than the king, and though it was death to speak of the un-natural magic that preserved him, we heard no less than four theories on the subject. We spent the afternoon replenishing our stocks of food and repairing our gear and clothes. That evening, Yorbez brought home a boy-whore with a handsome false smile and kicked Galva out, so the three of us played dice while trying to ignore the sounds of them in the next room.

At first light the next morning, I saw the whorelet washing makeup from his face at the yard's pump-well. He was just a bit younger than me. He turned his weary face my way as I stalked to the jakes, and though it wasn't candlelight, I could only just make out the shape of a rose tattooed on his cheek. Poor fucker had once thought himself a thief, but now the Guild had whored him. He was doing his armpits as I crossed back to my room. I flipped him a copper shave, and he snatched it from the air with-out meeting my eyes.

We left that day, the first of Vintners, heading for a small line of mountains called the Bitterns; these would be the last real mountains before the Thralls. The narrow kingdom of Oustrim would lie between, thick with pine forests and golden with un-killable wheat that fed Molrova and Middlesea when their crops faltered. Now, of course, overrun with giants. The air was grow-ing colder as the second month of fall came on, and faint traces of snow could be seen in the rock pleats, promising freezing nights and carefully husbanded fires.

Once, as we were marching along, I thought about those big-guns I saw in the witness coin, how broad they were as well as tall. My feet got heavier, and I had to concentrate to make myself keep walking west. It's like my feet were smarter than my mind, telling it, "Look, karker, you're telling us to go toward violent, man-shaped things the size of a house, not away from them, and we don't want any." The others in the party weren't slowing down or cold-sweating in their leathers, but they hadn't seen them, had they? I missed Malk now. He was the best-traveled of the bunch, being a sailor, and I could have talked to him. So I imagined him next to me, walking his bored cockerel walk toward the frontier. I asked him, in my mind, *Hey, Coldfoot, you ever see a giant?* And he said, *Every time I unbutton my pants,* and we had a laugh. Well, I had a laugh, and Yorbez looked at me like I was queer in the head. But I felt better.

Thanks, fucking Malk. Thanks for the good humor.

You're welcome, fucking Kinch. Watch out for giants!

And imaginary Malk thrust his imaginary pelvis at me twice, and I laughed again all by myself, looking at nothing.

Yorbez shook her head at me and lit a taback stub.

Norrigal and I had kept off lovemaking for no good reason; it's not like it profited Malk's bones wherever in the mud of Goblin-town they lay. But that first night of Vintners, a Lūnday and a full moon as the first always is, we stayed in an old brick horse barn mad with ivy just starting to blush red. She came to me wearing a pair of stag's antlers woven into a garland of ivy and goldenrod. She was playing the part of Marael, daughter of Haros and Cael Ilenna, the bright moon. Marael was said to roam the woods at the full moon, a human woman of great beauty, but horned like her father. You had to be careful of Lūnday night, or you might meet Marael's half sister, Solgra, Cael Ilenna's first daughter, whom she'd conceived with the wolf-headed god of war.

Solgra was just as pretty as her sister, and she'd sometimes wear false antlers to fool mortals. After the act of love, she'd turn wolf and kill you. You only knew it was her because she never lost her wolf's tail, so she would try to hide it in her skirts or wouldn't turn her back to you. The first thing Norrigal did was strip off and show me her backside, which was a very pleasing thing to look on, and would have been even if it bore a wolf's tail, which it didn't. So I took her like a stag would take a doe and tried to make Haros proud. She howled low like a wolf as I got close, and her voice was so husky and fertile, that did me. I spent before I meant to, and where I oughtn't have, and said, "Sorry," as I fell away from her. She ate my mouth with hers and said, "It's natural to try to make life after a death. Anyway, I've herbs for that, so you'll not be punished this once."

"You're two more weeks my wife," I said.

She nodded, her horns silvered by the moonlight.

"Eighteen sweet days and sweeter nights. What then?" I said.

"Then?" she said. "How should I know? Ask me then, you silly fond thing."

As the moon waned and we drew near the Bittern Mountains, Galva announced we had one more stop to make before we crossed over into Oustrim and made for its ruined capital.

"This bird I keep here," she said, gesturing at the spot on her chest where the tattoo was hidden beneath her chain mail, "her kind were made by magickers."

The Spanth looked even more solemn than usual as she said this, which I hadn't thought possible.

"In the war, there were two. Dalgatha and Bellu. They were magnificent. They tore the biters like fish. They saved my life many times. But Bellu is dead now, and his tattoo, over my heart, is his grave." Her hand rested over her left breast now. "His name means 'handsome,' and he was. The light made his black feathers a blue so beautiful my heart aches to think of him. The maker of these two I carry was a magicker of rare skill, and something even more rare—he pays no fealty to crown or Guild."

"You know this maker?" I said, suspecting this was the point she was building toward. It was unlike her to speak of her birds, or the war, or worst for a Spanth, her fucking feelings.

"I knew him in Ispanthia," she said.

This stilled me. A rare and great magicker from Molrova who

had lived and worked in Ispanthia? Galva was talking about Fulvir.

Fulvir the Dissolver.

Fulvir Lightning-Binder.

Fulvir who could make the dead talk.

"Hold on a moment. Fulvir—you know fucking *Fulvir*? *That's* who we're meeting in the Bitterns?"

"Who do you think inked Dalgatha into my skin? Who else made it so I could heal her in my skin even if she nearly died?"

Not only was Galva a duke's daughter, she bore a sleeper tattoo inked by a magicker as powerful as Deadlegs, whose warmth to Galva now made even more sense. My skin tingled with excitement. He was a bone-mixer like the great Galt Knockburr, his onetime partner who fell out with him over the ethics of mixing the bones of kynd with those of beasts. Knockburr had done it, as evidenced by Hornhead, but came to conclude it offended the gods and swore off the practice.

Fulvir, it was said, was none so delicate.

Another name for Fulvir was Father of Abominations.

Ispanthian mothers threatened their children with him, that he would come to them and change their heads to ravens' heads or their feet to roosters' feet. He was said to have a magical library unmatched in Manreach, coveted by witches from Goltay to Pigdenay. Galva had resolved that we should meet this infamous magicker, and I resolved that I would steal a book from him.

The Bittern Mountains weren't so large as the Thralls farther west, but what they lacked in height and depth, they more than made up for in treachery. The donkeys were having a time of it, and so were we. Norrigal in particular kept nodding off on her mount, which could be deadly on narrow mountain paths.

To help keep her in the saddle, she chewed a plant called fast-leaf that gave her energy but made her over-passionate about mundane things, and she talked a great deal, which normally wasn't her way. This small path over the mountains, while far harder than the main road farther south, and impassable to anything with wheels, was actually supposed to be a more direct route to Oustrim. In other words, gods preserve us all, a shortcut. It also had the advantage of taking us by Fulvir's bonegarden.

The afternoon we drew near the wizard's keep, I entertained myself trying to imagine what sort of spell books the old codger would be hoarding in his mountain fastness. Books on flight? Metamorphosis? Necromancy? Probably the lot. While I indulged my fancies, Norrigal, hopped up on the fastleaf, described how she once shrunk herself so she could ride a wolf.

"And he wasn't having any, so I had to use a bit of calming powder, which I mixed with my own spit and lamb's blood, you really shouldn't go anywhere without a bit of lamb's blood, it's in every spell, at least every spell out of Galtia, and you can get good silverwater, which'll keep the blood quick in its vial without spoiling its properties, I highly recommend it. Where was I, right, the wolf, an old fellow with white in his muzzle, and I slicked the powder and blood on my hand and held it out for him to lick, and you could just see he was thinking about biting the hand right off me, but he must have decided I was his friend, so lick he did, and then he was rolling on his back, and I gave him a rub, but I was already turning wee so my hand fairly disappeared in all that chest fur and—"

Here I interrupted:

"If I rolled on my back, would you give me a rub?"

"You've had rubs enough. Another one and you'll go tame and be no use to me. Where was I? Right, so I gave his belly a rub, and when he got up, it was one leg over . . ."

The story carried on. I resisted the temptation to make a lewd comment about *one leg over* and just listened. It's fascinating to hear about a girl four feet tall riding hither and thither on a wolf, though when she chewed that plant, it was nearly too fast to follow.

A fog had settled in, and it was getting strangely dark with sunset at least two hours away. I found myself following Norrigal's voice, feeling strangely at peace despite our harsh surroundings and her breathless fastleaf speech, and staring off to the sides of the path, where weeds or yellow grass grew, as if I thought I might find coins there. Before long, I *did* find a coin and, when I got off my donkey, snatched it up and wiped the dirt off. I couldn't believe my luck, because it was my favorite coin of all—a Gallardian owlet.

"How about that?" I said and held it up toward Norrigal's voice, which was still weaving her tale.

"And we were at a sort of brook, which looked too large for him to leap, but leap it he did, and that wolf smell of his all gamy and musky in my nose, and I got such a case of the giggles that I was afraid I'd fall off him, but dug my fingers even tighter in the fur at his neck, and he didn't mind, but rather seemed encouraged, and went faster yet, which I hadn't thought possible . . ."

I had fallen away from the party, though not by much and could still see their shadows in the murk.

"Hey, Norrigal," I said and hurried toward her with my coin held up in one hand, leading the donkey by the bridle with the other. I tried to follow her monologue, but I couldn't seem to close distance. That's when it occurred to me that I was being magicked. Was she doing it? I didn't think so. When you get to know someone well, their magic has its own feel and even smell; Norrigal's magic was warm and smelled like good, fresh mud, and honeycomb, and maybe pup's fur. This other magic was animal, yes, but old and dry and hard.

"Norrigal?" I said and pulled the donkey toward her shadow in the thick fog, but even as I moved toward it, it seemed to trot casually away from me at exactly the same distance, talking all the while.

I left my donkey and leapt at it now, and finally managed to close with the thing that had somehow taken her place.

49

The Golem

Where Norrigal had been riding, I now saw a sort of figure, smooth, but crude, like something a sculptor might roll out of clay with his fingers, only this was kynd-sized, just about my height exactly. It turned toward me now. Instead of eyes, it had two indentations like a thumb would make, and I thought I could even see the whorls of thumbprints in them. Its mouth was a round, small hole like a navel. The hole opened and closed and Norrigal's voice came out of it.

"Then we were in a thorn bramble, and the wolf was tangled so I got off, and did I ever bleed myself peeling thorns out of his hide . . ."

It slapped the coin out of my hand, which I found quite unfriendly, but things got worse quickly. It grabbed my arms now with its simple hands like clay gauntlets, and they were strong despite their mushy give.

"Hey!" I said and kicked it in the chest, a push-kick to get it off me, but my boot slid off, and the thing closed with me. Before I knew what to do, it had bulled me up against the rock wall by the side of the path, and now it was putting its potter's clay hand up over my nose and mouth to stop me breathing. I tried to turn my face away, and did the first two times, but finally, it managed to plug me up, and I felt my eyes bugging.

I saw that the donkey had caught up to us, and it hee-hawed at the struggle, though it was impossible to say who it was rooting for.

The clay thing moved its navel-mouth-hole up to my eye and kept talking at me in Norrigal's voice.

"And it took the rabbit in its mouth and bit, and there I was on the forest floor with it sharing its kill raw, the blood on my cheeks just the same as on its muzzle, and I realized we weren't so different, but now I wasn't wee anymore, and I knew the ride was over, and still I determined to ride a wolf again . . ."

I snaked my hands between its arms and braced my left knuckles under its left arm, slapping up hard with my right hand. A person would have broken their hold at that, falling off to their own right with ribs exposed for an elbow or a knife, but this thing? The arm came off of it with a wet clay sound, but at least it let go and I got a breath in me.

"Galva!" I yelled. "Norrigal! We're under attack!"

Where were they?

Had this lumpy bugger harmed my witchlet?

It picked its arm up and put it back on, still talking.

"You have to ride a wolf sometime, Kinch, you simply have to promise me you will . . ."

"Would you please shut up?" I said, then called again for my moon-wife and the birder. "You're not fucking Norrigal," I said and kicked its leg, meaning to trip it, but the leg came off. Of course. Why wouldn't it? It had its arm back on now and hopped so it hooked me around the neck and spun me so my head banged into the rocks, and I saw those little lights you see when you bang your skull a good one.

It fell with me and rolled over on me so my face was pressed in its soft clay chest, and that was bad. I pushed myself up a bit, but it hugged the back of my head, and thrash as I might, I couldn't get it off me to breathe. Since its arms were busy with my head, I got my knife out and started stabbing it deep, probing; sometimes an automaton will have a sheep's or a deer's heart in it to make it go, though I'd never seen a clay one before and didn't know how it worked. Its body seemed naught but thick, heavy clay. I was about to die, and I got that mad strength a drowning man gets; instead of thrashing wild, I grabbed its head with one hand and with the other cut its clay neck, right through a root's tendril that served it for a spine, until the head came off.

I learned enough about magic later to know it probably had a mandrake in its head, as mandrakes make great brains or hearts for animated figures, so with that severed, its arms lost most of their strength. I pushed it off and took big, ragged breaths. The homunculus was weakly feeling around for its noggin, hoping to make itself whole again. I couldn't have that, so I said, "No, you don't!" and gave the clay head a kick, spinning it on the ground.

From the thing's navel mouth, Norrigal's voice screeched, "Ooo, that's dirty! You're a dirty fighter, Kinch!"

"Right you are," I said and punted the head off the path so I heard it go "Eeeeeeee!" and thump down the stony mountainside. I wanted no more mischief from the creature, so I kicked its detached leg over, too.

It fought weakly to try to keep me from cutting its arms off, but it wasn't much good without the head. And yet, even as it tangled my arms up and tried to hinder me, I saw that the impression my face had made in the middle of its chest now bulged out from concave to convex so I was looking at a sort of death mask of my own face in its chest. The clay Kinch-face now spoke, and in my own voice, too.

"That's fine, that's fine," it said as I cut an arm off it, the hand grabbing on my sleeve, making it hard for me to pry it off. I chucked the arm off the road and reached for the other one, which it tried to keep away from me while my voice kept coming out of my clay face in its middle.

"That's fine," it said to me, its voice now thickening, taking on a foreigner's burr, "but you'll not have any of my books."

"What's that?" I said to me.

And now the face in the clay changed. It wasn't me anymore. It became an older man's face with deep lines bracketing the mouth and the tilted-up eyes you see in fair Gunnish men and darker

Molrovans. It spoke again, only this time its voice wasn't mine but a rich, melodic baritone voice with a thick Molrovan accent.

"I said, you impish little Galt, that you will not have any of my books. I heard you thinking you would steal from me, and you won't do that, will you?"

"No!" I said. "No!"

"Good!" it said, but its eyes in its chest lit like two coals and smoked. "I don't believe you." It stood up on its one leg and balanced itself by extending its one arm, and, wobbling, it said, "Are you afraid, boy? Galtish boy?"

I almost said yes, but before I could, it barked the word No! with great violence. "Do not insult me with the truth!" it said.

I said, "Fuck you, then, I'm not afraid."

"Are you tired?" it said, and I inventoried my aching, leaden muscles and said, "No, I could run the day long."

"Good! Are you hungry?" it said.

And I realized I actually wasn't hungry, so agitated from the fight was I, so I said, "Yes," because we were in Molrova and you lie, don't you?

So it grinned a wolfy grin and opened its mouth and shot a great jet of what I thought was fire at me, for it was hot, but as it gushed into my face and up my nose, and I shut my eyes against it, a bit of it got in my mouth, and I sputtered and coughed. It was soup. Hot soup, salty, peppered, some sort of fowl. Squab? Squab and black pepper soup?

"Ack!" I said. "I *love* this place!"

And it said, "Yes! And I am glad you are here."

I coughed and choked, my eyes still shut hard against the hot stew, and I realized I was sitting down. Someone was handing me a cloth, and I wiped soup out of my eyes and off my face. People were talking. When I managed to get my eyes open, I was bewildered, because I wasn't on a stony mountain path at all; I was seated at a table in a hall, and Galva was next to me, Norrigal on my right, and Yorbez smoking her stump of taback.

"Did you hear a thing I said?" Norrigal asked. "I was telling you a story, and you fell asleep and dropped your face in the soup."

"Was it a story about riding a wolf?" I said.

"What else?"

I blew a snort of soup out of my nose and said, "I heard it."

Then I remembered the cold chill I'd felt to think her gone and maybe murdered by a clay man, and I couldn't stop myself kissing her cheek, though in fact she turned at the last instant, and I smooched her weirdly on the corner of her eye.

"You fond knob," she said and smilingly shoved me off.

I became aware of an older man now, with a prominent forehead and lips that rested in a purse of disapproval between the parentheses of his deep wrinkles. He looked at me appraisingly.

"Kinch Na Shannack, student of the Takers Guild, third year physical, second year magical, and Norrigal Na Galbraeth, handmaiden of the Downward Tower, would the two of you like to see a library?"

"Not in the least," I said and got up to follow him.

50

Father of Lies

———— • ————

For the last few years, I'd been telling myself a marvelous fiction that, despite my laziness and love of being outside, one day I would get around to bending my neck over arcane books and learning deep magic; that being a thief was just a temporary diversion from my true calling; that with the right teachers and training, I could one day be a formidable wizard.

That's not how seeing Fulvir's library made me feel. What it made me feel was that I was an impostor, a decent thief, perhaps, but a mediocre spell-botcher who would be adequate on his best day and a dangerous liability on the others. Sure, I could break a fall, put a geezer to sleep, hold my breath underwater three times longer than you, but really, the people who wrote and cast spells from the books Fulvir had amassed made me look like a knee-pants barefoot serf's bastard who chopped the heads off wheat with a stick and thought himself a knight.

The library stood two stories up inside a house made entirely of white horse bones mortared with dark mud, a house you'd never see from the road but had to wind through narrow passes to find in its clearing. In the clearing stood piles and piles of skeletons, half of them from beasts that no longer walked our world or never should have. The house proper wasn't shaped like any other house in Manreach, but had the look of a hornet's nest or an onion, and the library was top and center. The wood for the shelves came from shipwrecks, unless that was a lie, which it probably was, but there was no need to exaggerate what they held.

Fulvir had 170 books if he had one, and that would sound impressive enough if we were discussing ordinary books written out by Gallardian scribe-slaves or Holtish scriveners. Magic books, however, that's another beast. He showed Norrigal and me books on how to speak with bears, dogs, and horses. How to call lightning up from the ground. How to bring the dead back to something like life and why you shouldn't. One book wouldn't open unless you bled on it and wouldn't close until you sang it a song, the song it asked for, and if you left it open, the next fellow to come along would be able to read your thoughts in it.

"Why are you showing us this?" I asked.

"Don't you know?" he said. "You are my son."

I just blinked at him.

He and Norrigal shared a look then, like they were both in on some joke just outside my ken.

"You heard me. When I go to the towns, which I used to do on my travels, I find bored wives and make sons in them. It is nothing."

"*Nothing?* That's a long way from nothing. Anyway, you're lying."

"I shit in the pan, I throw it in a hole. I am not sentimental about the functions of my body. But as you say, you are not my son, because I was lying."

What he said got me thinking, though. My da was a stoop-necked miner who knew nothing of the arts of love, while my mother was a beautiful woman who went heavy to the wedding.

"My ma was a beautiful woman," I said, letting that bit slip from mind to mouth.

"She was. Hair like spun copper, curly hair. A tiny woman, but lovely."

"And you passed through Galtia in those days, so they say."

"Making seagulls sing. Your mother was a good judge of their talents."

"The Isle of Ravens. *That* was my mother? Anyway, you said *we*. You used to travel with another magicker."

"I was in those days foolish enough to walk my paths with a Galt. Now he is as mad as an Ispanthian princess."

"Knockburr," I said.

His face lost its playful, mocking, smarter-than-me look. "That name is frequently spoken in this house. You are welcome to say it as much as you like."

I had a moment then, thinking about the name Knockburr. I had thought it a funny name, perhaps even vulgar, but now it came to me that a *burr* wasn't just a spiny plant-seed or a spur on metal but also a way of talking, and that the word *knock* might mean *the* Knock, the calamity that drowned the world. Calling that great old Galt Knockburr was as much as calling him the voice of doom.

I looked away from Fulvir to an open book on a small table, a book discussing the magical properties of blood from different animals. Apparently, lion's blood was the only thing more coveted than lamb's blood for spellwork but, as you'd imagine, a bit harder to come by.

"You have understood every book you have turned your eyes to here, I think."

"Not at all," I said. "And you. Your Holtish is ... not ... excellent."

"I speak sixty-one languages," he said. "How many do you speak?"

"Do you count handcanting?"

"Of course."

"Two perfectly. Three decently."

"Hm. Perhaps I was wrong. A son of my body would speak at least six languages. What besides Holtish do you speak perfectly?"

"Galtish, of course."

"Who taught you?"

"My mother. Do you speak it?"

"No," he said.

"I thought maybe my mother taught you, too, at least in the reality of the lie you've chosen to tell me."

"I was not with her long enough to learn a joke," he said, laughing.

"You don't have to be rude about it."

"I already didn't speak Galtish before she didn't teach me to speak it."

"Well, you should learn it, it's beautiful."

"Do you think so?"

"More than Molrovan."

"This is entertaining. Please continue."

"Molrovan sounds like a man getting kicked to death with hot broth in his mouth. It's a wet, spitting language for whore people with whore lips. Galtish is a poet's language."

"Yours is a difficult language. Too many ways to say things. Why should two people saying *we* be different from three people saying *we*?"

"Spoken like someone who doesn't understand poetry. If I say, 'My children are children of the moon herself and we don't need you,' *we* meaning the moon and I, it implies she's my lover. Very different from *we* meaning me and my children."

Norrigal spoke up then.

"As your wife for another week, I should tell you you're embarrassing yourself." She started laughing like a pot about to boil over.

"What? How?"

"You're speaking fucking Galtish right now, aren't you? And so is he."

She was right. She was speaking Galtish, too.

"When did we switch?"

She was laughing really hard now. "When you asked him if he spoke it and he said no!"

I could actually feel my face turning red, and I'm not usually a blusher.

"You did well against the clay man," he said. "You're a good fighter. For your size."

"But I'll never be a wizard."

"No."

"No for real, or Molrovan no?"

"Yes."

"Shyte, I hate this place."

"So leave," he said, walking away. "And take your temporary wife with the lightning ring on her thumb with you."

"Does that really mean stay another night?"

"As you wish," he said.

The door to the room we would sleep in that night swung open, and two books waited for us on the bed. On the left, where Norrigal always sleeps, was a Galtish book called *Charming Plants and Taming Poisons*. On the right, a beginner's treatise on magical tattoos. In Gallardian. Which he knew good and well I could read.

51

Father of Abominations

———— • ————

Curiosity devils me in the darkest part of the night. Was the mad old codger my da? I had turned the idea round in my head now and was leaning toward not. It felt too like a story your gran would tell when you were small, by the light of the hearth on a wintry night and all that. Not that my gran told stories. She lived alone in a leaning cottage, and toward the end of her life, she swore at mice and chased them naked with a shoe in her hand. But most grans, I guess. A magicker for a father, and a right mighty one at that? Not likely for Kinch Na Shannack from Platha Glurris, Prank of the Guild and debtor. I was at least a bit more like my poor, blacktongue da than this rich, pinktongue monkey. But enough *not* like dear ole da to leave no room for doubt. That's the thing about babies, isn't it? They all look enough like any man to reassure him, but not so much like the right one as to damn him—questions of skin or tongue pigment aside, that is.

And how'd he know my ma's hair was curly?

After I'd lost half the night's sleep tossing and turning over this business, I lit a candle and tried to read some of the magic tattoo book, but it made my cat tattoo itch and burn—I don't think the assassin liked me reading it—and anyway, I was too restless for sleep or letters. Norrigal slept like the dead, so deeply entombed in her blankets I couldn't see an inch of skin. I decided to have a look around this crafty old deceiver's demesne.

I had already seen a fair part of the house, so I chose to trespass in the many outbuildings behind. These were the same buildings Fulvir had warned us not to poke around in, but in Molrova, it was easy to mistake a prohibition for an invitation— or at least to claim you did. I scaled down the wall of horse bones and mortar, and nearly fell when I had the impression the house was about to pull itself out of the ground and rear like a horse. It did no such thing, but it was letting me know it could if it wanted to, so I got off it fast. I now understood the house could move, just pick itself up and leave. I also understood the bones that bricked the house were mortared together with blood, and not just horse's blood.

I crept past the first outbuilding, and keeping quiet, keeping to the moonshadows, for there was still half a moon in the sky, I peeked into the yard behind, where I saw what looked like a huge black hedge. It seemed to move just a bit in the breeze, then part of the hedge broke off and started coming toward me. It wasn't a hedge at all, of course. It was a whole pack of war corvids, just like the one that slept in ink on Galva's chest. The one killer bird who'd broken off from the rest came nearer and nearer. Did it see me? How? I grabbed myself around the legs and tucked my face so there'd be nothing to see. I made not a sound and hoped I made not too much of a scent.

I watched with just the squinted corner of my eye as the great, black murderous thing strutted by me on its taloned legs, shivering a wing as it passed either by chance or as if to say, "I know you're there but you've got permission," which I dearly hoped wasn't the case. It's no mischief at all sneaking around where you're welcome. It went by me, then broke into a run as it plucked something up from the ground. A mouse? I think it was a mouse, but I'll never know, for the corvid ate it down in one gulp, then croaked its pleasure.

Well, I thought, *I'm either harder to spot or less delicious than whatever that was.* The others croaked back at it, and it loped across the yard and rejoined them in their standing half sleep, the lot of them now turning slowly like a wheel in the wind.

*   *   *

I snuck around now to the front of the building I had been crouching behind and found its one door. The place had a roof of turtle shells, walls of ochre-colored brick and no windows to speak of. Over the door of fire-hardened oak I made out the word *bollisi,* which was the Molrovan word for "gods." It was the same word hanging over the Allgod house in Grevitsa, may its name be cursed forever. So my Molrovan false-father had a church in his yard, did he? I tried the door, and of course it was locked. I tried a simple unlocking cantrip, and of course it didn't work—magic was strong here.

I had one spell I'd been taught during my last month of study, and it was the strongest lock-magery I knew. I crouch-walked the ground slowly, so slowly the wheel of corvids wouldn't be alerted, until I came near several trees and soon found a dried twig in the grass. I took this and returned, saying certain words over it. I stuck the twig near the lock, said more words over it, then felt it turn into a key in my hand. I slotted this key and turned it slowly, so slowly, feeling the tumblers give. The door crept open with a slow push, and I slipped into the darkness within, closing it behind me and relocking the door. I may die for my curiosity, but at least I'd die knowing what sort of church a man like Fulvir kept. Surely that would be mischief enough for Fothannon.

Well, why don't you ask him? a voice in my own head seemed to say. *Well, what does that mean?* I thought back at the voice. My eyes took a moment to adjust to the full darkness, and as I did, I made out the sounds of breathing and sleep. I was in a gaol of sorts, where iron bars separated me from about a dozen close cells. Words hung over the cells. *Malmrana. Sava'av. Bolr.* These were the names of Molrovan gods, I was fairly sure, but I had little knowledge of them. *Bolr* was the Molrovan word for "bear," and that was their god of courage. I peered in the cave and saw a dark form sleeping, I could hear its snore, but could make nothing out. Sava'av appeared to be some sort of large bird, not so large as a corvid but bigger than an eagle, and the feathers on the wing it wrapped itself in seemed blue but could have been gray or brown as well.

My eyes were keen in the darkness, I had trained and magicked them to be so, but this place was dark. I could tell nothing at all about Malmrana, save it was hidden behind a pile of rocks and sticks. Logs crossed its cell, and the bars were closer together than the others. The name above the next cell caught my eye.

Fothannon.

My own god, the god of mischief.

What did it say about me that the word *sacrilege* only now occurred to me, with my own chosen deity parodied in flesh? I thought perhaps I should leave without looking in that cell, and I dearly wish I had, but how could I? I'm a man who'll always choose to know.

I crept over where I could get a better look. I saw what looked like a large fox sleeping, the way foxes do, all balled up like a fur hat with its pretty red tail over its nose. Every time I'd ever seen a fox came back to me at once, all their beauty and cleverness, how they play and bound over each other. I was always going to fall for Fothannon, even had he not been one of the deities sanctioned by the Takers Guild. I had loved him since I first met an old tinker who worshipped him and told me the story of the naughty fox, the sleepy drunk, and the lovestruck goat. I was reduced to a state of childlike awe and forgot I was a thief. For just that moment, I was a little boy again, and I was seeing the demigod I would devote my life to, and not in the tongue-in-cheek way Fothannon himself insists on. I was struck with wonder.

"Fothannon," I said.

The fox's head came up, and its nose twitched. It looked right at me. My heart skipped a beat. My godling stood up, and I was awed. The head of a fox sat squarely on the shoulders of a five or six-year-old boy. He had little leather pants with a hole cut in them so his bushy tail could peek out.

"Fothannon?" I said again, utterly bewildered.

I knew in my mind it was a mixling, but he was just as the legends described. He yipped like a fox now, then dropped to all fours and ran in a circle. The other gods were coming awake. I spared a look at Bolr and saw that the smallish bear or largish cub I had seen was peeking over its shoulder, but that it had a man's face. An old man with caterpillarish eyebrows and a confused look. I heard movement at Malmrana's cell and saw a serpent walk out on about a dozen pair of arms, flicking its tongue at me through the bars. Fothannon yipped. Sava'av stirred and began to beat its wings and I had no desire to see what they might hold aloft.

"*Braathe! Braathe ne byar!*" Bolr said.

"What?" I said to it.

It picked up a tin plate in its teeth and shambled toward its bars, dropping the plate near a slot in the ground, now pushing the plate with its nose.

"*Braathe ne* byar!" it shouted, its eyes mad, and wouldn't you be mad if you were a small bear with a geezer's face in a mad wizard's menagerie?

All the noise had of course roused the corvids, and I heard them croaking loud, menacing croaks just out the door, which was the only way in or out of this karkery. I was well in the shyte, but one thing they teach you at the Guild is never give up. I was just crouching there in the loud darkness trying to figure out what not giving up might look like in this awful situation when I heard Norrigal say, "Yer a fucking idiot."

Now she had me painfully by the hair at my temples and stood me up and shook me doglike, this from behind, where I couldn't actually see her. The corvids stopped their squawking, and I heard the tumblers in the door turn. The clay man I'd fought on the way up the mountain pass walked in the doorway holding before him a lamp that looked for all the world like a burning frog in a jar.

He saw me and fast-walked over, the corvids behind him. He turned away from me and bent over, walking backward at me, and I saw Fulvir's face on his arse. The face puckered its lips at me like it was going to whistle, then started blowing fire at me. I tried to run away but was caught fast by my hair. Now Norrigal's fists, or whoever's fists were wound into the hair at my temples, turned me around upside down as if in a dance so I could look behind me at her, but she wasn't there. Invisible! That was a good trick! And I was on fire. Then quite suddenly, I was in bed and Norrigal actually was there, and she let go of my hair and started spanking my arse. She seemed angry.

"Oh, thank the gods, it was a dream," I said.

"The devils it was," she said, and I smelled smoke and realized she wasn't just spanking my arse, she was putting it out. The wizard's clay man really had blown fire out of its bunger all over me in a gaol full of mixlings made to blaspheme the gods.

"You made me use my last dream-walk, and that's no cheap spell. I hope it was worth it." The way she said *I hope it was worth it* made it perfectly clear that it wasn't.

"You really do love me, don't you?" I said.

"I think so, yah, but ask me when I'm not tempted to cut your throat."

I saw out the window that first light was glowing in the sky.

Morning already? How long had I been wandering?

Norrigal slapped me in the face now, hard. I suppose because I wasn't paying attention, after she'd left her body to fetch me back and then put my burning arse out with her bare hands. Fair play.

"Sorry," I said.

She slapped me again, though less hard, to make sure I got the message.

Then she hugged me and held me to her.

"You confuse me dearly," she said. Then we both nearly jumped out of our skins as a hard knock fell on the door.

52

Bread and Butter

———— • ————

We had been invited down for breakfast, this by a steward with too much tongue in his mouth, slightly sharp teeth, and a tendency to pant when hot or tired. He seemed to be second in command here, for I saw him ordering about the hugely muscled man-bulls cut after Hornhead's pattern. We came down to find Galva and Yorbez already stuffing themselves with eggs, the yolks of which looked larger than they should have. When he saw us, Fulvir, from his post at the head of the table, motioned at two empty seats and bade us sit. A warm smell came from the kitchen, which was the iron heart of the bone-and-wood house, and a portly Molrovan woman followed it out.

"*Braathe ne byar,*" she said, setting down a wood block stacked high with sliced bread and a stone pot of butter beside it. I felt bad eating anything from the hand of a man who tangled up kynd and beast and kept the results in cages. As soon as I thought this, Fulvir looked at me and said, "Why don't you have some bread and butter?" I tried to say something back to him, I didn't even know what, but I found I couldn't speak. My hand reached for the bread, and I held it, trembling. The portly woman saw this and buttered it for me. My hand, quite on its own, brought the bread to my mouth, which opened, and I bit, chewed, and swallowed. I was outraged, but not so outraged I didn't notice it was damned delicious.

"When you eat your bread, thank the cat," he said in Holtish so all could understand, even though it was a Molrovan saying. It meant that for the grain to stay safe, mice had to die. It meant don't be a child. It meant that without his and Knockburr's experiments, we'd have had no corvids, and without corvids, goblins might have pushed us all the way to the Gunnish sea.

I ate the next bite without being forced to, or at least I think I did.

"You slept well, I trust?" Fulvir said.

The Ispanthians nodded. Norrigal shrugged.

I said, "Like a baby," and we all know how well babies sleep.

"Good," he said. "There is much to do and little time to do it. I have new intelligence that a giant army has moved well out of Hrava across the plains of Oustrim, and the chance they will pass by here has grown from minimal to probable. I will be moving south. Today. But not without leaving you with certain . . . gifts . . . to help you on your important mission." He made a gesture, and the doors that led to the library opened.

Now, as if they had been waiting behind the door, a trio of musicians came in and began to play. One man thumped a hipdrum, one woman blew wetly into a fife, one man squeezed and puffed his cheeks red wrestling a skreeking wail from a Gallardian cornemuse. They weren't very good musicians. We all watched the door they entered from to see what the gift would be, but when they finished their tune, they bowed and said their names.

"Bizh," said the drummer.

"Nazh," said the woman with the fife. I noticed now her large nose.

"Gorbol," said the piper, who sneezed all over himself, sorting out his snotty beard and mustache with a pocket-rag.

Galva seemed to be looking for something else, too.

"Were you expecting a horse and carriage? Take these three with you, and mind they don't die. They will try to die."

"That's hardly fair," said Bizh with a nasal quality to his voice and an accent I couldn't place.

"Aye," said Nazh, even more nasally. "All we've done is try to live."

"And we've done a good job of it," said Gorbol, who blinked a great deal.

Bizh beat a triplet on his drum to punctuate Gorbol's words.

Their names sounded Molrovan, but their accents remained a mystery. They didn't look particularly fit, and in this horseless world, that meant slowing us down. Were we really going to have to take these bastards with us?

"You will really take these bastards with you, and you will be sad if you do not," Fulvir said, and that was no lie, and that settled it.

After the "gift" of the musicians, we were ignored. Fulvir had a great deal to see to in preparing his household for a move. The doggish steward oversaw the efforts of the trio of man-bulls, and they buckled this and fastened that and dragged a great deal of furniture outside. The portly woman took all of the plates out of the cupboard and set them by the road.

Fulvir didn't even see us off.

I had wanted to see if I could worm something else about Galtia out of him, just to further plumb the chances he was my father, but I knew it would be futile. First, he probably wasn't any more my kin than a cornstalk. One of the greatest devices in confidence games taught at the Low School is to make a mark think they're more than they are. Many a fool has spilt silver for a honey-tongued deceiver bearing news of true fathers and unlikely inheritances. Even if I were a bastard, my blood da was far surer some local blandie who was half-comely for a month in his twenty-fifth year and never again, some once-lucky fisherman or dung-carter who winked just right or turned a pretty dancing leg for my ma when she'd a slow burn of cider under her skin at a gather-dance.

Second, Fulvir was sane enough to decide what to share and what to keep, and mad enough to turn any question on its head.

Father or no, he owed me nothing, not even a goodbye, and however likely we might have all been to die at goblin hands without his murder-birds in Manreach, I felt I owed him even less.

Especially when I saw further evidence of what Corvids could do.

When we approached the tree our donkeys had been tied to, we came upon a scene of terrible carnage. Three of the corvids I had seen last night were disemboweling a donkey, the one I called Anni. The one Norrigal rode. I hadn't named mine. I didn't like mine. But there was sweet Anni, dead as summer, with huge black birds greedily swallowing gobbets of meat and croaking in between. Donkey legs and other parts lay scattered on the ground.

"No. Oh, fuck no," Norrigal said, and sobbed once.

"*Dalgatha maia! Jilnaedus corvistus chodadus! Merdu!*" Galva hissed.

Somewhere in the distance, a donkey screamed.

"Fucking things!" I said and nocked an arrow.

"No!" Galva said, pushing my bow down with the closest thing to fear I had yet seen in her eyes.

We backed away.

We left on foot.

Just as we neared the breach in the rock wall that led away from Fulvir's clearing, the house unmoored itself from the ground and tottered on four tree-sized roots that had been hidden in the rocky soil beneath it. Raining dirt in a cape, the hive-shaped house pitched and swayed in the air and then started walking back the way we had come, balancing improbably on parts of the path that seemed too thin for it. We turned and kept our ways. We passed the clay man, inert in the mud, as dead now as he ever was alive, some small trace of blood running out of him and blending with the rivulets of rainwater that returned whatever soul was in him to the earth.

The last evidence of Fulvir's dominion here was the saddest, even if it was a deity. Bolr, Molrovan god of courage, gave us the farewell Fulvir hadn't felt bothered about. The small bear with the man's face shambled near us and watched us go. I was sure he was simple, that his man's face had no more than a bear's mind behind it, that he could do no better than scoot a plate and ask for bread and butter, but just before I looked away from him, he waved. I waved back. I saw that his eyes were red and knew his cheeks were wet from more than just the light rain that fell as we departed. He knew he'd been abandoned. Fulvir had turned Bolr out of his cage like he was just another unwanted table to leave in the rain. It occurred to me to kill the mixling for mercy's sake, but if Fulvir judged him capable of seeing after himself in this wilderness, who was I to deprive him of that chance? We all want to live, don't we? I would never know what became of Sava'av or Malmrana, nor whether Fulvir in his great generosity took little Fothannon along or simply had one of the man-bulls strangle him. Just as I was thinking that I couldn't hate the manipulative old prick any more, savior of Manreach or no, the musicians played a wretched, tuneless little song, and I did.

I hated him more.

"Stop playing before I cut your hands off," Galva said, and they stopped. Even if we were heading straight for an army of giants and our days were thinly numbered, I knew I was following the right woman.

53

The Oxbone Walls

———•———

One day later, we came to the walls that bordered and protected Molrova, called the Oxbone Walls for the whiteness of their stone, standing out against the darkness of the mountains they bridged. It was a sight to draw gasps, so gasp I did. The stones were massive, hinting at some feat of magic, engineering by the builders of Old Kesh—it was hard to picture Molrovans managing this. We were closer to giants than ever, so close I imagined a briny smell on the wind that could only be their sweat, or maybe it was iron in my nose, and that was their blood.

Our blood, I thought. *It'll be our blood on the rocks past those comely walls.*

Don't forget your shyte. One of those things steps on you, it'll squeeze your shyte out one end and your supper out the other, imaginary Malk said in my head.

What are you, twelve years old with all your talk of giants in your pants and shyte out my arse? I asked him.

No, you are, he said. *This is all your own invention. I'm fucking dead, aren't I? You poor kark of a bastard orphan.*

I laughed all by myself, looking into the middle distance.

We bribed our way through a small bronze gate guarded by a trio of joyless twats with bronze knives and cured sealskins, each of them hung with jewels they'd no doubt extorted from refugees heading east.

One of the men was black-handed and had scars on his lips

that looked as though his mouth had once been sewn shut. The walls were so thick the gate was more a tunnel, dark as death, and when we got through, our breaths smoking out before us in the cold, we saw that the mountains we had just passed were only the first and largest of a great many before us, all pressing close to one another, lean and hard and snow-cloaked, promising choked roads and rockfall. Each of us swore in our several ways, then marched on, the brass gate grating closed behind us.

Several times while crossing the Bittern Mountains, we were forced to abandon the road to let pass streams of refugees, every one of them thanking their dearest gods they'd escaped the land we were striding boldly toward. The people of Oustrim were fierce fighters, the blond-haired, gray-eyed seed of the Gunnish raiders who sailed to Hrava and down the rivers of Oustrim in the years of Ash, just after the Knock brought earthquakes and city-killing waves to topple Old Kesh.

If the Gunnish learned to use the plow, they never forgot where they hung their swords and went right on worshipping Wolthan, Tuur, and Hrael, the martial gods of their sea-raiding ancestors. To see beaten caravans of them shuffling toward the scant hospitality of Molrova was a sad thing indeed.

None of us had enough of their language to trade news with most of them, but one group was led by a clan chief with a Holtish wife. Galva asked her if there was fresh word from Hrava, the capital.

"The city is broken. Kynd have abandoned it, and it's too small for *them*," the wife said. "They say it's just bones and weeds, the people have gone up to the hills or down to the sewers. The giants pushed down into the valley and began to break the farms and eat our oxen. They mean to lay all our buildings flat and chase us all over the Bitterns. You're Ispanthian, yae?"

Galva nodded hard once, the way they do.

"Then you'll want word of the queen. It is said she lives, though I've not spoken to any who've seen her with their own eyes since Hrava fell. I hope she lives. I saw her once. She's better than King

Hagli." She cut her eyes at the square-headed, square-bearded man frowning at her left. "The king was a fool, and I can say that because my lord and protector here hasn't bothered to learn my tongue. He knows words like *brave*, though," she said, drawing that word out and smiling warmly at him, earning a proud smile back, "and *strong*, he likes that one, too." He poked his chin up a little. "But he was running like the rest of them when the giant kicked the house down. Have you seen one of them yet?"

Galva shook her head.

"Right, that's why you're going toward them instead of away. You'll be following us soon. Or you'll be dead. Got any beer?"

"No," Galva said.

"Too bad, we'd've traded for it. If you've any whiskey, don't say, he's got a nasty temper with whiskey in him, but whines like a dry hinge when the beer's gone. Ah, well. Good luck."

It was at her signal that the refugees started moving, but Norrigal put her hand up.

"Wait. You said you saw the queen."

"Aye, Queen Mireya. Before all this, of course."

"Why do you say she's better than her husband?"

"The king couldn't be bothered with people in the country. Just wanted to keep to the capital and be fawned on. She loved the land, even if it wasn't hers. She came to our town in the month of Ashers and made an offering of pigeons to Aevri, the rain-maiden, that dry summer three years back. Aevri must have liked the pigeons; she borrowed water from her mother Haelva-in-the-Lake, and rain came before the queen's procession was even out of sight. They aren't my gods, or they weren't, but now I cut pigeons for Aevri, too. Rain years we're rich, dry years we're poor. We were rich. Then poor. Poorer, now. Guess I should've been kneeling before Tuur since killing giants is what we need, and no one seems very good at it. Do you lot expect you're good at it?"

Galva opened her mouth as if to speak, but didn't.

Norrigal said, "Your love for your queen does you honor."

The square-bearded man grumbled something at his wife, and she hissed back at him in Gunnish.

"Knew he'd want beer," she said. "It was good to speak Holtish with you. Luck fill your larders."

"And yours," Norrigal said.

They went out of sight.

We weren't out of the mountains yet, but we were in Oustrim now.

One thing you'll remember about Oustrim if you ever go is the light. It's more golden somehow, and not just because we were into Vintners month. The trees were starting to splash yellow; not all of them, mostly one sort I'd never seen before whose leaves seemed to rattle and flicker in the wind. Not birch but like birch; its bark was easy to strip and came off white like expensive paper or not-so-new linen.

It was while we were coming down from the last of the Bitterns, camping near a stand of these trees, that Yorbez nearly killed one of the musicians.

It was the seventh night of Vintners, and I was on watch, doing the best I could to keep myself awake by getting up and walking every once and again, flapping my arms, or running in place to stir the blood. It had seemed altogether likely that it would snow before we quit the mountains, cold as it was, but the nights had stayed clear. The stars here were extraordinary in their brightness, and I was amusing myself trying to sort out the constellations. I had already traced the horns of the Bull and spotted the Axe-and-Lamb, but those were easy. I was just finding the thigh of the Summer Maiden, who wouldn't be coming much above the mountain before she dipped back down for her winter of coupling with the Happy Man, whose arms were up in good cheer or, as some cynics said, surrender.

"Get your *chodadu* hand from my pack, *bercaou*!" Yorbez said, and I looked to see her roll to her feet and unsheathe her bullnutter. I ran toward them, ashamed to have been caught stargazing, but it was all over before I got there. She moved so fast that I didn't see the blade until it stopped. Bizh yipped and danced in pain, his hands moving up to his nose. He took them away to gawk at the dab of blood that spotted one palm. I saw that the very tip of his nose was gone. He put his hand back up and painted a second dab on his palm.

"That is right!" she said to me. "That is right for thief so all may see his thieving when he comes. He steals from me bread."

Bizh made no attempt to deny it, just moaned a pitiful, sorry moan. Nazh and Gorbol came up now and put themselves between him and the angry Spanth, who seemed set to gut the drummer if he so much as looked up at her, which he wisely did not. The other two musicians were careful to move slowly and keep their hands in view.

"That true?" I said. "Did you steal from one of your journey-mates?" Galva had gone to stand near Yorbez, her Calar Saram, and Norrigal walked up behind me. How quickly we divide ourselves by nation, whatever nation the musicians were from—I still had no inkling about their accent and never heard them talk else but Holtish.

Nazh spoke for Bizh while he went *oh oh oh*. "He probably did steal, but it is not his fault. She left her pack open at the top so he could see the bread, and he can't help himself when he sees bread. None of us can. We love bread."

"Who doesn't," I said, remembering the bear man saying, "*Braathe ne byar!*" and wondering if he was yet dead or in a cage.

"I'm soooooo sorry," Bizh said through the shirttail he had up to staunch his bleeding nose. His white, skinny belly shone in the starlight. When the shirt came briefly down so he could find a fresh spot to stain, I noticed crumbs in his sparse beard. He looked thirty, but that beard belonged on a lad just fourteen.

"Well, will you do it again?" I said.

He nodded pitifully. "Y-y-yessss. Unless she closes her paaaaaaaack," he said, crying the last bit.

Nazh and Gorbol folded their arms protectively around him. Galva deferred to Yorbez in this matter. The older swordmaster looked back at Bizh, and I thought sure she was about to stick him liver-deep, but she flicked a drop of blood off her *spadín* in contempt, then wiped and sheathed it. I had nothing to say.

It wasn't like I never stole anything.

"Fucks to you," she said, pointing at the sobbing drummer. "*This* time I only close my pack."

The next day, when we stopped near a stream that cut across the foothills just west of the Bitterns, four of us walked a bit away from the three newcomers who were arguably musicians. They had played a couple of times, and it had been so awful, we threatened them with stoning on the first occasion and decapitation on the second. We still had not the first idea why we were to tolerate them. Whether or not to continue this policy was a matter of some contention, and it seemed the more one profited from the use of magic, the more tolerant that person felt toward the trio.

"I think the old man was playing us a joke. These are useless, and he know it. He laugh at us to take them, it save him the rope to hang them," Yorbez had said.

Galva was of the same mind. "I do not see what they do for us besides eating our food and slowing us down."

Norrigal crossed her arms and said, "If any of you are sensitive to magic, you'll know these bunch raise the hairs on your arms. There's something to them. I think we leave them back or harm them at our peril, and I'm against it. I say we keep them."

"Besides which," I said, "their playing drives the scavengers away."

Even Galva laughed at that.

And so they stayed.

For the moment.

54

The Dogs of Hrava

———— • ————

A Dirge for Hrava, City of Long Winters.

Sailors lament the rocks in your treacherous bay, the kynd-killing eels in your brackish lake; bad poets rhyme about your lepers dying in saffron robes on Bald Island, so named because they cut all the wood for fires, or because they shave the lepers' heads, the poets won't agree.

Here's a health to your memory, Hrava, ringed with mountains half around, your tower of two colors leaning after the earthquake thirty years gone. Proud Hrava with your king's palace of timber, called the Hall of Shields because your warriors were your strongest walls, or so you bragged, but then they fell. Pilgrims from the Gunnish islands farther north that spawned your strong, blond heirs came to leave their father's fingerbones in the ossuaries at your temple of Tuur. And there stood stony Tuur in statue form, as if guarding the temple door, with his golden mustache and wooden Tree-Tall spear, his beaten copper helm gone green, and the spiral tattoo on his stone chest inlaid gold. Tuur, slayer of giants, fifty feet tall on a ten-foot pedestal of volcanic rock.

I even remember a song about you, westernmost capital of Manreach:

Hrava hath a summer sweet
Forty days on lamblings' feet
A fall so bitter, bare and cold
You'll swear the gloaming's taken hold

And when the winter icefall brings
For firewood you'll sell your rings
So when the spring at last returns
You've nothing left to eat nor burn

Hrava, Hrava, stone and wood
And little else to do man good
Save fur and iron, flesh and bone
Hrava, Hrava, wood and stone

When the giants had come to Hrava this year, they'd found a proud, rich city just starting to go soft in the middle, like an old warrior now too fond of beer and bench, a once-feared sword hanging up with its first cobwebs on it. They'd found a beautiful city cut with canals and tall new houses with slate roofs and gardens of strange winter plants. That was not what I found on this tenth day of Vintners, a week and a day later than my Guild told me to get here.

I found a graveyard of rubble and thrown boulders.

I found a playground of free thieves.

I found so much blood between cobblestones that thirty rains might not wash it all away.

I would soon find the statue of the giant-killing god toppled and lying on his face, in three huge pieces, the gold and copper stripped off him like jewelry off a victim. The city of Hrava had been well and truly murdered.

The rest of the party stayed in the foothills close to the dead city while I went in to see what I could find out. Galva entrusted me with the map of Hrava Rough Fucker had provided; it was the first time I'd had a good look at it. She just handed me the map and nodded at the ruins. Turned her back before I could say anything. Not that there was anything to stay.

I was a thief, and thieves scout as well as steal, don't they?

I hadn't Norrigal's power or the Ispanthians' swords, but I had luck and training. This was my moment.

And if I could find that wayward witch-queen, it might just win me enough to have my own leaning house on a windy Galtish bluff with no one to answer to but me, and naught to do but read old stories and count my filthy silver.

Besides, I wanted to impress not only Norrigal but that Spanth birder, too. It struck me funny that I should care so much what Galva thought, but so I did. I don't know if it was the noble birth or the Ispanthian blood, but the last daughter of Braga had a way of making you feel like you were just one stupidly brave deed away from finally earning her respect.

Maybe walking into a city that had been crushed by giants was more stupid than brave, but there was nothing for it but to point my toes and swing my legs.

I walked by the cold, calm lake with my strung bow around me and a dozen arrows in my quiver; my long dagger oiled and my feet up on the balls, ready to move. The sun was on the water like coins, which made me think of my own Platha Glurris, or Shining River, back home. Water looks more or less the same everywhere, or everywhere I'd been. Poets enough had spilled ink about the green shallows in the Sea of Tigers, or the turquoise bays off Istrea and Beltia, and maybe oceans were another class. But it seemed to me that a river was a river and a lake was a lake. This one was just really far north and really far west.

What the fuck was I doing here, anyway?

Oh, that's right. Betraying my Guild for love of a woman, friendship with a Spanth, and hatred of the Takers.

Onward!

Soon, I heard the chunks and haws of a tongue I'd never heard before, and I hid myself quick. Crouching low, I saw one party of looters, squat, dusty-brown-haired hardboys and sharpgirls draped in finery and bristling with spears and hatchets, pulling a cart laden with spoils. They were on the road, and I was well away from it, keeping to the high grass already yellowing with the start of Vintners month.

I squatted like a mother quail and waited for the larcenous bunch to pass—I didn't feel like trying to fight or flee the six of them to keep them from adding my few possessions to their trove. I had to wonder how long they'd be able to keep it. Larger, tougher groups of looters and highwaymen prowled the roads around the broken capital—unless they were allied with one of these, their merrymaking would be brief.

I passed what had once been a sort of town square, its proud, tall blue firs mostly snapped and fallen, dozens of kynd-sized boulders strewn about, mixed in with the rubble of a fountain that once honored Aevri, the Gunnish goddess of rain. Her beautiful white arm—I think now not unlike Norrigal's when first I saw it at the Downward Tower—seemed to beckon to me since she'd found no help from Wolthan, the Sky-Father, that arm had once lifted toward.

I found a canal stained with blood on both sides, pocked where great rocks or massive axe-heads had smashed cobblestones—the fallen city wall behind it told me that a second stand had been made here at the canal, that it was probably just too wide for a giant to leap. It was too wide for a normal kynd to leap, or even me without a cantrip behind me.

One street advertising glovers and tanners had fared better than the rest in that most of the buildings were still standing, but their insides had been gutted; it looked like each window and door had coughed or vomited rubble into the street. At first, I saw people only at a distance; shadowy figures in twos or threes who were as eager to avoid me as I was to avoid them, though I would need to talk to someone before long if I were going to be able to find this non-Guild thief Ürmehen that Rough Fucker said might help us.

Stray dogs started following me near the wrecked temple of Tuur. At first, it was just one or two, then another half dozen joined, and they stalked nearer.

"This is all I need," I said.

I readied my bow. I really didn't want to shoot a dog. I walked through the trash in the street until I came to the three pieces of the fallen statue of Tuur, the rather less than successful deity charged with keeping giants in line. The dogs, skinny and sick and desperate, started to ring around me, the leader edging forward with his head down, his lieutenants stalking close behind. If I shot him, they'd probably scamper, but I thought I'd see what good dodging them might do. I used Tuur's stone belt and scabbard as footholds and scurried up to stand on the top of Tuur's arse, which I now saw had been defaced by men as well as giants—a vandal of some artistic talent had used pitch or black paint to draw a number of phalluses all in a circle pointing where the humbled god's bunger would be. Fair play, too. He'd had only one job, hadn't he? People putting their fathers' fingerbones in a great stone chest to pray for protection from giants had a right to be disappointed when an army of giants wrecked their capital.

The giants had done their share, too. Someone must have let on to the bigguns what Tuur's line of work was, because a coil of poo only a giant could have manufactured adorned poor Tuur's helmetless head. When and if I got down from here, I was going to have to find something to write with and add *Tuurd* with an arrow pointing at the offending matter. The thought made me chuckle. The lead dog paced back and forth in frustration at finding me out of reach, and huffed two low barks. I barked back at him. I don't know what I said, but it might have involved his mother, because he began to growl.

"Ah, don't take it hard," I said, leaping the six feet or so between Tuur's arse and his back and shoulders. "I'm sure your sisters have fleas up their squinnies, too."

He barked again.

I barked back. This conversation might have continued until well after dark had not the children arrived.

From one of the shadowy side streets that spilled into this square like the spokes of a wheel, I heard a whistle. The dogs looked up. Now a small mob of children came, somewhat less skinny and desperate than the dogs, and they started yelling and pelting the dogs with rubble from the street. The little bastards could throw, too. Soon the dogs, after a few half-hearted lunges at the new pack, decided to find better odds and trotted in a dignified retreat down one of the other spokes of the street-wheel. The scene was so amusing, I momentarily forgot I was more than just a spectator. What I should have done was sprint down one of the other streets before I got myself surrounded, but by the time I thought that, they were too close.

They came up to where I perched and held their hands up to me, saying the Gunnish words for *money* and *food*. I showed them a copper shave, and they said, "*Je! Je!*" so I threw a half-dozen coins down at them, but the kids who got those just hid them away and kept saying, "*Igeldi! Esnok!*" I thought about threatening them with an arrow, but I would have felt nearly as bad about shooting a child as I would have about shooting a dog. Also, the thought of the score or so of them raining busted brickwork at me was manifestly unpromising.

Inspiration came to me, and I shouted, "Ürmehen!" Which stopped them. I turned it into a question. "Ürmehen?" I said and pointed down different streets. They started speaking to each other. A ginger with a black eye and a wicked short spear seemed to be in charge. He said, "Something-something-something Ürmehen?" which I assumed to be "What do you want with Ürmehen?" or "What will you give me if I bring you to Ürmehen?" so I held up a silver owlet and said *je*, which sounded enough like a Norholter's *yae* that I assumed it must mean yes.

The leader started climbing up toward me, but I don't know what would have happened when he got there, because a horn sounded. A really big, nut-shrinking horn that rattled my teeth in my head. The smaller children ran, but the ginger's close hench-men stayed near him and, though he now climbed no farther, he held his hand out insistently. The horn sounded again, and I felt it in my sternum. Something big was moving down one street, making big steps. The ginger and I both looked wide-eyed into the darkness of that street, then he looked my way again and shoved his empty palm at me. He was just that little bit more greedy than scared, which I understood completely.

His lads clutched at his sleeves, but he wasn't going anywhere until I paid him the toll for safely exiting the square. Ballsy little sprumlet, anyway. I threw him the owlet. He took it and ran, be-hind the others. When the horn sounded again, I thought about shooting him through the thigh and scooping up the coin when he dropped it; I was pretty sure his boys wouldn't turn about to help him with a giant almost here, if one of them even noticed he had dropped off, but I didn't shoot. I almost liked him. I was glad for my generosity later. Mostly. Now, though, I got down and ducked behind Tuur's arse, watching to see what was coming from the alley.

The streets leading to Tuur's temple's square, brilliantly called Temple Square if the signs were to be believed, were merchants' alleys, their crowded buildings leaning in so the apartments over shops nearly kissed windows over the streets they plumbed in shadow. Down a street called Martyr's Way, I saw one dusty shadow, fifteen feet high if an inch, duck to avoid the bottom of a balcony. He wasn't the first one to enter the square. First came kynd, six of them, their necks collared, breaking into sunlight so it shone on their pale, northern skin. Next, the giant's fist holding the ropes attached to the collars, steering them as hunter's hand might guide a pack of leashed hounds. Next, the giant himself. It was the first one I had seen in real life, not counting the blurry images in the witness coin.

"Fothannon put a jape on my lips," I mouthed, feeling panic rise up in me. Two more giants walked behind the first, one holding a horn that came off some beast whose dimensions defied belief—a hillox, as I believed, native to the giantlands past the Thralls.

The giants wore greaves made from bones and leather to protect their shins, and knee-length skirts hung with strips of bronze. Great leather girdles two inches thick and likewise tiled with bone rose almost to their teats, arching in the center to shield the breadbasket. They wore no shirts or mail coats. The leader's pierced teats hung with bronze rings like door knockers on rich houses, and staring eyes tattooed over those teats. Fuzzy, blued tattoos covered their muscly arms, and their hair hung in matted locks. I would later learn this marked them as a lower caste; that the upper sorts had hillox-bone combs, and these before me weren't allowed to touch combs.

Terrified though I was, enough of my reason remained to note that these giantfolk had armored themselves where the weapons of kynd could easily reach—I couldn't imagine trying to drive a spear or sword through those greaves or past that girdle. I would later see the great wicker shields they used against arrows, shields woven by human slaves, but this lot weren't arrayed for battle. They were out for sport. Worse, they were drunk. How like dogs they heeled their leashed kynd—of course. This was how they looted. They were too large to go into the buildings that still stood, so these they sent inside to find gold or silver or other kynd.

Hell, I'd done it again. I had stared too long. I broke and ran. The giant saw and barked a hoarse syllable after me, it sounded like *Go!* But I spoke no giant or thought I didn't. He let two of the kynd slip their leash. The very drunk giant with the horn blew it again, and the other laughed. I got to an alley, then turned with my bow. The running men saw me drawing on them, but ran at me with half-closed eyes anyway, scared of what I would do to them, more scared of what was behind them. I shot the first one in the groin, and he fell, tripping up the second. The giants loosed two more to chase me, yelling now to rattle teeth, I suppose in anger that I had slain one of their trained pets.

The alley I'd chosen was, I now realized, the same the children had taken. Had that only been a moment before? It felt like half a day. It was too narrow for the giants, too littered for kynd to easily run down. I ducked and hopped and slid, holding my bow with one hand, a ready arrow in my fingers. The fresh kynd-hounds had made the alley—they were fast, picked no doubt for running. One yelled at me and I thought he said *stop* in Galtish, but that was scarcely likely. I said, "Sorry about this, mate," and shot him through the eye.

I came out onto a street whose buildings had mostly collapsed, offering not as much cover as I'd have liked. I saw a sort of crack in the street, then saw it close.

The sewers!

I ran for that, stopping to stab the kynd-hound that tried to tackle me. I did it sneaky, hiding Palthra in front of me so he couldn't see, then sort of slipping hard left, driving the blade down and right, just at gut level. It's a very popular Guild move, one of the first things they teach you at Low School, because it works. He grunted, but the knife stuck in him. He balled himself around the knife and slid to a stop on his side, no longer concerned with me or his giant masters, one of whom was stomp-stomping drunkenly around the corner, slobberingly blowing his hillox horn. Bollocks if I was going into the sewers of a strange city without that dagger. I poked him in the eye with my thumb, and when he moved his bloody hands to defend his face, I ripped Palthra free from him, and sheathed her wet. Yeah, I know, I'm a bastard, let's see how nice you are with your best knife hilt-deep in a fucker and three giants and their slavies coming to kill you.

I grabbed the iron ring and heaved at the stone sewer lid, only just strong enough to move it. The giant was less than forty yards away now, the kynd slave closer. I dropped into the hole, holding up my bow, not knowing how far I was falling or onto what. Only ten feet or so, as it turned I hit dry, foul-smelling stone; a sort of landing, with steps below I could only just make out. I took the first ten steps, then hit another landing. I looked up at the rectangle of sky above me and saw three slavies look down and point. They only did that an instant before they were yanked brutally away and a huge head and shoulders blacked out the sun near completely. I looked back down and couldn't see where the next steps started, so I shot an arrow where the sun used to be and heard a giant yawp. The rectangle of sunlight magically reappeared. I hurried down the steps just as the dead hound-man was hurled at me, one of his legs clipping my shoulder, almost knocking me off my feet—but I'm nimble, thank Fothannon.

My descent into hell was unimpeded.

55

The Upright Man

———— • ————

The sewers beneath Hrava weren't the worst sewers I'd ever seen. I'd sooner eat a dead man's foot than go underground again in Pigdenay, as we had to more than once at the Low School. But Hrava? Cold, as Pigdenay was normally cold, which is good for sewers if you have to be in them or above them, but Pigdenay was built five hundred years before. Apart from having all that time to collect filth and fall into ruin, the art of building shyte-tunnels was much improved by the time the wild Gunnish thanes decided they, too, wanted a city, here in the mountains between the river and the lake.

These sewers were fairly wide and, thanks to the sudden depopulation of the city, not so full of shyte. Not new shyte, anyway, which is something. Not that I was thinking about pitching a tent and having my letters sent here, but it wasn't so bad is what I'm saying. And as such, it was a very popular place. While a good many Hravi died when the giants came, and even more fled to the wilderness, I soon realized that a tenth of the city was now below ground.

And who could blame them? Giants were serious business. How the hells were the armies of kynd supposed to stand up to those things? Pikes fifteen feet long would help, but I'll bet a hail of twenty-pound rocks would bust a phalanx pretty fast. Ten thousand longbows shooting poisoned arrows might serve, but if kynd could make a shield wall, the giants could as well. And how long could archers keep their feet planted and their boots unwatered with a wall of ten-foot shields driving toward them? Those things could move, too, with plenty of muscle under what fat they had, and if their strides looked lumbering, it was all a matter of scale—just a few strides and they were across a field. I better understood Galva and her goblin-troubled sleep—I would be dreaming of the goblins we had faced on the island, but more so now I would hear thundering steps, a hunting horn, see kynd leashed like dogs running after me, and after them, their masters with their long, long shadows.

Hrava had become a whole city of long shadows.

Within a hundred steps of the entrance, I found myself passing ordinary folks getting by as best they could without sun or fresh air. Here was a new mother suckling her babe on a pallet of scrap wood while two broken-looking beardy men sagged against their spears. Here were twenty sad bastards hunched around a smoky tallow lamp while one read a Gunnish saga about another giant war, one that men had won to drive them over the Thralls seven hundred years before. The firelit glimpses of their faces said they regarded what they heard as mere fables—the giants they had lately encountered were worse than anything in those books. I passed a few groups who'd strung furs or sailcloth to screen their couplings and their dungings from their neighbors, but most lived in the open. And few did more than turn a sideways eye at me as I passed to assure themselves I was benign.

At a juncture of several tunnels, I came to a large stone room that served as a sort of agora. Dim orange light flickered from a very few walled torches and carefully guarded candles. People had spread cloths and even set up rickety tables in the dry middle part, selling buckles and scraps of leather, wood for burning, a few bolts of soiled cloth. A chandler dam with a ready axe and a very skinny leashed dog displayed a few dozen beeswax candles you'd need silver to take away.

The most popular table, one with a large crowd around it,

belonged to a group of hunters who had just returned with a few ducks, a doe, a handful of fat rabbits, a box of straw and eggs. These women had the look of thanes—the tough Gunnish nobles who were to their folk as knights were in Holt. You'd have to have good swords and a reputation to make it through a starving city with fresh game.

I saw that those around their table had on dirty velvets and fine, worked leather rather than filthy hemp and wool. People started yelling prices, bidding against one another, a small scuffle broke out but was quickly beaten down, and soon I saw the glint of real gold going into these hunters' hands for a duck. I saw a sword worthy of fable, two hundred years old if an hour, scrawled with runes and humming faintly with magic, go to the hunters as a crying man with a horde of children at his feet and several women behind him took the doe. Within a quarter hour, the last egg was gone for the price of a night in a fine inn, the thanes had drunk off a skin of what smelled like fruit mash liquor, and they were off again to dodge bigguns and try to fell another priceless deer.

I saw arrows for sale in a bucket, different sizes, some no doubt perfect for my bow, and I was about to ask the birthmarked fletcher's lad how much, when I felt a hand on my sleeve. I turned, stepping back, in case the stranger's free hand held a dirk, and backed straight into another body, the hands attached to which grabbed my belt. I covered my knife so they'd not have it out of its sheath, and then I saw them. The ginger lad and a dusky boy who'd been with him by the fallen statue of Tuur. He showed me an open hand to say, *Calmly, we're not here to fight,* and I relaxed my hand on the knife, though didn't move it far.

I shot a look at the belt-grabber, and he let go, but two more urchins had moved up behind him. I looked at the ginger. He said, "Ürmehen," and nodded down one tunnel, which yawned like a mouth of sheer black. "Ürmehen, *je,*" I said. I consulted my luck heading down the tunnel with the boys, and it was swimming near normal. I was not heading for immediate tragedy, in any case, or if I were, I had even odds to escape it.

Ürmehen was my first experience with an Upright Man, an underworld boss not feal to the Guild. In that regard, he was a sort of relic—a museum piece to show what crime looked like before the Guild put a Hanger's House in every city, and a Problem to run it, and three Worries under the Problem, and any number of Pranks, Fauns, Fetches, a small army of Scarecrows, and perhaps a Famine to do their bidding. Not to mention the assassins.

But all of that was gone when King Hagli kicked them out a decade ago, his new Ispanthian bride Mireya at his side. How had he gotten away with it? How had no Assassin-Adept poisoned or gutted them? That was a question for another day. Now I strode into a sort of mossy hallway that had been turned into a tavern and brewery. A sign, in Gunnish, read, *The Worming Vault.*

Witchmoss, a rare phosphorescent lichen that mostly only grows in the caves of the far north, had been cultivated here and ran in mad streaks like glowing embers along the walls. In a far corner, I saw lads and lasses stoking a fire under a yeasty vat. I saw a bunch of planks laid across the heads of broken statues serving as a bar, precious candles flickering in their hollow eyes and mouths. Proper whale oil lamps burned steady behind the bar, where the formerly wealthy drank real beer poured by a tough-looking swinish fellow of twenty with an unbecoming chin-strap beard. Not that there's any other kind of chin-strap beard. You wear a beard like that, you're basically saying, *I have no hope of getting laid but you won't like what happens if you punch me.*

Lamps also glowed behind a sort of throne made from barrels, upon which a thirtyish man in striped southern catfurs sat, having his bare feet rubbed by a girleen of twelve or so using an expensive-smelling oil. At a small table to his left I saw an impressive pile of coins, a bottle of Gallardian wine, a few books, and if I didn't miss my guess, a Towers deck. Two strong-looking adolescents in full chain armor stood near him with war crossbows and short spears at hand. The kids escorting me entered and knelt and jerked at my sleeve so that I knelt, too.

"*Tou esc Gallard?*" the man on the makeshift throne asked.

"*Nou, mesc iei lei paurel am puel,*" I replied.

Took me for a Gallard! Made sense, though, since his lad peeled an owlet off me. He shooed the foot-rub girl away and leaned closer.

"You a Holter?" he said in the singsong Gunnish accent, but he really just wanted me to open my mouth again.

"Technically," I said and had barely gotten it out before he saw my black tongue wagging and hissed, in wonder, "A Galt!"

I said, "That's as I am."

"You are very far from home."

"That's the truth."

He rubbed his chin and smiled gleefully. "I never fuck a Galt before."

That staggered me, but I tried not to show it.

"Well," I said, "unless my whore cousin's been following me all this way, I don't guess you soon will. Unless you like your meat cold," I said, running a thumb across my neck and closing my eyes in pantomime of a throat-cutting.

He took a moment to understand what I said, then laughed hard, showing good teeth. A few lickspittle types standing near laughed with him, though I doubt they had the slightest idea what I said.

"I am thinking I like you," he said. "Good hand with a bow. Very good. Killed two *Jetenhunden*. Maybe three? *Je?*"

"Three," I said, "but one was with a knife."

"Even better," he said, glancing at Palthra in her rosed sheath. "I can see the blade?" he said. I pulled her most of the way out, enough to show half her belly and let him cover the ashmetal pattern.

"Good knife," he said. "Magic?"

"No," I allowed, "but you might think so to watch me use it."

He liked that. "Ha! *Je,* good fighter. Maybe not such a good thief? You owe this Guild some monies?" he said, pointing at my cheek. Was I about to get slapped? Buggered? Both? Anyway, toss him, I was a fairly good thief.

"I'm a good thief," I said. "Fairly."

"Maybe," he said. "Maybe me, too. So what are you wanting of me that you ask for me at Temple Square? Janliff says you gave to him a good coin to see me."

"Could this be discussed in private?"

"No. Everyone here is loyal."

"Fine," I said. "I heard the king is dead."

"Everyone is knowing this. He crossed your Guild, your Guild start the war with the giants sending men dressed like Oustri."

He saw my mouth fall open.

"Ah, this you did not know. Many from outside Hrava do not know, but it is so. King Hagli sent away the Guild, this is known. They could not kill him. So is it surprise that they sent to him angry giants? Your Guild is like this. They play to win."

"Why couldn't they kill King Hagli?"

"Because he is protected by the queen."

"How so?"

"She is like the Queen in Towers," he said, gesturing to the deck beside him. "She is finding the traitors. Most of them."

"But how?"

He smiled. Shook his head at me like I was a slow learner. Maybe I was.

"I was speaking of the king, Hagli. He led his picked soldiers at the canal, and there he fell. Like in a saga, but with one sad ending for him. For us, it is not so bad. We have a monopoly on beer. Some brewers were trying to make beer down here, we make them show us how, then take this place from them. Anybody else who makes beer, they get a big fire. Is best money in town, but hunting, better than looting now that the houses are all stole from."

"And the queen? Where is she?"

"This nobody is knowing."

"Nobody?"

"Nobody who wants to say." He smiled impishly.

"What will it cost me to learn?"

He looked at the pile of gold on the table near him. "I have more gold than I can spend here."

My eyes cut to his table.

"You have magic?" he said.

Now I looked at a ring on his finger, white gold, that practically hummed with some powerful spell beaten into it.

"I can do a little, but I have no weapons or rings."

"Pity."

"I can get you a ring that shoots lightning."

"How much lightning?"

"One bolt."

"Pffft."

"Well, what do you want?"

"I am already saying it."

"When?"

"Eeearlier," he said, drawing it out, his eyes winking with mischief.

Oh shyte.

"I thought you were making a joke."

"Yes and also no. Please know that I am a man of my word. Janliff is taking your coin for a meeting, now you have one. I did not have to do this. You lay with me, I tell you in private what is come to the Ispanthic queen. Unless your cousin comes, then if she is pretty and have a black tongue, I fuck her instead. Is all the same to me. All of these you see have been my lover. Except the bartender. He is ugly. But a good fighter. Maybe one day I drink enough to fuck him, too. *Hä, Keln? Je?*"

Keln said, "*Je*," then slurped foam from a beer over his chin strap.

"He is not speaking Holtish," Ürmehen said.

Just my luck. The one man in Hrava who can tell me what happened to Queen Mireya is too rich to bribe but will fuck anything that moves, and a special premium put on Galts. And you know, I thought about it. Fellas aren't my flavor, but everyone's made to fuck a teacher or two at the Low School—they want you ready to do anything to get the score. Anything. And they don't want you squeamish about a cock up your arse if that's the only way. Just in case you were thinking about signing up for the glamorous life of a thief, I mean.

He was waiting for an answer. I smiled coyly like I was thinking about it, thinking instead, *Fothannon, make me clever.* In my mind, a fox-headed man appeared to me and replied, *I will, but only if you bugger me,* and he laughed and danced away holding his tail in his teeth. That's my god. Ürmehen was about to speak again, no doubt to express displeasure in my delay, when my eyes lit on his table and inspiration hit in a flash. My heart lit up warm with the foreknowledge of good luck. I smiled my most wicked smile at him.

"I have a proposition for you. Instead of trading, why don't we wager?"

"Oh?" he said.

"I'll play you Towers for it."

He sat like stone for a moment.

Then he looked at his Towers deck, and back at me, saying, "*Ha!* I knew I was liking you! You have a deal—but *varatt!*" he said. "Look out! I am almost never losing at the Towers."

And that's the true story of how on the tenth day of Vintners, I ended up betting my arse on a card game in a sewer under an army of murdering giants at the very top of the wicked world.

56

Towers

———— • ————

Towers is a vicious game. Some call it Thieves and Towers, some call it Traitor's Towers. You get sixty cards to a deck, made of Archers, Sappers, and Thieves (the Servants), Soldiers, Queens and Kings, and Towers, of course (the Masters). The most powerful cards are the Fates—one Death, also called Plague, and one Traitor. Some decks, called Mouray decks after the Gallardian city, also include a Doctor to stay death's hand, but purists don't like that. It seems unrealistic. Death always wins, doesn't it? You get those nicer Mouray decks at court. In taverns, you'd better have a Lamnur deck. From Holt. The art's not as good—the Thieves are just a hand—a fucking hand!—but the play's more brutal. Fewer Coins, more Bees and Archers. Bees and Coins are the Means cards—you need them to fuel your Masters. I won't bore you with the whole set of rules; just know Towers is like a war right there on the table, and it sucks money out of purses faster than a two-squinny harlot. Starts more fights than religion and politics together. And it's addictive.

We decided to play with matched pots, whoever had the most at the end of one Game wins, one Game consisting of three Tourney rounds—where you jockey for position, saving back cards for the final—then the War round, which is no joke.

Ürmehen had a special table rolled out, a great tree's trunk that had somehow grown around the skeleton of a man. It had been cut just over the cavity with the man lying fetal, like a cut view of a giant's womb, and glassed over with thick, greenish glass from Pigdenay, bubbles in it and all.

We used a brass cup for the ante pot, a copper bowl for the War chest. The distinctive sound of Towers, heard in taverns, brothels, and monasteries from Ispanthia to Hrava, is the double clink. When you bet on a Tourney round, the same goes to the War chest—that's where the money gets made. *Clink-clink.* A shave to you, *clink-clink.* Goin' to bed, see you at the War. I'm in for ten, *clink-clink,* and ten besides, *clink-clink.* A lucky or clever man could win or bluff his way through the Tourneys and make as much money as whomever won the War, but if you won the Tourneys, you likely had good cards to save back for that last round. This is what often got me chased out of taverns, running for my life. My luck draws strong cards.

Though not always the obvious ones.

Ürmehen dealt first, smiling with his wildcat furs and his tousled, ink-black hair, his arched libertine's eyebrows. Now that he was closer, I felt magic coming off a ring he had, a silvery ring in the shape of a cat wrapped around his finger, biting its own tail. It seemed to jar something in my memory, but I was too distracted by the game to make the connection. Here came my first six cards! I got a Coin, two Bees, two Thieves, and a Sapper. He won a decent little pot, and I let him run me because any folded cards are forfeit, so I didn't fold.

He had four Bees and two Towers. I could have smashed a Tower with the Sapper and robbed off two of his Bees, but he still would have one Tower standing, and me with no Master to beat it and all my good cards spent. The Coins and Bees are perishable, they can't be banked back. But I kept those Thieves and that shovel-wielding, Tower-killing Sapper. He kept the Towers, because he had Bees to feed them. Servants don't need feeding. Think of it like the lower classes are good at surviving; Thieves steal their food, Sappers grow gardens, Archers hunt. Armies, castles, and monarchs? Machines for eating and spending, no good without gold and honey.

The second Tourney, I led with a Soldier and Sapper, threw one more Soldier, one Tower. No Means at all. As far as he knew, I was dry, and had what's called a *starveling hand.* Useless, as good as dead. He led with Bees and Soldiers, nothing impressive, but all fed and ready; he stayed in, so I knew he was saving a wallop. I hoped it wasn't the Traitor, but I guessed I'd feel a luckless chill if he had one. My guts told me he had a Queen.

I threw the King down second to last and bet hard. He bet harder, hoping I had drawn the Death card and meant to bluff. You see, if Death visits your hand, your most powerful card got sick and died. You can't fold with the Death card, either, not until you play him. You let on that you've got it, your opponent will drain you dry. But if, just if, you manage to make them fold, you get to keep that Death card for the War, and in the War? Death is your friend. You can send him like an arrow to the heart of any card the other plays. And the best thing about that move is that they won't see it coming. Towers is a card-counter's game, but there's just enough chance in it you can't account for everything.

So brass-balled Ürmehen, scared of Death after all, called me on it, bet hard, and when I *clink-clink*ed my reply, he flipped his Queen. When I showed him the Coin, which brought my King and one Tower to life and won the hand for me, he stood up and paced away, issuing what must have been a chain of Gunnish oaths fit to make old Wolthan blush. He reined himself back in and sat, even offered me beer. He got to save his Queen for the War. It was still anyone's game. It usually is, until the last card falls.

The third Tourney was his. He bet the moon, and I let him do it because I got two Archers and two Sappers, and I had to play them to keep them. He ran me nearly out of money, then banked a King to balance mine, a second Queen, and one more Tower to make three. He was going into the War round as rich as Old Kesh, but my luck felt good.

And now came the War round. But first, Ürmehen wanted a break. A fiddler came in, an old woman with a long, skinny braid wound around her belt, and she played a sweet air. When she was done and I'd thrown her a copper shave, I asked to play her fiddle, a scratched, warm old Gunnish thing, and she handed it over. I said,

"This song, from my native Galtia, is called, 'I Lost My Arse at Towers, and It Hurts to Ride My Horse, but I Haven't Any Horse, So You Can Ride My Ass,'" and those who spoke Holtish laughed. Ürmehen translated, and the rest laughed, too. I played a jolly reel. This moved my host to bring out the hard stuff, and we drank the last of his wodka. I was starting to like the bastard. Down we sat again.

How you sculpt your War deck is of the utmost importance in Towers. You get exactly ten cards, you see, but you can't save Coins or Bees, so you have to hope to draw some. Go too heavy on Masters and you might not draw enough Means to fuel them, especially if your enemy has Thieves, which he knew good and well I did. He had a crushing advantage, but dared not use it all. So, as I figured out later, he sacrificed his Soldiers, hoping to draw enough Means to beat me. He drew well, as it turns out.

I was making sacrifices, too. I knew he had a King to tie my King, and I could never out-Master him, nor would my one Tower serve. But I was rich in Servants, so on my Servants I laid every hope. I left my mighty King and Tower out of the draw, *going low,* as they say; a very risky gambit.

It was my deal, which gave me an advantage. Gods know the cards didn't. I had all Servants, and almost all the Servants in the deck; four Thieves, three Sappers, and three Archers—great luck that I had not drawn Bees or Coins, which would have been useless to me. The bugger started with two Queens and a King, two Towers, two Bees, and a Coin. As if that weren't imposing enough, he also drew both the Traitor and Death.

He could have won with that hand, had he known what I had, but there's the rub. Ürmehen threw down his two Bees to watch my Thieves snatch both up. He played a Queen I swiftly killed with an Archer. He tried two Towers, humphing as my Sappers pulled those Towers down one after the other, but yet he hoped to wear me out.

Out came another Queen, who drew another Archer of mine to kill her, but he threw the Death card down to that Archer's misfortune, saving the good lady. He now had a Queen on the table, and myself naught but his two stolen Bees. He played his King. I sent another Archer, and reluctantly, he used his mighty Traitor to snatch that up for himself and hold in his hand—I'm sure he'd wanted to save the Traitor for the King he'd seen me save.

Now he played a Coin to feed his Queen, but here came a wicked Thief of mine, which he promptly slew with his stolen Archer. You can't kill a Thief with a fucking Archer, unless this was some weird Gunnish rule, which I took it to be since nobody raised an eyebrow. I closed my mouth before I even opened it, as we say in Galtia, and took a deep breath.

And then I smiled.

He was going to lose, anyway.

He had a King and Queen on the table and a Coin to feed them both. But he was out of cards, wasn't he? And here came the last squinnying Thief in the deck, my Thief, me, to filch that Coin. And him still out of cards. I played my third Sapper, a miner, covered in shyte and dirt. And with those Bees, he had buckets of honey he didn't even need while Ürmehen's King and Queen starved to death in the field. Had he known I had all four Thieves, he might have played Death and the Traitor against them and kept his Coin. But he was saving his strength for a King of mine I'd shoveled under.

The game was so exciting I nearly forgot I was nowhere safe at all and at the mercy of the man I had just thrashed. I had almost hoped he'd show himself a graceful loser, but I knew that losers, graceful or otherwise, don't long last in command. He slid the copper bowl full of War winnings toward me, greater as it was than his winnings in the Tourneys.

With all his den's eyes on him, and me sweating in the cold cave, he said, "And now, we play again. Double or nothing." As I looked about, with the eyes of the three score vicious youths on him, some of them watching for a hint of weakness to exploit, I didn't even hold it against him.

With feigned enthusiasm, I said, "Fair play!" and shuffled the deck.

It would be my deal first.

Of course I threw the second game.

Ürmehen slept in a natural cave off the sewers, a small cave, but holding barely any whiff of foulness, unless I'd simply grown inured. It had a proper bed with a wood frame, a straw-filled mattress and a bearskin. A bear skull daubed with witchmoss glowed in a glass cube. A bookshelf sagged in the middle, and a rack winked with odd weapons. A light blue silk tapestry depicted a rich fat man in white robes decorated with gold crescent moons holding a cage with a beautiful white bird in it, a Molrovan snowhen by the looks of it. Ürmehen lived in seedy luxury.

Once he had me past his bolted door, his spearguards outside, ready for orders, he invited me to sit on the bed.

"Let's just have done with it," I said. "You know this isn't to my liking."

"I'll tell you what's to your liking!" he yelled, but then whispered close, "Shut up, Galt. I told you I'm a man of my word." He waited for a moment, watching me, then looked at the door. "Now make some little noise like I fuck you."

I grunted.

"Yes, this is good. I almost believe you. Again."

I groaned and ended on a yelp.

"Yes! A natural actor!" he hissed. "You could make your living in an actor-wagon or carnival!"

He now grabbed the frame of the bed and rocked it once.

"Mph!" I said.

He waited a heartbeat and then did it again.

I exhaled a held breath.

"Good! It is almost like we actually fuck together!" he whispered into my face with his beery wodka-tart breath.

"Don't get excited," I whispered.

I saw then that a fox-foot pendant had fallen out of his shirt.

"Fothannon?" I said.

"Yes. Here we call him Reffra, but it is the same. The chief of thieves. My actual god, not fucking Wolthan or worse, that laughing-sack Tuur, who failed us. You saw perhaps the cocks I drew on him."

"Yes. Good work. Quite lifelike."

He laughed once, like a fox yip, pleased with himself.

"Are you ready?" he said.

"Er . . . for what?" I said.

"We held the queen down here. We held her for almost a moon. We kidnap her after the king died, hoping to ransom her back to Ispanthia. They are sending an army here to get her. If we can wait for the army, they pay us in gold. But it is hard, she is hard to keep down here, but I think it makes more mischief if I do not tell you why. Even your Guild did not know I had her, even with their merchant man and their fat wizard. Even with their killers on Bald Island. But at last the Guild find out. Even I am not so strong to avoid death from them, their assassins, so I agree to sell her to them. To the Full Shadow. He is giving me money like I never seen before. He is giving me a ring that I fall like a cat. To jump from third story is nothing now."

The ring of Catfall.

And when he had told me all he felt like telling me, he kissed me chastely on the forehead. He then shame-walked me out of his chambers like he'd cleaned my chimney good.

But he hadn't.

He was a man of his word.

He didn't dare to.

He probably thought I'd have killed him.

So he didn't.

Not even a little.

And if you believe that, I envy you the life you've lived thus far.

It wasn't until I was well away from my fellow fox-follower's den that I spat his Catfall ring into my hand and pouched it.

57

Behind the False Wall

———— • ————

Stars winked in the night sky above me. I squinted like a mole, hoping I wasn't pushing up the stone lid just near the heel of a biggun who'd step on me when I was half out. As I slid up into the street, my body actually tensed, anticipating being crushed. No giant's heel awaited me, though, and I slipped from the darkness of the sewer to the darkness of the house with no one to see but stars.

This house was where the Full Shadow had taken the Queen once he had her, Ürmehen had told me. The thought of finding the Full Shadow inside it now scared me more than getting stepped on by a giant. A squashing would at least be quick. I had neither means nor will to fathom the cruelties that lay ahead for me if I were caught here.

But my luck was high, and the house proved empty. It was a narrow, three-story affair with arched doorways throughout, delicate off-white brickwork and nails where the rich tapestries the merchant used to trade in had hung. It was also now missing one wall and teetering like a good breeze would tumble it, clinging as if drunk to its neighbors, both of which were in somewhat better shape. A strange, smelly grease covered the wood on the main floor as well; I would find out later it was human fat.

I searched the basement, which was unlocked. I smelled where sacks of Urrimad tea had once stood, and telltale hairs from the pelts of southern beasts like the one adorning Ürmehen's

shoulders, but I soon found a hidden door behind a swinging
panel of false stones. This door was locked, and carefully, but
yielded to my lock-picking skills after a short while. I knew the
door was likely to be trapped and relaxed a little after I tripped
and avoided the first iron needle with its drop of poison, probably
stillheart. The second needle almost got me.

A series of cells waited behind the false wall and Guild-locked
door; a proper dungeon. Whoever or whatever had occupied
these dank, frigid rooms was long gone, and good luck to them.

The queen. Queen Mireya, infanta of Ispanthia.

There were four small cells and one larger one, complete with
benches and iron rings to which chains or ropes might be se-
cured. Faint bloodstains marred them all. One closet held all
manner of tongs and scalpels, which made even me shudder, and
I'm no dewflower.

These were questioning rooms.

My search turned up no further false doors, so I headed
back up.

It was on the main floor that I found a tunnel, cleverly hidden
in the hearth, under the ash grate. I only figured this out because
of the way the ash was spilled—it had been tipped to the back.

I went slowly, using the fireplace poker to prod the steps down,
expecting one of them to shoot poison spikes up, but they never
did. I made my way along the tunnel, which, past the hearth's
false entrance, was surprisingly wide, a real piece of engineering,
using every sense I could; I prodded and poked with the poker;
I felt for magic's prickle; I plumbed my luck, ready to freeze on
my heels as soon as the chill of impending misfortune gripped
my heart.

I padded on without incident for perhaps a hundred yards.

That's when I saw the dead boy.

He had been skewered from above by an iron spike that entered behind his collarbone and exited right of his bunger, poking a hole in the stone floor below. Probably a great stone weighed

down the spike and had propelled it through a cylindrical chamber. Pity it missed his head—his agonized expression suggested it had taken him a moment or two to die. His mates had left him here, there was naught else to be done save trying to cut him loose, a job a butcher would have quailed to do. They'd left his good boots on him. Either they were too fond of him to loot him, too scared to stay, or wanted none of his bad luck. He hadn't done anything wrong, just failed to skirt left, where the tunnel got wider, and caught a tripwire.

I said, "Samnyr pipe you somewhere better," and carried on.

As I walked, I consider all that Ürmehen had said. That the Guild had provoked the giants while posing as Oustri; that they had orchestrated Oustrim's destruction as retribution for having been expelled from the kingdom. I knew my Guild were brutal bastards with their fingers in every pie—that was half their appeal to an aspiring thief—but to set in a motion a plot of that scale? I wouldn't have thought it, even of them.

Ürmehen had said also Queen Mireya was like the Queen in Towers, hunting out the traitors. This had the ring of truth, as she and her husband had thwarted three attempts on their lives, a rare feat for someone the Guild meant to see dead. I remembered the mummers' play in Cadoth, with the infanta Mireya's monkey prophesying to her, warning her of her rat of an uncle's plan to kill her father and usurp the throne. Was that how it was? Could Mireya use an animal's nose to sniff out lies and know the hearts of those before her?

But there were no answers to be had in this tunnel. Over the next several miles, I found and avoided three more tripwires, one bear-pit, and one false ladder up, which I believe would have decapitated me had I taken it, before I got to the true ladder and a face full of fresh, cold air and nearly blue sky.

It was morning.

I had surfaced in the Starehard Hills.

I saw tracks leading up a goat path—someone had tethered a

donkey here, and the party, including the Full Shadow and possibly their royal captive, had ascended into the hills here. It had been more than a day ago. I was tempted to go on before the tracks were gone completely, but I needed the others. Norrigal was a better tracker and, anyway, had that magic-sniffer. This bunch was strong in magic.

Lovely Norrigal. The thought of seeing her face again pleased me, and I put the clovenstone in my mouth, hid behind a bush, and, lying on my side because it felt more comfortable than lying on my back, fell right to sleep.

58

Come the Giants

———— • ————

"You look like . . . you had a difficult time," Galva said.

"Shyte," Norrigal said. "You could have said he looked like shyte, because he does." And then, more intimately, she said only to me, "You do," and softly kissed my lower lip.

"Tell us," Yorbez said. "Tell us where is our Mireya."

We followed the trail for hours, Norrigal wearing her false nose, me checking for donkey tracks, up gentle hills crowned with old cairns and down rocky passes; past an old well with Sterish writing promising cold snowmelt water but which turned out mucky and nearly dry; past the huge image of an elephant carved into the white stone of a green hill, the style of that one looking Keshite, probably a tribute to the bygone glory of the mountain folks' ancestors.

We came to a tor crowned with a sort of round wooden henge, probably a calendar. I climbed it for a bird's-eye view, doing my best to dodge the abundance of sheepshyte carpeting the place. I suppose sheep like a nice view, too. The countryside *was* beautiful, with stands of yellow trees smattered about and blue firs and faraway lakes, poor Hrava lying dead behind us, but as I looked east and south where the path continued, I saw no sign of the party we were chasing.

Back on the path, I now took a good look at the pain-in-the-ass musicians and noticed that Gorbol had a pair of black eyes to go with Bizh's shortened nose, so I could only guess that he had tried to pilfer someone's pack or had gotten up to other mischief. The musicians refrained from playing anything, which was a blessing, but by mutual accord, the rest of us all started walking faster. Gorbol, Nazh, and Bizh fell behind, struggling to keep up but receding. They were useless, and helpless, and sure to die without us. I almost felt bad. No, actually, I did feel bad, but Galva had her queen to catch, and you never knew if the quarter hour or half day they cost us might be the difference between Mireya's life and her death.

They were almost out of sight behind us when we found the donkey, dead, its head smashed flat. Two dead giants lay near, their faces blackened with having been dead awhile, and a less-than-fresh dead man in leper's saffron robes, also lying flat as a frog in a wheel rut.

"Shyte," I said.

Galva and Yorbez stood agape. They had likely never seen a real giant before, not in anything but old engravings, and the size of them is breathtaking that first time. And really, every time after.

I looked closer at the saffron-robed fellow, cleaved and mashed as he was, one eye horrid with looking up at us from the mess of his head. In the north, they put saffron robes on lepers to warn others of their coming. This man, though wrapped in dirty bandages, was no leper. Where some of his bandages had come off with the violence of his death (being ground into pulp with the bloody fifty-pound bronze axe-head stuck in the dirt near the road was my best guess), I saw that his skin was covered not in sores but tattoos in various languages, not unlike Sesta's. This was no sick man. It was an Assassin-Adept, one of the Guild's elite killers disguised to pass as a leper on the road. That was how they had hoped to get out of Oustrim, we surmised, crossing into Molrova where the Guild operated unhindered and going back underground with the queen.

But where was she?

The flies were thick here—all this had transpired a day or two ago.

We didn't see the log flying at us until it was too late.

The giant must have thrown it from a hundred yards off, and to be fair, when I call it a log, to her, it was really just a hunting-stick. It was a good throw, too. A bull's-eye. It caught Norrigal low and plowed her off her feet, snapping both legs, and if the gods are kind, one day I will forget how that sounded, though I haven't yet and don't expect to. We know too much about the gods to hope for their benevolence, do we not?

Norrigal was on her back and thankfully insensible, though at the time, I did not know she was not dead. The log, six feet long if an inch and too wide for a big man to throttle with his hands, had skidded to a halt near a plume of settling dust, and I looked back the way it had come. Three bigguns long-legged the dwindling square acre between us, quivering the earth with their footfalls.

"There! A cave!" Galva yelled, pointing at a sort of frowning slit-mouth in the rocky hill's face. It might or might not be tall enough for a man to slide through. It might or might not admit a giant, but it seemed a better gamble than the road. The man I'd been a month before would have huffed it up that hill and mourned Norrigal later, but that man had died with an oath under a dark sky. Quick as a snake, I bent and stripped the false nose from her, pinched the real one to try to wake her—she moaned but didn't wake.

There wasn't time to pick her up with care, and scooping her careless might be the death of her.

"Not without Norrigal!" I shouted. In that instant, I saw Galva consider the possibility her queen was in that cave and weigh it against the dishonor of leaving a comrade to die in the road. She nodded and shook her horse-staff into life, mounting the clock-work beast.

I took my strung bow off my shoulder and readied an arrow. Yorbez huffed a breath to ready herself and drew her sword, about to put all those mornings running uphill to use. I can't believe I'm saying this, but we charged the fucking giants.

Two of the bigguns were male, one female. The first fellow had even bluer, fuzzier tattoos than the ones in Hrava, his dark red dreadlocks roughly the same color as my hair bouncing as he ran, his bronze axe glinting in the weak sun. The woman who threw the log because she had no weapon now in hand, had the same almost-to-the-teats girdle as the men, her exposed dugs flopping, her muscly arms as powerful-looking as those of her fellows. The last giant had a wicked-looking flail with three heads, and a thought came to me I had no time to muse on at the moment, but which I later explored at length; we were goblins to them. We were little, fast, dirty-fighting fuckers fit to beat with flails and clubs. Only we didn't bite and were even smaller in comparison. When at last we came together, we would have likely died but for the sound of the cornemuse.

The smaller cousin of Norholt bagpipes, the cornemuse is popular from Ispanthia west to Molrova. Some people love the wail of the high, reedy pipes, and some people find them not unlike the strangling of a cat. I had been in the latter camp, but now? I love them. They sound like mercy and good luck. They sound like the very voice of Cassa, goddess of second chances, telling you your death is not today.

The sound of a cornemuse came up now, the pipes keening with the air squeezed out of Gorbol's underarm bag. The musicians, who had begun a stumble-run toward us when they saw the giants coming down a far hill, were now close enough to be heard. The tattooed giant was swinging for me, but his axe slowed down. Not a lot. Just enough so the bronze blade cut air as I dodged just out of its nearly horizontal arc.

I ducked between his legs, brushing my head on the bottom of his leather-stripped skirt and getting an unfortunate whiff of him. The female bellowed as Galva on her stone-and-wood horse similarly thwarted the giant's attempt to swat her with a paddle-hand, then cut her arm with her bullnutter. Flail had tried for Yorbez, but he was moving slower, too, and only sprayed dirt. The older Spanth wasn't close enough to touch him yet—bullnutters with their two-foot blades aren't the ideal weapons for giants—but got behind him. We were all behind the giants now. We kept running, wanting to lead the battle away from where Norrigal lay, then turned.

The giants ran off the path and split to surround us, but their running looked wrong. Now the drummer, Bizh, had started beating his hip-drum, and I noticed something odd—his drum-beats exactly matched the steps of the lead giant, and as his drumbeats slowed, so slowed the giant's legs. Nazh was playing her pipe at the same drowsing tempo. It was a careful, powerful bit of magic. They had started playing at the same beat the giants moved to find accord with them, then slowed, and slowed the giants.

"*Ha!*" I shouted, shooting an arrow that Flail just managed to catch with his leather bracer—I don't think that one even drew blood, but then I shot both of his eyes out. Galva and Yorbez ran at him and finished him, cutting his legs above his boots until he fell to his knees.

Yorbez then stabbed his neck while he grabbed Galva off her clockwork horse, which turned staff again as soon as the Spanth was off of it, and tried to fling her to her death. At full speed, he would have vaulted Galva three stories in the air, but as it was, he just sort of pushed her off, then looked down to see his beard and belly soaking red. Axe was coming for me now, moving like he was underwater, tears of frustration forming in his eyes as he gritted his teeth. I understood how he felt. One of the great truths of magic is that it is profoundly unfair. On the other hand, so is being twelve feet tall.

I did for Axe now, tossing down my bow and drawing Palthra,

using first his boot and then his girdle as steps up, then cutting, with difficulty, the main of his neck and starting the fountain of his blood. As with the biggun felled by the Spanths, *that* came out fast, the first spurt sending a great ruby gout of it against the powder-blue Oustrim sky, no small part of the next spurt jetting on my arm and face. I was blinded myself and fell. So by the spell's logic, and every spell has logic, blood once out of the body wasn't bound by the magic. I hit the ground, sleeved blood out of my eyes and only just rolled away in time not to be pressed forever into the earth by the weight of the slow-falling bastard.

That's when the tree hit the musicians.

The female biggun had uprooted a dead, leaning tree and, if she could not throw it for her lack of speed, she could push it out of her hands at them. Caught up in the music-making, I supposed no one of them wanted to be the first to flee and break the spell, so none of them fled, and the spell was broken anyway as they were crushed.

The sound brought it home, the screams of Gorbol and Bizh, the surprised yelp of Nazh, the terrifying crack of dead wood hitting flesh, earth, and bone. The screaming of the injured musicians turned into peeping. Gorbol's and Bizh's clothes now flattened, empty, and a mouse ran out of Gorbol's sleeve. The mouse that had been Bizh was too badly injured to run away and went in a sad circle, then he rolled on his back and died.

The giant, fast again, kicked a spray of dirt and stones at Galva and Yorbez, who had started at her, forcing them to hunch and cover against the hail of debris. I grabbed my bow off the ground, shot arrows at her face, sticking one eye so she howled in rage and pain, and distracting her so that the Ispanthians, charging her again, could cut her down while I rained arrows into her.

She died just as a cloud passed over the sun.

I saw the shadow rolling across the rocky earth, then saw the shadow's end and the sun's frontier returning.

I may have been delirious, but I thought I spied the shape of a wolf in the trees now slinking off. Not that I really believed the gods were physical realities, but at that moment, I didn't believe they weren't.

"Thank you, Solgrannon, god of war, for strengthening our arms against our foes," I said, "and I'll drink to you, Fothannon, when next I have drink, for the mischief these musicians made."

Now if I could just figure out who to pray to about Norrigal.

59

In the Cave

———— • ————

The cave was dark, lit at first only by the light from outside, which spilled in from the entrance with us. I carried Norrigal's shoulders, Galva had her broken legs bound in a shirt. My moon-wife was awake now, unfortunately. She panted with pain, blowing a lock of hair in and out of her mouth, hurting too badly even to crack wise about how poorly I was carrying her. Yorbez took up the rear, watching to make sure nothing and no one followed us up from the rocky pass.

I peeked back that way.

One last dead giant lay quite near the cave's mouth. We hadn't seen him at first for a stand of bushes, but there he lay as we made for the cave, a swarm of flies worthy of the world's end around him. His blackened face seemed to be caught mid-sneeze, his hairy, tattooed arm pointed toward the entrance, his treelike legs tangled behind him toward the pass. Whatever had killed him and his fellows might well be in this cave with us. Norrigal had the best eyes for darkness, what with the cat's eye sigils on her lids, but she was a bit distracted at the moment. Galva and I laid her down on the flattest bit we could find. Yorbez came in now.

A woman's voice, barely more than a whisper, fell from the darkness slightly above us.

"*Varatt!*" it said. "*Datt eer Jeten.*"

Accented Gunnish.

Beware. There is a giant.

* * *

My eyes were adjusting, helped by some patches of dying-coals witchmoss on the walls and floor. Yes, there was a giant. A female. Lying against the far wall with tent cloth around her and her massive, blood-crusted hands closed around something she didn't seem to want to let go of. She looked ill. She looked banged up. Old blood embrowned her forearms and legs, what I could see of them. She was covered in tattoos I could not make out. She watched us with heavy-lidded eyes, her face moist with sweat despite the cold.

How had she got here? The frown-mouth of the cave was too narrow for the likes of her.

Galva moved forward as if in a trance—she recognized that voice. Even in another language. Even on the farthest end of Manreach.

"*Infanta Mireya?*" Galva said, her voice cracking.

"*Non,*" said the voice from above, now in Ispanthian. Very weak. "*Raena Mireya.*"

No. Queen Mireya.

"Holy knaps, that's a big one," Norrigal managed, in Galtish, more awake now, having made out the giantess against the wall.

The giantess spoke.

"I am the smallest of my family"

I understood her because although what she said wasn't precisely Galtish, it was damned close. And Galva's princess-queen was somewhere in the cave. Too much was happening at once.

The Spanth went toward the sound of Mireya's voice.

"You do see *that,* don't you?" I said to her in Holtish, meaning the giant. I knew as I said it that she wouldn't care. I put my bow together, got an arrow ready. I only had three left. I hadn't any idea what good my arrow would do against the giant should she decide to start chucking rocks at us. Not that she looked like she had the strength to chuck anything. She was covered in nasty lacerations like her skin had split in places.

"We won't hurt you," I said to the giant, not knowing if it was true.

"Good," she said. "I am hurt enough."

What was she holding?

I realized I was still hearing flies even though we'd left the giant outside.

As my eyes adjusted, I became aware of dead kynd in the cave. One very fat one in fine sage-green robes stared at the ceiling. Looked to have been dead a day. Two more dead lay toward the back, smashed so flat there would be no separating them from their saffron robes.

Galva was beginning to realize she couldn't climb the rocks up the shelf from which the voice of the infanta came—they were steep, sharp, slick, and cruel. It would take a bird to get over them.

The knight asked her a question in Ispanthian, probably, "How did you get up there?"

"*Voilei.*"

I flew.

"So fly down," she Spanthed at her.

"I can't," Mireya Spanthed back.

"Why?"

"I'm not a bird anymore."

See? It *did* take a bird to get up there.

Now she said, "Galva?"

"Yes," she said. *Os.*

"I knew it would be you," she said, and by the way she said it, I knew they had been lovers. I'm not especially keen. I just knew, and you would have, too, if you'd heard it. Galva had been the lover of the infanta Mireya, the queen of Oustrim.

I looked again at the sweating giant, the dead men.

Various trunks and traveling packs.

The ruins of a small, painted cage.

I stroked Norrigal's hair.

"What by the right tit of any goddess happened in here?" she managed, in Galtish, through her pain-breathing.

"I will tell you," the giantess said. "If you will hear it as my death-song."

"Your death-song?" I said.

"Yes. The dead cannot speak until they are given back their tongues. Only the truthful may speak, and they speak in songs in the valley of fruit and flowers. Those who lie walk tongueless down to the valley of smoking hills and mudded water and grunt and moan like torn beasts. If I speak my death-song to you, the Father of Stars will come to you in dreams and ask what I said to you. If I tell it truly, I will grow a tongue of gold."

"So, wait, giantkind aren't supposed to lie?"

"Some do. Not my tribe."

That figured. Leave it to giants to get holy about the truth. It's always the big, thick wankers saying, "Don't lie," isn't it?

Only the strong, the rich, and the dying think truth is a necessity; the rest of us know it for a luxury.

"I will hear your song and speak for you in my dream," I said, taking care she didn't see the black, black tongue in me.

60

Her Death Song

———— • ————

My name is Misfa. I am a chief's daughter, though he is not a great chief—a chief over three families only. I grew up in the vale on the other side of the Thrall Mountains, where my people live. I have no children, so a second husband was given to me, but I still have no children, so my womb was named hollow and I was sent to learn war and watch cattle. We all knew war with the small kingdoms was coming, though there had not been such a war for five spawnings. Now they were harming us. Two of my brothers had been killed by Oustri bearing the banners of Hrava—for a year or more, parties came over the mountains, killing giants or stealing them.

I was stolen. I saw a bright light flashing from a hill near the cattle I was minding, and I knew I shouldn't go to see, but something in the light called me, and I couldn't help it. I woke up in a dark stone room, chained down, my mouth gagged with iron bits. I was pricked with needles while voices spoke over me. Dead small-men lay near me. I refused food, but water was wrung from cloths into my mouth through a bit that held it open. Still they pricked me, taking images from the dead men's skin and putting them on me. They tattooed me for half a moon at least, and then the Fat Man, who you see dead in this cave, spoke words that made me small. It was not easy for him to do this—it made him sick.

I was taken into the city and hidden in a basement under the Rich Man's house. I stayed under his house for many years. The Fat Man, who they called Bavotte, burned incense that made me want food, and so I ate. Bavotte played music for me from flutes that made me sleepy and tame. I came to want the sound of the flutes. I wanted the sound of the Fat Man's voice, when he came to speak words over me, words I now know had been keeping me small.

One day, the ground shook, and dust from the stones over my head fell down on my face. I knew my people had risen against the small-men of Oustrim, had called a Taking-Up-of-Stones. Other tribes from farther west will have come, among them the Wood-Binders who knew how to build machines for crushing walls, and the People of the Bright Cloud, who worked bronze and traded axes and armor with the rest. There was talk the city people, farther west yet, may join the war as well. But they are wicked, and their god is a god of fire.

I lay in the dark and listened to the new war, wishing I could fight, wondering if my father or brothers or husbands would know me in my tiny, crippled body covered in ink. If I could not fight, I wished the house would fall and crush me, and the earth would hug me in its arms of Warmth-Beneath-the-Ground. The house did not fall. Instead, I was brought up in chains, where three men in the yellow robes of the scab-men made ready in a house full of dead. They had killed the servants of the Rich Man, and the Rich Man was now wearing yellow robes, thinner than he had been. Bavotte, the fat smallman, was there and still fat, with a pretty white bird in a cage.

The four of them took me and the bird in its cage and all their goods down into tunnels that led out of the city and to these hills, where a donkey was tied and waiting for them. First, smallmen of the hills tried to rob them, but the yellow-robes showed them a book, which killed them when they looked in it. Just outside this cave, giantkind, five of them, from a neighboring clan to mine, saw them despite the magic of the Fat One, and came to kill them. They killed one of the yellow-robes, but the other smallmen used poison and magic and killed the giants, and ran with me into this cave.

The Fat One was using too much magic, magic to keep me small, magic to keep the bird a bird, magic to hide them, magic to fight. His heart died in his chest, and he fell. I felt the small-making magic die with him, and my limbs began to grow. I began to choke on my iron collar but my neck was stronger than the collar and broke it, as my wrists and ankles broke their bands. I was angry at the deaths of my neighbors and at all that had been done to me. Growing so fast hurt me, but I started fighting from the moment I was free.

I killed the Rich Man with my fist, and the last yellow-robe hurt me with a blade, but I pulled his arms and head off, and mashed him with a rock. The cage of the bird broke in the fight, and it flew up to the rock-shelf. Then it became a woman. I was not sure if I should kill her if she came down, but she has not come down. I was too big now to get out of this cave, and there is no water, so I knew I must die. I will go to the Father of Stars with my face blooded and because the deeds against us demanded blood, the blood on my face is righteous, and he will smile upon me and learn by my death song that I should have a golden tongue.

Before I could die, I saw something move out toward the cave-door. I thought it was an animal. I caught it in my hand and saw it was that book, the one that killed the smallmen with bad runes. It bit me. It wanted to leave. I knew that it was wicked and should not be able to do what it wanted so I stopped it and held it, and I hold it still. It poisons me, but I will not let it go, and I will fight you if you try to take it. Though I do not think I can win now. I am weak.

"Shyte," Norrigal said, through a groan. She was the only other one that understood the giant's story. Now it made sense. The Guild had been hiding in the merchant's house, the one where'd I found a basement full of interrogation rooms, and on Bald Island, the leper colony. The Guild had sent those smallkind over the Thralls to attack the bigguns unwarranted, provoking the giants, hoping to cause Oustrim to be toppled. It had worked. The Full Shadow of Oustrim and the Shadows under him probably didn't believe their own luck. There's a Galtish expression, *cnulth touidáh,* which means, roughly, "fight luck," or opportunity arising in a fight. When you're wrestling a geezer on the street, all clenched up and desperate, and you notice your elbow will reach their head, you start throwing that elbow, knocking their dome on the cobbles. Pretty soon, they're asleep, and you're on your feet again. That's *cnulth touidáh*—trying something out and having it work beyond your wildest hopes. No doubt that's how this tickle-the-giants gambit had gone. The Guild got the whole karking kingdom overthrown. Then the Guild had managed to kidnap the queen that had exiled them and turned her into a bird to hide her.

What I didn't yet understand was their interest in Misfa the giantess.

Why tattoo her?

Why shrink her at great cost in magic and try to smuggle her out?

I walked closer to her, ready to run if she made any threatening gesture. I didn't think she would. I wanted to get a look at those tattoos on her. There were hundreds, it seemed, if the hidden parts of her were as closely tattooed as the parts I could see.

"Gods and their bastards," I said, close enough now so I saw where witchmoss lit the giant's skin.

"What is it?" Norrigal said, gritting her teeth. "What are the tattoos?"

"Sleepers," I said, looking at the crudely drawn but somehow beautiful, somehow individual, beasts in her skin, with their manes, muzzles, and fetlocks, with their sweet, patient eyes. "Horses. This giant is a treasury of real fucking horses."

"Good," Norrigal said.

And slept.

61

The Witch-Queen

———— • ————

The queen was too weak to even try to climb thirty feet down the sheer, loose rock-face leading up to her shelf. I could climb it, though, thanks to training and luck, and a ring of Catfall to (hopefully) save me a leg-break if I did tumble. So up I went and brought the queen water. Before she drank, she asked if there was more. When I said no, she only took a small sip but kept the skin near her. I also gave her Norrigal's second kirtle to cover her nakedness.

I had never seen a queen before, not close; when Conmarr of Holt made his progresses through Holt's Galtish lands, he never bothered with a place as small as Platha Glurris. When he came through Pigdenay, which he did twice while I studied there, he made a point not to bring his Gunnish wife, Birgitta—Pigdenay's courtesans were the best in Holt and you don't bring beer to a tavern, do you? This Mireya was everything I expected a queen to be, and nothing about her seemed mad. She was kind and powerful and generous. When I addressed her, I turned my gaze down as I seemed to remember Ispanthian protocol demanded, but she took my chin and pointed my face up until I met her eyes. People looked in the king's eyes in Oustrim and in all the frank, northern Gunnish lands.

Mireya was beautiful, her face worn but showing good bones. What small gray had begun to frost her hair only served to show how black the rest was. Those eyes she insisted I look into were hazel as a cat's, neither brown nor blue nor green, but all and none of them. She spoke no Holtish, nor Galtish, and I knew only the barest Ispanthian, so it was up to Galva, below us, to translate.

"You can speak with the giant?" she said.

"We have nearly the same tongue."

"What did she tell you already?"

I told her.

"My husband the king forbade his subjects to go over the Thralls. He did not kill or kidnap giants. It was the Takers, to punish us for closing their Guildhouses."

After Galva finished translating for her, the queen looked at me, said something in rapid Spanth to Galva. Galva replied, and Mireya looked at me again, her eyes softer.

"What was that?" I asked the birder.

"She wanted to know if you are Guildron. I said that you were, but now you were against them. I am correct about this, yes?"

"Yes," I said.

"Good. Because I swore on my death."

The queen now spoke some words into the waterskin I had offered her, sending the hairs on the back of my neck standing up with the prickle of magic, and sent me down to offer water to the half-dead giantess. She saw in my eyes that this would be half a swallow for a creature her size, and she said:

"Pour it into her mouth from above. There will be enough."

I did as she asked. The giant wouldn't let go of the book she held, but suffered me to stand on a near rock and pour the water for her. I dearly hoped she wouldn't take it in mind to do to me what she'd done to the Full Shadow and the other dead man in yellow robes—I was too close to her to be sure I could get away before one of her huge hands grabbed and flattened me.

Misfa's tongue worked in her open mouth as she swallowed down the water, which, to my wonder and surprise, kept gurgling out. I didn't have to lift the bottom of the flask as it emptied, because it wasn't emptying. The queen of Oustrim, the infanta Mireya of Ispanthia, was an actual witch!

She is hard to keep down here, but I think it makes more mischief if I don't tell you why.

Now I understood in my bones why Deadlegs and Norrigal and even Fulvir in his way had been devoted to our journey—if Mireya took the throne of Ispanthia back, she would be the first witch-queen since well before the Goblin Wars. And she could chase the Guild out of Ispanthia the way she'd done it in Oustrim. For the first time in my life, I had glimpsed a future in which the Guild might not control everything under the sun and moon.

They could never let that happen.

Mireya, now that she was out of their grasp, had to die.

62

The Murder Alphabet

———— • ————

I had given water to Norrigal, who was in and out of sleep, and
had helped her chew on some roots from her pack that dulled
her pain without making her any sleepier. Then, with hammered
spikes as anchors, I strung a rope Galva could get up to help the
weakened queen down from her high shelf. I didn't understand
everything they said to each other, but I did get one exchange.

"Are you hurt? Why are you so weak?" Galva said.

"You try being a bird for ten days."

For some reason, Yorbez found this so funny she almost in-
haled the taback she was smoking. Galva stood near the queen
on one side of the cave. I went toward the center of it to rifle the
pouches of the dead Guild magicker named Bavotte, the one who
had turned the giant small and the queen into a bird. There I
found a small fortune in Oustri gold and silver, but alas, no owlets. I did him the favor of shutting his sunken-in eyes and putting
his scarf over his face to save it from the ministrations of the flies
busying around him. A torque around his neck seemed to hum
with magic, so I took that, though I had no idea what it did. Was
this the Hard-Stone Torque I had heard of at the Hanger's House
in Cadoth? No way to know.

I looked at the giantess, and she at me.

Something struck me about the book she held—she said it
had killed the men who tried to read it. Clearly, it was written in
the Murder Alphabet, which was some of the darkest magic the
Guild had. But she'd said she caught it trying to get away. This
stirred a memory I had about the Guild's upper echelons.

CHRISTOPHER BUEHLMAN

I reached into a pouch, put on my proofed goatskin gloves.

"May I have a look at the book you're holding?"

"It will kill you," she said.

"Not me. But it's poisoning you."

She held it yet, just looking at me with her two eyes, each the size of a huge apple, and yet they looked small and beady in her great head. She had said she would fight us for the book, but that was before we gave her water. Three more deep breaths while she considered me, and she passed the book to my hands. If you want to imagine my hands shaking, I'll not say they weren't.

The book read, in large, gold leaf Gallardian:

Lį Livēre dil Ouchure Comblēct.
The Book of the Full Shadow.

At the bottom of the book's greasy leather, in smaller gold script, it said:

Louray chē bulay echēre mirdēct.
Read if you wish to be bitten.

Those rhyme, if you'll notice. Very clever. No one will say those bastards aren't clever. Set into the leather binding, at the frontiers of the square cover, pointing out but not poking past the edge, were rows of sharp teeth, all small, but different sizes of small. Cats, martens, foxes, any number of yipping, skulking things had contributed. Parts of the binding seemed to have been armored with lacquered crab shell.

As I turned the book in my hands, I saw it grow yet greasier. I knew that sheen. Thieves' dew. A contact poison that will nauseate in small doses and kill in large ones. At the Low School, we spent many queasy evenings because they put it on our door-handles and in our beer. By the time we finished our first year, we were effectively immune. Still, I was glad for the gloves—if the secrets of the Full Shadow of the west were in this book, a mere Prank like myself might not be welcome to handle it, and the poison might be stronger.

It was a heavy book.

I knew it was full of the Murder Alphabet, but what I didn't know was if it would kill a Cipher like me. Back in school, when I first heard of it, I had a theory it might not. The way I understood it worked, those who knew the Murder Alphabet by heart were unaffected, but you had to *know* it before you tried reading words or phrases. The thing was, there were hundreds of characters, and nobody went around teaching it except to the highest ranks of the Guild. You didn't start learning it until you were named a Shadow and had a city to answer for. It was possible to learn it because no one letter would kill you, but if you were reading a word or phrase and stopped because you failed to understand something, that confusion was what invited your death in. Maybe this was why the Guild was so powerful—no thick bastards in charge.

Monarchy is a bad system because, no matter how smart you are, you can still squirt a moron out of your plumbing. Maybe you get lucky and your son or daughter is at least half as smart as you—what about your grandchild? Probably a knob, and when they inherit the throne, everything you built falls to shyte. Not so with the Guild. If you were stupid, you never went to a True School. If you weren't brilliant, you'd never make it to the upper tiers, but if you did, the Murder Alphabet was waiting for you to make a mistake so it could kill you.

"Are you going to read that book or drool on it?" Norrigal said, slurring for the drugs in her.

"Yah," I said. "Still deciding."

I desperately wanted to open the book and see what was in it, see if I could really read it. My heart glowed warm when I thought of it—my luck was in. If the characters of the Murder

Alphabet were going to strike me dead, I would have felt a chill going all the way to my heels at the thought of chancing it. Would I trust my life to that feeling? The gods knew I had before.

I was so scared, I half wanted to piss myself, but the difference between the strong and the weak isn't that the strong don't piss themselves. It's that they hitch their pissy pants up after and go through with it. I jerked the book open to a random page, toward the end, and focused, knowing I would either understand what I saw or die.

The words at first appeared in a blur but before I could finish thinking, *That's it, I'm dead,* they came into focus.

> *The Magickers are less powerful in Hrava than Molrova or Holt, the Gunnish too thick for magic—they are strong swordsmen and spearmen, but no better against giants than house cats against bears. The queen alone has thwarted us, but she has fallen into our hand now that the kingdom topples. Better that Hrava and all Oustrim fall and lose smaller Guild revenues so that other crown lands see what happens when the Takers Guild is cast out. As when all horseflesh stumbled, we reshaped the world to our profit, serving the Forbidden One hilariously in this and all things, may laughter keep us young and malice keep us rich.*

I read on. There was confirmation of what Deadlegs said in the Snowless Wood—the Takers had the Magickers well in hand, had made a straw school of them. They wanted there to be no magic in the world they did not control.

But it didn't end there.

From the sound of this, they had the Carters, Runners, Builders, and Seafarers Guilds in their grips as well. Good business, that, in a world that must suddenly make do without horses.

The mention of the horse plague was particularly disturbing. It was certain that the Guild had profited massively from the

Stumbles we all blamed the goblins for, but was this saying they manufactured that calamity themselves? The answer to that was *very* important, wasn't it?

I looked back down at the spiky figures to read more, noticing now the small eyes inked on the upper corners of each page, but that was when the book shifted slightly in my hand like something alive. The eyes seemed to have moved, too.

I know now that it was becoming aware of me, reading me even as I read it. It saw everyone in the room and inventoried their strength, their magic, their significance to the Guild. It opened itself in my hand now, flipping to a page near the very front, where I saw an illustration of a crab. Before I could shut the book, that crab had leapt from the page and onto a wall.

The Book of the Full Shadow was alive.

63

Lightning in the Dark

———— • ————

The crab, black and spiny, hard to see in the cave's gloom though now grown to the size of a dog, poked my face with a pincer, just missing my eye, and scuttled from the wall to the floor. I leapt back and drew Angna, my rondel dagger, meaning to punch the rotten thing right through its middle, but it crawled, fast, straight for Norrigal.

Understandably alarmed by the sight of the leggy, spiny black thing rushing at her, my crippled witchlet pointed her ring-thumb and loosed a bright, hot bolt of lightning, which hit the book-crab and burned it to cinders. Temporarily blinded by the bolt, I ran to stand in front of Norrigal as the Spanths shielded their queen near the far wall.

Bastard of a ring, that. Norrigal yipped now as the glowing circle of metal burned her, she peeled it off her thumb and threw it to the ground, where it smoked and dissolved into nothing. As my sight returned:

"By Cassa's holy squinny," I said, trying to understand what had just happened.

Norrigal blinked, also trying to get her sight back.

"Are you well, Kinch?" she said, at not much above a whisper in the stunned, wary silence of the cave.

"Yah," I told her, then said, "Ow!" at a hot pain in my arm. I jerked up my sleeve, which was spotted with blood.

"Oh no," I said, realizing what must be happening. My tattoo was gone.

"Rao," said the blind, gray tabby, Bully Boy, stalking in a figure eight on the floor.

Of course, he wasn't alone.

I saw her eyes first. My Assassin-Adept. Sesta. Her arms, tattooed black from shoulders to fingertips, flashed and then she struck me in the head with one of those arms, knocking me aside like driftwood. The pain was blinding, the blow sharper than a hand should have been. I saw now a sigil glowing coal-like on one of her black shoulders that said *Iron* and I understood. *Arms of Iron.* Not a spell she could burn for long, but while it went, her arms and hands were as hard and strong as bars of iron. I sheathed the rondel, reached for my bow, nocked an arrow.

The Spanth warriors crossed the cave fast as blinking.

The adept blocked a sword blow from Yorbez with an arm, making sparks as she did, then her black lower lip glowed and she spat into Galva's eyes, which smoked. Like a spitting cobra from the hot hills of Urrimad, the killer had blinded her!

She kicked Yorbez's leg out from under her, then I saw a sigil on her leg that said *Up.* Before I even thought about it, I shot my bow over her head, my heart glowing warm with the spark of coming good fortune. My luck was in. She leapt for the far wall almost too fast to see, meaning, I think, to kill the queen with her arms of hard iron.

She didn't get to.

My arrow stuck that bitch like a quail.

In the kidney and out the liver.

She jerked in midair, skewing her trajectory so she thumped into the wall and fell. To her credit, she didn't let herself groan. Yorbez got to her in two steps and stabbed her through the heart. Blood came out of her mouth as she grinned. She moved her hand up to her chest. The hands of the clock now seemed to stick out of her flesh. She reached for it. A sigil that had been invisible before it lit up glowed, reading, *Go Back.*

"*Moch!*" I yelled.

"Shyte!" Norrigal said in Holtish, as if translating. "Don't let her!"

Yorbez deftly withdrew her sword, getting a spray of heart's blood on her for her trouble, then cut at the assassin's hand to stop her touching the clock. Yorbez's sword broke on the assassin's iron arm. The killer coughed one more gout of blood and jerked the clock-hand.

64

The Rabbit and the Wolf

———— • ————

"Ow!"

A pain shot through my arm. I jerked up my sleeve and saw that it was spotted with blood.

"Oh no," I said, feeling even as I said it that I'd said it before. My tattoo was bleeding.

Again?

Or just now?

"Rao," said Bully Boy, stalking blindly in a figure eight on the floor.

Sesta! She's breaking free!

I saw the Assassin-Adept's eyes first. Then I saw her arms, tattooed black from shoulders to fingertips. The arms glowed for an instant like coals. I thought, *didn't this just happen?* and while I stood bewildered she struck me in the side of the head so hard she tore the top of my ear.

Shyte, that hurt.

I saw now a sigil glowing on one of her shoulders that said *Iron*. But I somehow already knew she was using a powerful spell called *Arms of Iron*. Guzzled magic, she wouldn't be able to burn it long. Arms and hands as hard as castle-gates.

I put Angna away, reached for my bow, and nocked a shaft.

It seemed obvious to me I would stick her through.

Yes!

Here came Galva and Yorbez, motioning the queen to stay where she was.

This is as it should be.

That's what my mind said, but my luck-sense was saying something else.

Sparks leapt as the adept used one ferrous-hard forearm to turn Yorbez's blade, once, twice, then twisted her opponent's arm and almost stripped the sword. Galva stepped in now and had a blow parried. Sesta spat at Galva's eye, but only got one, which smoked, the pain making her grunt.

No. This is wrong. It's going wrong.

I saw a sigil on the back of the assassin's leg glow, reading *Up,* and before I could consider what I was doing or why my actions felt at once familiar and doomed, with the chill of bad luck running in me from tits to kneecaps, I shot above the assassin's head.

But she didn't go up.

Not straight, anyway.

She flew left, kicking herself off a stalactite and making straight for Mireya on the other side of the cave. I heard my arrow snick against stone in the far darkness.

The witch-queen stood but had no weapon. Galva, fast as a cat, leapt between them and thrust for the killer's middle, feinting first so her hard arm missed the parry. Still the assassin rolled so it only nicked her, feinted left, then leapt right, striking out with a spade-like hand straight into Yorbez's throat even as the other arm covered her own neck, raking sparks from Yorbez's sword, which otherwise would have gorged her.

Yorbez stood, dead on her feet, expelling her final breath in an awful bloody wheeze, her windpipe crushed, her neck mercifully broken. I doubt she knew what happened. My next shot just missed the back of the assassin's neck and cut a groove in dead Yorbez's cheek, cutting whatever weird string had kept her standing so she dropped like a bag of rocks. I drew my knife. We all anticipated another run at Mireya, so I leapt in that direction—but adepts don't do what you think they will. She jumped backward and made for Norrigal. Out of the corner of my eye, I saw the giant trying to get up, but sinking back down again.

My own heart exploded in my chest as I saw Norrigal holding her small, ritual dagger up, helpless as a babe, but smiling all the same.

The assassin kicked the witch's head, then punched her in the chest so hard she staved in her ribs and wrecked the plumbing around her heart. Then the killing bitch leapt off toward Galva and Mireya.

"*No!*" I screamed, going to Norrigal, my love, my wife until the new moon. She sputtered and looked at me with a rolling, dying eye.

She held the knife up to me, handle first. I heard Galva grunt in pain, then heard the assassin yelp.

The giant yelled something.

Norrigal couldn't speak, just gestured with the knife.

The garden in the Snowless Wood.

The rabbit and the wolf.

I understood, or thought I did. It made sense and disgusted me at once, the way it always does when you get a glimpse of the world's true workings, the bones in the knees of creation. All in an instant, I remembered the feel of the rabbit doe's ears in my hand and the feel of Hornhead's tough neckpipes cutting, the wash of his hot blood, finding it sticky on my arms later, especially on the inner bend of my elbow, the coarse hair on him, the musky, fuggy smell of him suddenly overwashed with hot brass, the intimacy of it, how I hated doing it even to an enemy. Far, far worse than stabbing or arrowing. That was all I had time to think in that moment, and that quick as blinking twice, but later I would think on it at length. The whiteness and smoothness of her neck, how her sweat-heavy hair clung to it, how you could see her heart beating in it, and how I was now supposed to cleave in twain before she died, and died with no way out of it.

No swivel home.

I'd been shown what would happen.

I just had to believe.

The rabbit's ears in my hand.

The place her voice was born now under my knife.

Her dying in a moment anyway, and for nothing.

No reason why not.

It's just a neck.

Move, hand.

Fucking *move.*

It moved.

I did it.

I cut sweet, sweet Norrigal's throat.

In the space of two heartbeats, Norrigal was gone, and in her stead, the old witch called Deadlegs, true to her name, tottering on corpse's legs that were nearly skeletal, bracing herself up with a cane.

As the rabbit whose throat I cut in that long-ago garden had swapped places with the wolf from the Downward Tower, so now had these two witches done. Or was it *two* witches? Although I had no time to dwell on it, in a glimpse, I saw the two faces very much the same, one young and fair, one older and barrel-shaped.

This one's eyes burned with fury. I dropped the small knife and drew Palthra, leaping up and rushing at the assassin, who was down on one knee, blood streaming from where Galva had badly cut her hip. Galva was on her stomach, her arms flailing, her legs inert. *The bitch broke her back!* Even as Sesta stood, cut in several places, Galva rolled over as best she could and started trying to get her mail shirt off so she could free the corvid, but she hadn't the strength.

The assassin rushed at the queen, who had found Yorbez's sword. I rushed at the assassin's back and stabbed down hard at the base of her neck, but she spun and elbowed me crushingly in the side; I felt a rib snap as I fell hard.

As I went down, she stripped the knife off me. The giant had stumbled and fallen—whether from weakness or some further poisoning, I couldn't say—and was struggling unsuccessfully to rise again. The queen assumed a credible fighting stance, but before the assassin could kill her, for I was sure she would, the cave wall beyond Mireya began to rumble and shake, throwing dirt and gravel. The magic happening now was so strong the hair briefly stood up on everyone's head.

The dead Full Shadow, the dead Assassin-Adept in leper's robes, and the fat, dead magicker all rose and lurched as fast as their ruined limbs allowed into the cave walls, which smoked where they passed. Now a rumble shook the walls, and three figures made of dirt and rocks, with tufts of glowing witchmoss for eyes, now leapt from the cave wall near Sesta like martial cousins of the dirt-wight servants who had poured drinks for us in the Downward Tower. They formed a wall between the killer and the queen, but the Assassin-Adept was not discouraged. Not yet. She used those iron arms to smash the first stone-wight to rubble. But the spell was costing her. She was slowing down. The queen, who had edged away from the wall, moved to stab her, but Deadlegs, who had also hobbled closer to the fight, pulled her back by her hair, that's right, a queen, by the hair, saying, "Not you, girleen. We'll do for this whore."

The assassin was getting the hot piss beat out of her. Not wanting to get in the middle of the storm of stone, iron, and flesh that was the fight between Sesta and the wights, I picked up my bow with its last arrow. I felt my heart glow warm. I shot that killing bitch right above her navel. She knocked the head off a second wight, and it crumbled. Her arms went white then. The spell had burned out. She absently reached a hand to where the clock had been, but that tattoo was used, and she only touched bare white flesh. The last and largest wight fetched her a kick to the side of the head, and she went sprawling. The wight was damaged, too, though, and took some effort to rise, moaning eerily as it did so—perhaps some part of Bavotte remained awake inside it and lamented its servitude and impending second death. Sesta got up to her knees, bleeding freely from her skewered belly. I picked up Galva's bull-nutter and moved closer to her.

"Look at you, you crawling cunny," she said. "Me in this shape, and you scoot and inch like a castrated slave and hope a man of rocks will do your work for you. What, are you numbering the times I saved your worthless life? From bandits. From goblins. You *weakling*. I killed your lover, and I was glad to do it. Will you hold me to account, you fucking runt, or let another take the glory?"

Deadlegs whispered some things in old Galt under her breath, then said, "At least fight him in your own hide, you skinny devil." She gestured with a claw hand, and seemed to cast something away. When she did, the rest of Sesta's magical tattoos flew off of her as puddles of ink on the ground. All of them. She tried to get off her knees and couldn't. The rock man had collapsed, nothing but a pile of rubble, the witchmoss that had been his eyes going dull. I took the bullnutter and staggered over to Sesta, raising it above my head to cleave her skull in two. She lifted not an arm. It was the first time I saw her scared, kneeling there, gut-stuck and naked, stripped of her magic, too weak to use her training. Sesta's mouth was open and she was sucking breath, barely able to stand. I lowered the blade. I said, "Get out of here."

Before Sesta could get to her feet, if she could have at all, Queen Mireya of Oustrim, and the rightful queen of Ispanthia, decapitated her.

65

Running West

———— • ————

I found Bully Boy after the fight was done, raoing softly in a corner, scared as a cat ever was. It wasn't until I draped him across
my shoulders and wore him like a stole that he purred. He felt
safe on me, I suppose, the little blind fool. Wearing him so, I took
him over to where Deadlegs and Mireya were seeing to Galva.

I never knew there was magic in the world strong enough to fix
a broken back, but that's exactly what the old witch now did for
the ruined Spanth. I took the chain mail shirt off Galva and set
it far enough away it wouldn't weaken the spell. Deadlegs fixed
her as good as new, and maybe better. She had me leave the cave
and fetch Galva's staff where it still lay in the grass near the road
where we'd fought the giants. Deadlegs took that staff, with its
clockwork horse magic in it, and had me break it with a stone—it
was important to break it such that it would snug back together,
so with a smaller spell she salted it and made it brittle first. She
then dipped the broken ends in some of Galva's blood and spit,
chanted over it for the better part of an hour, then joined the
pieces together. Then off with the salt, on with wine and some of
my blood to strengthen it. But I was glad to give it. Galva cried
out, and when Deadlegs raised the staff from off the ground, she
stood, too, like a marionette with its strings jerked tight, looking
vigorous and hale. Next, the old witch laid her palm over Galva's
blinded eye and drew out the poison Sesta had spit into it, flicking the venom onto the cave floor as if it had missed in the first
place.

That eye would always be a shade paler than its mate.

The first thing the birder did with her healed body was to go to the body of Yorbez. Galva smiled down at her old teacher. "You found her," she said in Ispanthian. She kissed both of her cheeks. "Thank you, Mistress. I will see you both before long." I realized I didn't know if "Mistress" was Yorbez or Dalgatha, the Skinny Woman. I always thought maybe these Death-lovers were faking it, putting on a brave mask if you will, but the woman seemed genuinely glad to see the body of her sword instructor and friend lying there with a blue face from having her pipes crushed, because that meant her spirit was frolicking somewhere with their jolly, winged lady skeleton.

I'll never get the Spanths.

I looked at Deadlegs now and saw that her hair, which still had some browny-gray color in it when she arrived, had become a hoary storm of white. One of her eyes bugged, and she seemed unwell. Even a witch of her power had limits; between the swivel spell, the stone men, and healing Galva, she'd nearly killed herself, and unless I missed my guess, getting us out of here would tax her further yet.

The giantess groaned in discomfort, and the witch saw to her as well, dusting her with a powder from Norrigal's pack that perked her up, healing the lacerations from her overfast growth. Perhaps the younger witch had been saving the powder for herself, with her legs smashed as they had been. Perhaps she hadn't wanted the giant to murder us all as she'd done for the exhausted thieves. Perhaps she hadn't the strength to work a spell on herself, as much pain as she'd been in. Deadlegs answered my curiosity, after a fashion.

"That'll keep her from dying," the witch said, "but shouldn't make her feel well enough to kill us all."

"What's become of your . . . great-niece?" I said. "Is she dead?"

Deadlegs smiled at me. "She cannot be while I live. And when I die, which I'm like to do before I see the Snowless Wood again, she'll make another, younger, and she'll be the old one."

"Is she . . ."

"She's back where you found her. She'll heal, but you'll not see her soon, if ever."

"I'll get back to her," I said, "one way or another."

"*By earth or by water,*" Deadlegs started.

"*By fire or crow,*" I finished.

"You must hide from the Takers. You'll bring that book with you and find a way to translate what it says. What's in there will rend your Guild to tatters. Do that, and it'll pay all the blood spilt so far. Do that, and you'll be a man worthy of his father."

I hadn't time to consider the possible import of that last, because the book, as if understanding it was being spoken of, stirred from where I'd left it and began moving for the cave's mouth again. I hit it with a rock, and it lay still.

Galva told Mireya what Deadlegs said, and Mireya spoke to her.

Galva started to protest, but the queen interrupted her and insisted. The knight walked over to me, seeming none too happy about the news she carried.

"My sovereign, Mireya, has told me to come with you, Galt, to keep you alive and make sure you do what is right with that book."

"How nice for both of us."

"Now help me with one more thing," Deadlegs said, handing me a saw-knife and gesturing at the dead assassin. She sat heavily on the cave floor and pulled her own rotted legs off, casting them aside like damp firewood, then looking at me expectantly.

"Well?"

I glanced at Sesta's headless form.

Thank the gods her head was turned away from me.

I wasn't made for cutting legs off. I was what the Galts call *mud-brave,* meaning I'd get my hands in the shyte to get a job done, but I had never been blood-brave.

"Don't make me do it," I said.

"Why?" Deadlegs said and nodded at the killer's corpse. "Were you planning on taking her home with you?"

The way she said it was so like Norrigal, so Galtish, so casually awful.

I missed my moon-wife so dearly then, it felt as if I'd known her my whole life instead of, what, six weeks? I'd met her not sixty days past, and now spending an hour without her made no sense at all.

If you've never fallen hard in love and lost your heart's sovereign, go on and laugh at me. If you have, have a drink and dab an eye.

I would do what needed to be done with this murdering Guild book, then I would return to find Norrigal, be she in an upside-down tower or a right-side-up grave. And if the gods were kind enough to show her to me living once again, I would promise myself to her for as many moons as she had want of me.

Deadlegs must have been reading my thoughts as she had in the Snowless Wood, for she said, "As if Norrigal Na Galbraeth would look twice at your sort again. You're as like to fuck an elf."

Again, just the rhythm Norrigal would have used.

I looked at her.

"It can't be," I said. "It just fucking can't."

The old witch grinned.

How'd her legs get dead anyway?

Norrigal hadn't just been her great-niece.

A giant threw a tree on them.

Norrigal *was* Deadlegs.

Long ago and also now.

Somehow.

"This needs thinking about," I said. "I'll just—"

"Get the legs."

"I'll just get the legs."

Before I could do that, though, she bit me.

On the arm.

Hard.

And smiled bloody.

"What the fuck was that for?"

"Something to remember me by."

The giants came soon after.

A dozen or more of them, one of them a cousin of Misfa. They reached their ox-long arms and their sow-sized heads through the cave mouth and Galva made to fight them, but Mireya wouldn't let her. I was glad of it. We'd barely beaten three, with one of mighty Fulvir's spells to help us. Misfa got shakily to her feet and made her way to the opening, which neither she nor her kin could wholly fit through. She grabbed her kinsman's hand and he told her how strong she was, that the war went well, but that an army of smallmen approached.

"That'll be the Spanths or the Holtish," I said, "those armies from Middlesea. And how the devils are we going to get out of here? Do we have to fight these bigguns?"

"Sure and we don't," Deadlegs said. "They'd mash us like turnips. I've got about one more big spell in me before I need to sleep for a week, and if these bigguns aren't to kill us, someone's got to get their kinswoman out of this cave. First, though, Kinch, you have to free a horse from her."

"What? The sleepers? I can't."

"You'd best learn. Your future's not in taking, lad. It's in making."

We proposed a deal with Misfa, and she agreed.

Deadlegs guided me through a spell to crack a sleeper tattoo. It was the strongest magic I'd yet done, stronger than I'd ever dreamed of working, and I had no idea what I was doing. But at the end of it, a hoof broke free from the giant's skin. Then a head and mane, a horse's startled eyes. Soon, the whole thing was out, clopping on the cave floor.

Bloody with her blood, as if it had just foaled from her thigh.

A stallion.

A young, strong stallion.

Something Manreach hadn't seen in twenty years. The plague killed all the boy horses and most of the mares, so that now even those were old and mostly died out. This creature, this brown, lovely, sweet-smelling, warm creature, this heavy, grass-loving dog, this saddleless bearer, was nothing less than a miracle.

Galva shivered when she heard those hooves on stone, and when it exploded a whinny in the confines of the cave, she sobbed openly and might have dropped to her knees in thanks and wonder if she hadn't had a better idea. She went to the animal and gave him an apple. If I live a thousand years, I'll see few things as beautiful as that Spanth feeding the last, or first, or only stallion in Manreach an apple. Even the giants outside the cave were transfixed, lying on their bellies to look in the slit at us.

Then came our part of the deal.

Deadlegs's specialty was magic to do with minerals—it's why her stone men and dirt-wights worked so well, why she had been able to sink a tower upside down in the earth. So she spoke to the stones of the cave and asked them wouldn't they like to stretch a bit, wouldn't it feel good? The cave started to shake then, gravel and dust rained on us, turning the lot of us white.

"Fothannon, is it going to fall on us?"

"Might do," she said, seemingly unconcerned.

But it didn't.

What it did was to triple the size of the cave mouth so two women could ride a horse through it and a giant could duck.

We went out with the dust on us like a procession of ghosts. It turns out giants really are an honorable lot, or at least this bunch were. Misfa limped out to them, to their thunderous embraces and laughter not so different from the laughter of kynd. They backed straight off from us as Deadlegs and Mireya rode the horse out, a horse Mireya had plumbed its name for and found to be Ēsclaer, Gallardian for *lightning*. I don't know how much of the giants' reverence was gratitude for the return of their kinswoman, how much was the value of their own word, how much was liking for our trust in going out among them, and how much was plain fear of Deadlegs, who had made a small mountain open its mouth. That last they needn't have bothered with—there was barely enough fuel for spells left in Deadlegs to fling a pebble at a field mouse, not until she slept and ate and bathed.

She leaned half-asleep on Mireya's back.

"Where are you off to?" I asked her.

Half slurring with exhaustion, she said, in Galtish, "To find the Ispanthian army and see if they like their witch-queen so well as her usurping uncle, Kalith."

"Sounds risky," I said. "What's to stop them from breaking out bullnutters and hacking each other to pieces over it? Or one of them to kill her in her sleep?"

Deadlegs's weary eyes moved back and forth, trying to focus on me. "You got a better idea?"

"Can't say I have."

I saw the chance in it, at least. Mireya seemed very much a queen, *was* a queen, had ruled a kingdom and kept her king alive—for a time—with the deadliest legion of bastards in Manreach trying to kill them both. And Spanths were horse-mad to their bones. If Mireya couldn't charm and command the loyalty of an Ispanthian army from the back of the world's only stallion, she'd never do it at all.

"Besides," Deadlegs slobbered, "it's not like we're going west, over deadly mountains and to the giantlands, hiding from the whole of the Takers Guild with little magic, one good sword, and a biting arsehole of a murder-book in our pack."

"Fair point," I said. "And my family? Will you? Can you?"

She nodded slow against the queen's back. "I'll have them hid and warded. No promises. Except to do all I can."

Which might be much. If she could get word east, she could have my family moved out of Platha Glurris and Brith Minnon. The Guild would spare no expense to find me and the book, but how much energy they'd spend trying to find my tired old mum, handful of siblings, and stammering niece was another matter.

Meanwhile, if I could milk the book of its secrets and find a way to make them known, I could make life hard for the Takers. If it turned out they'd killed the horses out from under us for their own power and profit, they'd be hard pressed to hide anywhere. It would be like every one of the fuckers had a tattoo of a noose on their necks, and drinks on the house to any mob good enough to string them up.

"Now. For the love of Samnyr," Deadlegs said, "and all the gods besides. Shut up. And let. Me sleep."

And she was out.

Mireya, who had just finished a hushed talk and a long stare with Galva, whose eyes were no drier than hers, nodded at me hard once and wheeled the horse.

A horse.

A real and actual horse I had brought back into the world under my own hand. If I died the very next day, and it didn't seem unlikely, I'd done something, hadn't I?

Galva and I ran west, me with the cat over my shoulder, my pack on my back and the poisonous book in a second bag carried under my arm; an oilskin sack the Full Shadow had, probably for just this purpose. A ring of Catfall on my finger and a torque that did I know not what on my neck. The sky was dark in the west, and I knew we'd be rained on before nightfall, but the day's last warm sun was shining on us.

"I'll keep carrying you for a bit, but if you shyte on me, it's over," I told Bully.

He didn't reply.

"So, Bully," I said, "are we going to be killed in the giantlands?"

He said nothing.

"Would you like to see Galtia someday?"

Nothing.

Well, he wasn't much at prophecy, but I was glad all the same for his warmth and goodwill. I had many cold nights before me and, for company, only a Spanth who'd rather sharpen a sword than talk. I missed Norrigal like a part of myself that I hadn't known I had. She was back in the Snowless Wood now, I thought it likely, her legs wrecked until she made a maiden of herself, however that was done.

Galva and I ran through the foothills of Oustrim. We ran past copses of gorgeous yellow-leaved trees hissing in the wind, and past broken houses giants had wrecked, and past streams that burbled as though there wasn't a trouble in the wide world. When we got a chance to rest, I'd have to see about getting Bully Boy back into my skin.

But for now, it was good to have the little beast on my shoulder. I could tell Bully liked having the sun on his face and a breeze in his whiskers; a blind cat's pleasures are few.

Let him stay awake for a little bit.

Let him smell the autumn and the fires on it and the voles and mice and birds he'd never catch preparing for the winter.

"Rao," he said.

I like to think that was thanks.

Acknowledgments

Among the many to whom I owe some debt for this story, I want to start with its champion and midwife, editor Lindsey Hall; how she learned so much so young is beyond my ken, but no sharper knife than hers has cut a book's baggage or defended its heart.

Likewise, this story would not exist without my steadfast, talented, and insightful agent, Michelle Brower, who asked me some years ago what genre I might like to write besides horror.

I want to thank Kyle and MaritaBeth Caruthers, whose Dice Cup Lounge provided a cool and welcoming haven on many a hot day at the Scarborough Faire in Texas, and who were always happy to listen to newly minted passages; thanks also to Marc, Maggie, Hunter and Teri, Sarah and Cyrus, John, Rhonda, Bob, Stefan, and any others who found themselves willingly or otherwise formed into an audience for said readings in said place.

I am grateful to the early readers who commented on the manuscript: Allison Williams, Ian MacDonald, Kate Polak, Skip Leeds, Kelly Cochrane, Jamie Haeuser, Andrew Pyper, and Kelly Robson; I owe you all a drink in the Quartered Sun whenever next we get to Edth.

And lest I forget, thanks to Michael and Stephanie, Byron and Aaron, Liam, Chris K., and the other eager players of Towers who helped me turn it from an author's fancy into a brutal and addictive betting game. Most ardent among this group of test players is my wife, Jennifer; my playmate, my comfort, my strength.

I also wish to acknowledge those who blazed this trail; J. R. R. Tolkien, of course, who is every modern fantasy writer's common ancestor; but also publisher Tom Doherty, who helped bring him to an American audience and who runs the company that brought this book to light. George R. R. Martin inherited not just Tolkien's middle initials but his genius in world-building and set an astonishingly high bar for the rest of us—the audio books of A Song of Ice and Fire, brilliantly narrated by the late Roy Dotrice, have smoothed many a long mile on my road and remain, for me, the gold standard of storytelling excellence. The works of modern masters Joe Abercrombie and Patrick Rothfuss influenced this author, it is fair to say; in a world so full of good books and so short on time, theirs are among the stories I gladly revisit.

Lastly, to Luther. He showed up on my doorstep in the summer of 2015 and raoed to be let in. He was a handsome boy, but sickly, with only a few short years to give. Though his eyes didn't work, I had been the blind one and had never loved a cat.

He taught me a few things about that.

About the Author

CHRISTOPHER BUEHLMAN is an author, comedian, and screenwriter from St. Petersburg, Florida. He tours the country most years, writing fantasy and horror and performing at Renaissance festivals. He and his wife, Jenn, travel with their rescue dog, Duck, and a black cat named Jane Mansfield, who is proficient in ninjutsu.

christopherbuehlmanauthor.com
Twitter: @Buehlmeister
Goodreads: Christopher Buehlman